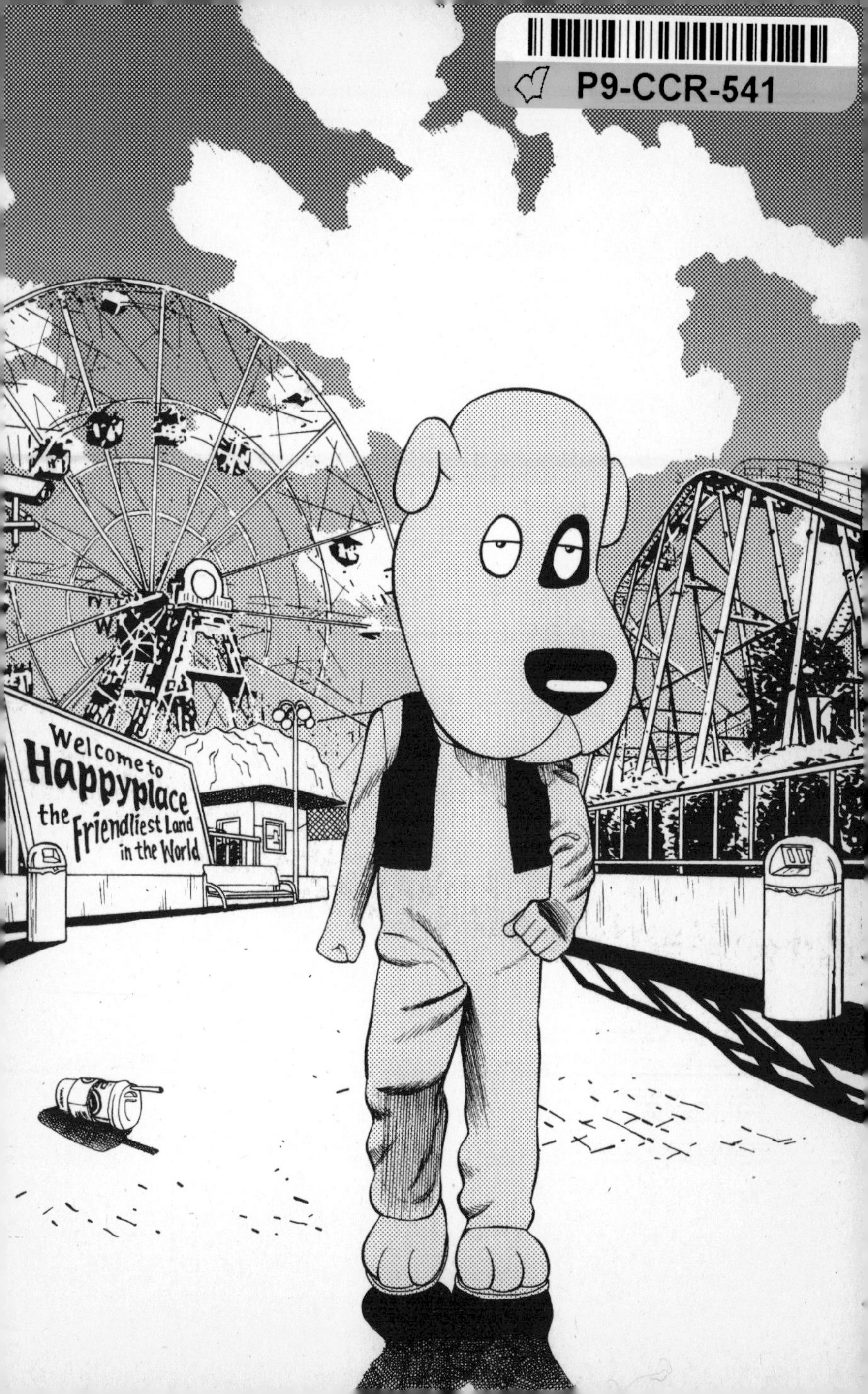
Welcome to
Happyplace
the Friendliest Land
in the World

Dogby Walks Alone
Created By Wes Abbott

Production Artist - Lucas Rivera
Cover Layout - Jason Milligan

Editor - Luis Reyes
Digital Imaging Manager - Chris Buford
Managing Editor - Lindsey Johnston
Editorial Director - Jeremy Ross
Editor-in-Chief - Rob Tokar
VP of Production - Ron Klamert
Publisher - Mike Kiley
President and C.O.O. - John Parker
C.E.O. and Chief Creative Officer - Stuart Levy

A  Manga

TOKYOPOP Inc.
5900 Wilshire Blvd. Suite 2000
Los Angeles, CA 90036

E-mail: info@TOKYOPOP.com
Come visit us online at www.TOKYOPOP.com

ISBN: 1-59816-582-8

First TOKYOPOP printing: June 2006
10 9 8 7 6 5 4 3 2 1
Printed in the USA

DOGBY WALKS ALONE

BY
WES ABBOTT

TOKYOPOP®

HAMBURG // LONDON // LOS ANGELES // TOKYO

CONTENTS

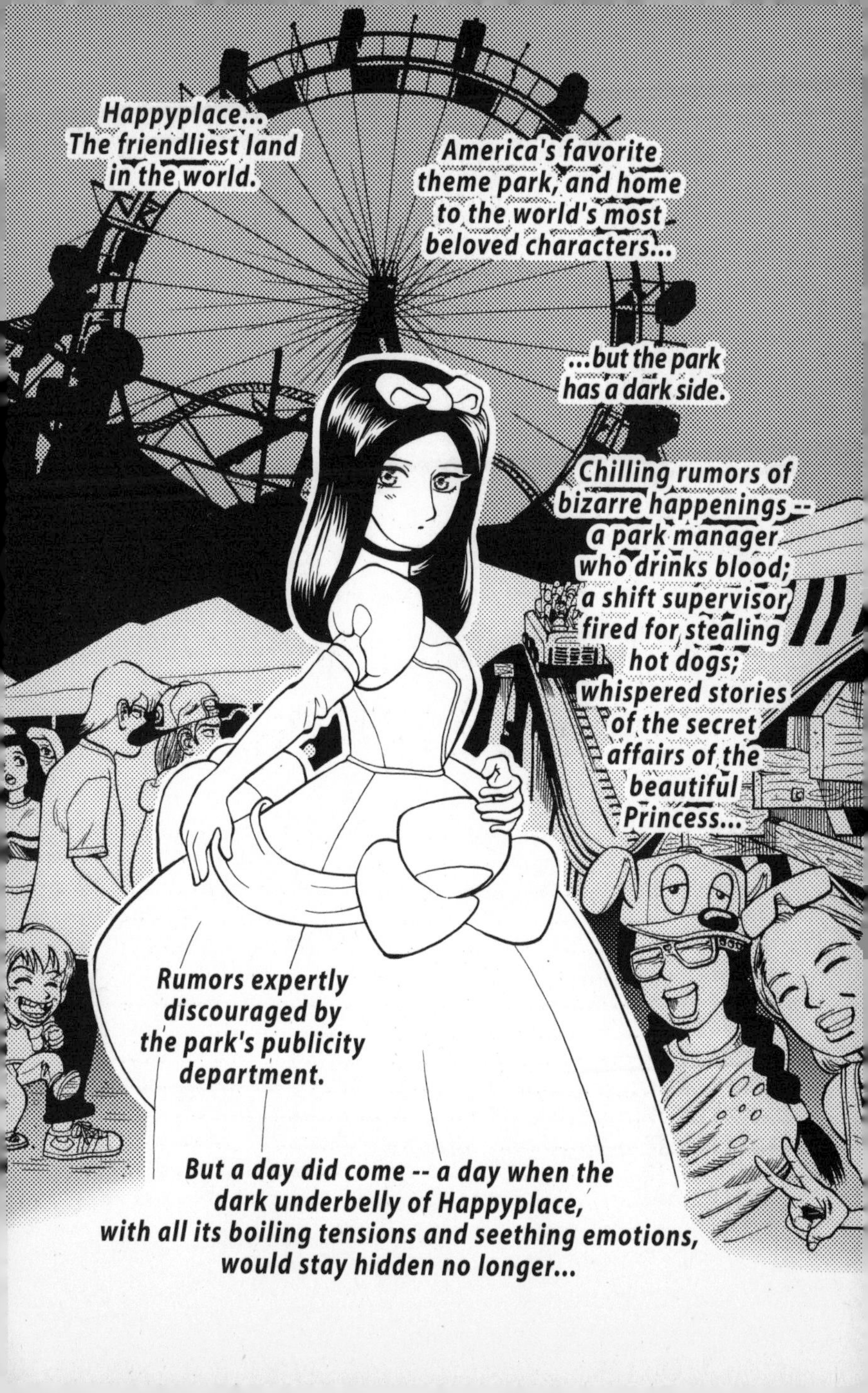
Happyplace... The friendliest land in the world.
America's favorite theme park, and home to the world's most beloved characters...
...but the park has a dark side.
Chilling rumors of bizarre happenings -- a park manager who drinks blood; a shift supervisor fired for stealing hot dogs; whispered stories of the secret affairs of the beautiful Princess...
Rumors expertly discouraged by the park's publicity department.
But a day did come -- a day when the dark underbelly of Happyplace, with all its boiling tensions and seething emotions, would stay hidden no longer...

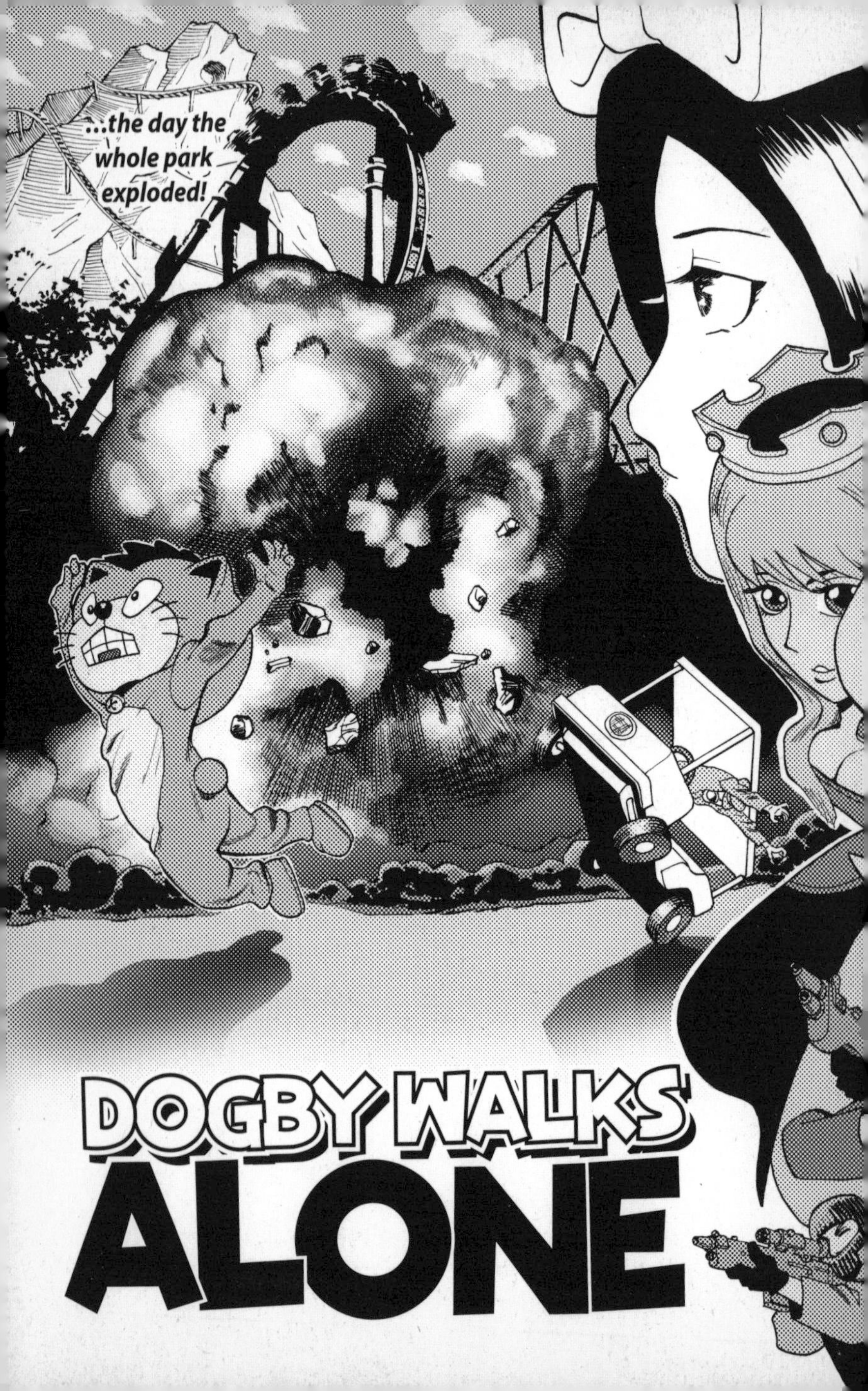
...the day the whole park exploded!
DOGBY WALKS ALONE

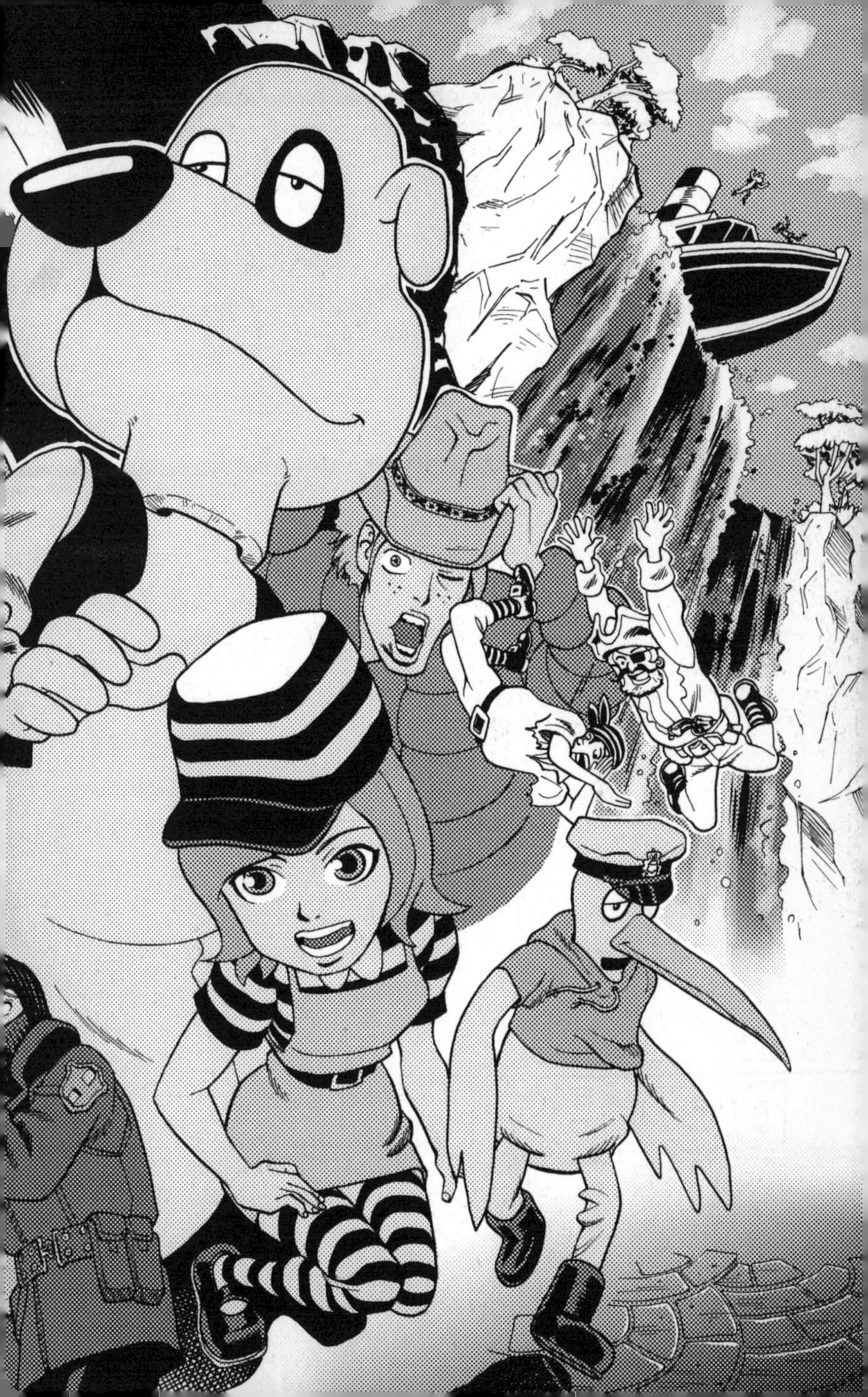

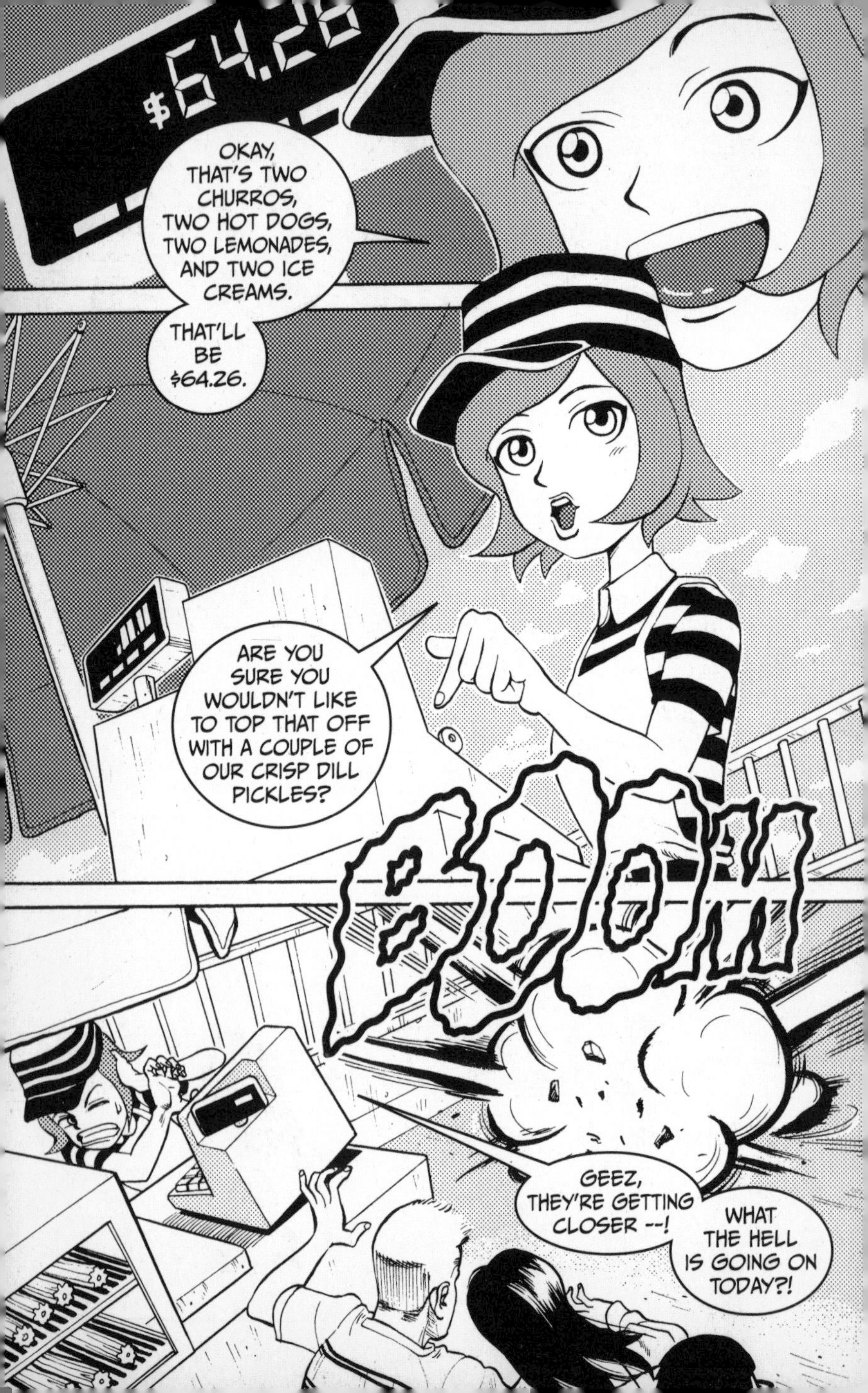
$64.26
OKAY, THAT'S TWO CHURROS, TWO HOT DOGS, TWO LEMONADES, AND TWO ICE CREAMS.
THAT'LL BE $64.26.
ARE YOU SURE YOU WOULDN'T LIKE TO TOP THAT OFF WITH A COUPLE OF OUR CRISP DILL PICKLES?
BOOM
GEEZ, THEY'RE GETTING CLOSER --!
WHAT THE HELL IS GOING ON TODAY?!

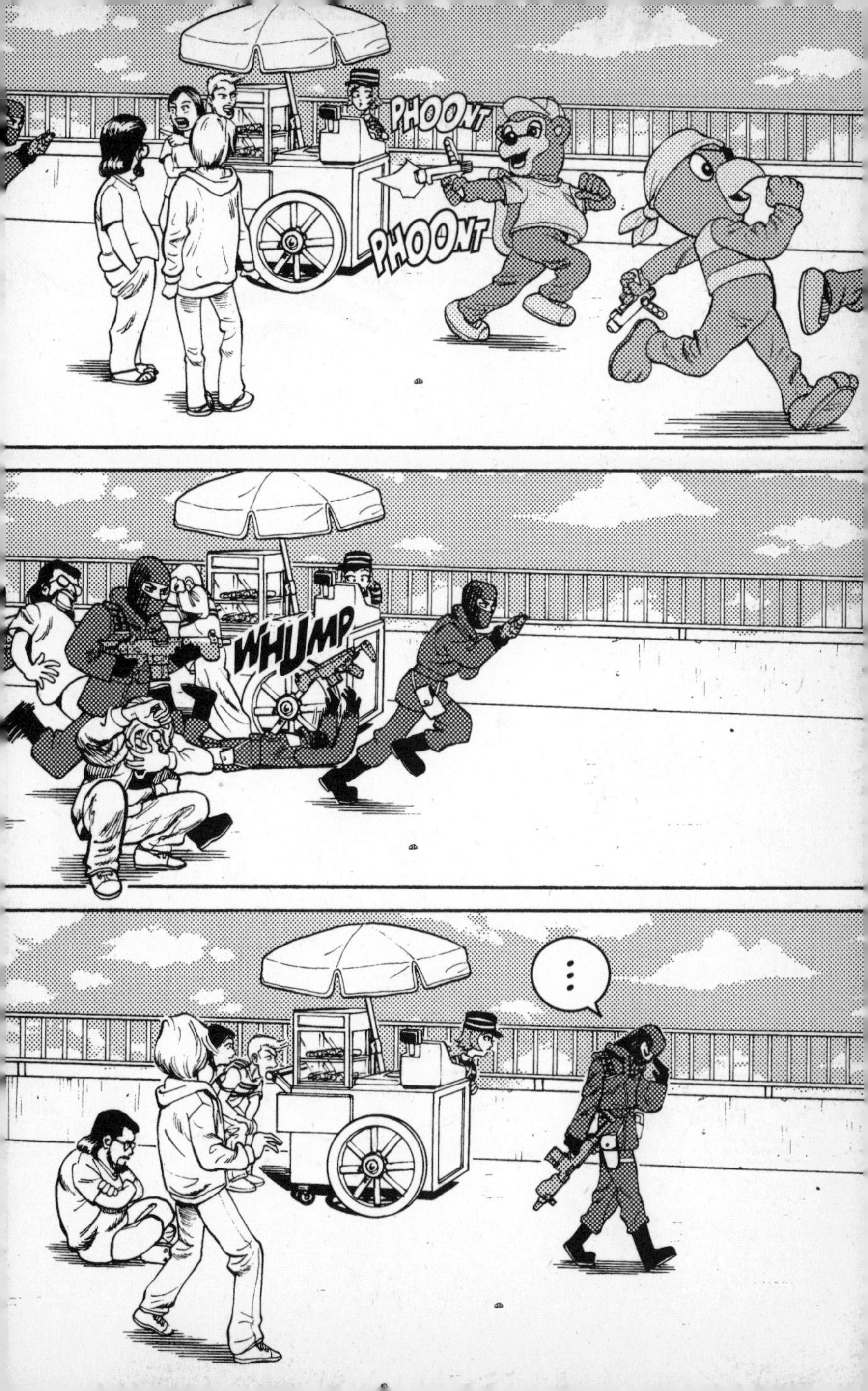
PHOONT
PHOONT
WHUMP
...

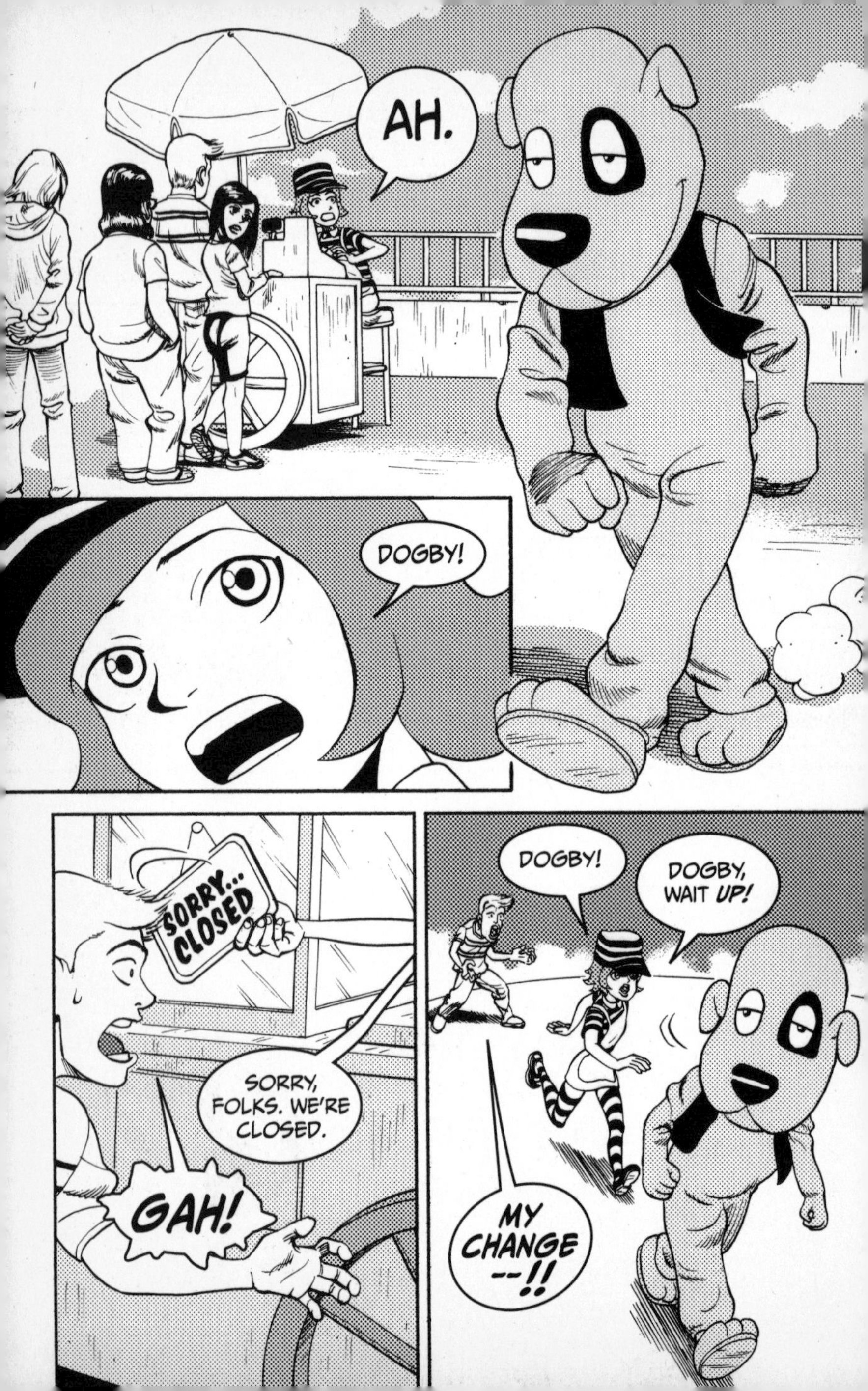
AH.
DOGBY!
SORRY... CLOSED
SORRY, FOLKS. WE'RE CLOSED.
GAH!
DOGBY!
DOGBY, WAIT *UP*!
MY CHANGE --!!

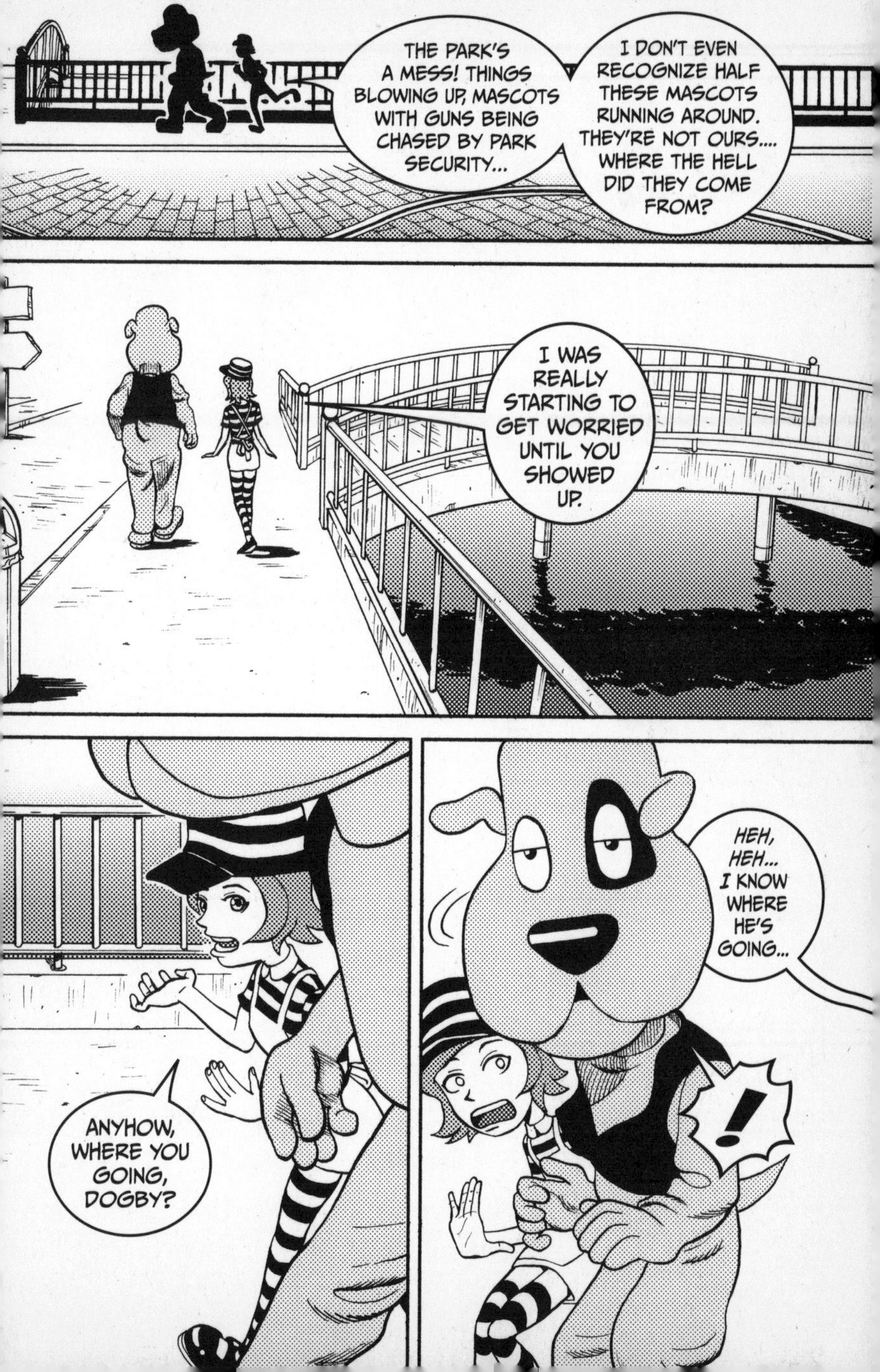
THE PARK'S A MESS! THINGS BLOWING UP, MASCOTS WITH GUNS BEING CHASED BY PARK SECURITY...
I DON'T EVEN RECOGNIZE HALF THESE MASCOTS RUNNING AROUND. THEY'RE NOT OURS.... WHERE THE HELL DID THEY COME FROM?
I WAS REALLY STARTING TO GET WORRIED UNTIL YOU SHOWED UP.
ANYHOW, WHERE YOU GOING, DOGBY?
HEH, HEH... I KNOW WHERE HE'S GOING...
!

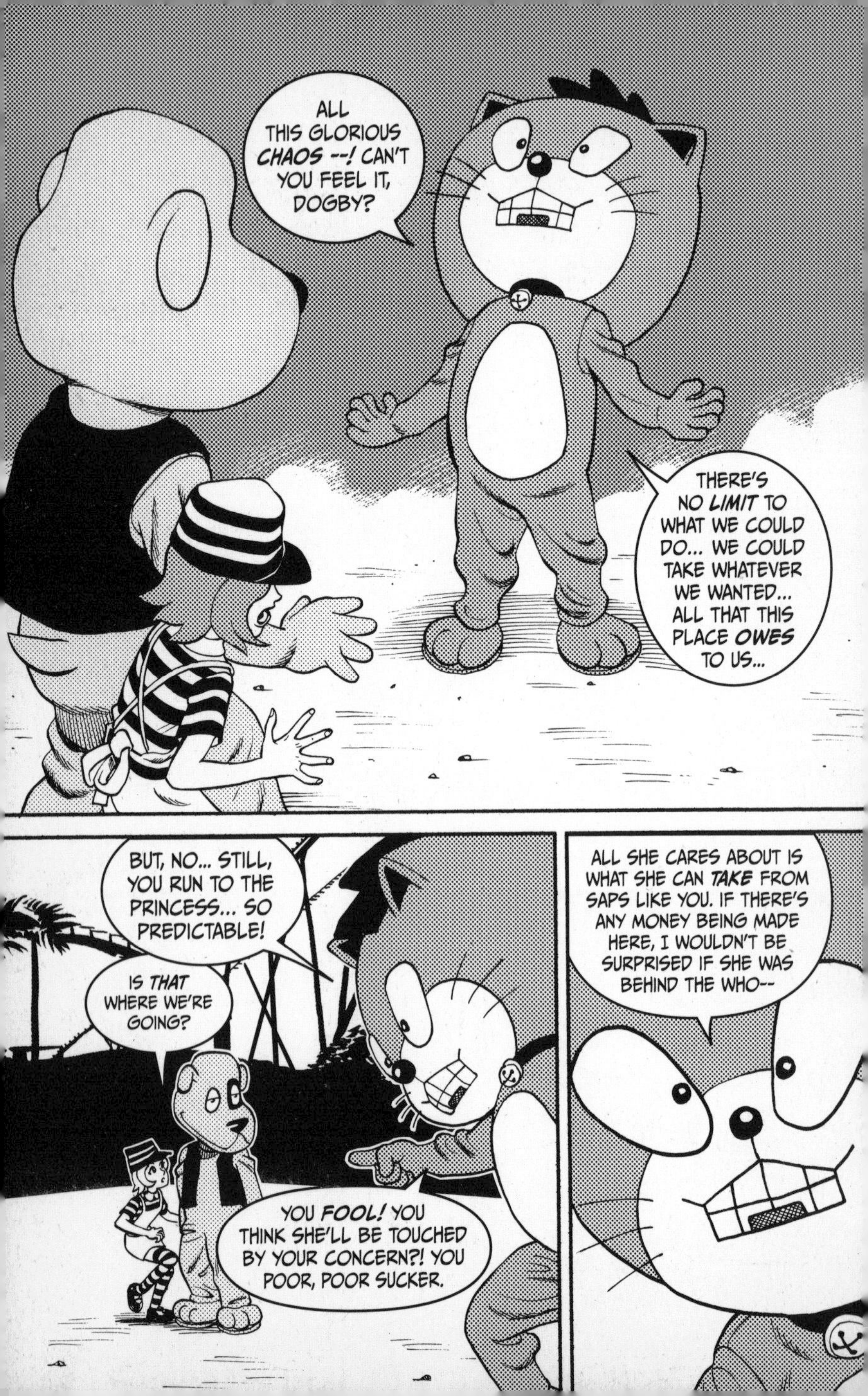
ALL THIS GLORIOUS CHAOS --! CAN'T YOU FEEL IT, DOGBY?
THERE'S NO LIMIT TO WHAT WE COULD DO... WE COULD TAKE WHATEVER WE WANTED... ALL THAT THIS PLACE OWES TO US...
BUT, NO... STILL, YOU RUN TO THE PRINCESS... SO PREDICTABLE!
IS THAT WHERE WE'RE GOING?
YOU FOOL! YOU THINK SHE'LL BE TOUCHED BY YOUR CONCERN?! YOU POOR, POOR SUCKER.
ALL SHE CARES ABOUT IS WHAT SHE CAN TAKE FROM SAPS LIKE YOU. IF THERE'S ANY MONEY BEING MADE HERE, I WOULDN'T BE SURPRISED IF SHE WAS BEHIND THE WHO--

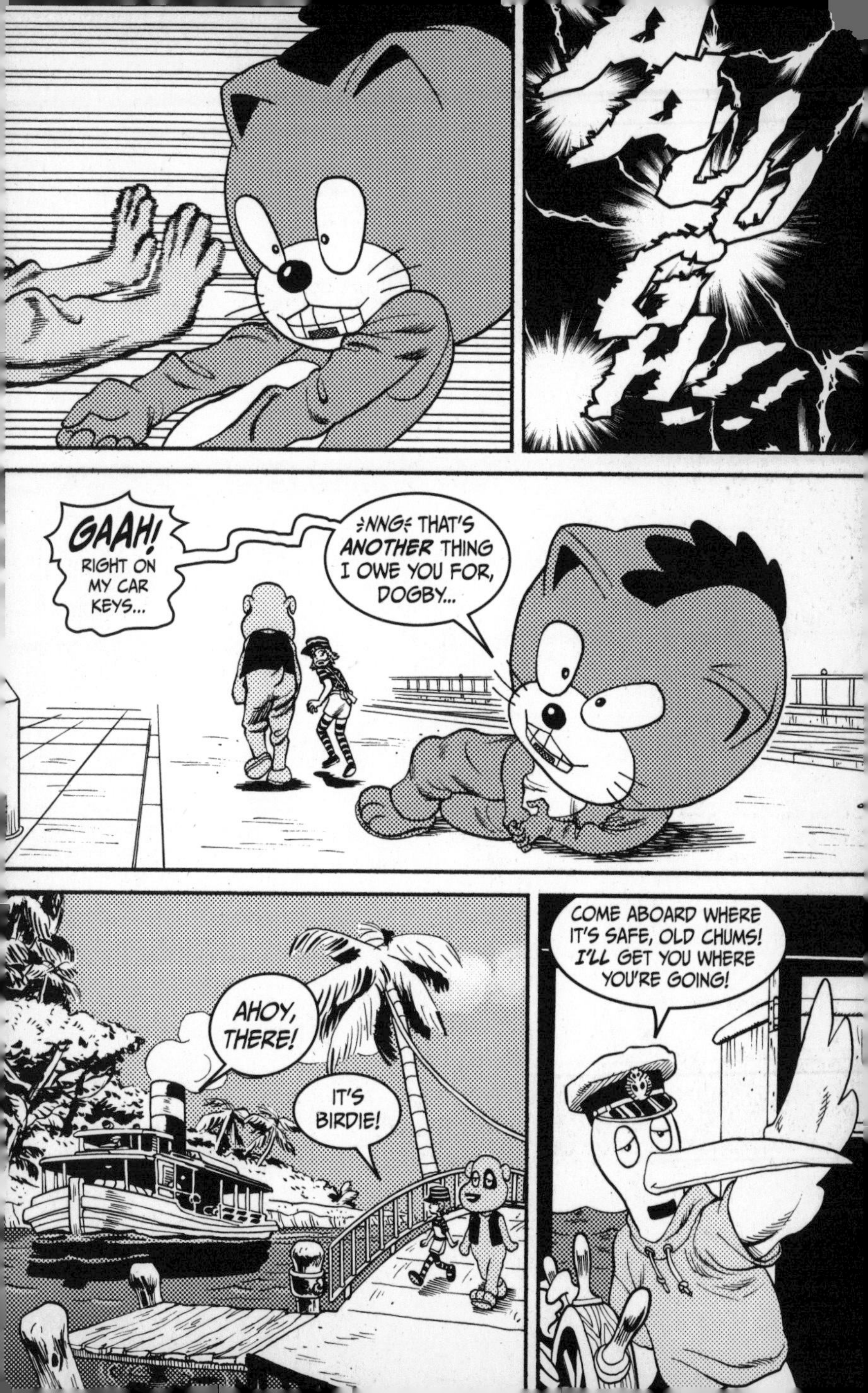
GAAH! RIGHT ON MY CAR KEYS...
≠NNG≠ THAT'S ANOTHER THING I OWE YOU FOR, DOGBY...
AHOY, THERE!
IT'S BIRDIE!
COME ABOARD WHERE IT'S SAFE, OLD CHUMS! I'LL GET YOU WHERE YOU'RE GOING!

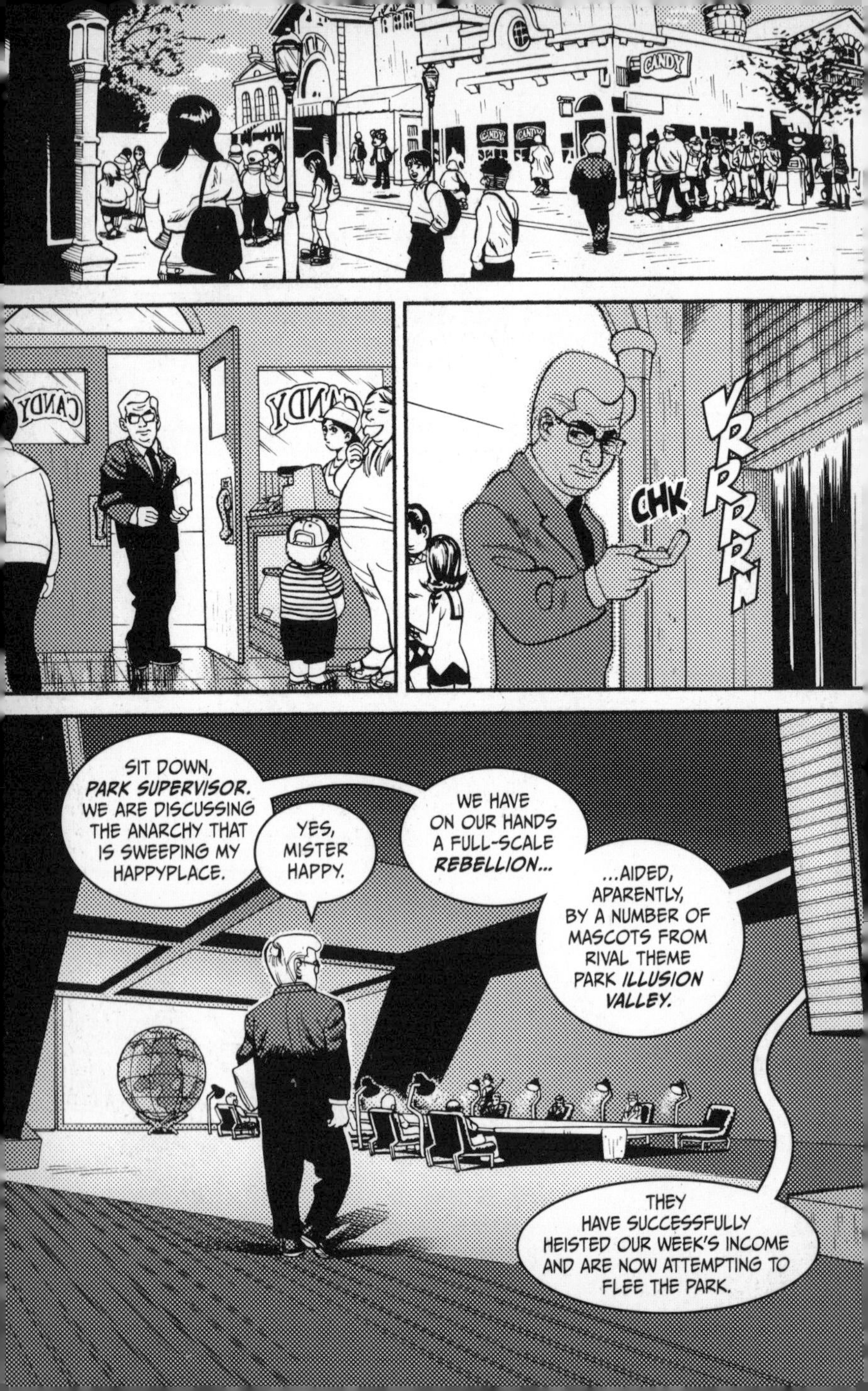
CANDY
CHK
VRRRRN
SIT DOWN, *PARK SUPERVISOR.* WE ARE DISCUSSING THE ANARCHY THAT IS SWEEPING MY HAPPYPLACE.
YES, MISTER HAPPY.
WE HAVE ON OUR HANDS A FULL-SCALE *REBELLION...*
...AIDED, APARENTLY, BY A NUMBER OF MASCOTS FROM RIVAL THEME PARK *ILLUSION VALLEY.*
THEY HAVE SUCCESSFULLY HEISTED OUR WEEK'S INCOME AND ARE NOW ATTEMPTING TO FLEE THE PARK.

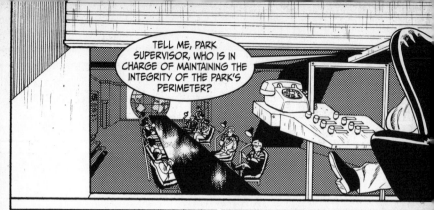

TELL ME, PARK SUPERVISOR, WHO IS IN CHARGE OF MAINTAINING THE INTEGRITY OF THE PARK'S PERIMETER?

THAT IS AMONG THE DUTIES I DELEGATED TO PARK-UPPER-MANAGEMENT-GUY EARLY LAST WEEK. APPARENTLY, HE WAS NOT UP TO THE ADDED RESPONSIBILITY.

T-THAT'S NOT FAIR --! I WASN'T GIVEN THE MANPOWER TO--

PLEASE -- NO PATHETIC EXCUSES, P.U.M.G...

YOU *ARE* AWARE OF THIS BOARD'S POLICY ON *FAILURE*, ARE YOU NOT...?

G. Howard

Sco

P.U.M.G.

Park Supervis

YES. I MEAN--

NOOOOOOO!!

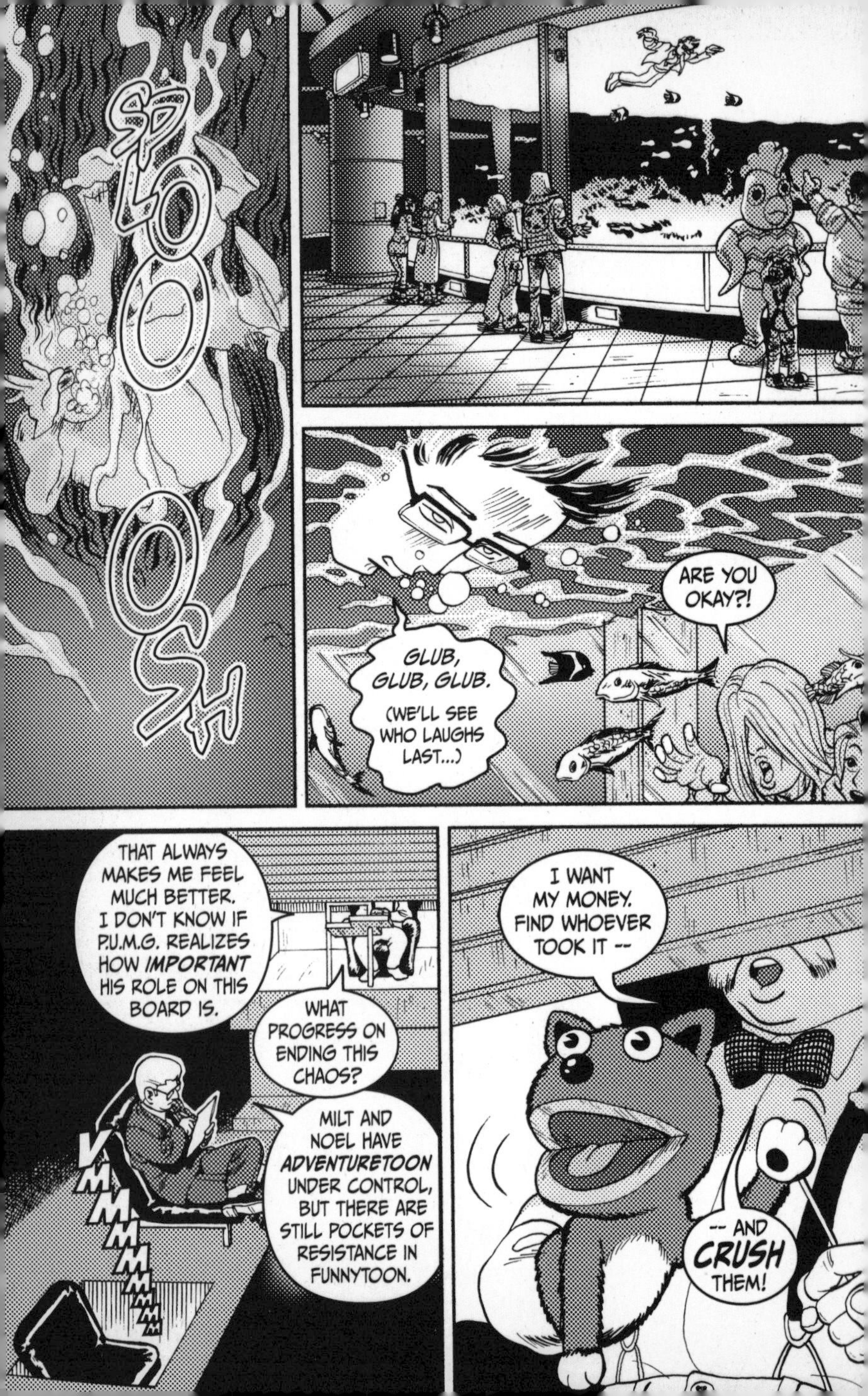
SPLOOOOSH
GLUB, GLUB, GLUB.
(WE'LL SEE WHO LAUGHS LAST...)
ARE YOU OKAY?!
THAT ALWAYS MAKES ME FEEL MUCH BETTER. I DON'T KNOW IF P.U.M.G. REALIZES HOW *IMPORTANT* HIS ROLE ON THIS BOARD IS.
WHAT PROGRESS ON ENDING THIS CHAOS?
MILT AND NOEL HAVE *ADVENTURETOON* UNDER CONTROL, BUT THERE ARE STILL POCKETS OF RESISTANCE IN FUNNYTOON.
VMMMMMMMMMM
I WANT MY MONEY. FIND WHOEVER TOOK IT --
-- AND **CRUSH** THEM!

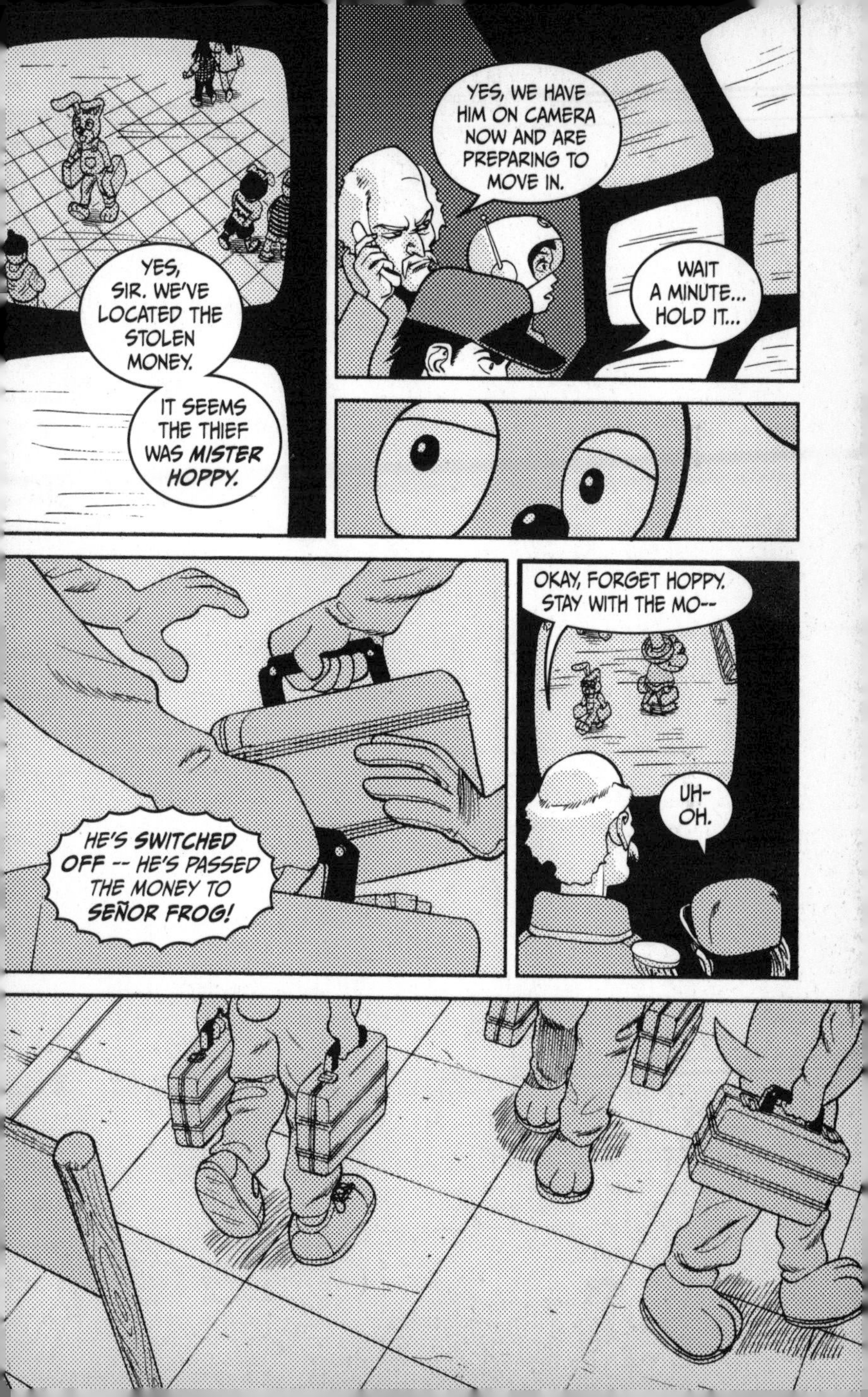
YES, SIR. WE'VE LOCATED THE STOLEN MONEY.
IT SEEMS THE THIEF WAS *MISTER HOPPY.*
YES, WE HAVE HIM ON CAMERA NOW AND ARE PREPARING TO MOVE IN.
WAIT A MINUTE... HOLD IT...
HE'S **SWITCHED OFF** *-- HE'S PASSED THE MONEY TO* **SEÑOR FROG!**
OKAY, FORGET HOPPY. STAY WITH THE MO--
UH-OH.

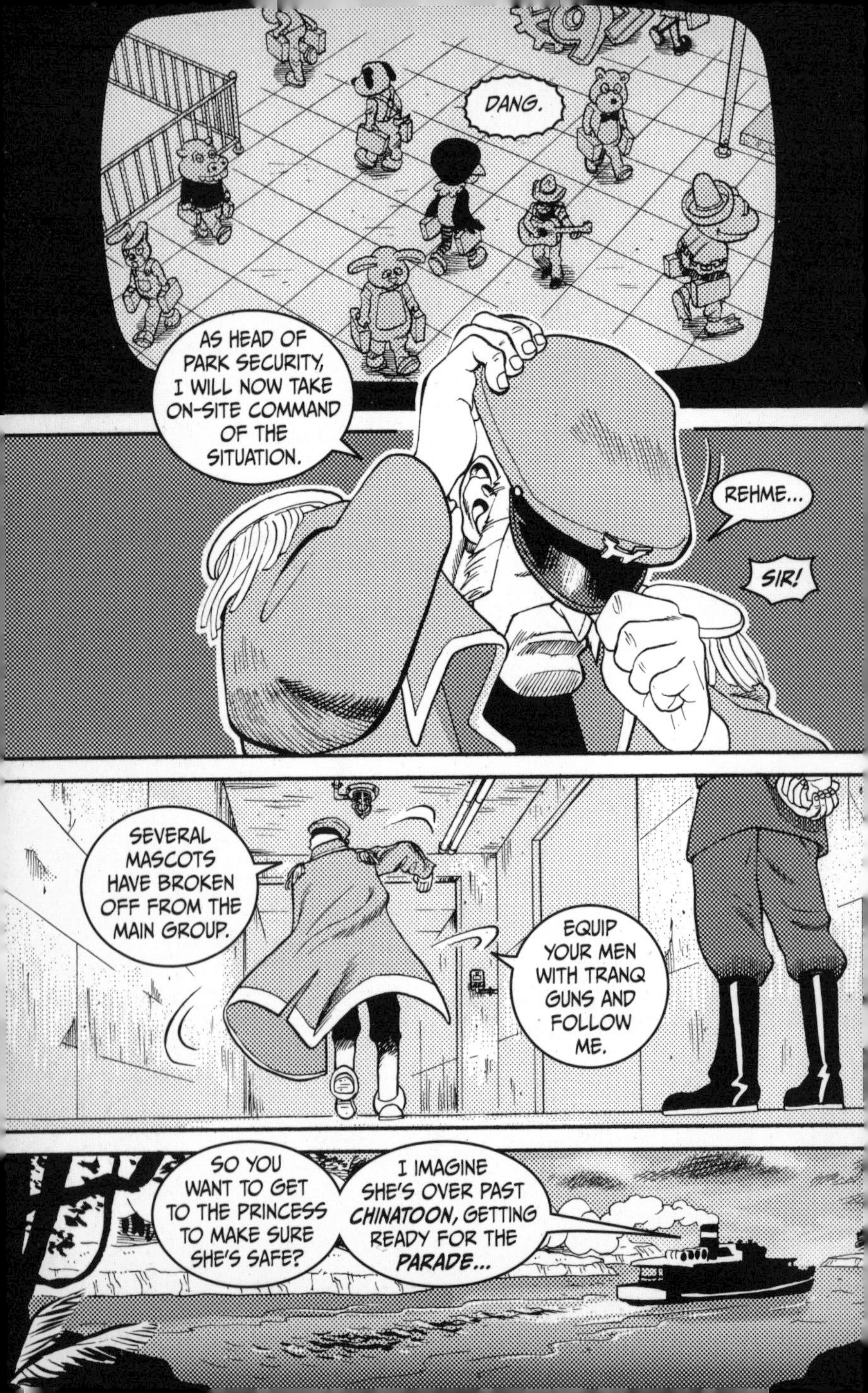
DANG.
AS HEAD OF PARK SECURITY, I WILL NOW TAKE ON-SITE COMMAND OF THE SITUATION.
REHME...
SIR!
SEVERAL MASCOTS HAVE BROKEN OFF FROM THE MAIN GROUP.
EQUIP YOUR MEN WITH TRANQ GUNS AND FOLLOW ME.
SO YOU WANT TO GET TO THE PRINCESS TO MAKE SURE SHE'S SAFE?
I IMAGINE SHE'S OVER PAST CHINATOON, GETTING READY FOR THE PARADE...

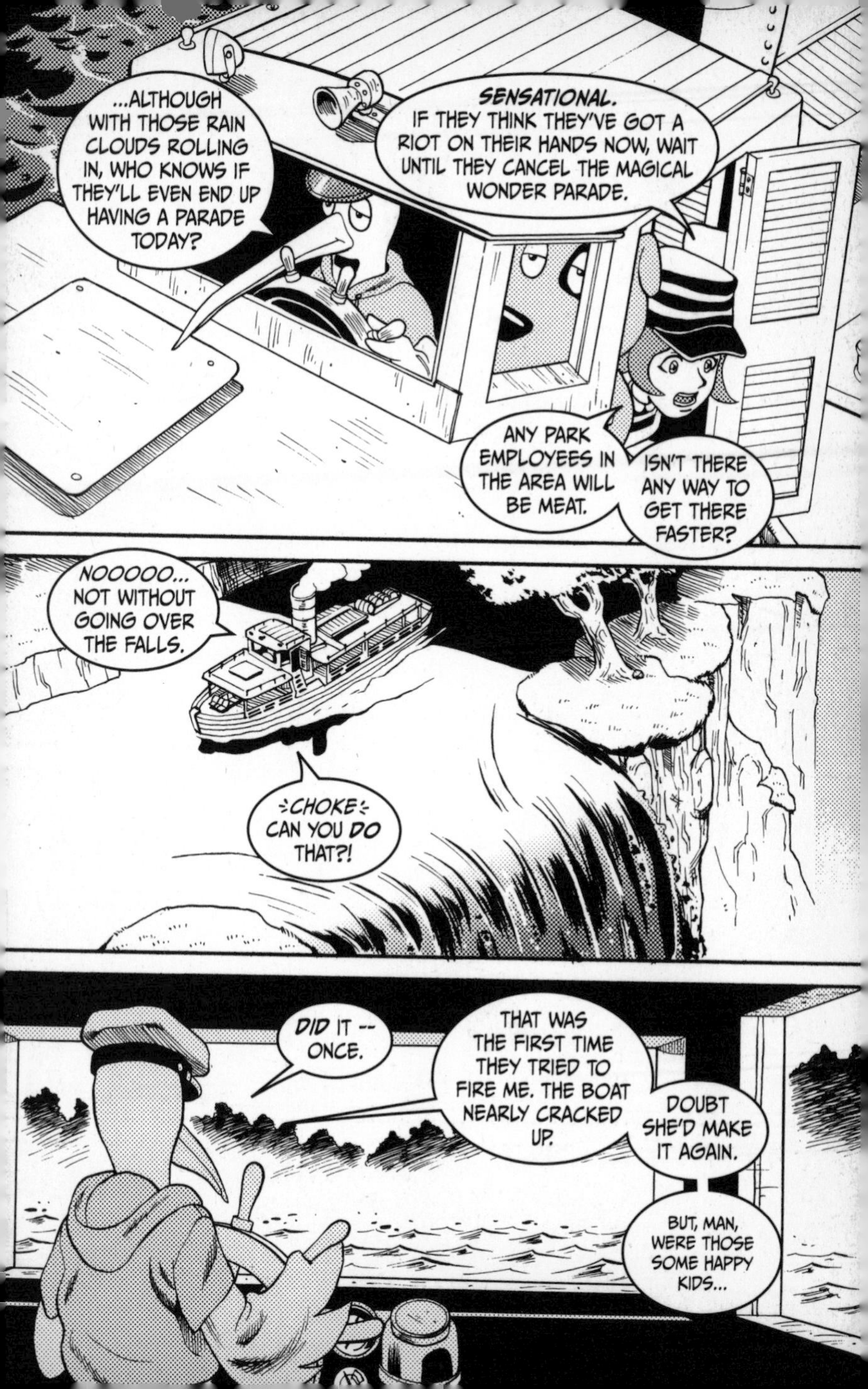
...ALTHOUGH WITH THOSE RAIN CLOUDS ROLLING IN, WHO KNOWS IF THEY'LL EVEN END UP HAVING A PARADE TODAY?
SENSATIONAL. IF THEY THINK THEY'VE GOT A RIOT ON THEIR HANDS NOW, WAIT UNTIL THEY CANCEL THE MAGICAL WONDER PARADE.
ANY PARK EMPLOYEES IN THE AREA WILL BE MEAT.
ISN'T THERE ANY WAY TO GET THERE FASTER?
NOOOOO... NOT WITHOUT GOING OVER THE FALLS.
CHOKE CAN YOU DO THAT?!
DID IT -- ONCE.
THAT WAS THE FIRST TIME THEY TRIED TO FIRE ME. THE BOAT NEARLY CRACKED UP.
DOUBT SHE'D MAKE IT AGAIN.
BUT, MAN, WERE THOSE SOME HAPPY KIDS...

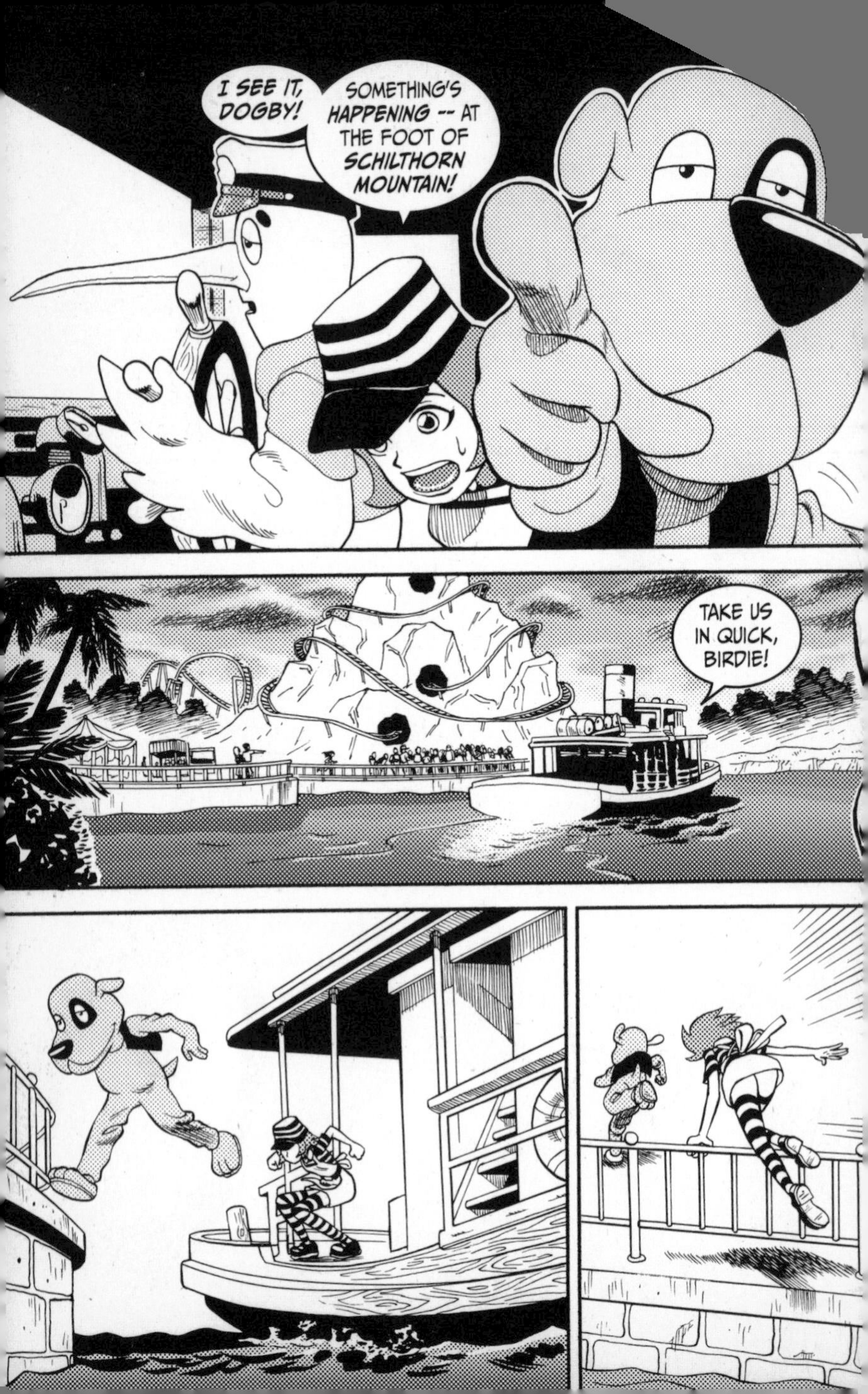
I SEE IT, DOGBY!
SOMETHING'S HAPPENING -- AT THE FOOT OF SCHILTHORN MOUNTAIN!
TAKE US IN QUICK, BIRDIE!

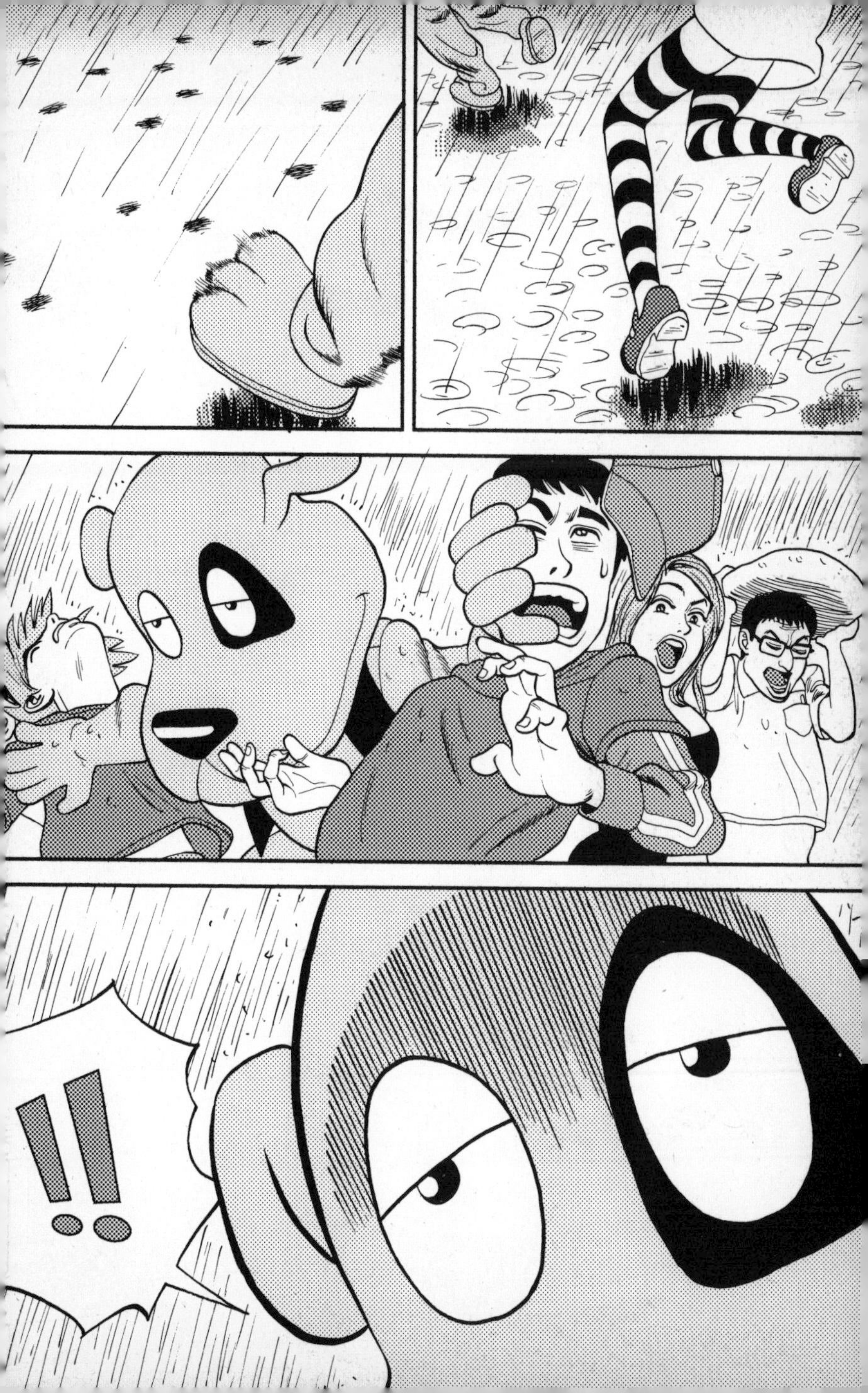
!!

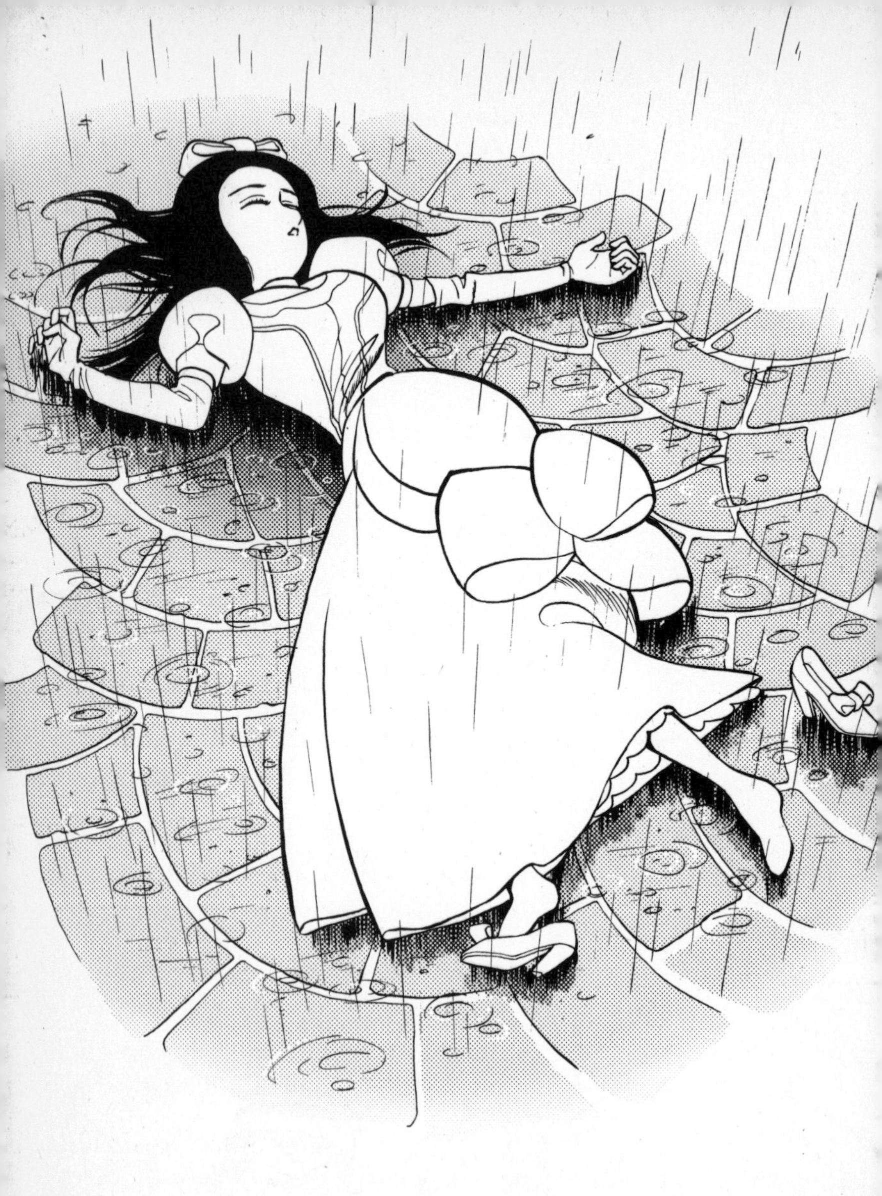

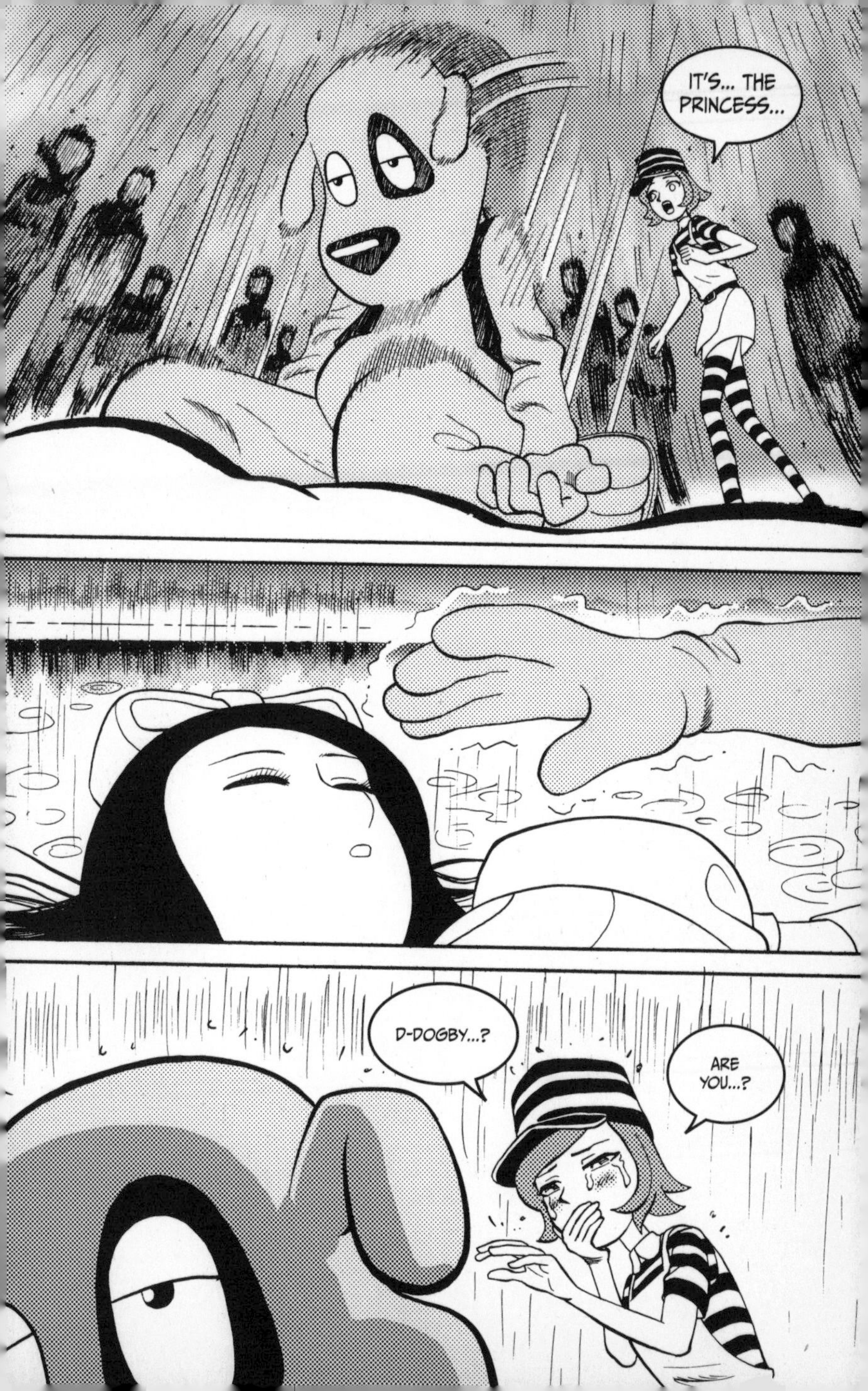
IT'S... THE PRINCESS...
D-DOGBY...?
ARE YOU...?

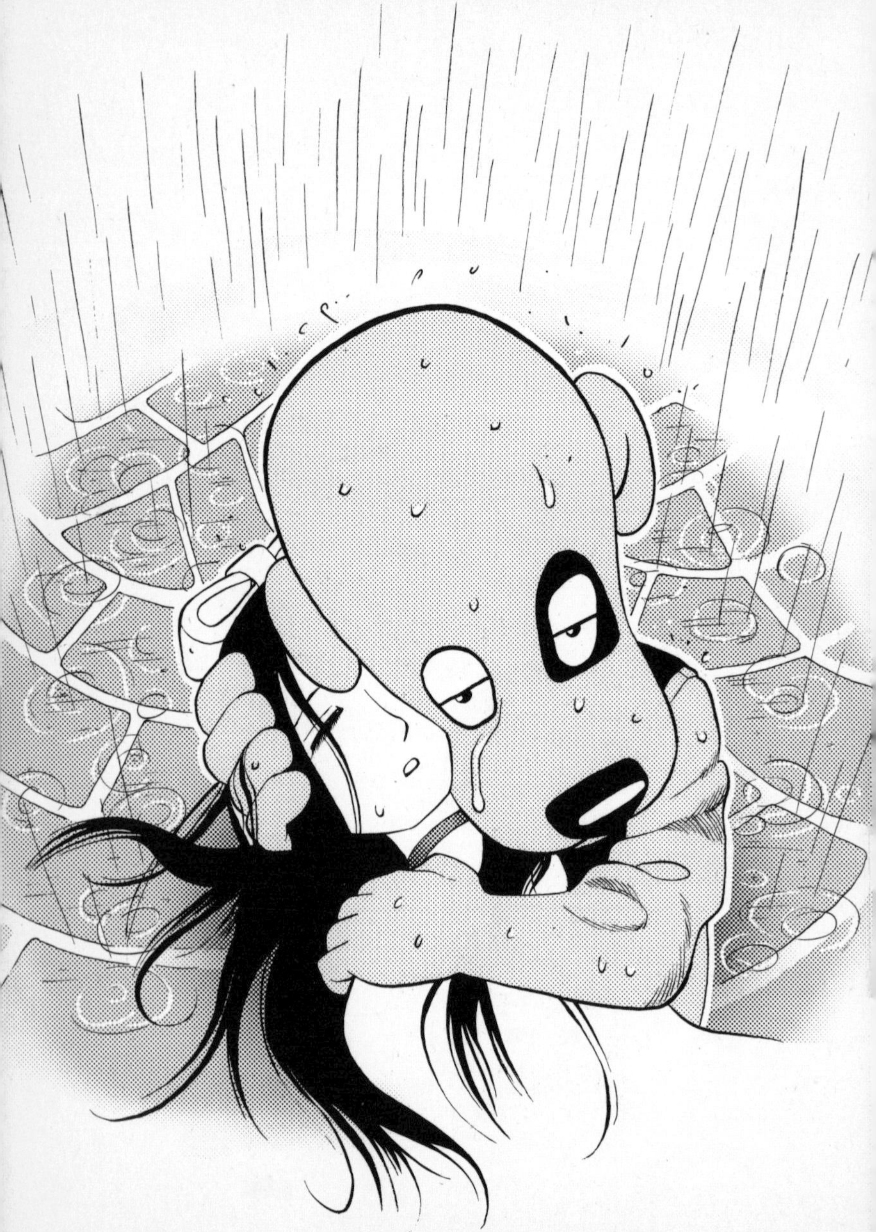

chapter 2

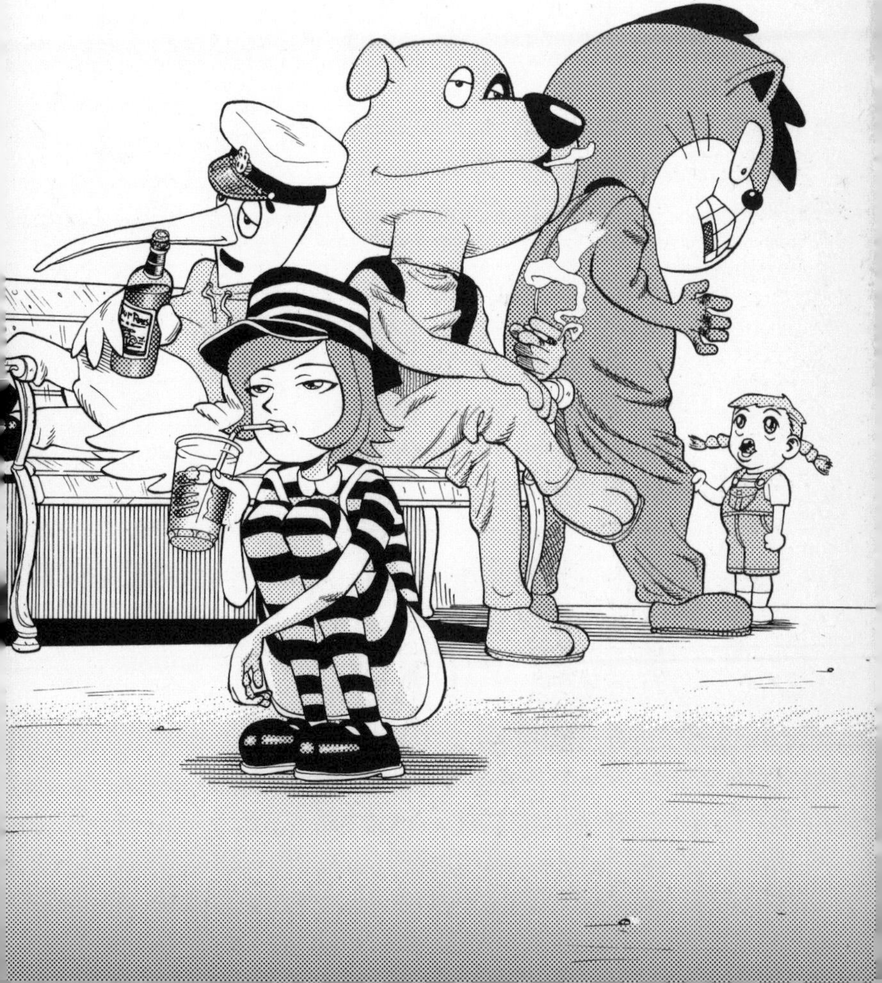

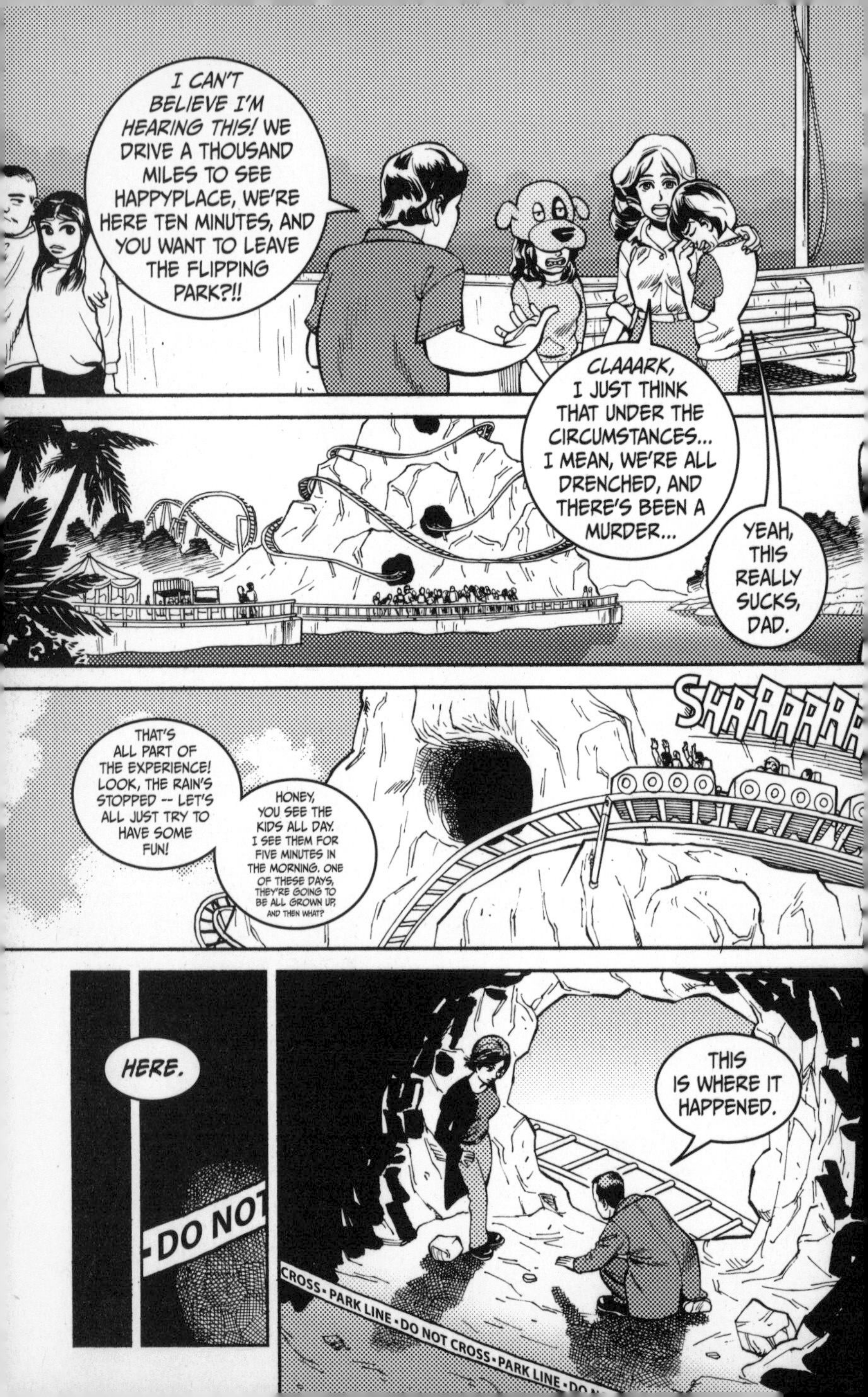
I CAN'T BELIEVE I'M HEARING THIS! WE DRIVE A THOUSAND MILES TO SEE HAPPYPLACE, WE'RE HERE TEN MINUTES, AND YOU WANT TO LEAVE THE FLIPPING PARK?!!
CLAAARK, I JUST THINK THAT UNDER THE CIRCUMSTANCES... I MEAN, WE'RE ALL DRENCHED, AND THERE'S BEEN A MURDER...
YEAH, THIS REALLY SUCKS, DAD.
THAT'S ALL PART OF THE EXPERIENCE! LOOK, THE RAIN'S STOPPED -- LET'S ALL JUST TRY TO HAVE SOME FUN!
HONEY, YOU SEE THE KIDS ALL DAY. I SEE THEM FOR FIVE MINUTES IN THE MORNING. ONE OF THESE DAYS, THEY'RE GOING TO BE ALL GROWN UP, AND THEN WHAT?
SHAAAAAA
HERE.
DO NOT
THIS IS WHERE IT HAPPENED.
CROSS • PARK LINE • DO NOT CROSS • PARK LINE • DO

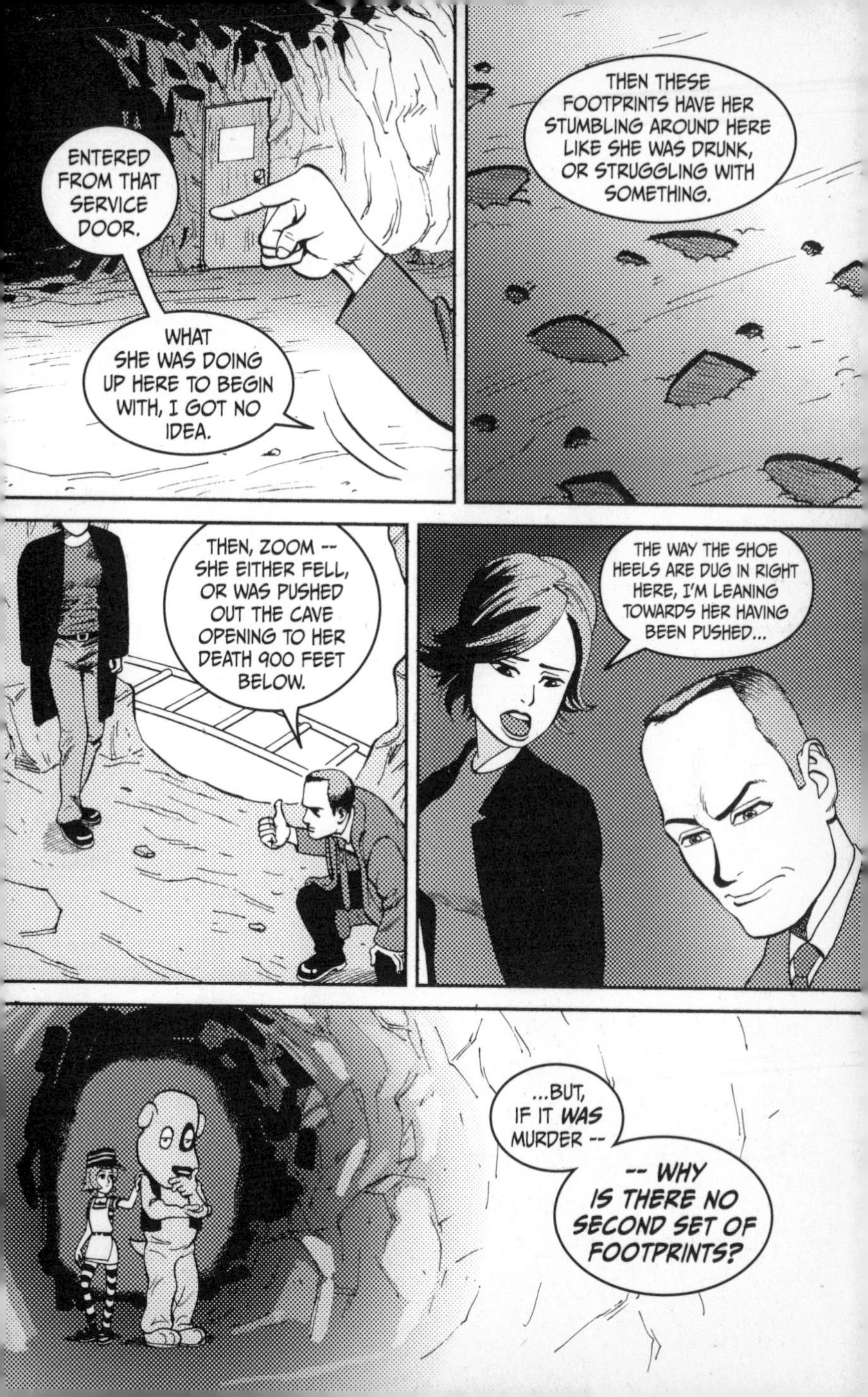
ENTERED FROM THAT SERVICE DOOR.
WHAT SHE WAS DOING UP HERE TO BEGIN WITH, I GOT NO IDEA.
THEN THESE FOOTPRINTS HAVE HER STUMBLING AROUND HERE LIKE SHE WAS DRUNK, OR STRUGGLING WITH SOMETHING.
THEN, ZOOM -- SHE EITHER FELL, OR WAS PUSHED OUT THE CAVE OPENING TO HER DEATH 900 FEET BELOW.
THE WAY THE SHOE HEELS ARE DUG IN RIGHT HERE, I'M LEANING TOWARDS HER HAVING BEEN PUSHED...
...BUT, IF IT WAS MURDER --
-- WHY IS THERE NO SECOND SET OF FOOTPRINTS?

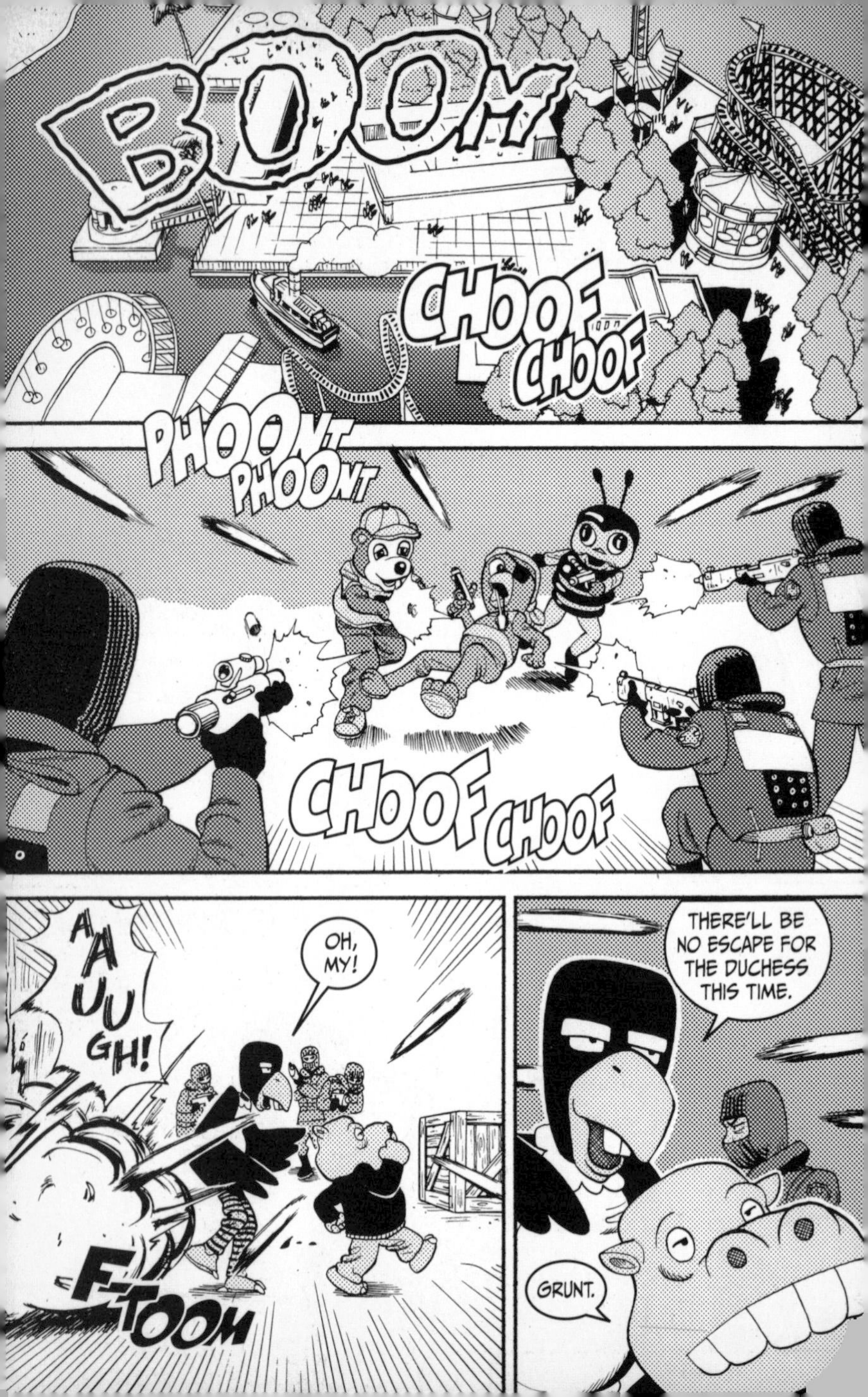
BOOM
CHOOF CHOOF
PHOONT PHOONT
CHOOF CHOOF
AAUUGH!
OH, MY!
F-TOOM
THERE'LL BE NO ESCAPE FOR THE DUCHESS THIS TIME.
GRUNT.

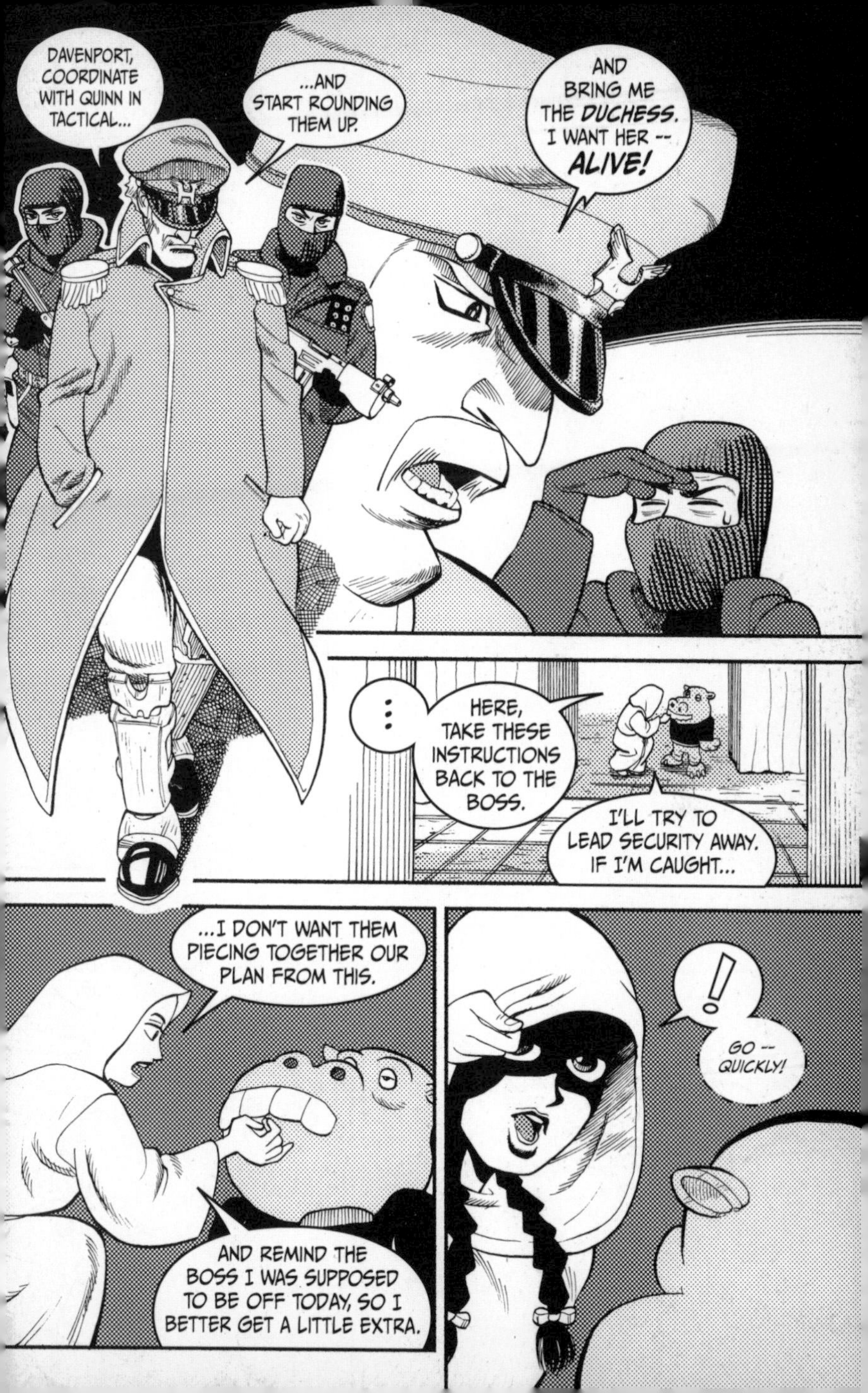
DAVENPORT, COORDINATE WITH QUINN IN TACTICAL...
...AND START ROUNDING THEM UP.
AND BRING ME THE *DUCHESS*. I WANT HER -- **ALIVE!**
...
HERE, TAKE THESE INSTRUCTIONS BACK TO THE BOSS.
I'LL TRY TO LEAD SECURITY AWAY. IF I'M CAUGHT...
...I DON'T WANT THEM PIECING TOGETHER OUR PLAN FROM THIS.
AND REMIND THE BOSS I WAS SUPPOSED TO BE OFF TODAY, SO I BETTER GET A LITTLE EXTRA.
!
GO -- QUICKLY!

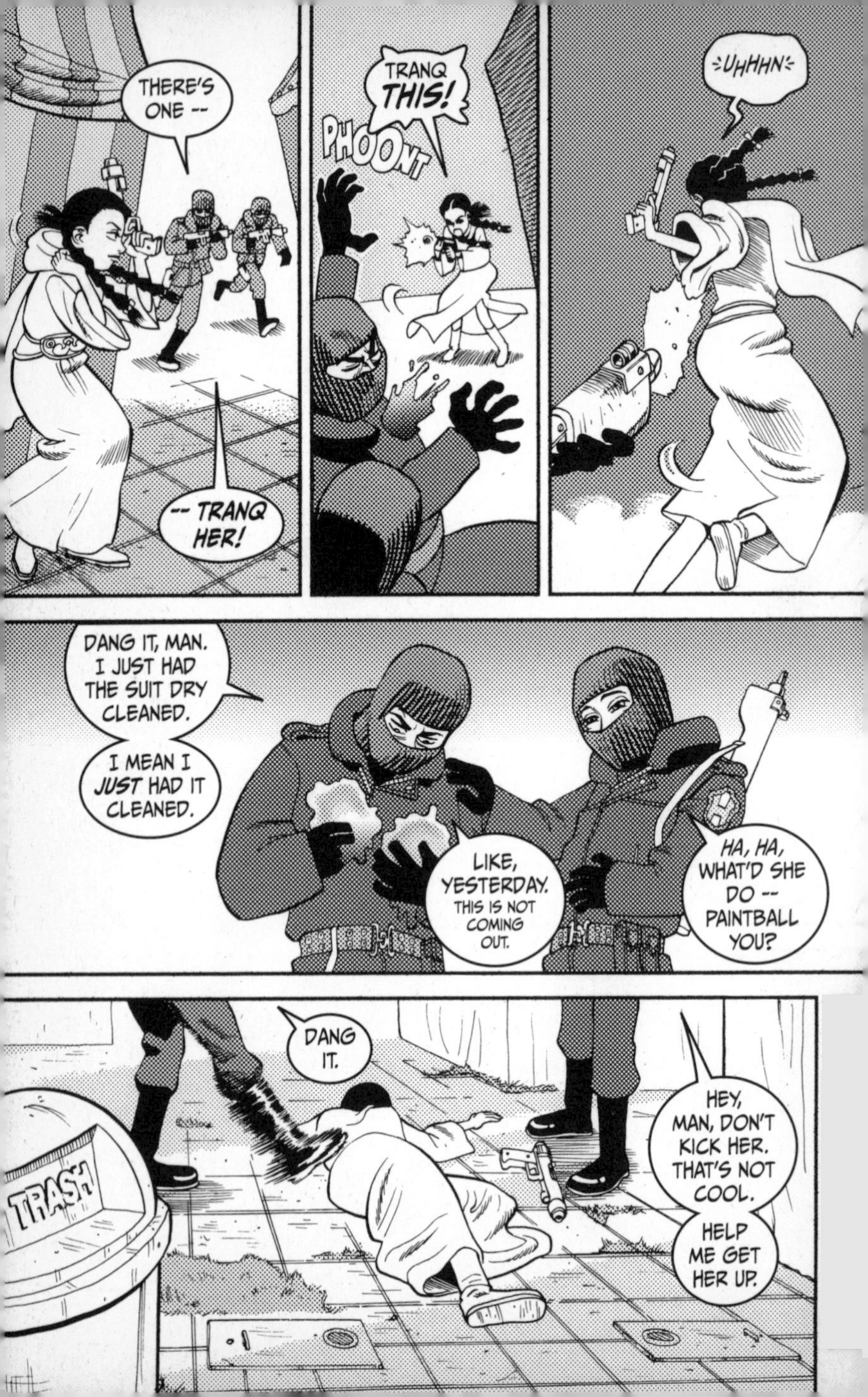
THERE'S ONE --
-- TRANQ HER!
TRANQ THIS!
PHOONT
UHHHN
DANG IT, MAN. I JUST HAD THE SUIT DRY CLEANED.
I MEAN I JUST HAD IT CLEANED.
LIKE, YESTERDAY. THIS IS NOT COMING OUT.
HA, HA, WHAT'D SHE DO -- PAINTBALL YOU?
DANG IT.
TRASH
HEY, MAN, DON'T KICK HER. THAT'S NOT COOL.
HELP ME GET HER UP.

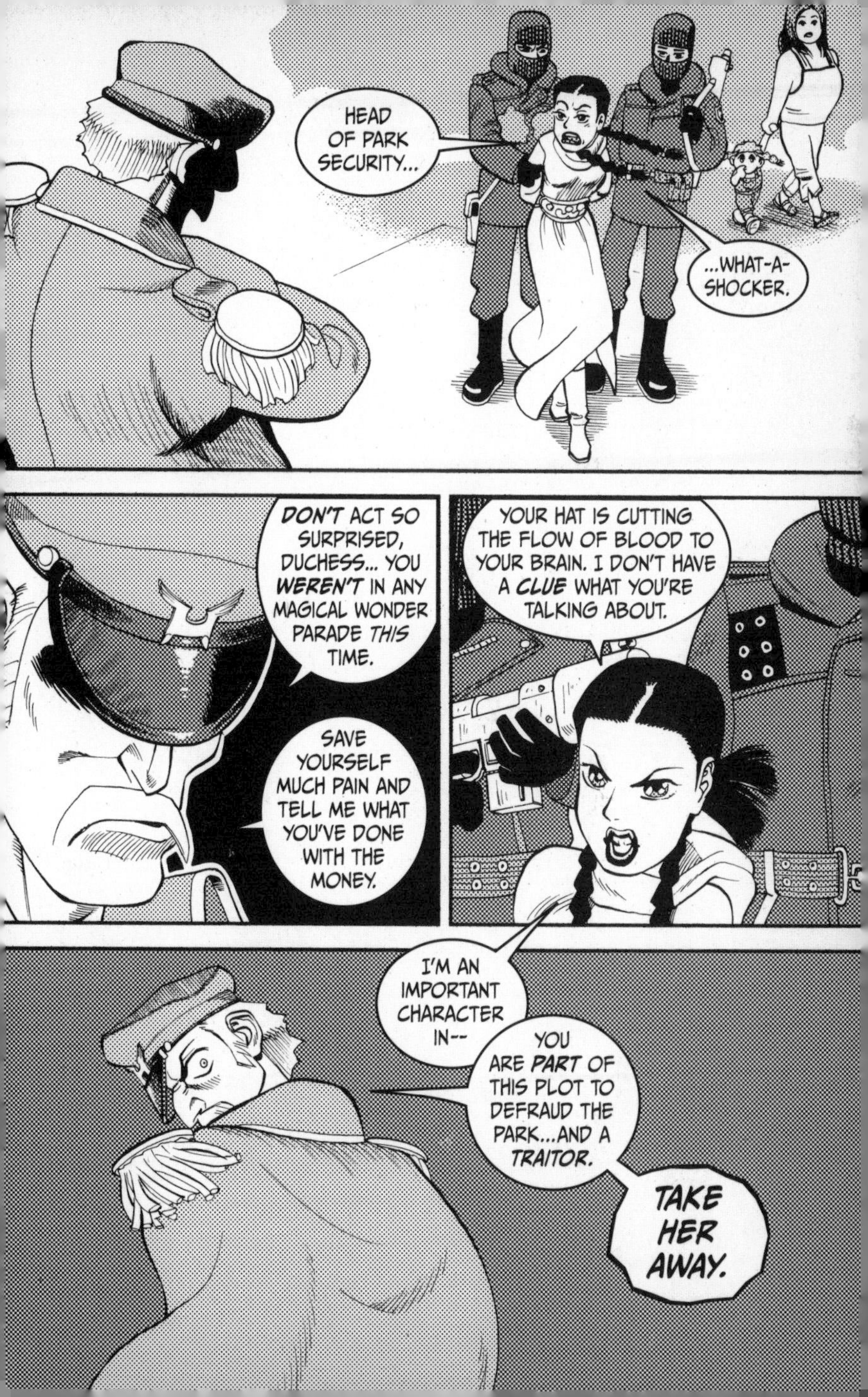
HEAD OF PARK SECURITY...
...WHAT-A-SHOCKER.
DON'T ACT SO SURPRISED, DUCHESS... YOU WEREN'T IN ANY MAGICAL WONDER PARADE THIS TIME.
SAVE YOURSELF MUCH PAIN AND TELL ME WHAT YOU'VE DONE WITH THE MONEY.
YOUR HAT IS CUTTING THE FLOW OF BLOOD TO YOUR BRAIN. I DON'T HAVE A CLUE WHAT YOU'RE TALKING ABOUT.
I'M AN IMPORTANT CHARACTER IN--
YOU ARE PART OF THIS PLOT TO DEFRAUD THE PARK...AND A TRAITOR.
TAKE HER AWAY.

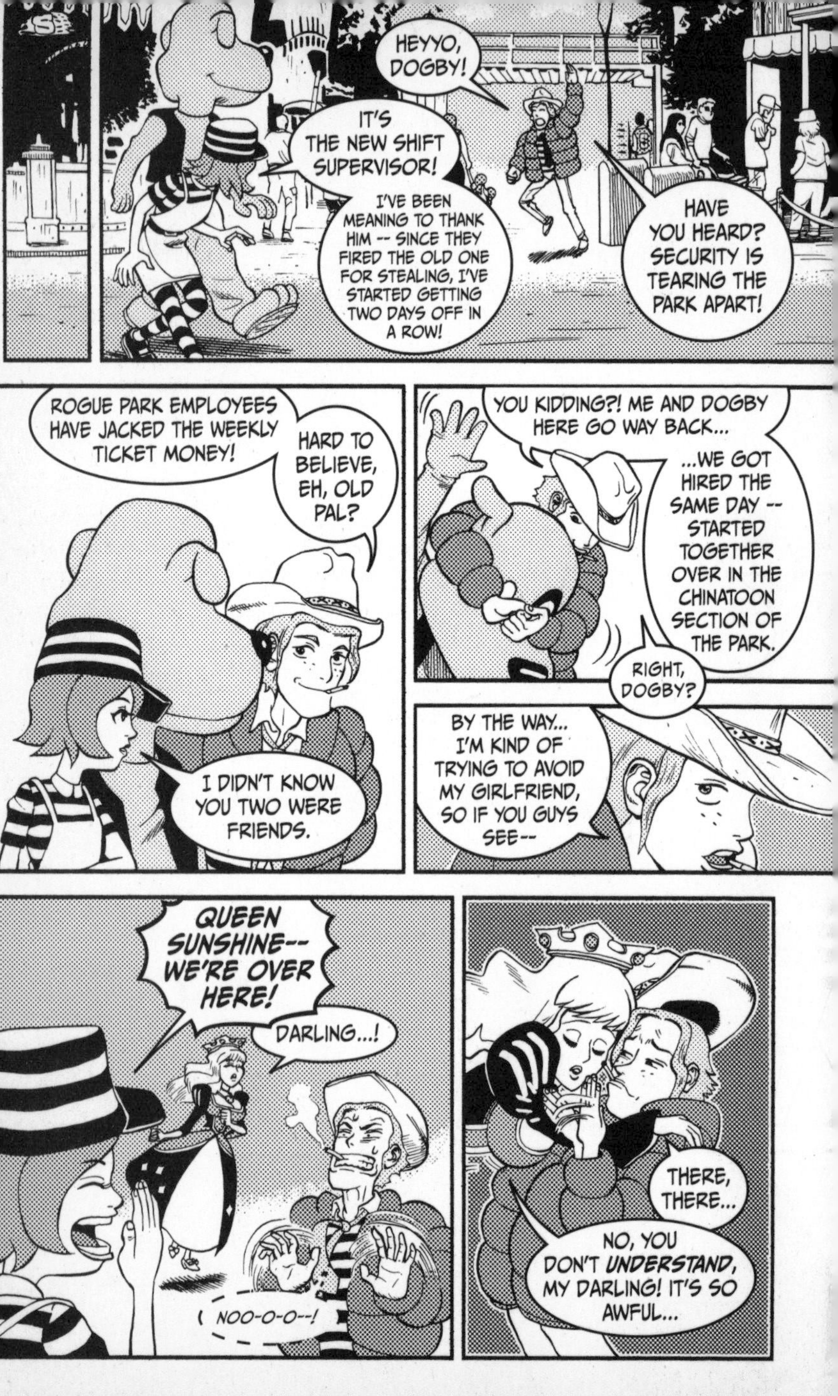
HEYYO, DOGBY!
IT'S THE NEW SHIFT SUPERVISOR!
I'VE BEEN MEANING TO THANK HIM -- SINCE THEY FIRED THE OLD ONE FOR STEALING, I'VE STARTED GETTING TWO DAYS OFF IN A ROW!
HAVE YOU HEARD? SECURITY IS TEARING THE PARK APART!
ROGUE PARK EMPLOYEES HAVE JACKED THE WEEKLY TICKET MONEY!
HARD TO BELIEVE, EH, OLD PAL?
I DIDN'T KNOW YOU TWO WERE FRIENDS.
YOU KIDDING?! ME AND DOGBY HERE GO WAY BACK...
...WE GOT HIRED THE SAME DAY -- STARTED TOGETHER OVER IN THE CHINATOON SECTION OF THE PARK.
RIGHT, DOGBY?
BY THE WAY... I'M KIND OF TRYING TO AVOID MY GIRLFRIEND, SO IF YOU GUYS SEE--
QUEEN SUNSHINE-- WE'RE OVER HERE!
DARLING...!
NOO-O-O--!
THERE, THERE...
NO, YOU DON'T UNDERSTAND, MY DARLING! IT'S SO AWFUL...

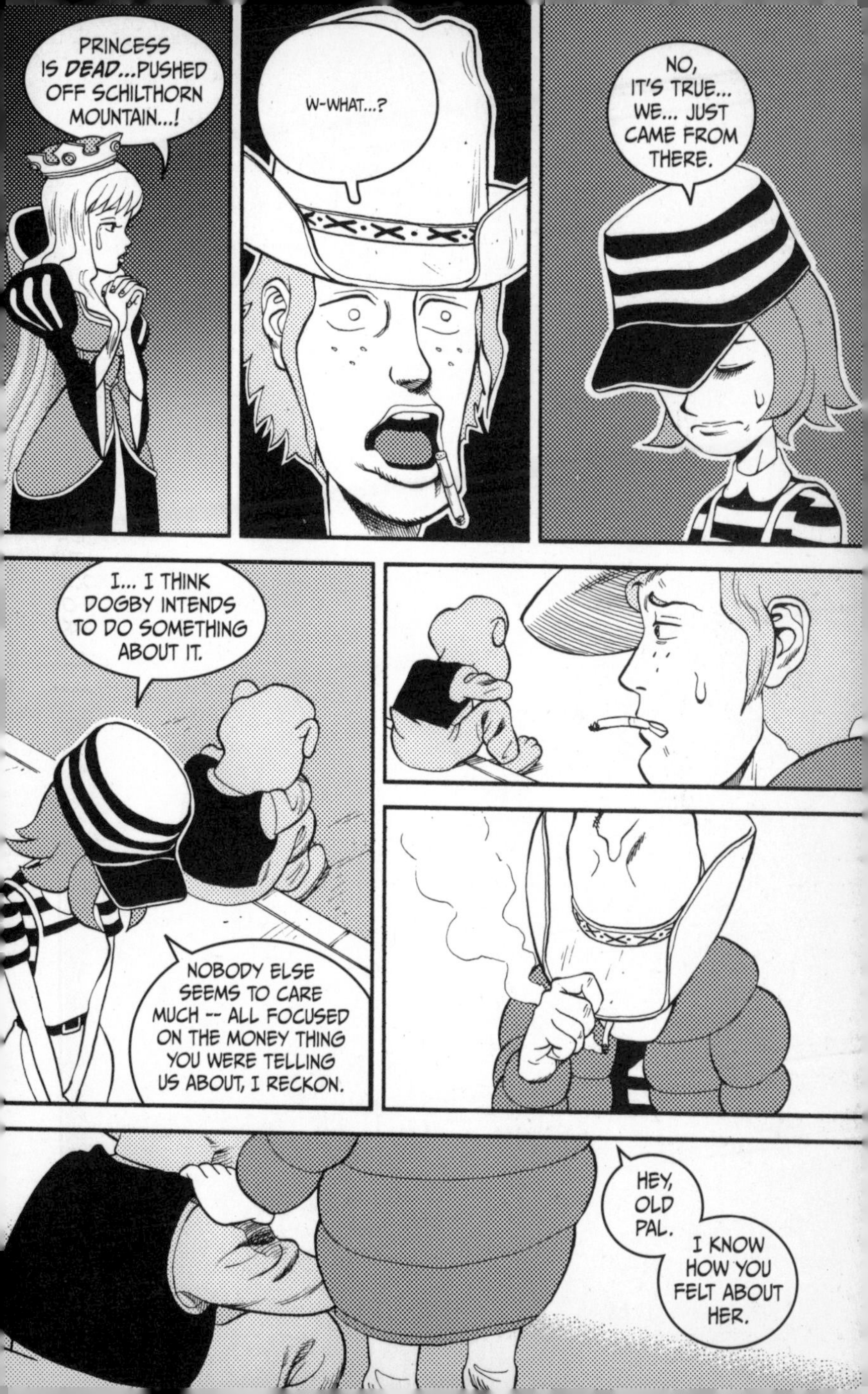
PRINCESS IS DEAD...PUSHED OFF SCHILTHORN MOUNTAIN...!
W-WHAT...?
NO, IT'S TRUE... WE... JUST CAME FROM THERE.
I... I THINK DOGBY INTENDS TO DO SOMETHING ABOUT IT.
NOBODY ELSE SEEMS TO CARE MUCH -- ALL FOCUSED ON THE MONEY THING YOU WERE TELLING US ABOUT, I RECKON.
HEY, OLD PAL.
I KNOW HOW YOU FELT ABOUT HER.

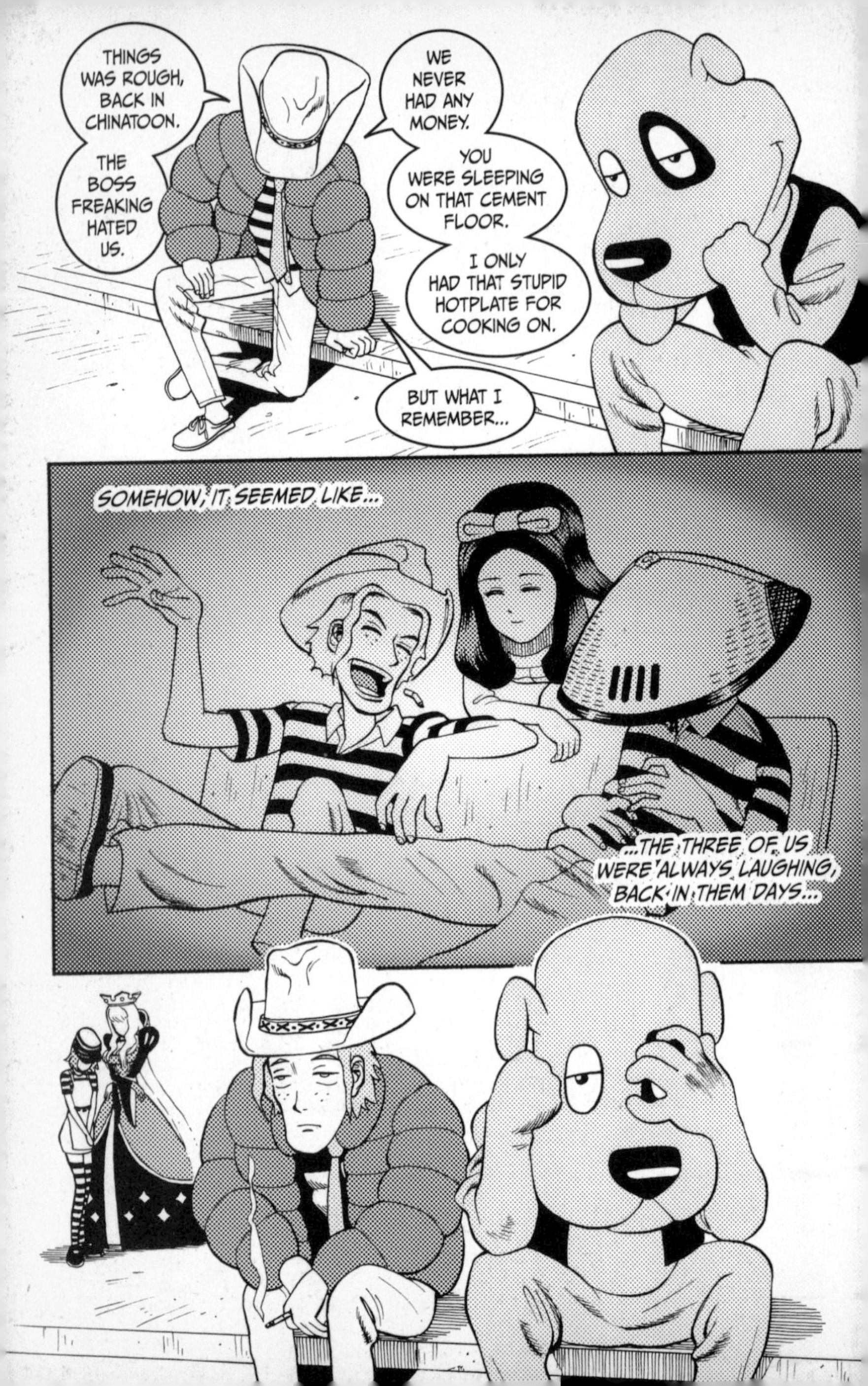
THINGS WAS ROUGH, BACK IN CHINATOON.
THE BOSS FREAKING HATED US.
WE NEVER HAD ANY MONEY.
YOU WERE SLEEPING ON THAT CEMENT FLOOR.
I ONLY HAD THAT STUPID HOTPLATE FOR COOKING ON.
BUT WHAT I REMEMBER...
SOMEHOW, IT SEEMED LIKE...
...THE THREE OF US WERE ALWAYS LAUGHING, BACK IN THEM DAYS...

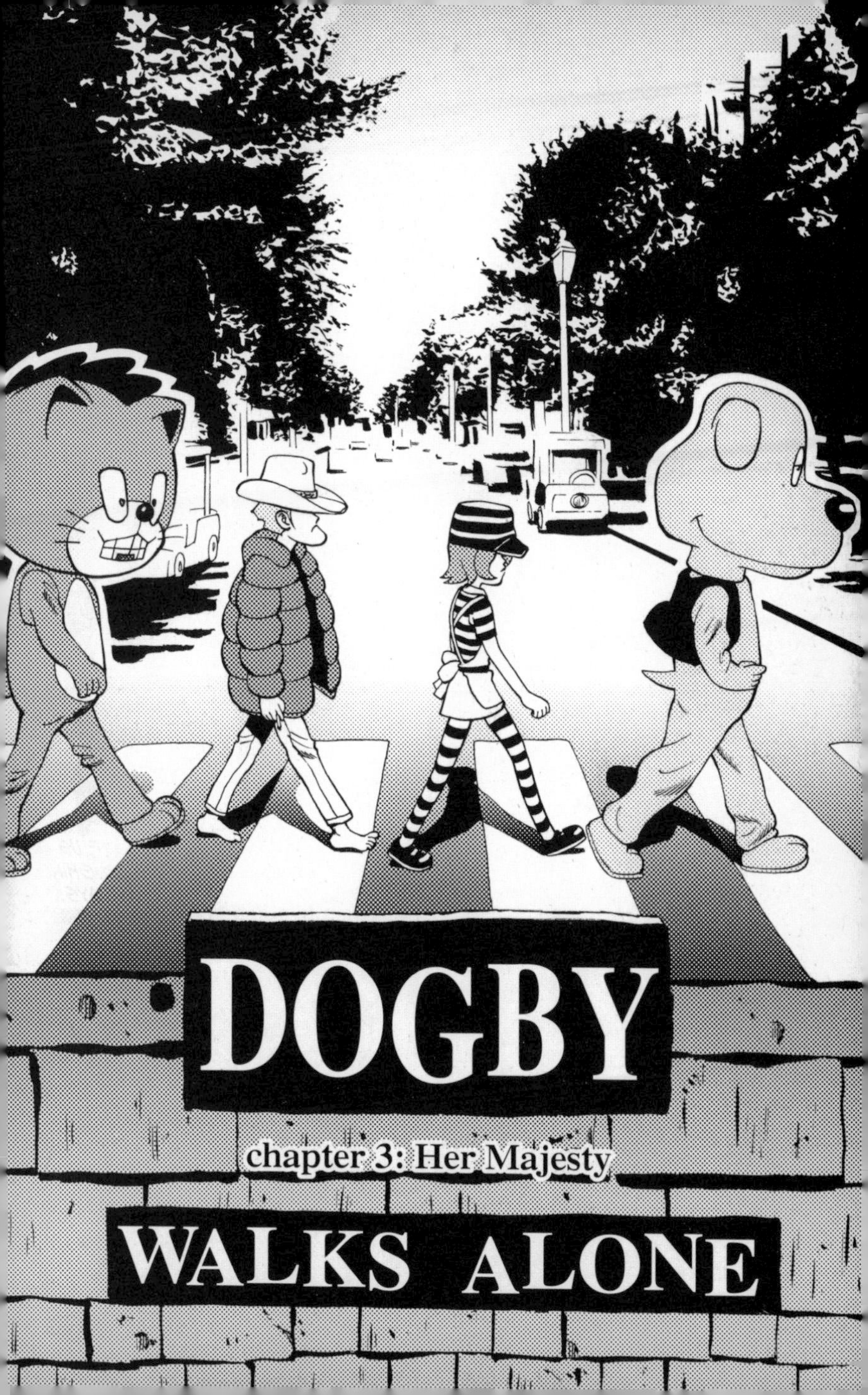
DOGBY
chapter 3: Her Majesty
WALKS ALONE

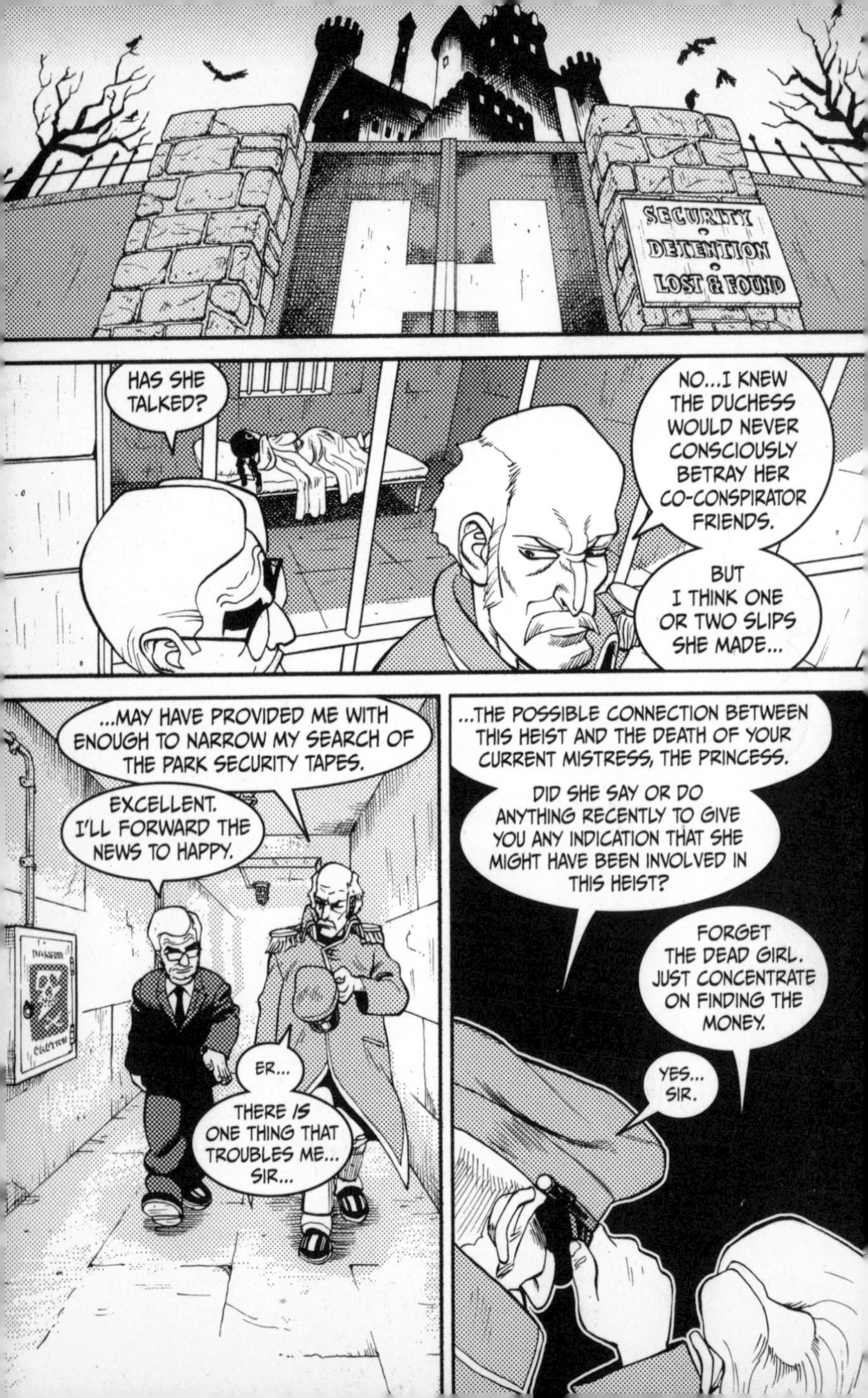
SECURITY • DETENTION • LOST & FOUND
HAS SHE TALKED?
NO...I KNEW THE DUCHESS WOULD NEVER CONSCIOUSLY BETRAY HER CO-CONSPIRATOR FRIENDS.
BUT I THINK ONE OR TWO SLIPS SHE MADE...
...MAY HAVE PROVIDED ME WITH ENOUGH TO NARROW MY SEARCH OF THE PARK SECURITY TAPES.
EXCELLENT. I'LL FORWARD THE NEWS TO HAPPY.
ER...
THERE *IS* ONE THING THAT TROUBLES ME... SIR...
...THE POSSIBLE CONNECTION BETWEEN THIS HEIST AND THE DEATH OF YOUR CURRENT MISTRESS, THE PRINCESS.
DID SHE SAY OR DO ANYTHING RECENTLY TO GIVE YOU ANY INDICATION THAT SHE MIGHT HAVE BEEN INVOLVED IN THIS HEIST?
FORGET THE DEAD GIRL. JUST CONCENTRATE ON FINDING THE MONEY.
YES... SIR.

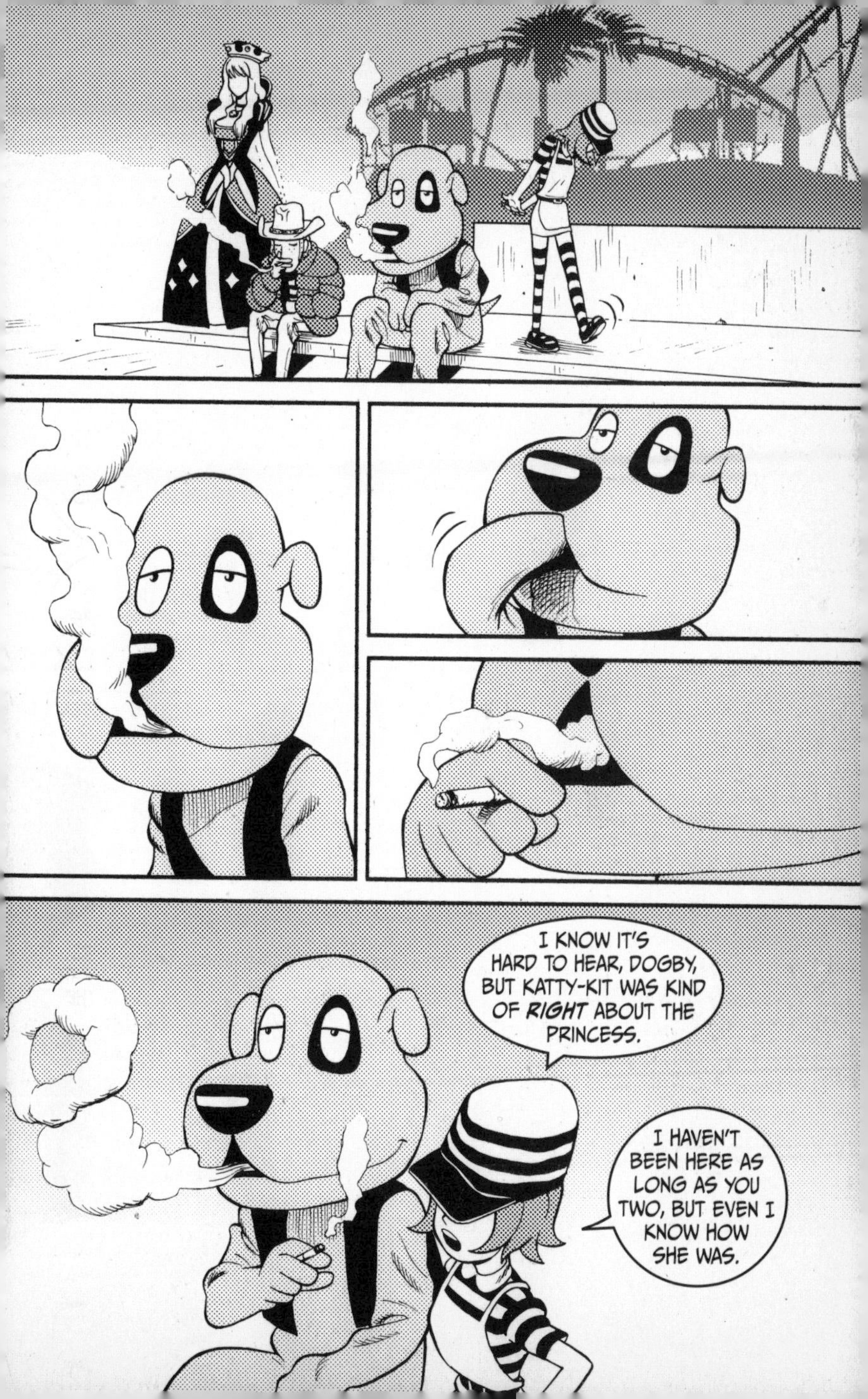
I KNOW IT'S HARD TO HEAR, DOGBY, BUT KATTY-KIT WAS KIND OF *RIGHT* ABOUT THE PRINCESS.
I HAVEN'T BEEN HERE AS LONG AS YOU TWO, BUT EVEN I KNOW HOW SHE WAS.

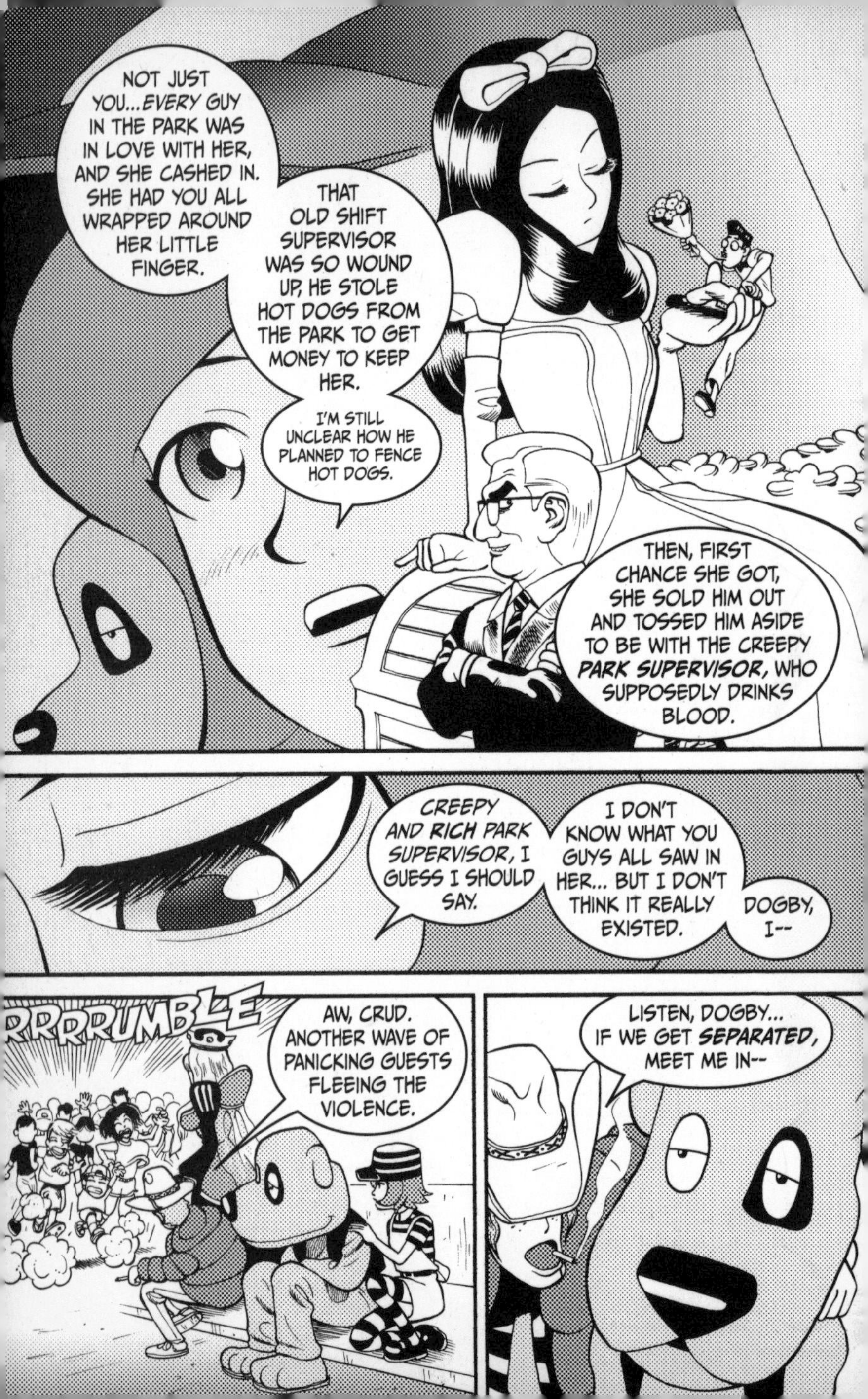

NOT JUST YOU...EVERY GUY IN THE PARK WAS IN LOVE WITH HER, AND SHE CASHED IN. SHE HAD YOU ALL WRAPPED AROUND HER LITTLE FINGER.
THAT OLD SHIFT SUPERVISOR WAS SO WOUND UP, HE STOLE HOT DOGS FROM THE PARK TO GET MONEY TO KEEP HER.
I'M STILL UNCLEAR HOW HE PLANNED TO FENCE HOT DOGS.
THEN, FIRST CHANCE SHE GOT, SHE SOLD HIM OUT AND TOSSED HIM ASIDE TO BE WITH THE CREEPY PARK SUPERVISOR, WHO SUPPOSEDLY DRINKS BLOOD.
CREEPY AND RICH PARK SUPERVISOR, I GUESS I SHOULD SAY.
I DON'T KNOW WHAT YOU GUYS ALL SAW IN HER... BUT I DON'T THINK IT REALLY EXISTED.
DOGBY, I--
RRRRRUMBLE
AW, CRUD. ANOTHER WAVE OF PANICKING GUESTS FLEEING THE VIOLENCE.
LISTEN, DOGBY... IF WE GET SEPARATED, MEET ME IN--

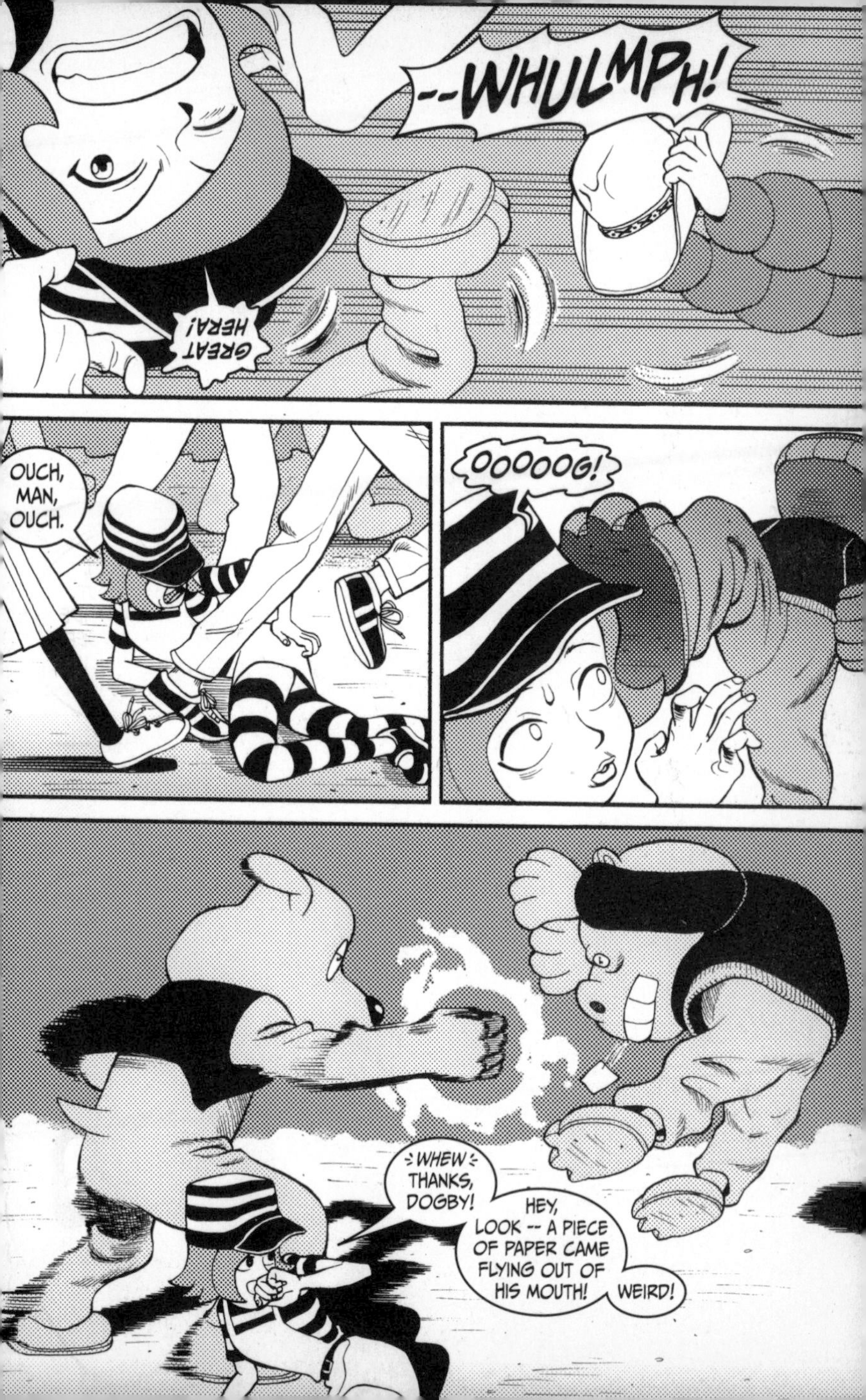
--WHULMPH!
GREAT HERA!
OUCH, MAN, OUCH.
OOOOOG!
WHEW THANKS, DOGBY!
HEY, LOOK -- A PIECE OF PAPER CAME FLYING OUT OF HIS MOUTH!
WEIRD!

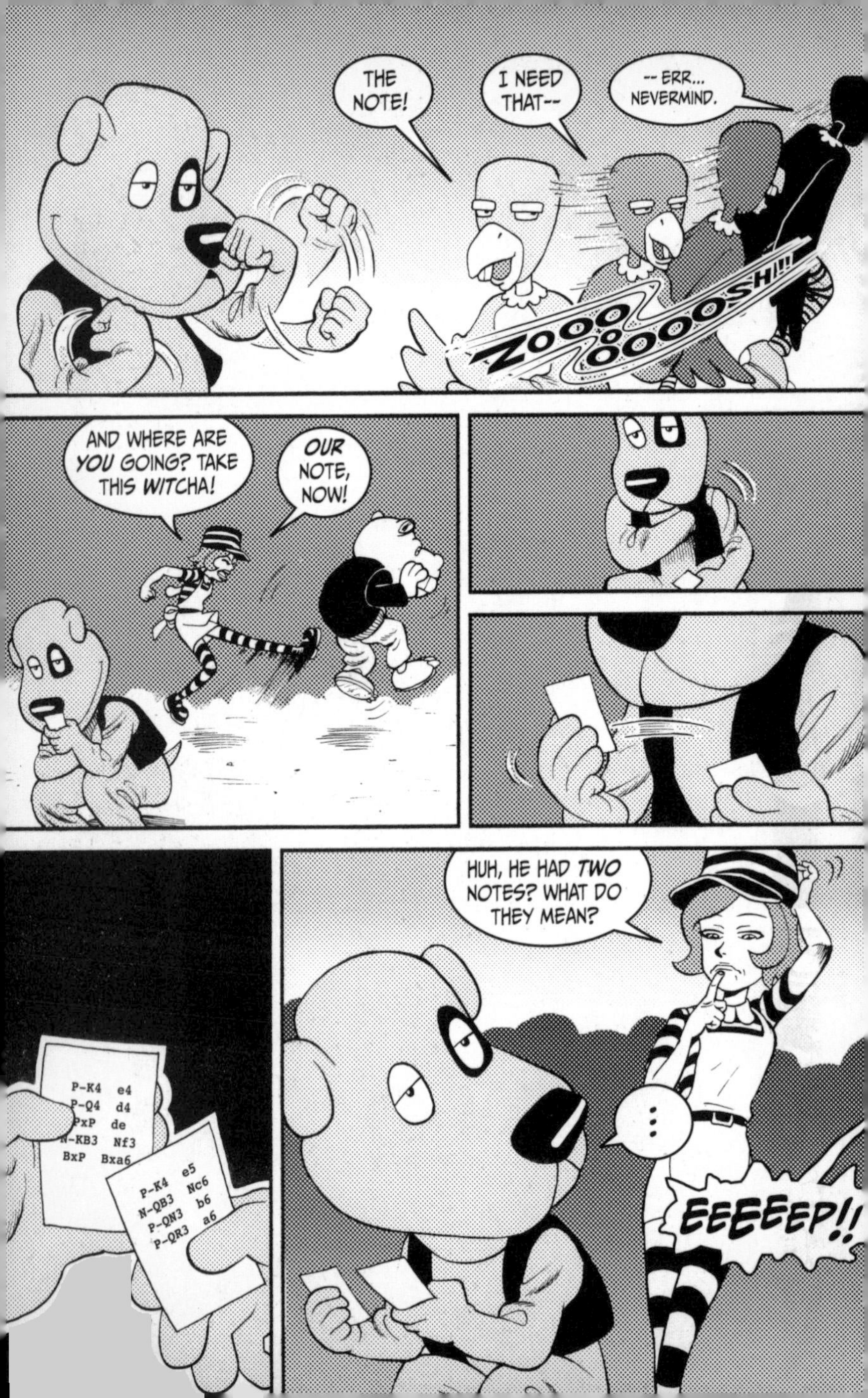
THE NOTE!
I NEED THAT--
-- ERR... NEVERMIND.
ZOOOOOOOOOSH!!!
AND WHERE ARE *YOU* GOING? TAKE THIS *WITCHA*!
OUR NOTE, NOW!
P-K4 e4
P-Q4 d4
PxP de
N-KB3 Nf3
BxP Bxa6
P-K4 e5
N-QB3 Nc6
P-QN3 b6
P-QR3 a6
HUH, HE HAD *TWO* NOTES? WHAT DO THEY MEAN?
...
EEEEEEP!!

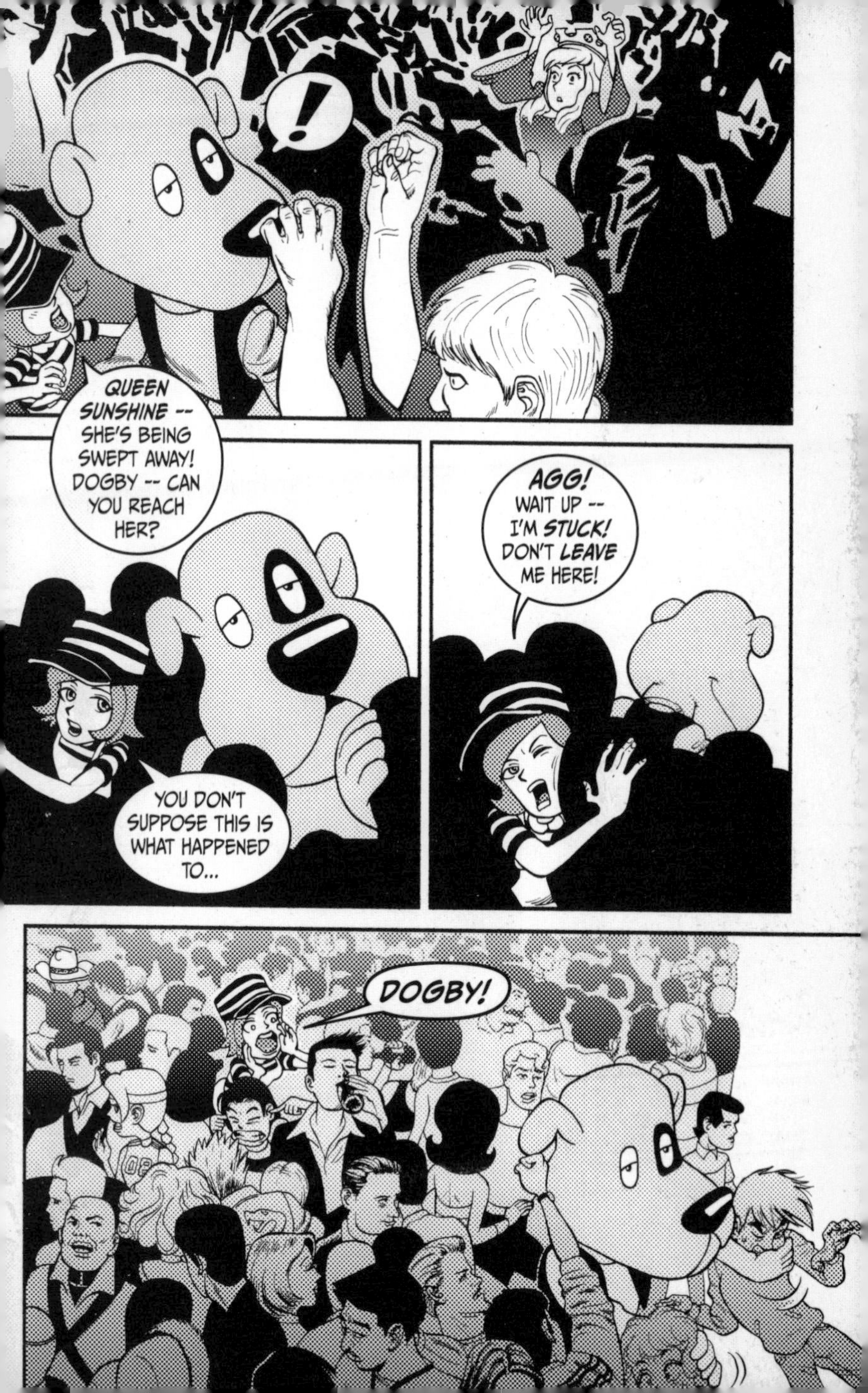
!
QUEEN SUNSHINE -- SHE'S BEING SWEPT AWAY! DOGBY -- CAN YOU REACH HER?
YOU DON'T SUPPOSE THIS IS WHAT HAPPENED TO...
AGG! WAIT UP -- I'M STUCK! DON'T LEAVE ME HERE!
DOGBY!

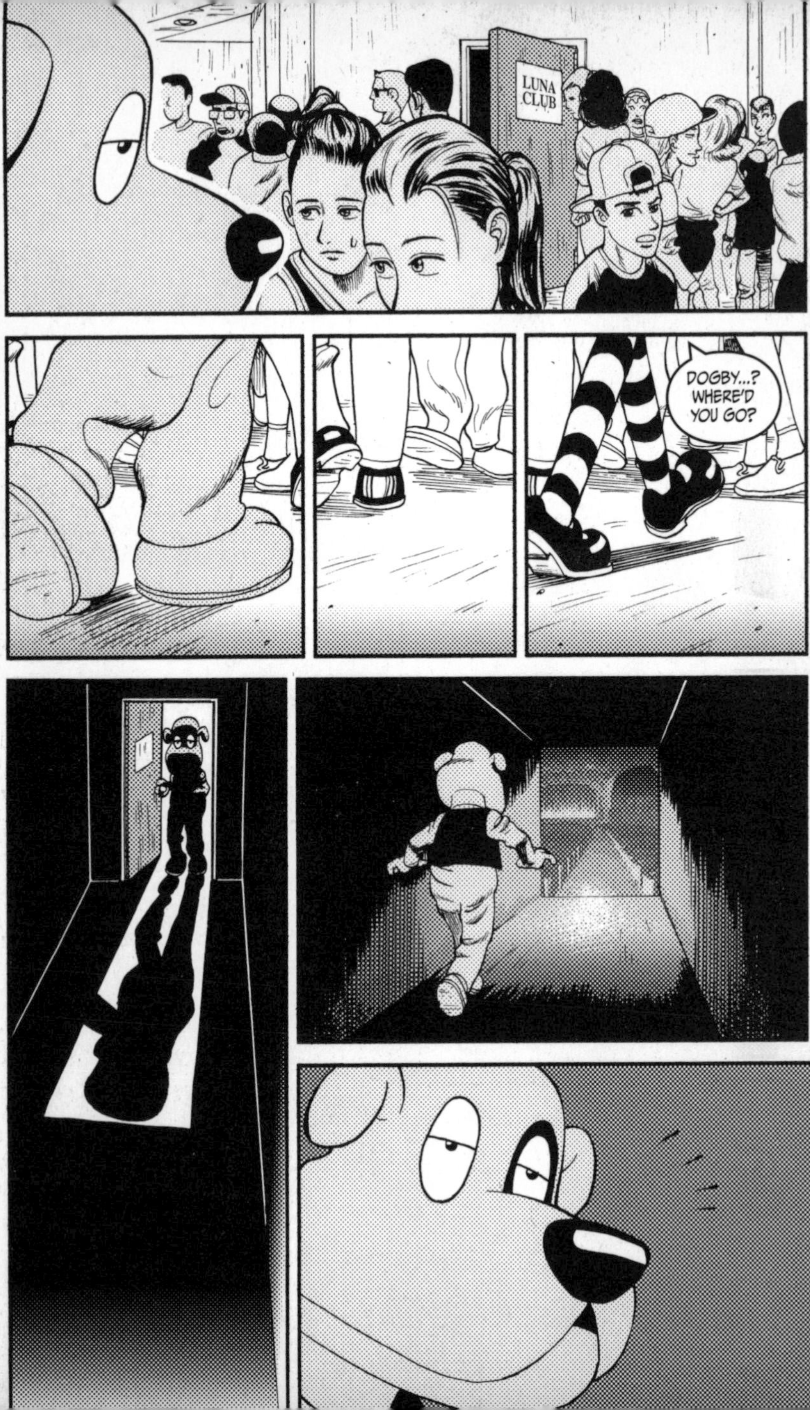
LUNA CLUB
DOGBY...? WHERE'D YOU GO?

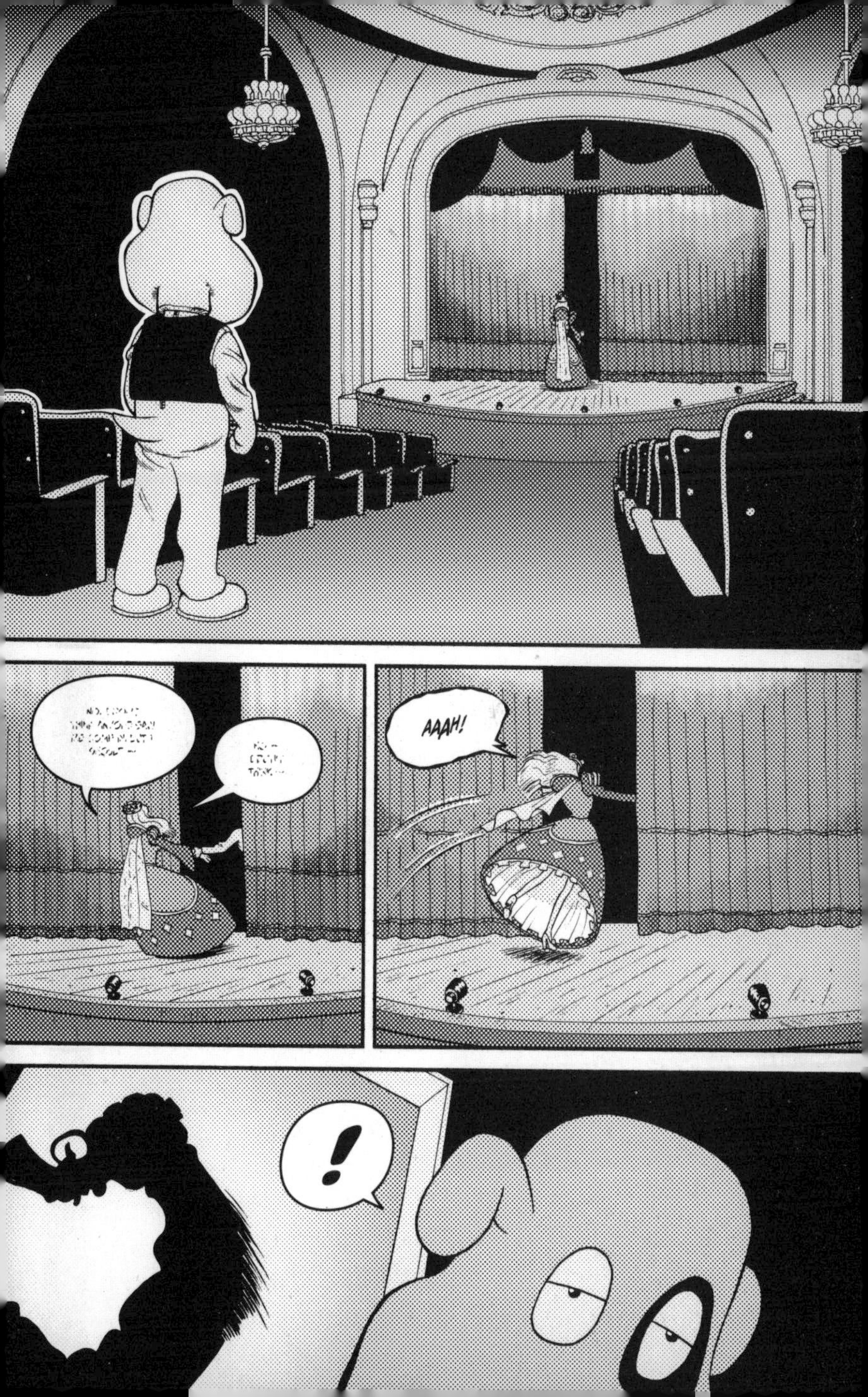
AAAH!
!

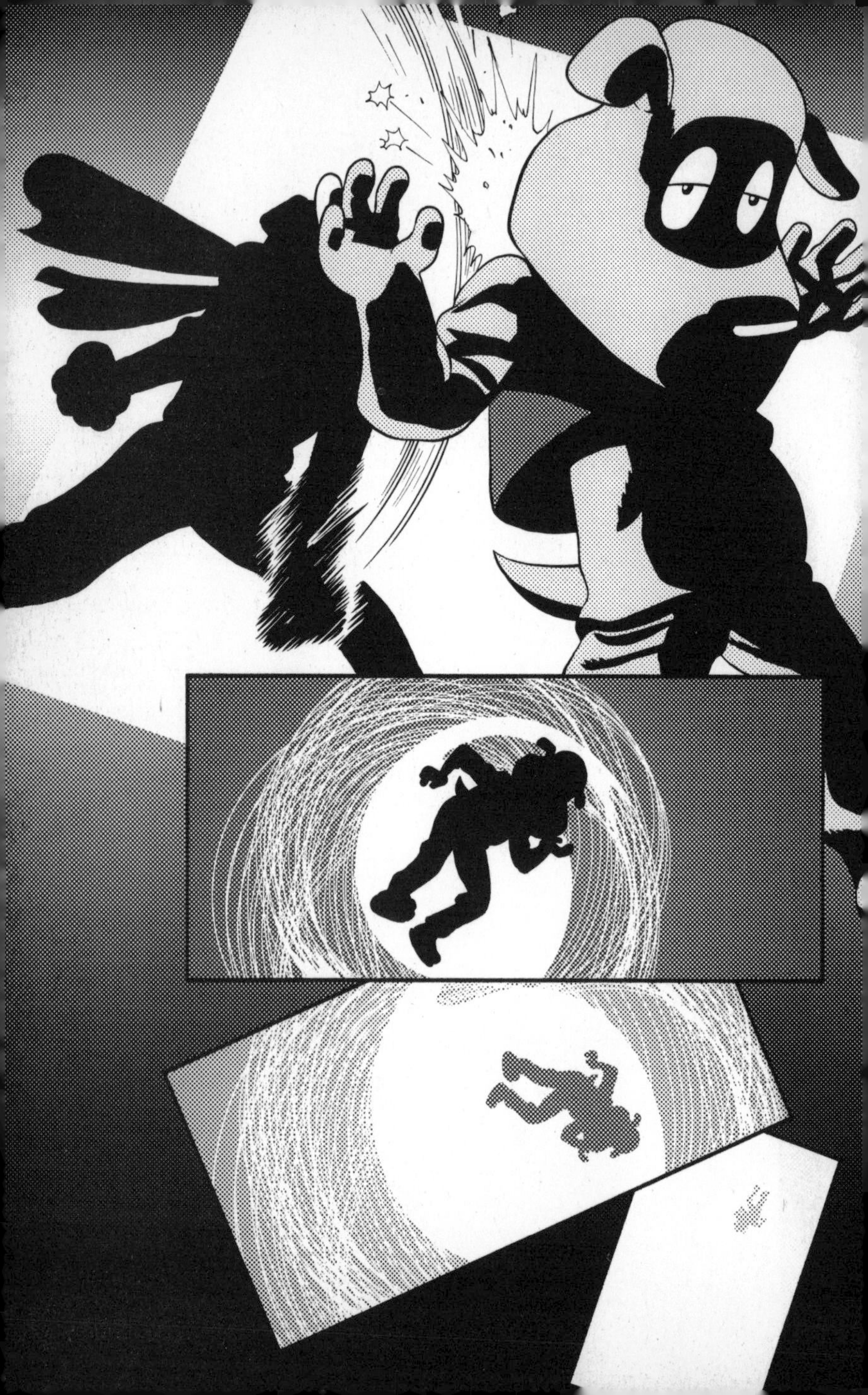

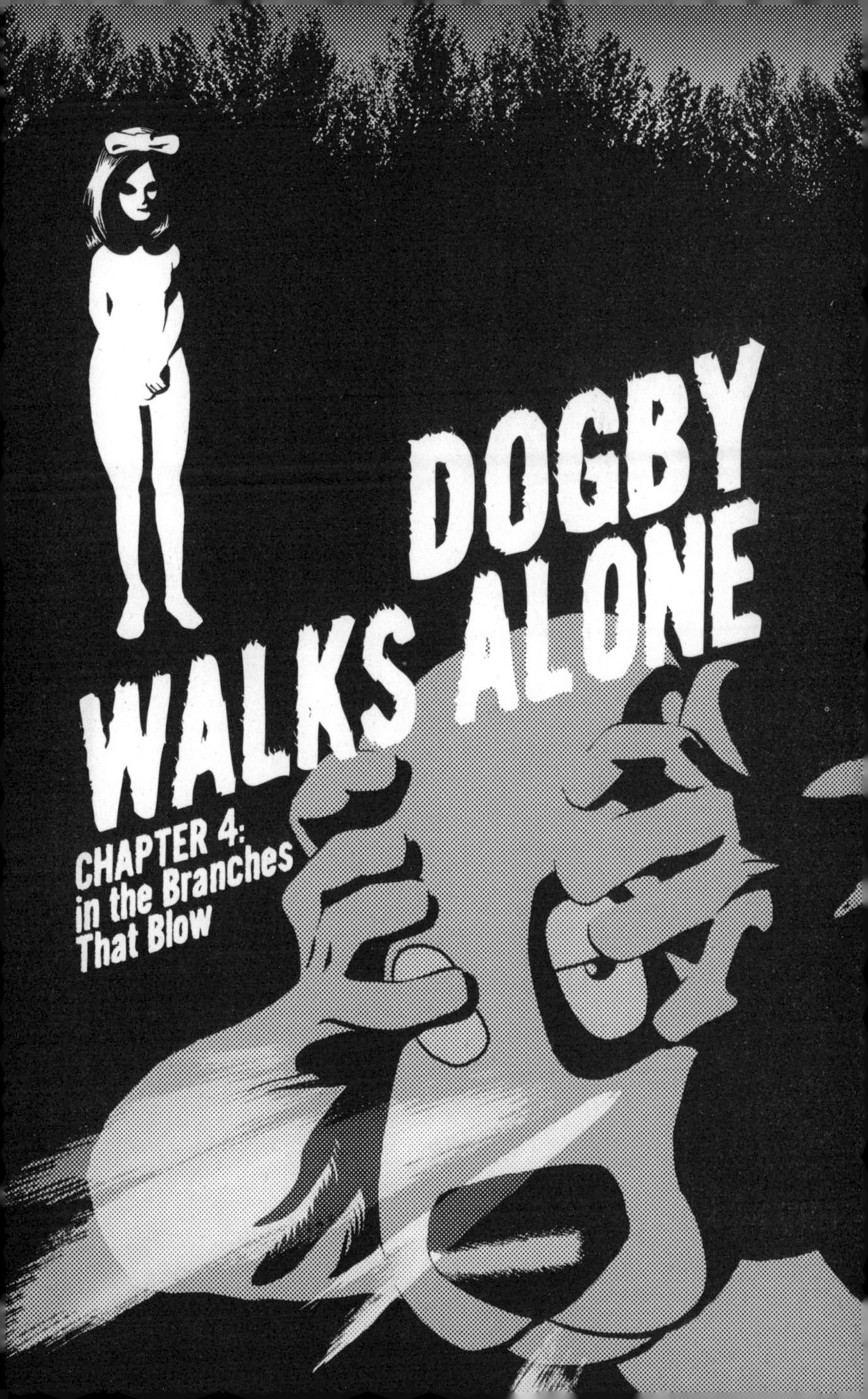
DOGBY
WALKS ALONE
CHAPTER 4:
in the Branches
That Blow

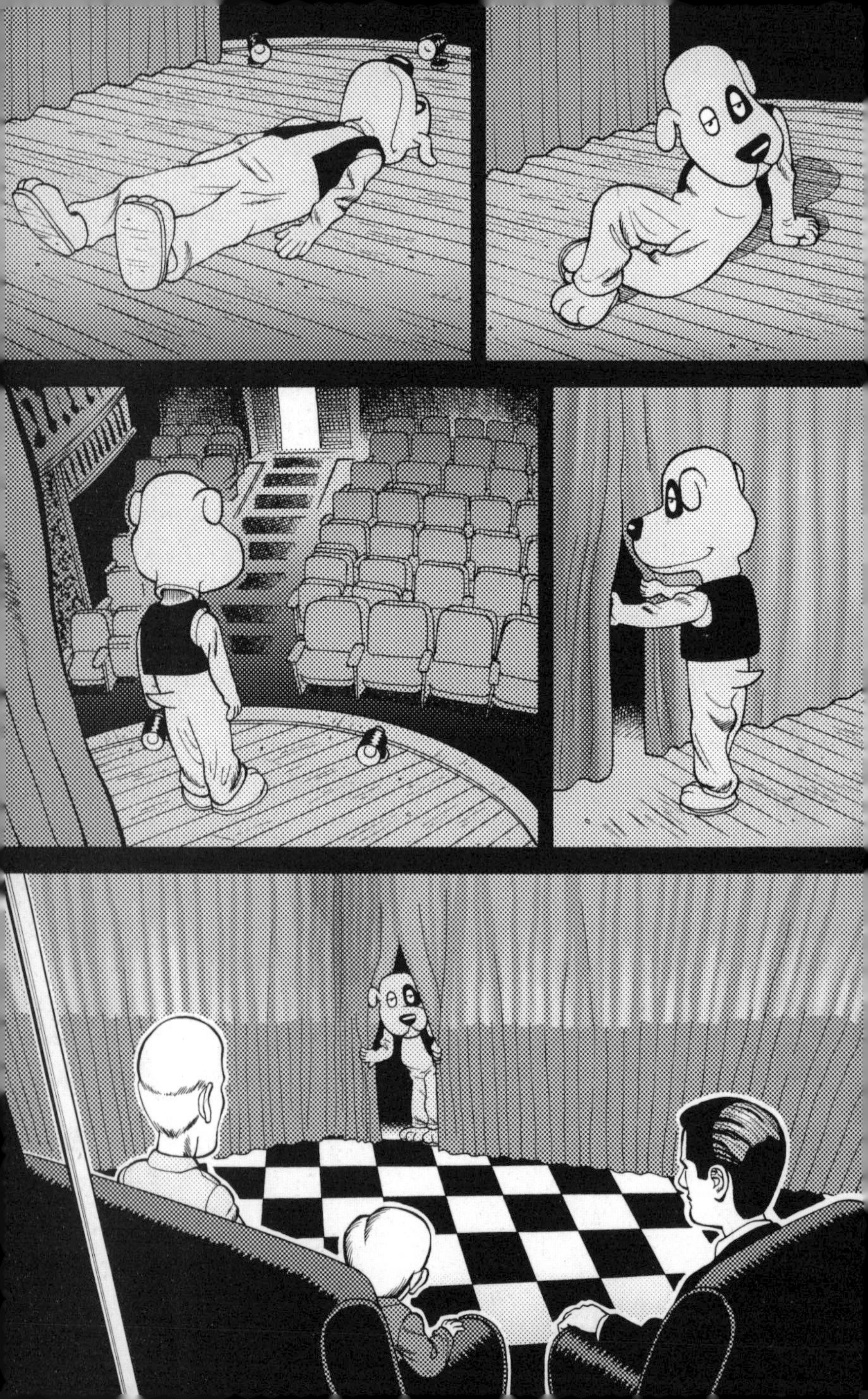

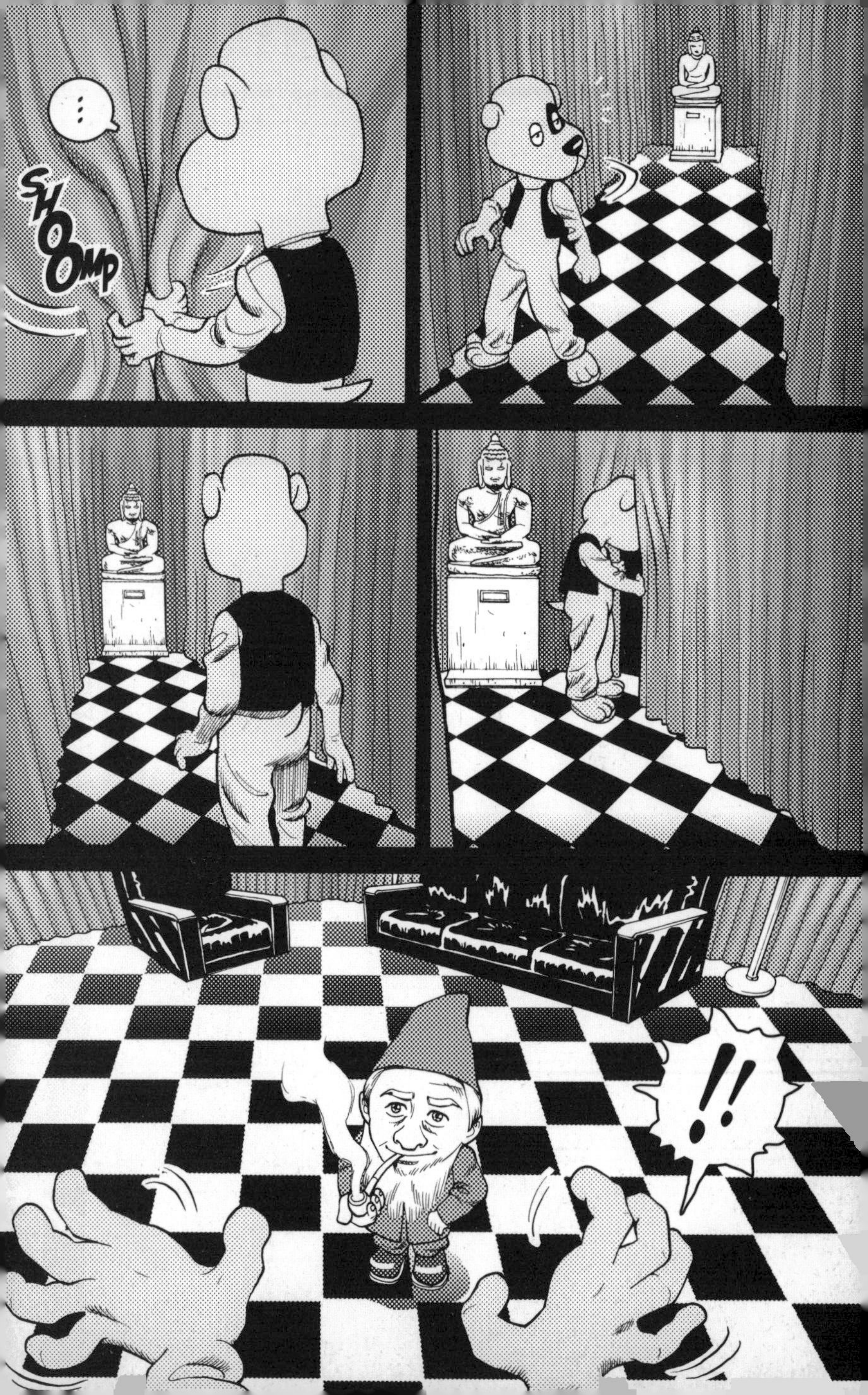
...
SHOOOMP
!!

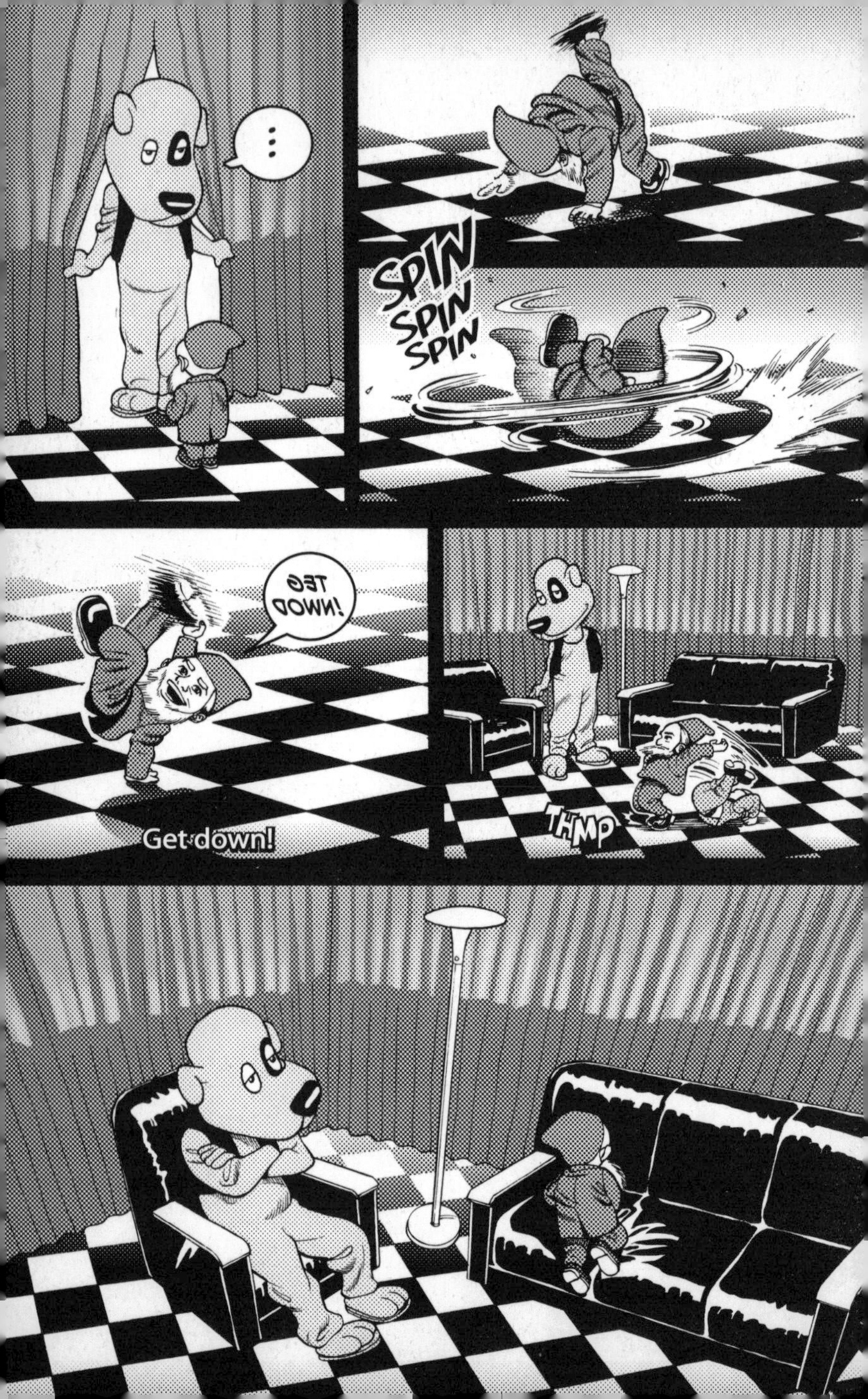
...
SPIN
SPIN
SPIN
GET DOWN!
Get down!
THMP

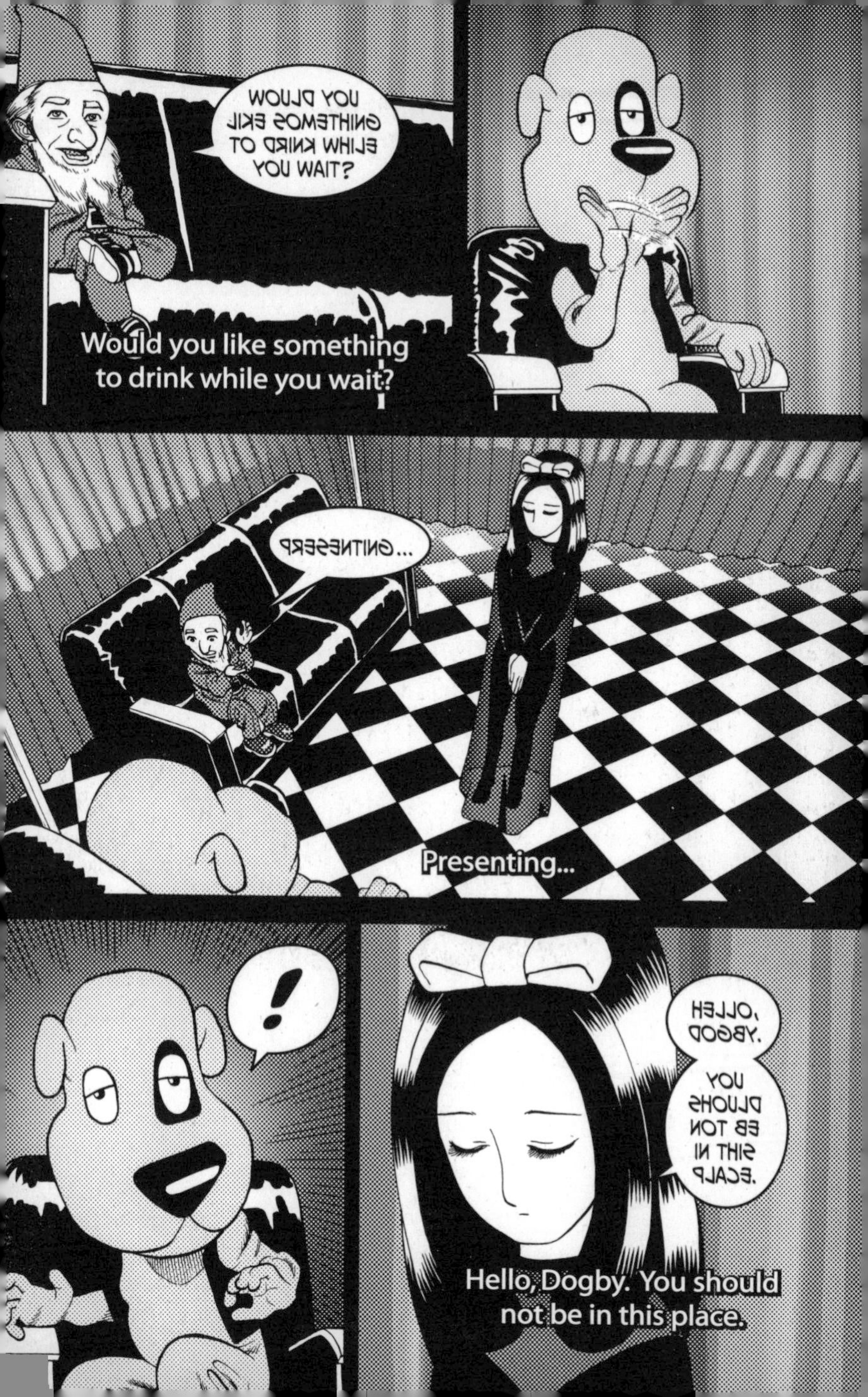
Would you like something to drink while you wait?
Presenting...
!
Hello, Dogby. You should not be in this place.

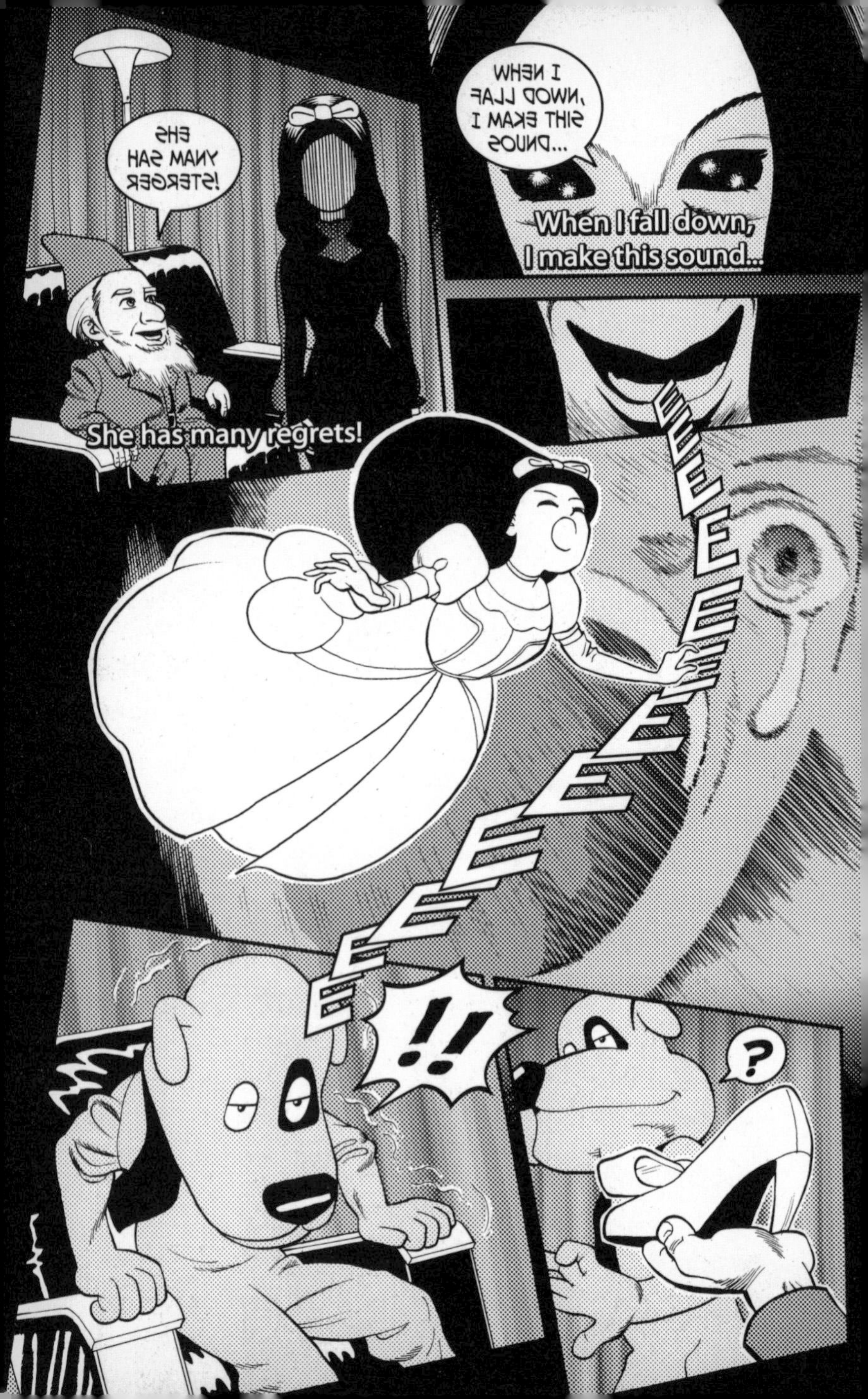
She has many regrets!
When I fall down,
I make this sound...
EEEEEEEEEEEEEEEEEEE
!!
?

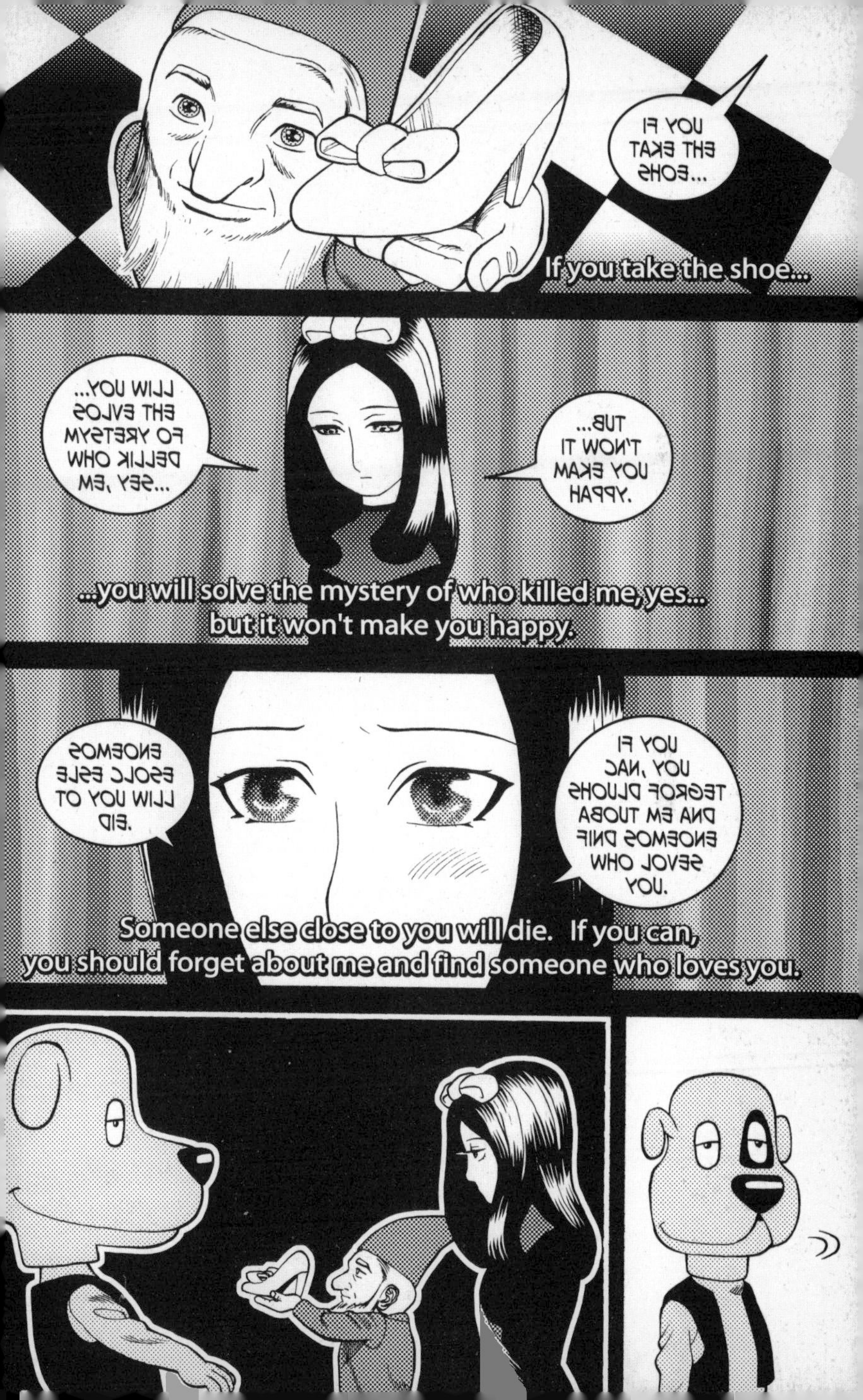
IF YOU TAKE THE SHOE...
If you take the shoe...
...YOU WILL SOLVE THE MYSTERY OF WHO KILLED ME, YES...
...BUT IT WON'T MAKE YOU HAPPY.
...you will solve the mystery of who killed me, yes... but it won't make you happy.
SOMEONE ELSE CLOSE TO YOU WILL DIE.
IF YOU CAN, YOU SHOULD FORGET ABOUT ME AND FIND SOMEONE WHO LOVES YOU.
Someone else close to you will die. If you can, you should forget about me and find someone who loves you.

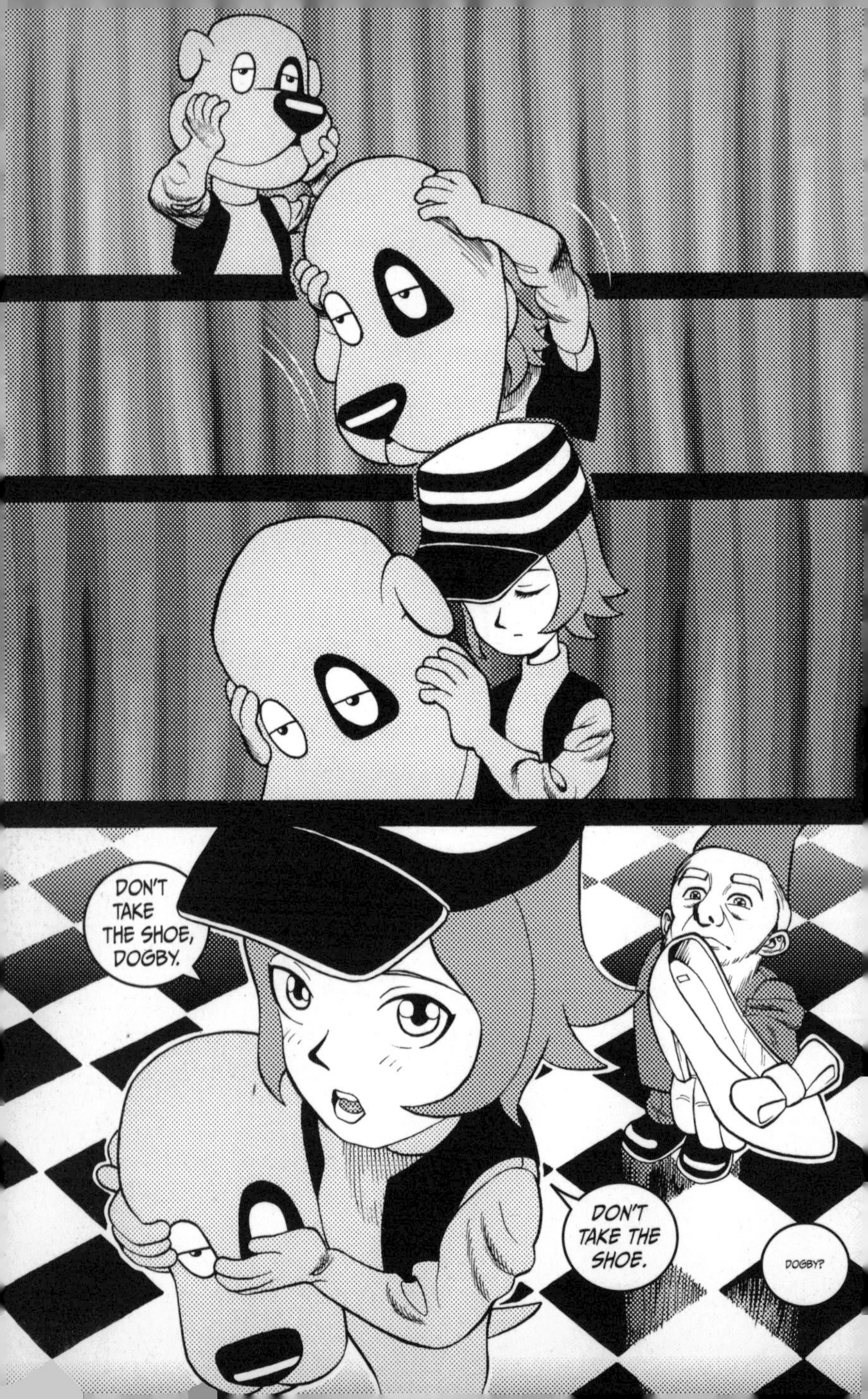
DON'T TAKE THE SHOE, DOGBY.
DON'T TAKE THE SHOE.
DOGBY?

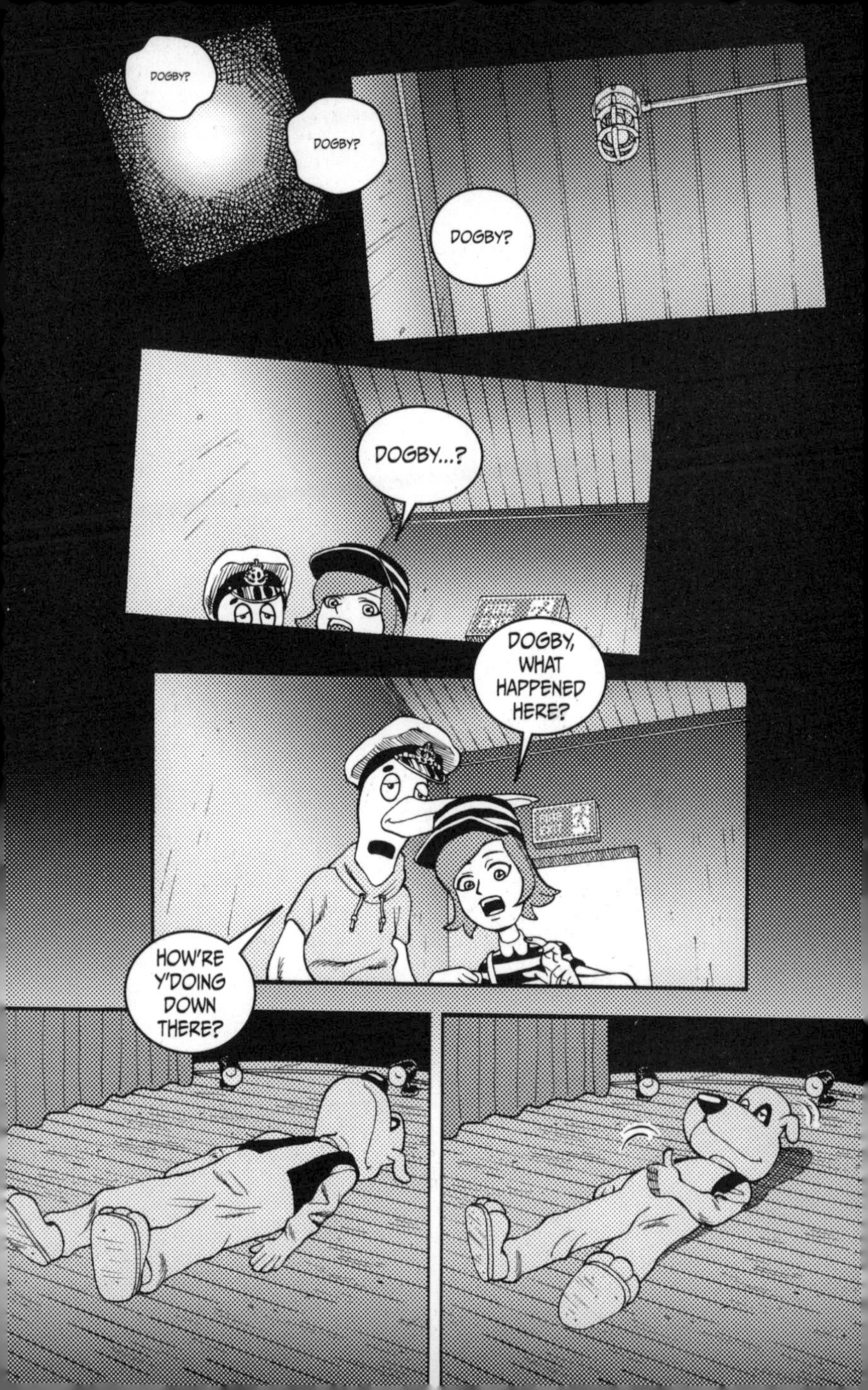
DOGBY?
DOGBY?
DOGBY?
DOGBY...?
DOGBY, WHAT HAPPENED HERE?
HOW'RE Y'DOING DOWN THERE?

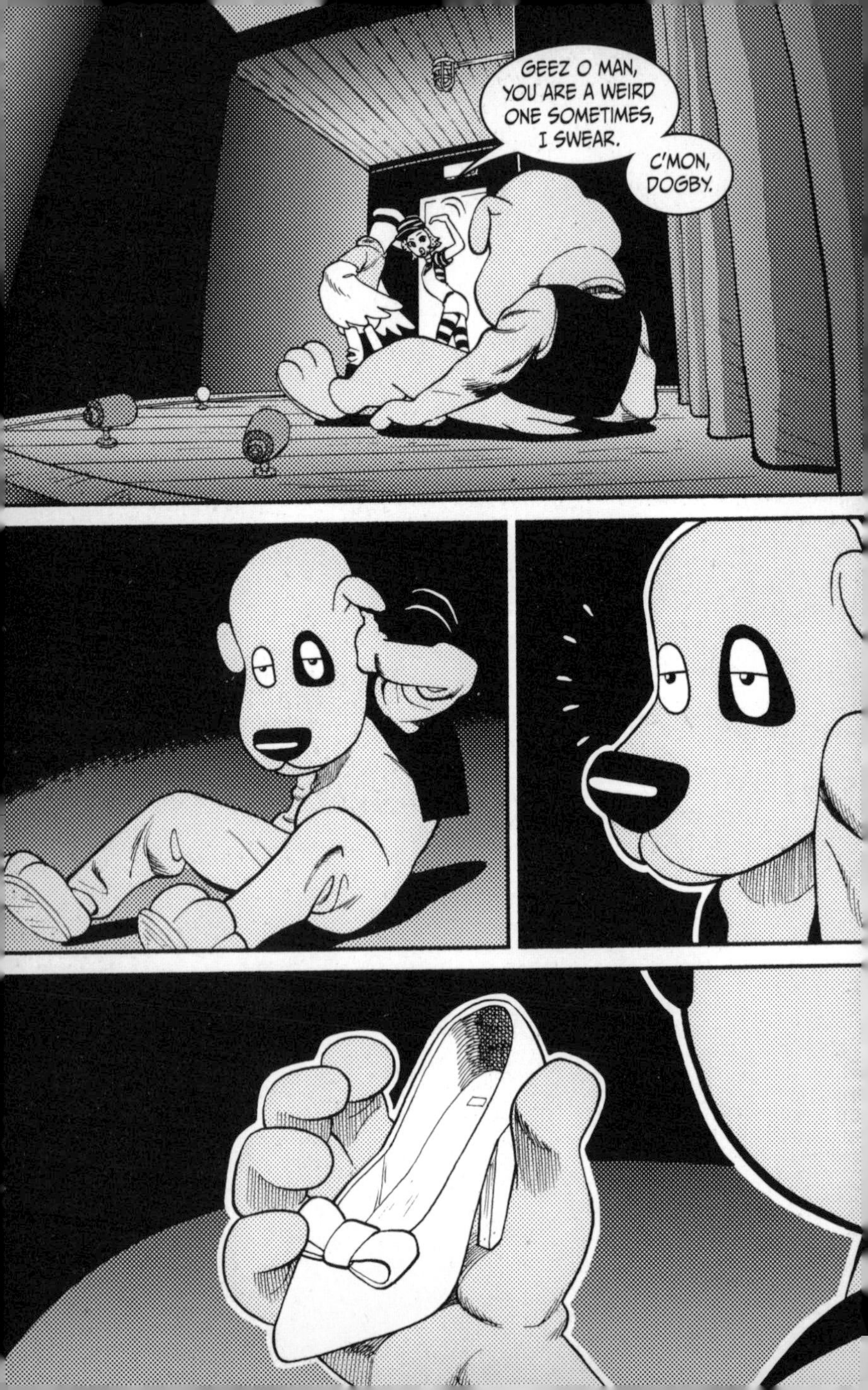
GEEZ O MAN, YOU ARE A WEIRD ONE SOMETIMES, I SWEAR.
C'MON, DOGBY.

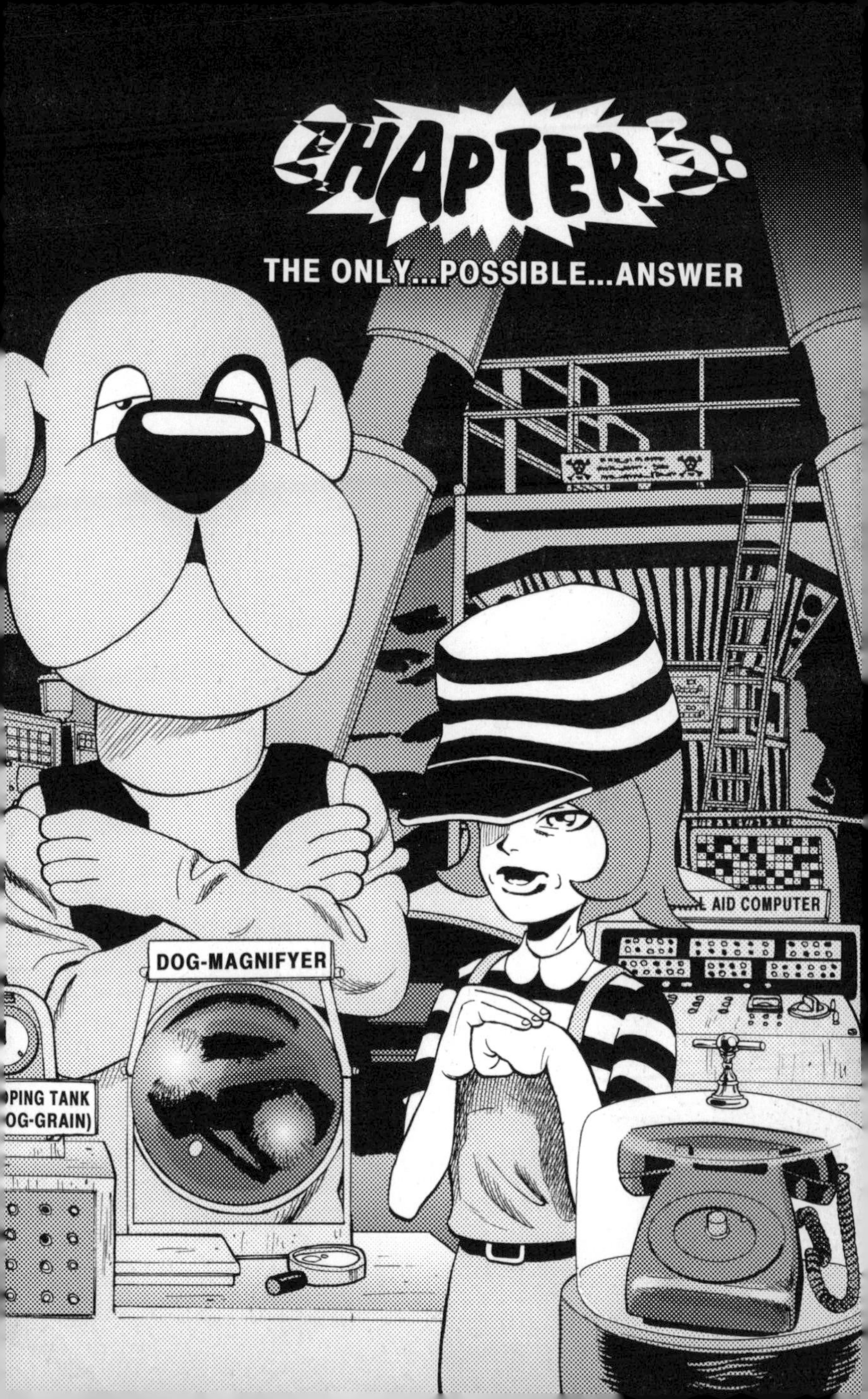
CHAPTER 3:
THE ONLY...POSSIBLE...ANSWER
AID COMPUTER
DOG-MAGNIFYER
PING TANK
OG-GRAIN)

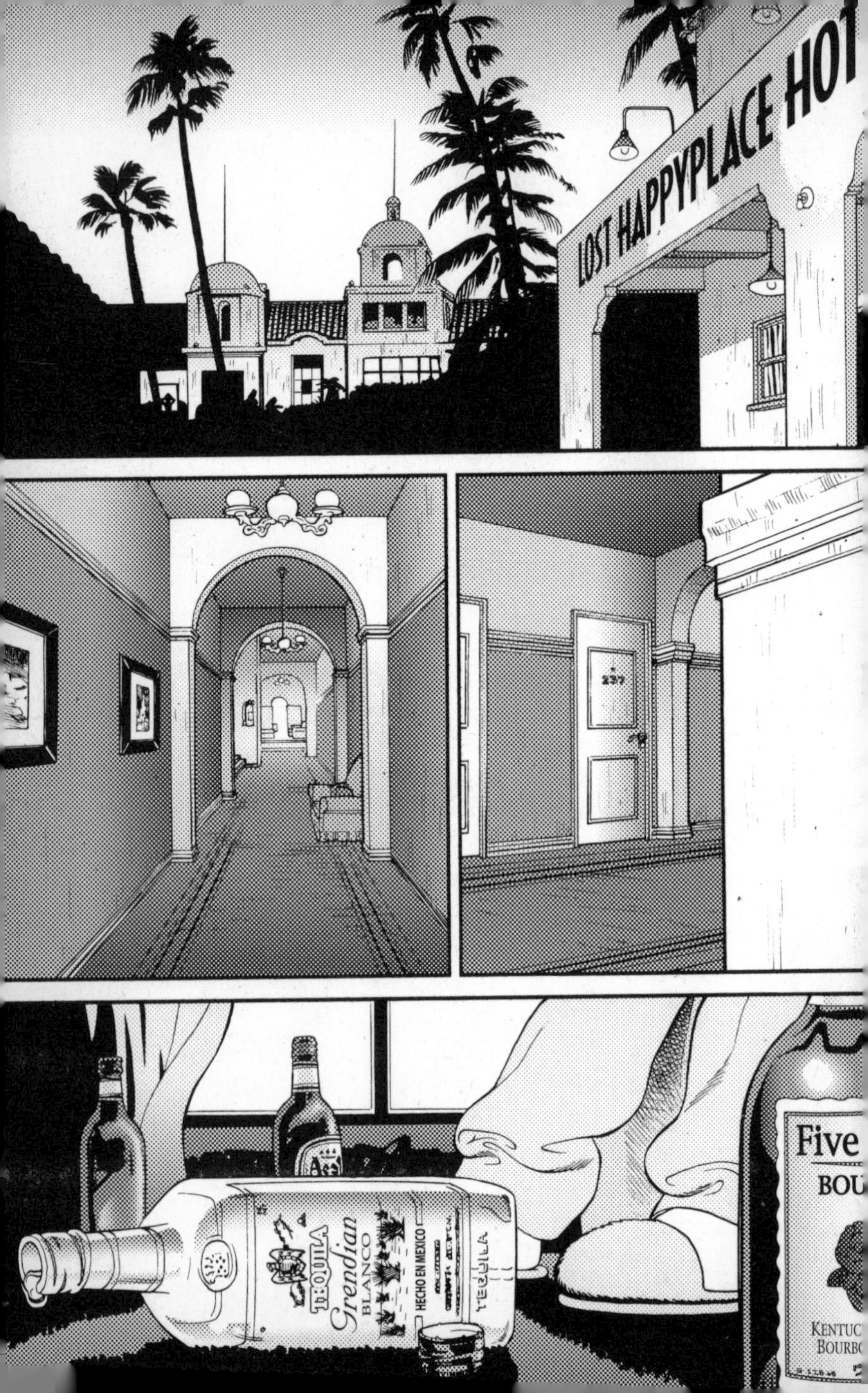
LOST HAPPYPLACE HOT
TEQUILA
Grendian
BLANCO
HECHO EN MEXICO
TEQUILA
Five
BOU
KENTUC
BOURBO

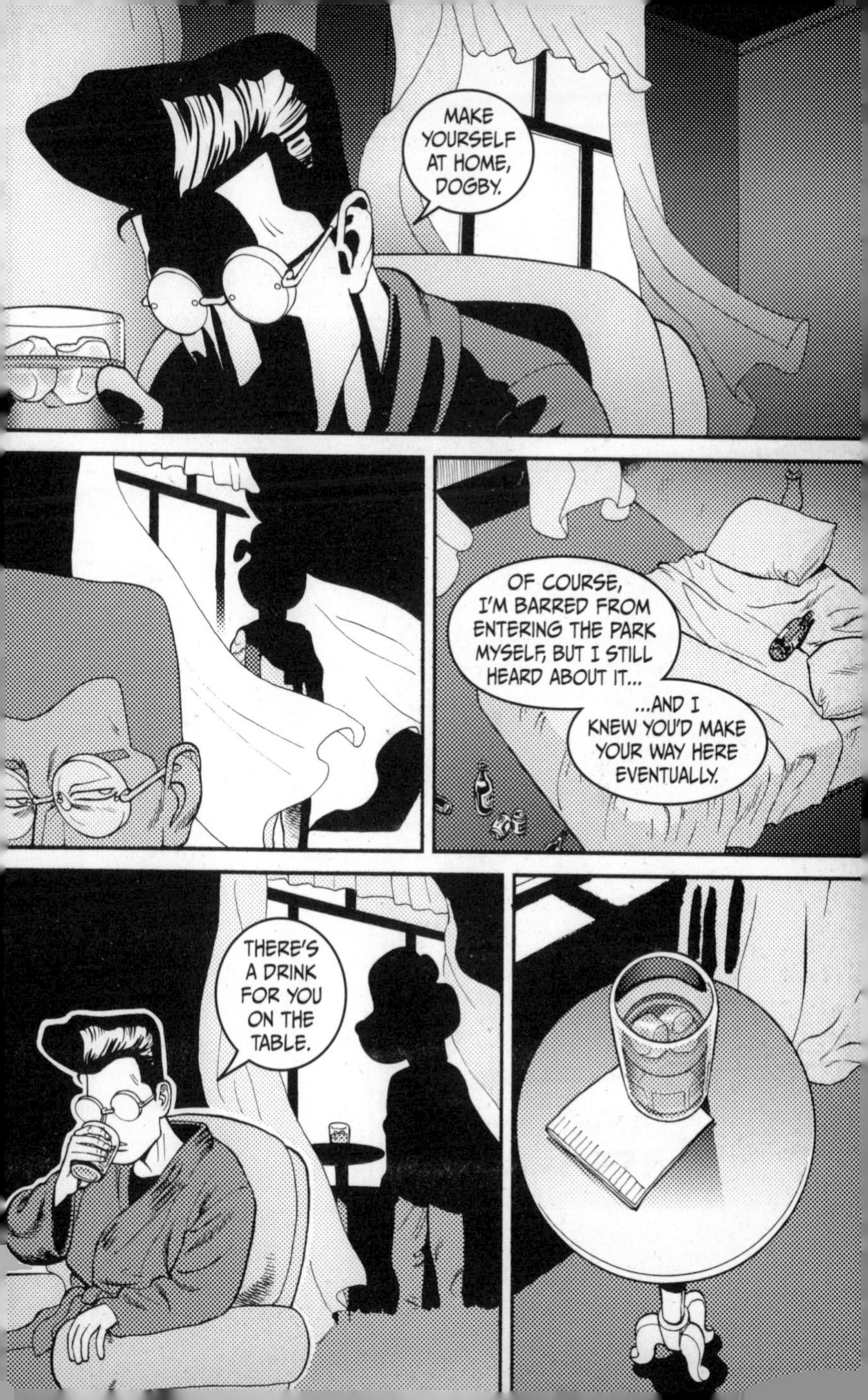
MAKE YOURSELF AT HOME, DOGBY.
OF COURSE, I'M BARRED FROM ENTERING THE PARK MYSELF, BUT I STILL HEARD ABOUT IT...
...AND I KNEW YOU'D MAKE YOUR WAY HERE EVENTUALLY.
THERE'S A DRINK FOR YOU ON THE TABLE.

I ALWAYS HATED YOU... BUT NOW YOU'RE THE ONE PERSON IN THIS WORLD I CAN STAND TO HAVE AROUND.

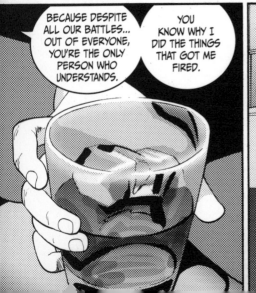

BECAUSE DESPITE ALL OUR BATTLES... OUT OF EVERYONE, YOU'RE THE ONLY PERSON WHO UNDERSTANDS.

YOU KNOW WHY I DID THE THINGS THAT GOT ME FIRED.

BUT I KNOW YOU'RE NOT HERE TO CHIT-CHAT WITH YOUR OLDEST FOE.

YOU WANT TO KNOW...

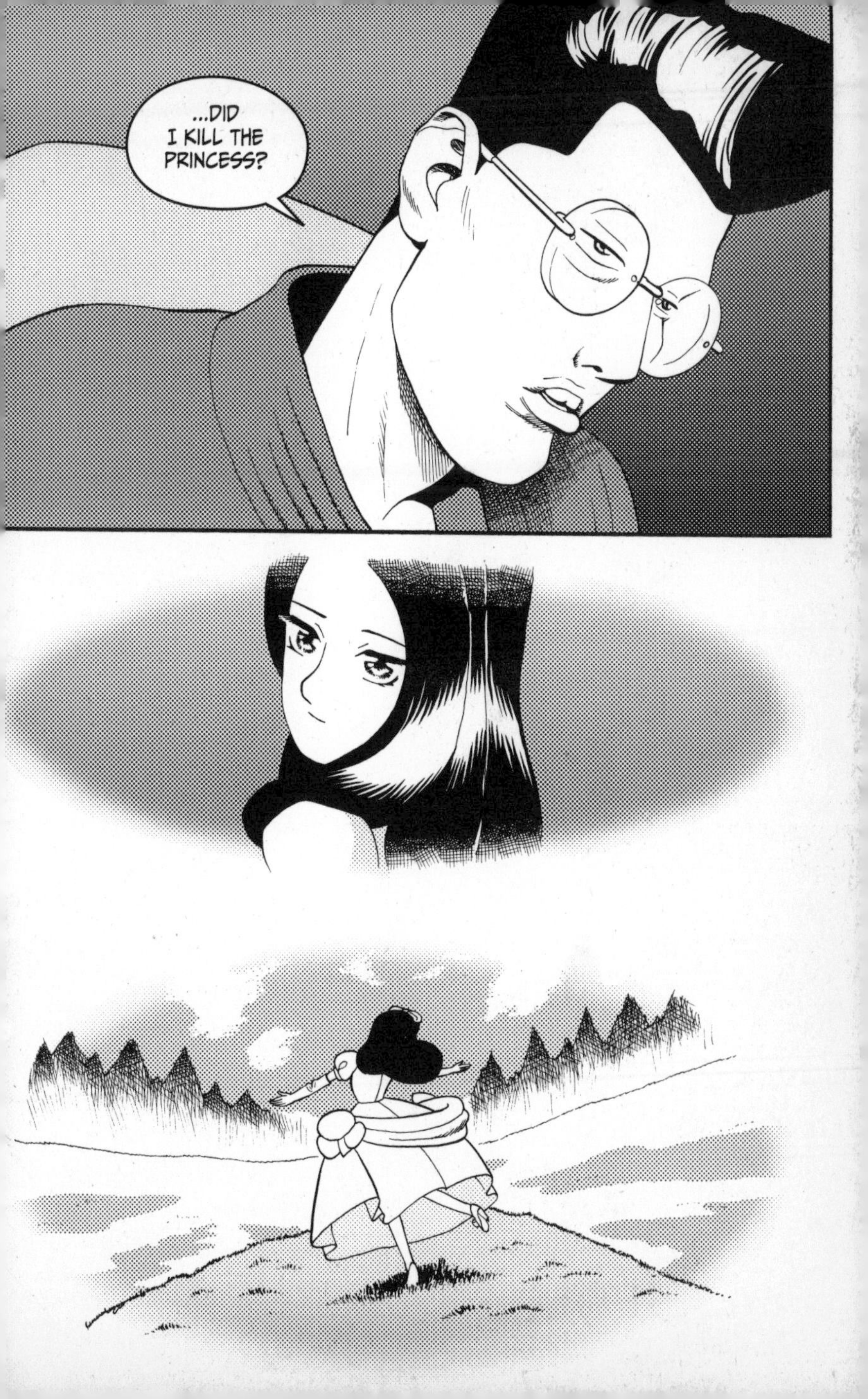
...DID I KILL THE PRINCESS?

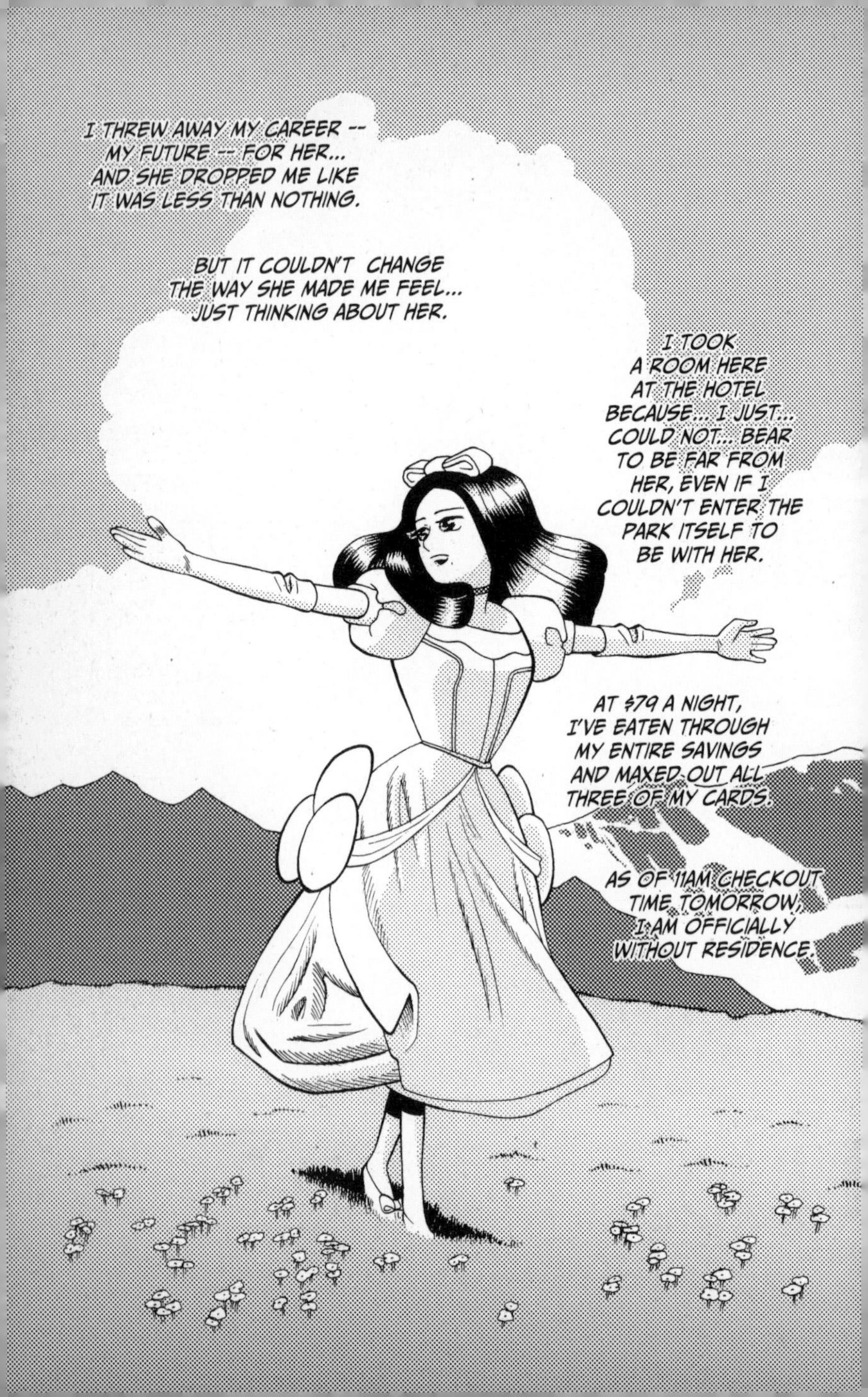
I THREW AWAY MY CAREER -- MY FUTURE -- FOR HER... AND SHE DROPPED ME LIKE IT WAS LESS THAN NOTHING.
BUT IT COULDN'T CHANGE THE WAY SHE MADE ME FEEL... JUST THINKING ABOUT HER.
I TOOK A ROOM HERE AT THE HOTEL BECAUSE... I JUST... COULD NOT... BEAR TO BE FAR FROM HER, EVEN IF I COULDN'T ENTER THE PARK ITSELF TO BE WITH HER.
AT $79 A NIGHT, I'VE EATEN THROUGH MY ENTIRE SAVINGS AND MAXED OUT ALL THREE OF MY CARDS.
AS OF 11AM CHECKOUT TIME TOMORROW, I AM OFFICIALLY WITHOUT RESIDENCE.

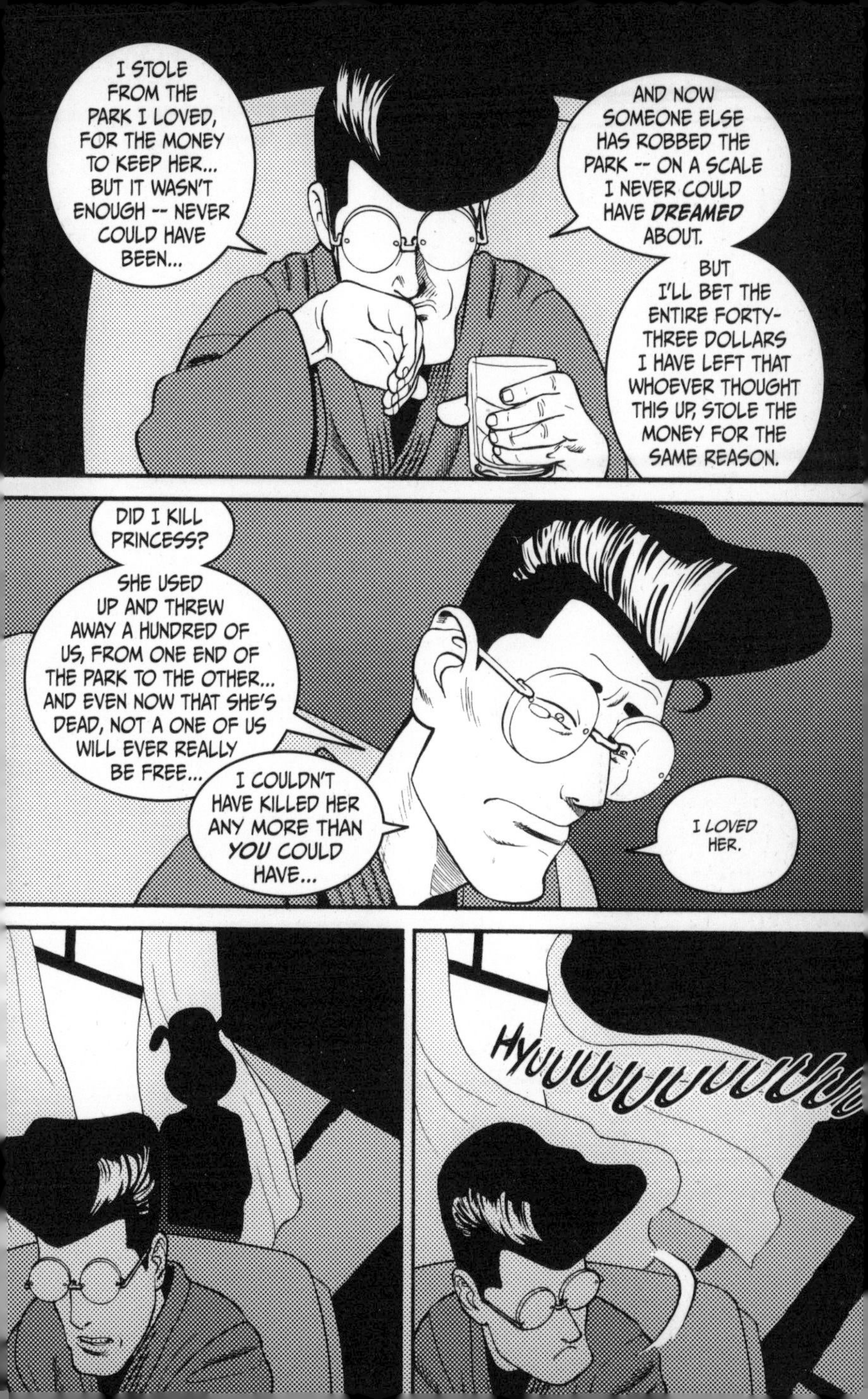
I STOLE FROM THE PARK I LOVED, FOR THE MONEY TO KEEP HER... BUT IT WASN'T ENOUGH -- NEVER COULD HAVE BEEN...
AND NOW SOMEONE ELSE HAS ROBBED THE PARK -- ON A SCALE I NEVER COULD HAVE *DREAMED* ABOUT.
BUT I'LL BET THE ENTIRE FORTY-THREE DOLLARS I HAVE LEFT THAT WHOEVER THOUGHT THIS UP, STOLE THE MONEY FOR THE SAME REASON.
DID I KILL PRINCESS?
SHE USED UP AND THREW AWAY A HUNDRED OF US, FROM ONE END OF THE PARK TO THE OTHER... AND EVEN NOW THAT SHE'S DEAD, NOT A ONE OF US WILL EVER REALLY BE FREE...
I COULDN'T HAVE KILLED HER ANY MORE THAN *YOU* COULD HAVE...
I *LOVED* HER.
HYUUUUUUUUUUUUH

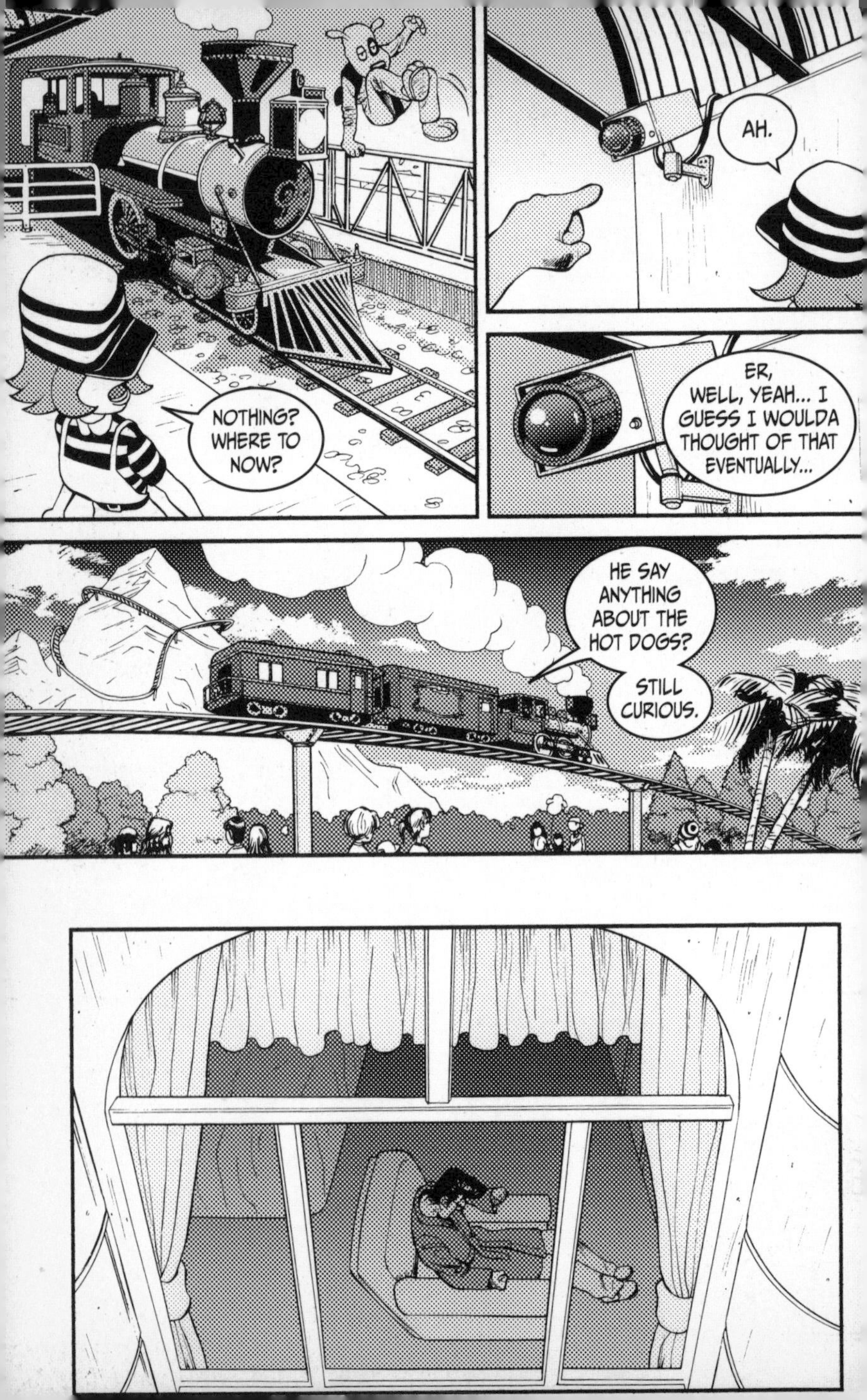
NOTHING? WHERE TO NOW?
AH.
ER, WELL, YEAH... I GUESS I WOULDA THOUGHT OF THAT EVENTUALLY...
HE SAY ANYTHING ABOUT THE HOT DOGS?
STILL CURIOUS.

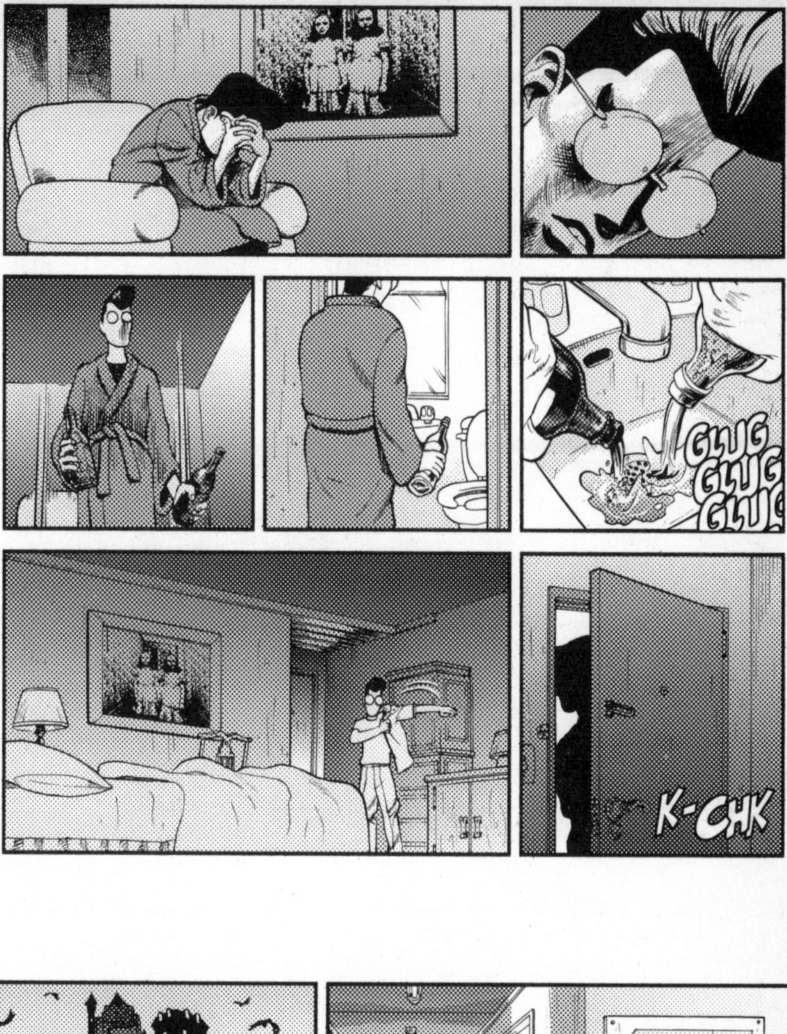
GLUG
GLUG
GLUG
K-CHK

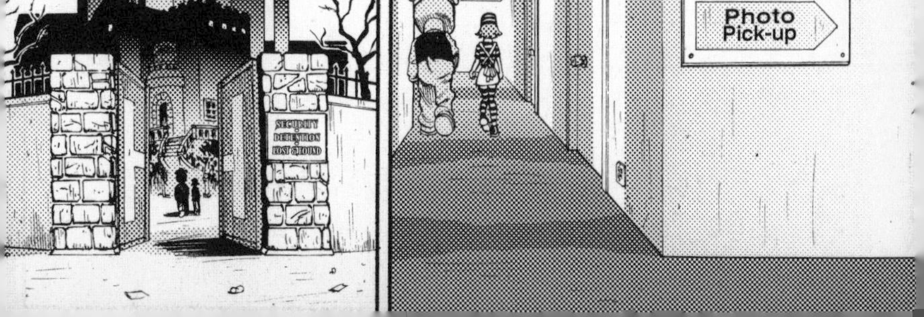
SECURITY
DETENTION
LOST GROUND
Security
Monitor Room
Photo
Pick-up

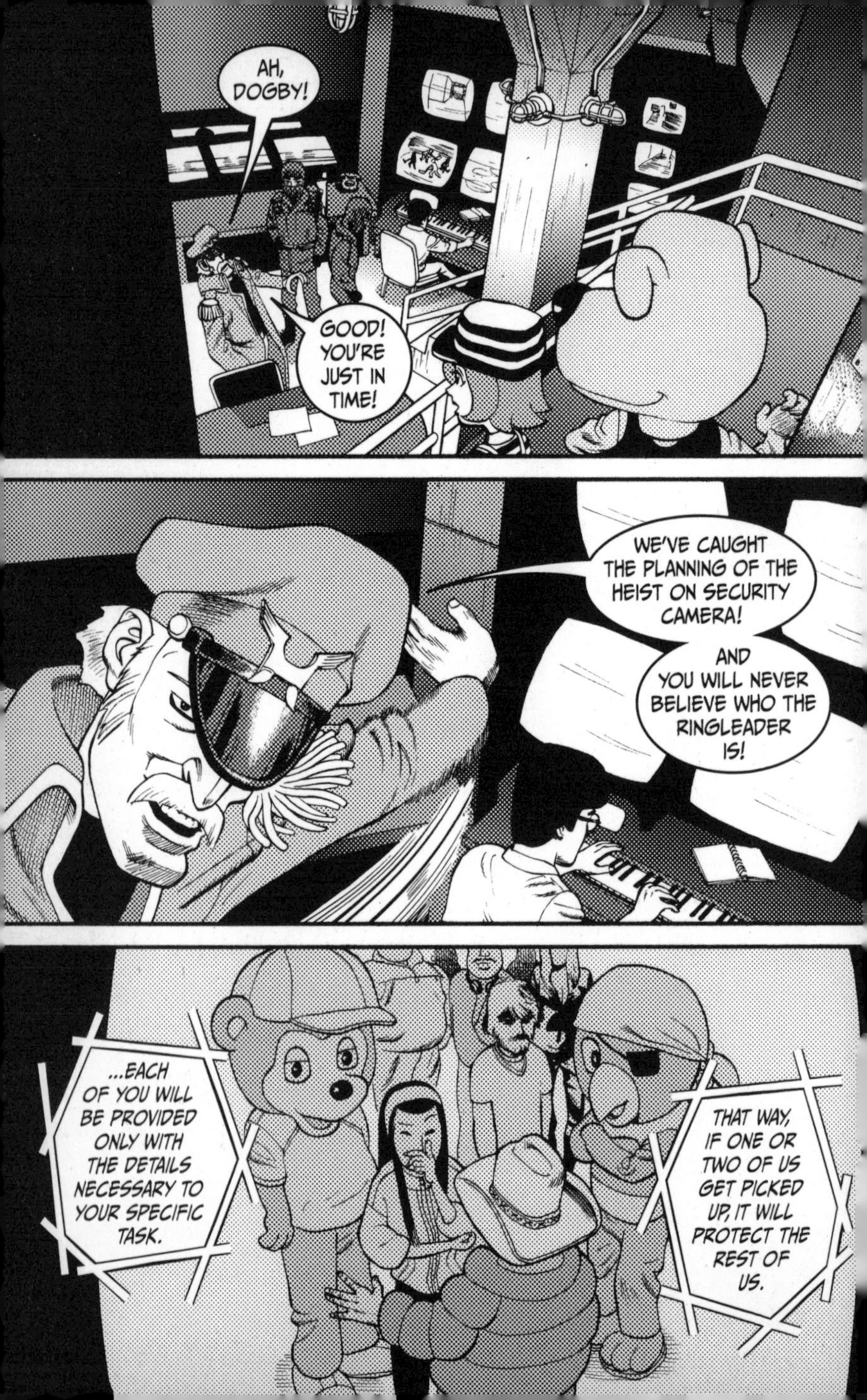
AH, DOGBY!
GOOD! YOU'RE JUST IN TIME!
WE'VE CAUGHT THE PLANNING OF THE HEIST ON SECURITY CAMERA!
AND YOU WILL NEVER BELIEVE WHO THE RINGLEADER IS!
...EACH OF YOU WILL BE PROVIDED ONLY WITH THE DETAILS NECESSARY TO YOUR SPECIFIC TASK.
THAT WAY, IF ONE OR TWO OF US GET PICKED UP, IT WILL PROTECT THE REST OF US.

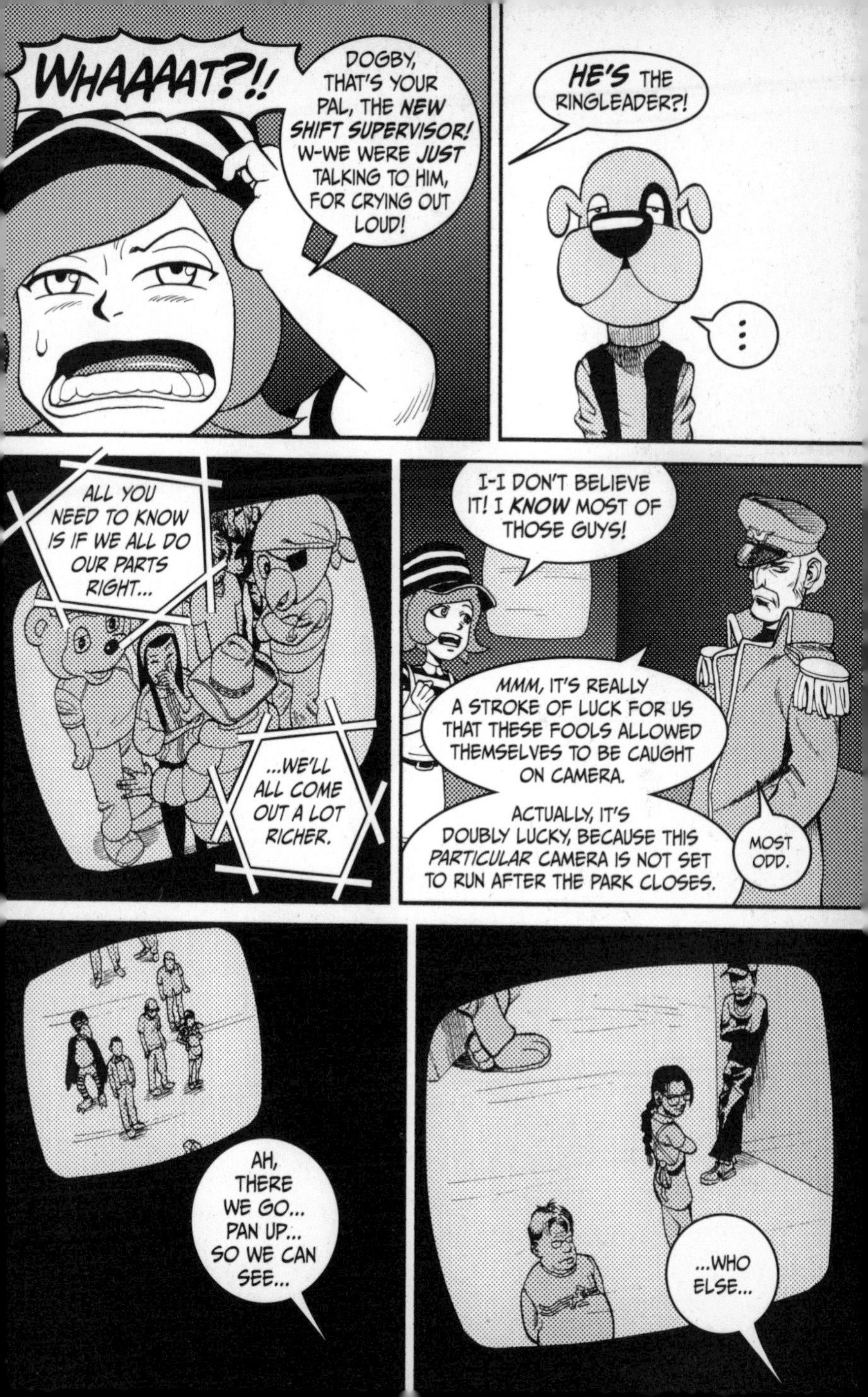
WHAAAAT?!!
DOGBY, THAT'S YOUR PAL, THE *NEW SHIFT SUPERVISOR!* W-WE WERE *JUST* TALKING TO HIM, FOR CRYING OUT LOUD!
HE'S THE RINGLEADER?!
...
ALL YOU NEED TO KNOW IS IF WE ALL DO OUR PARTS RIGHT...
...WE'LL ALL COME OUT A LOT RICHER.
I-I DON'T BELIEVE IT! I ***KNOW*** MOST OF THOSE GUYS!
MMM, IT'S REALLY A STROKE OF LUCK FOR US THAT THESE FOOLS ALLOWED THEMSELVES TO BE CAUGHT ON CAMERA.
ACTUALLY, IT'S DOUBLY LUCKY, BECAUSE THIS *PARTICULAR* CAMERA IS NOT SET TO RUN AFTER THE PARK CLOSES.
MOST ODD.
AH, THERE WE GO... PAN UP... SO WE CAN SEE...
...WHO ELSE...

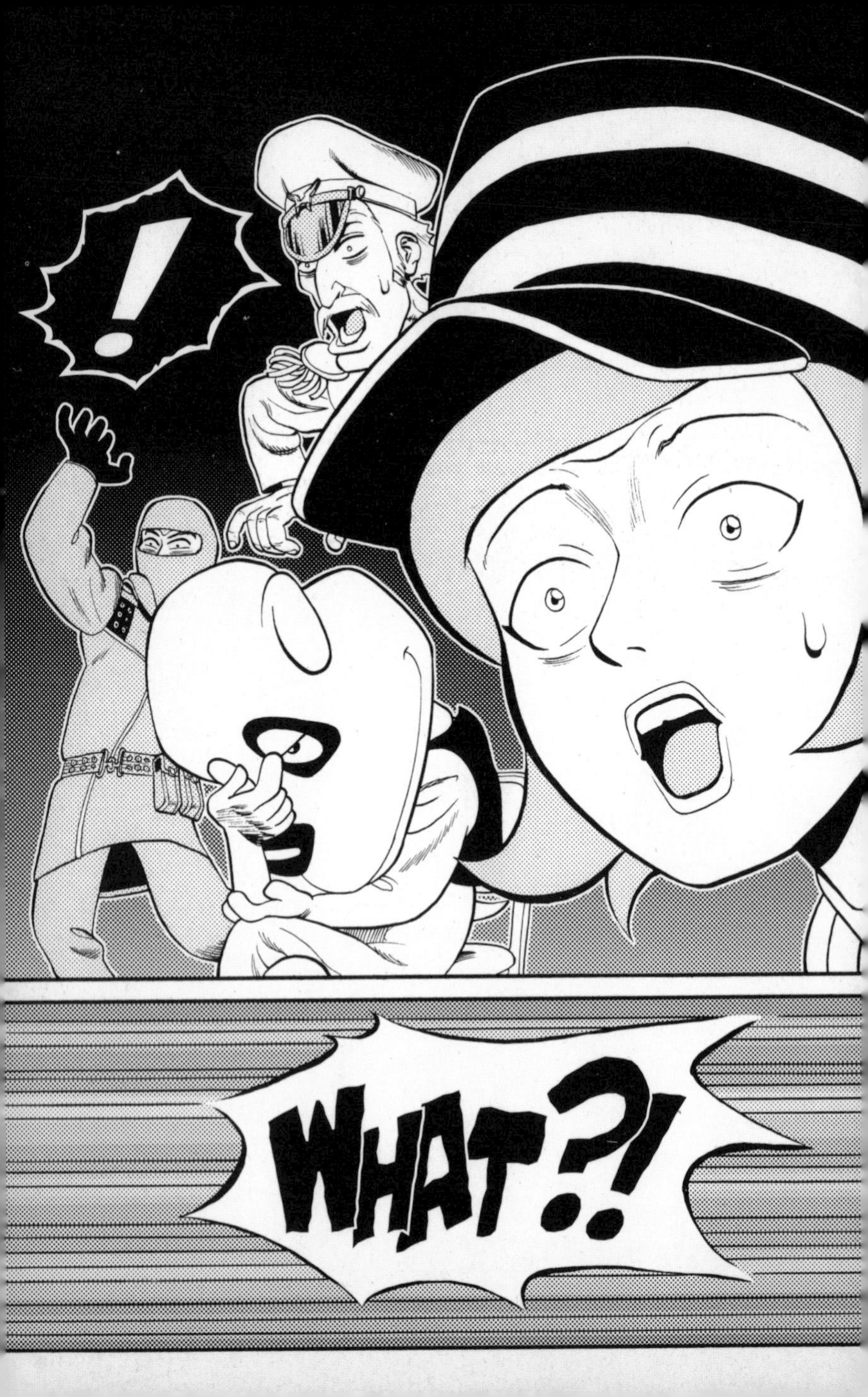
!
WHAT?!

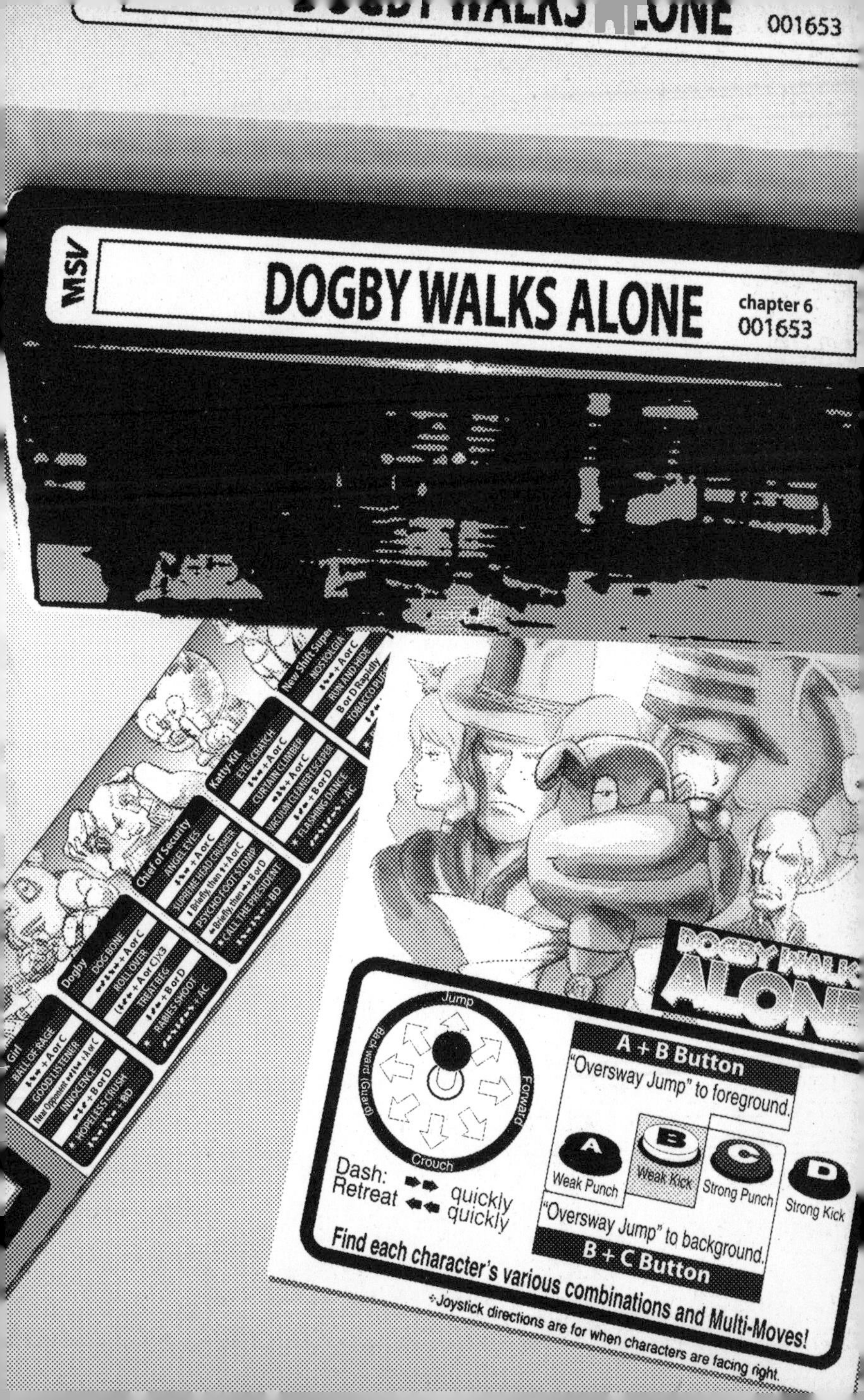
001653
MSV
DOGBY WALKS ALONE
chapter 6
001653
Girl
BALL OF RAGE
GOOD LISTENER
INNOCENCE
HOPELESS CRUSH
Dogby
DOG BONE
ROLL OVER
TREAT BEG
RABIES SHOOT
Chief of Security
ANGEL EYES
SUPREME HEAD CRUSHER
PSYCHO FOOT STOMP
CALL THE PRESIDENT
Katty-Kit
EYE SCRATCH
CURTAIN CLIMBER
VACUUM CLEANER ESCAPE
FLASHING DANCE
New Shift Super
NOSTALGIA
RUN AND HIDE
B or D Rapidly
DOGBY WALKS ALONE
Jump
Backward (Guard)
Forward
Crouch
Dash:
Retreat
quickly
quickly
A + B Button
“Oversway Jump” to foreground.
A
B
C
D
Weak Punch
Weak Kick
Strong Punch
Strong Kick
“Oversway Jump” to background.
B + C Button
Find each character’s various combinations and Multi-Moves!
✧Joystick directions are for when characters are facing right.

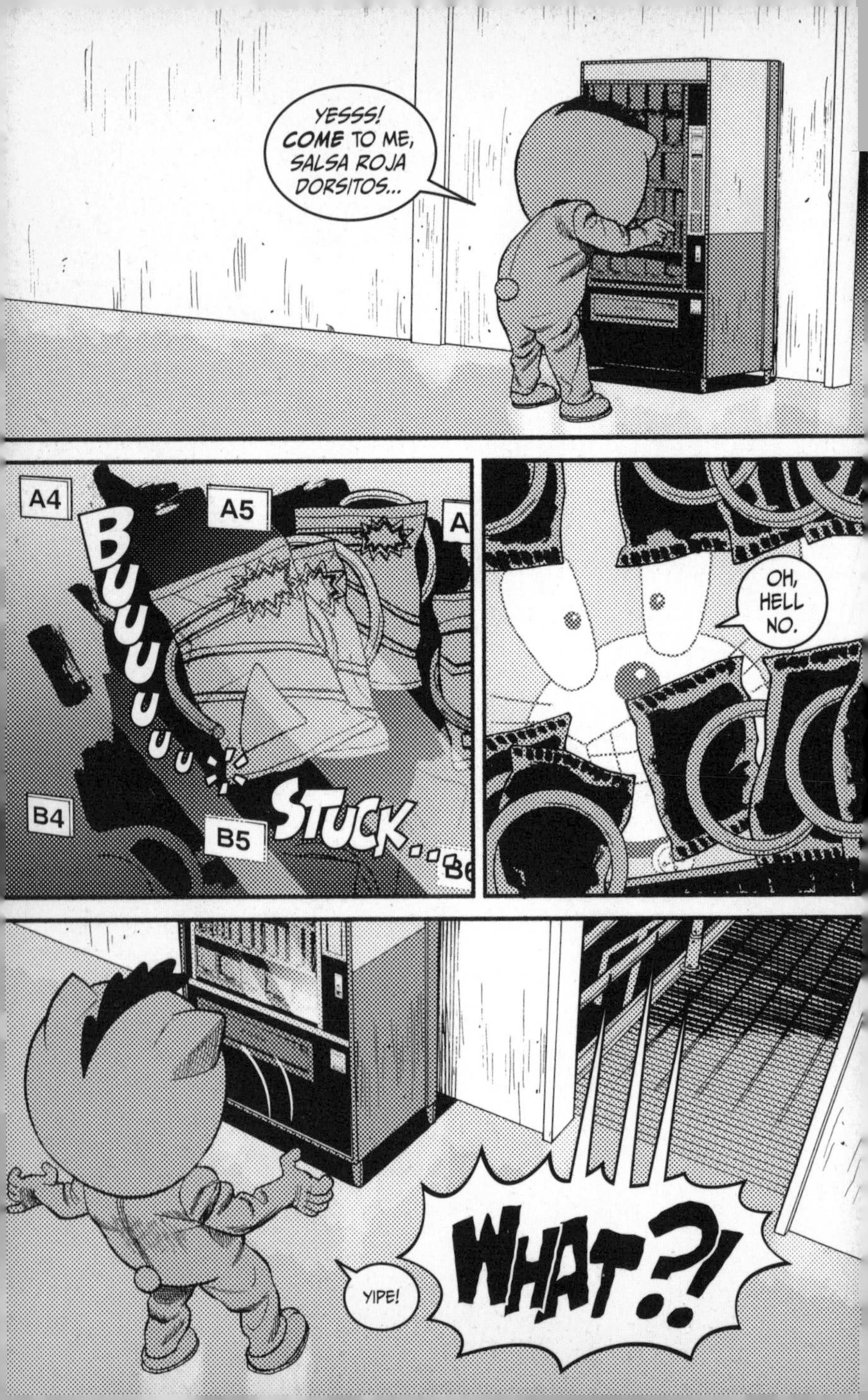
YESSS! COME TO ME, SALSA ROJA DORSITOS...
A4
A5
BUUUUUU...
STUCK...
B4
B5
OH, HELL NO.
YIPE!
WHAT?!

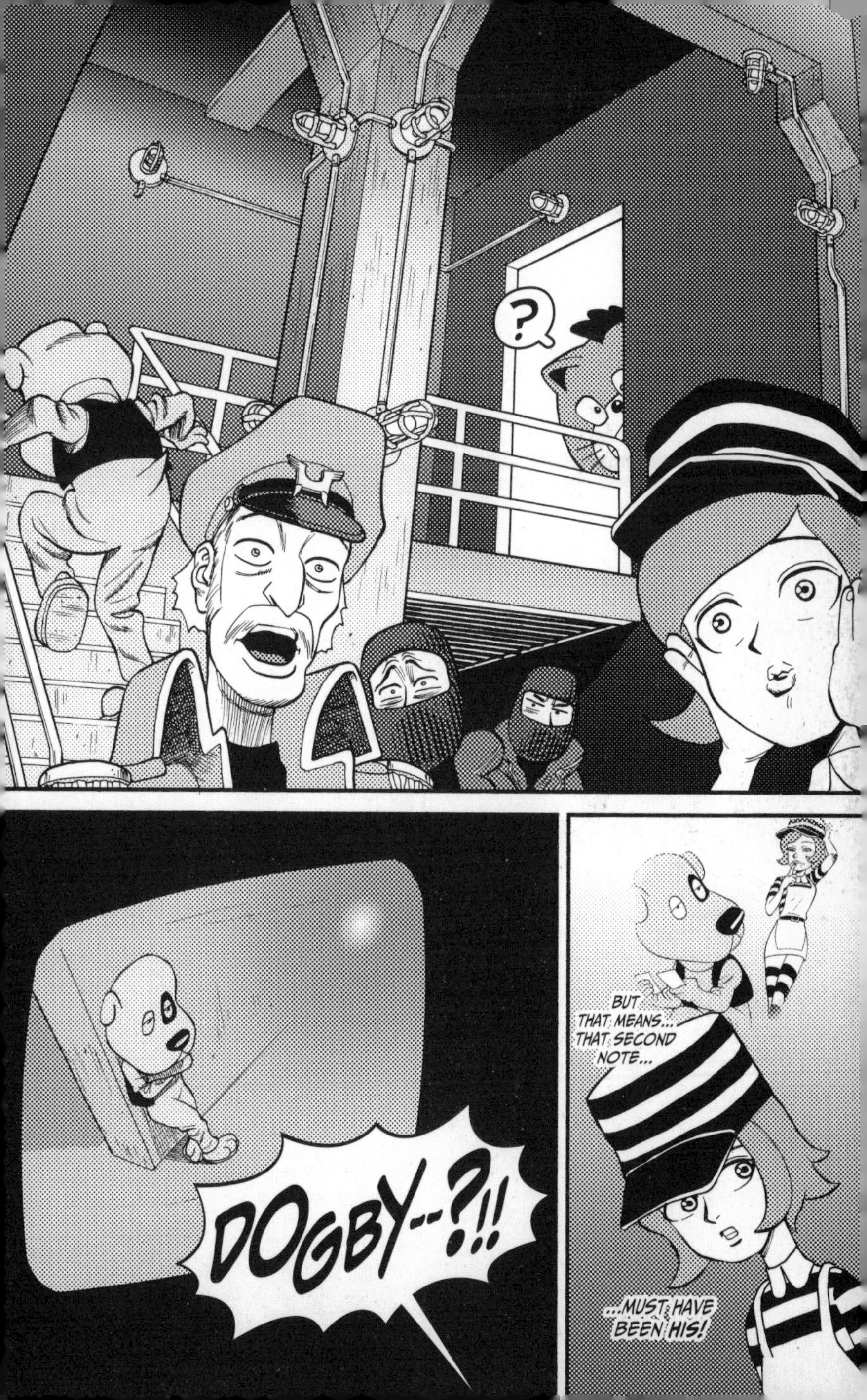
?
DOGBY--?!!
BUT THAT MEANS... THAT SECOND NOTE...
...MUST HAVE BEEN HIS!

STOP HIM!
HOLD IT, YOU CRUMB BUMS...

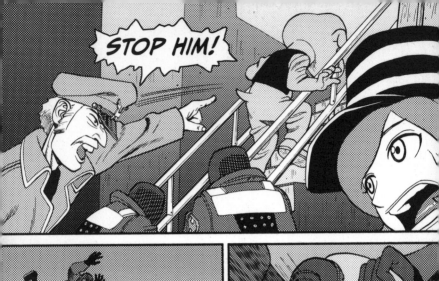

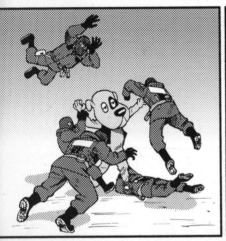

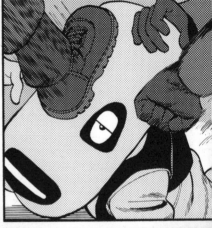

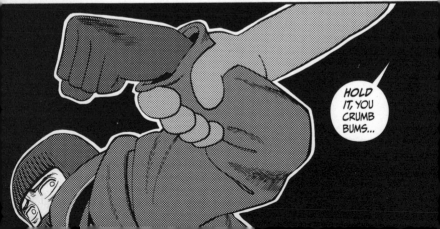

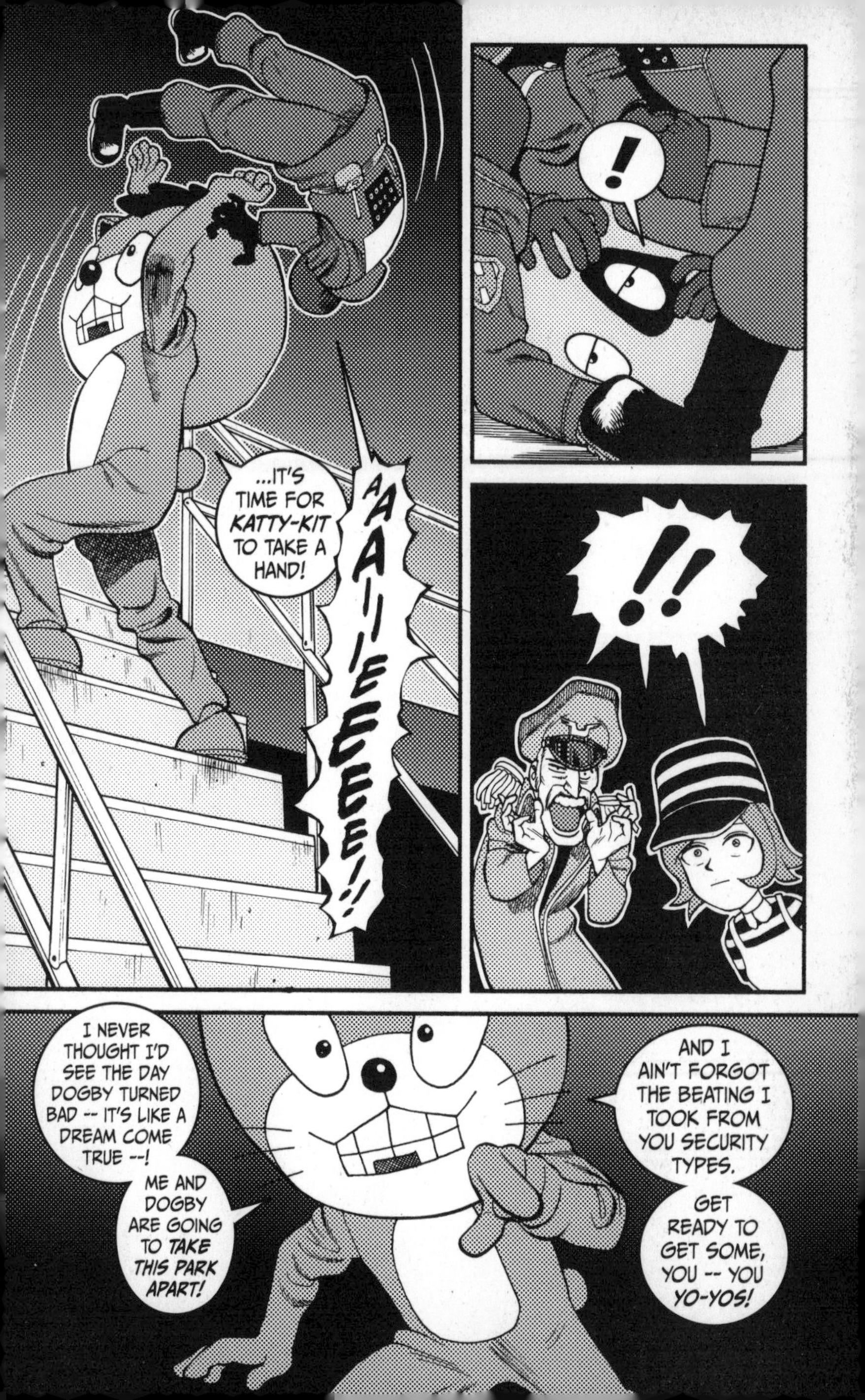
...IT'S TIME FOR KATTY-KIT TO TAKE A HAND!
AAAIIIEEEEEE!!
!
!!
I NEVER THOUGHT I'D SEE THE DAY DOGBY TURNED BAD -- IT'S LIKE A DREAM COME TRUE --!
ME AND DOGBY ARE GOING TO TAKE THIS PARK APART!
AND I AIN'T FORGOT THE BEATING I TOOK FROM YOU SECURITY TYPES.
GET READY TO GET SOME, YOU -- YOU YO-YOS!

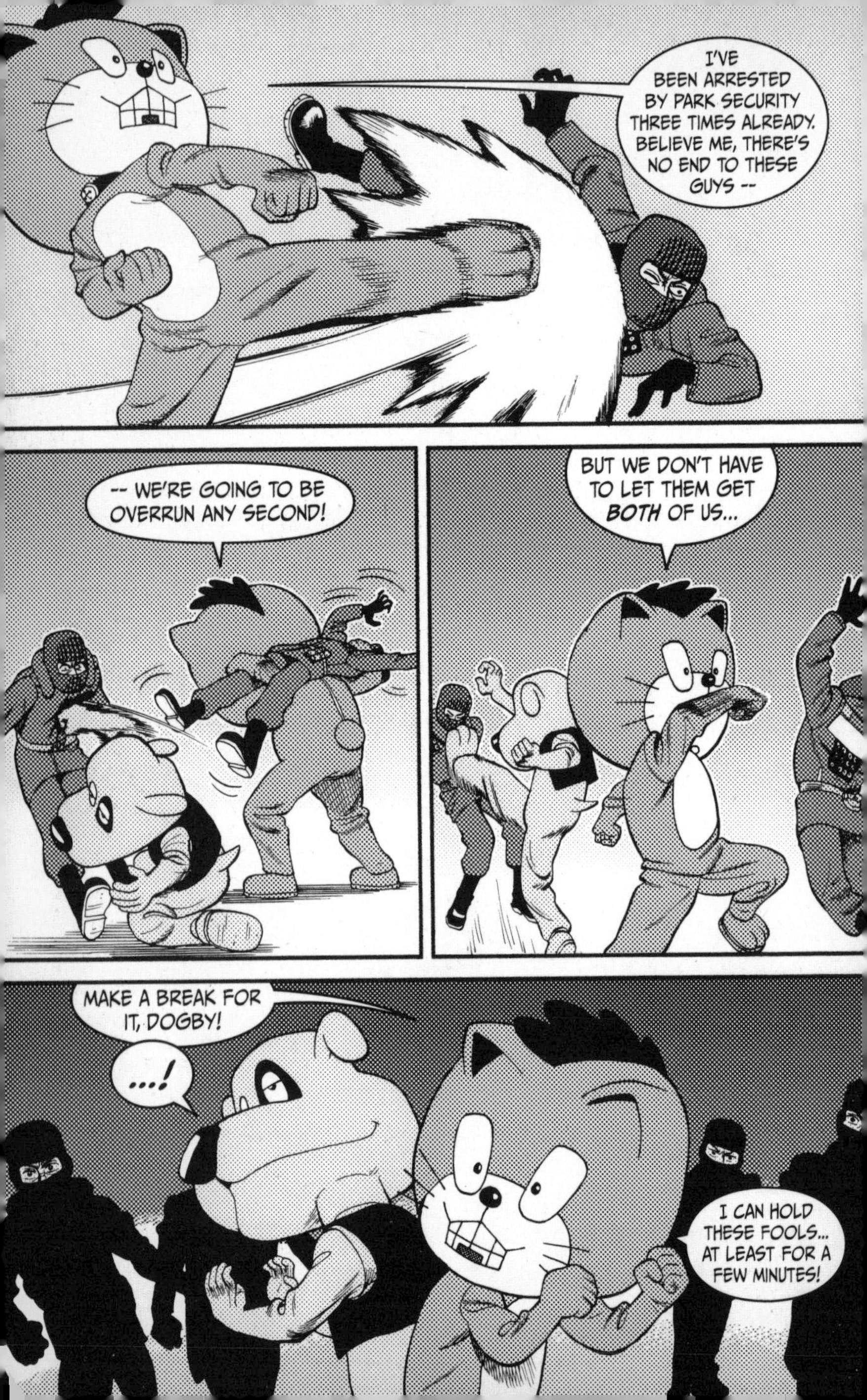
I'VE BEEN ARRESTED BY PARK SECURITY THREE TIMES ALREADY. BELIEVE ME, THERE'S NO END TO THESE GUYS --
-- WE'RE GOING TO BE OVERRUN ANY SECOND!
BUT WE DON'T HAVE TO LET THEM GET *BOTH* OF US...
MAKE A BREAK FOR IT, DOGBY!
...!
I CAN HOLD THESE FOOLS... AT LEAST FOR A FEW MINUTES!

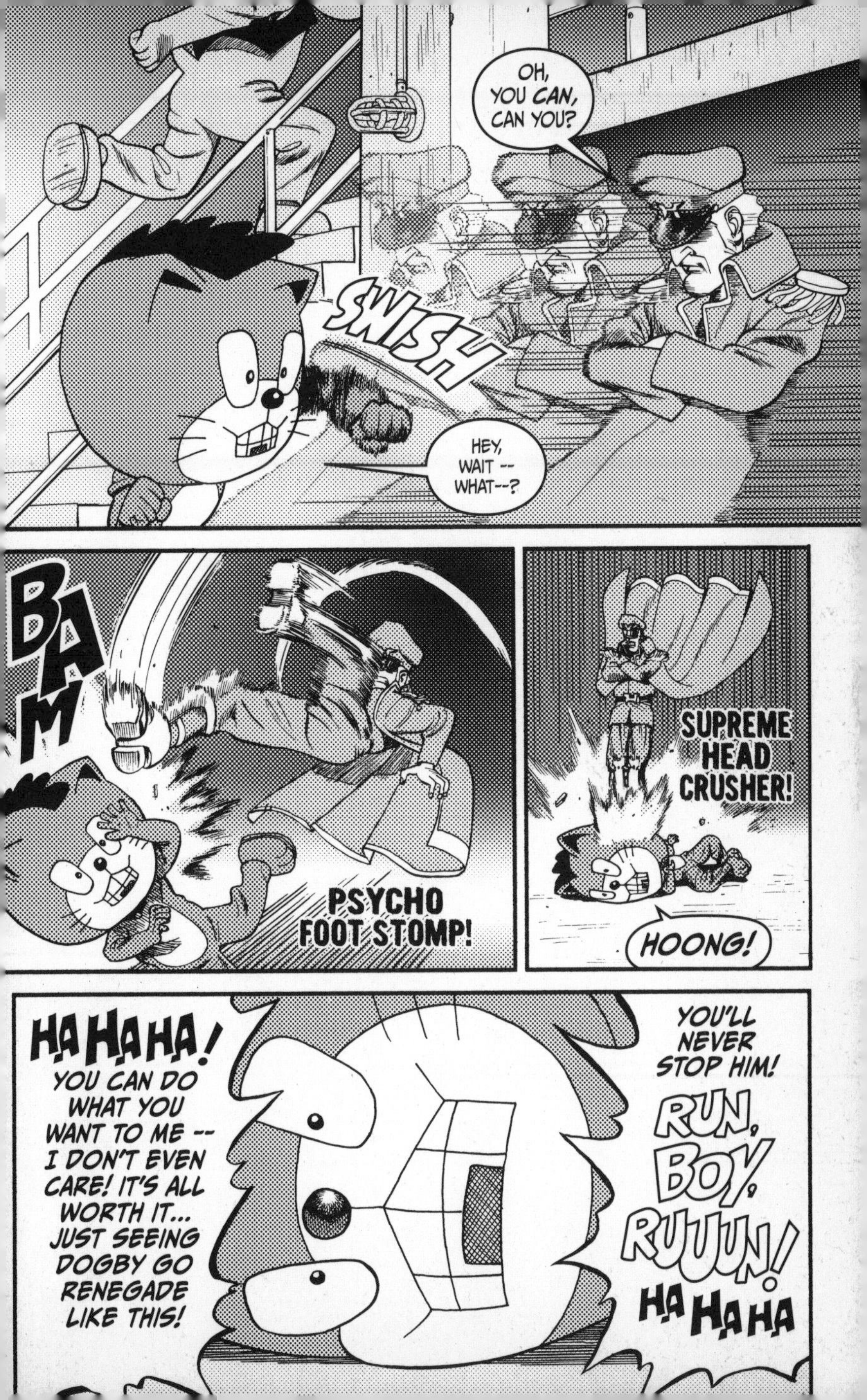

OH, YOU CAN, CAN YOU?
SWISH
HEY, WAIT -- WHAT--?
BAM
PSYCHO FOOT STOMP!
SUPREME HEAD CRUSHER!
HOONG!
HA HA HA HA!
YOU CAN DO WHAT YOU WANT TO ME -- I DON'T EVEN CARE! IT'S ALL WORTH IT... JUST SEEING DOGBY GO RENEGADE LIKE THIS!
YOU'LL NEVER STOP HIM!
RUN, BOY, RUUUN!
HA HA HA HA

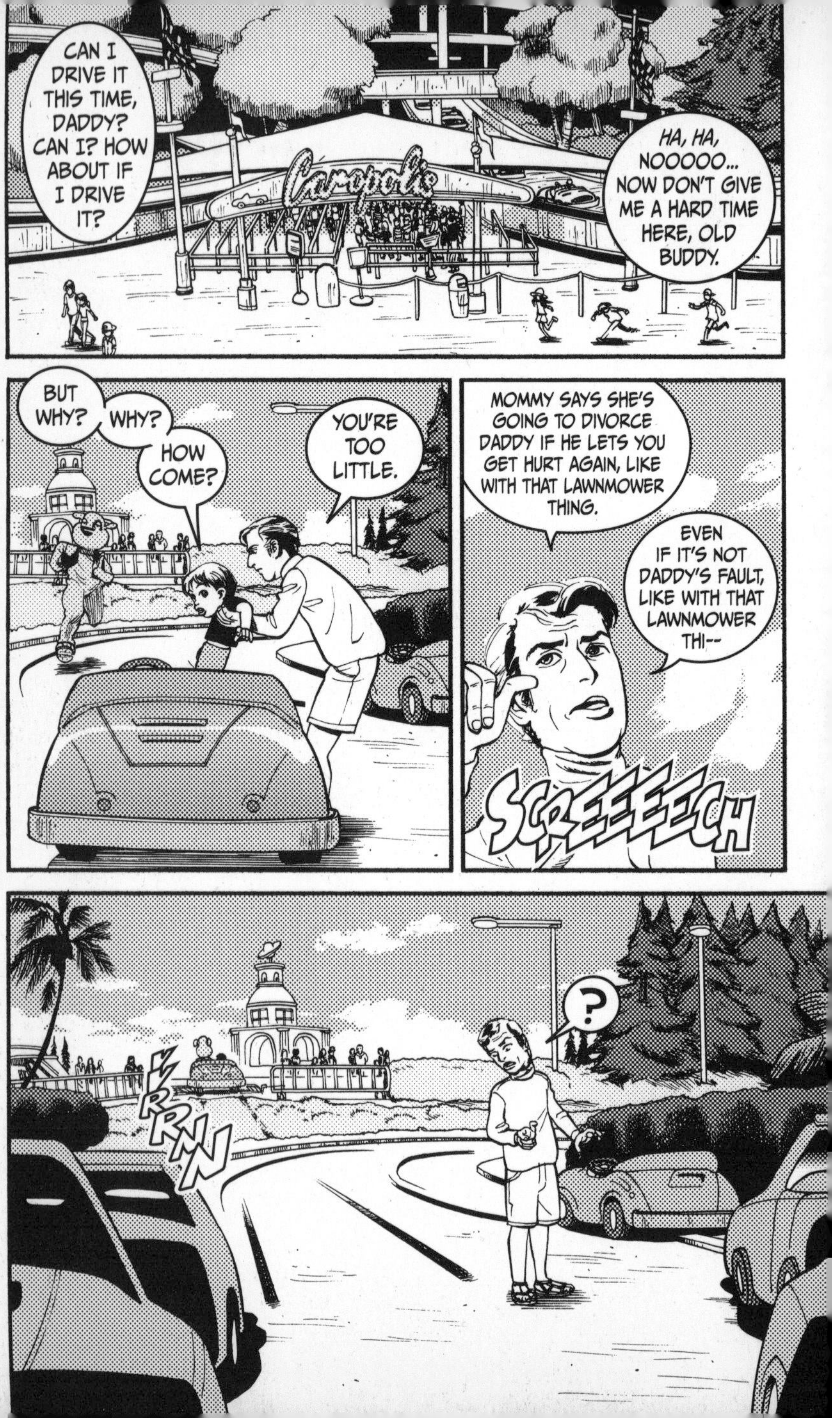
CAN I DRIVE IT THIS TIME, DADDY? CAN I? HOW ABOUT IF I DRIVE IT?
Caropolis
HA, HA, NOOOOO... NOW DON'T GIVE ME A HARD TIME HERE, OLD BUDDY.
BUT WHY?
WHY?
HOW COME?
YOU'RE TOO LITTLE.
MOMMY SAYS SHE'S GOING TO DIVORCE DADDY IF HE LETS YOU GET HURT AGAIN, LIKE WITH THAT LAWNMOWER THING.
EVEN IF IT'S NOT DADDY'S FAULT, LIKE WITH THAT LAWNMOWER THI--
SCREEEECH
?
VRRNN

chapter 7: CATCHING THE KATY with the SELF-PRESERVATION SOCIETY

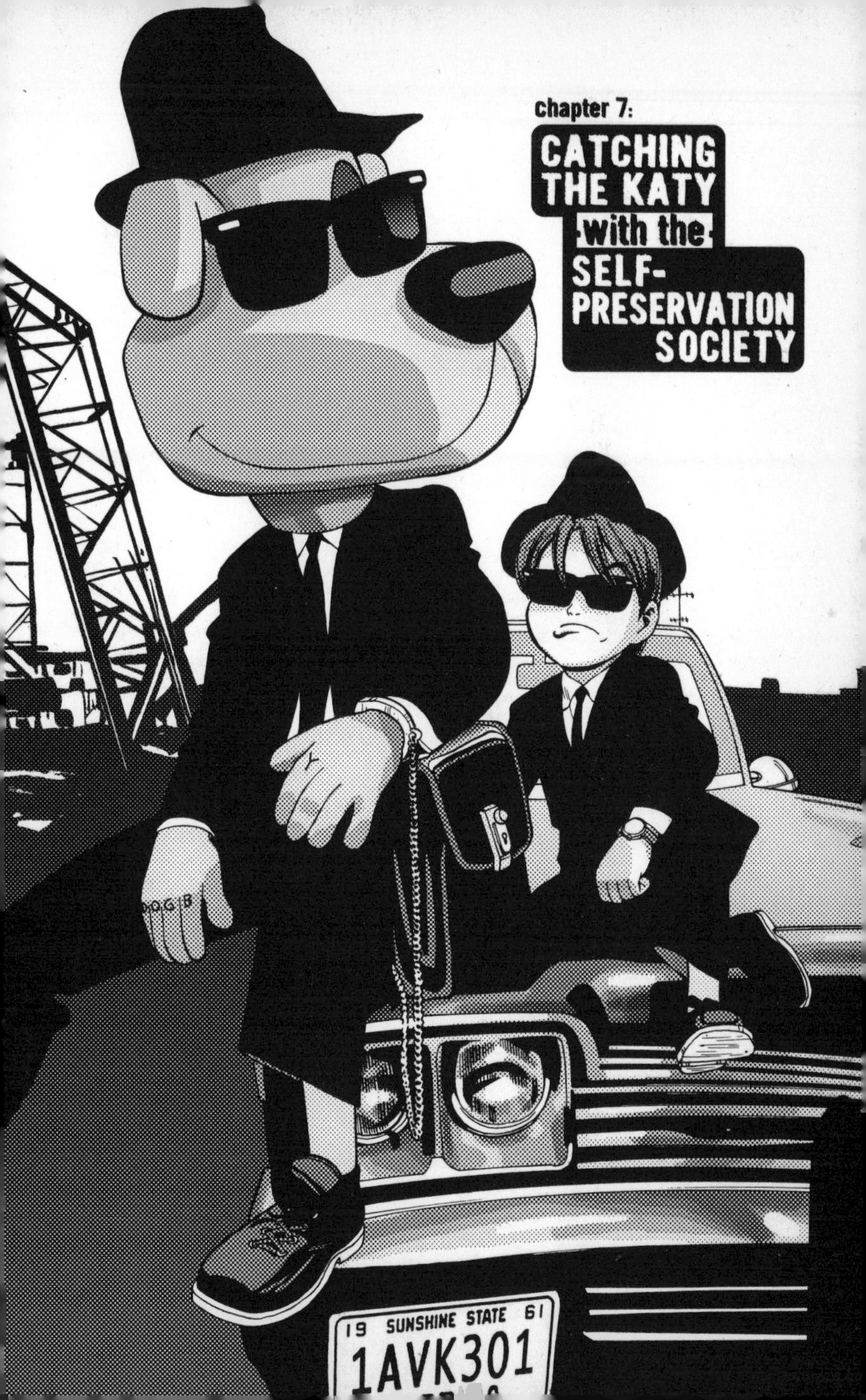
19 SUNSHINE STATE 61
1AVK301

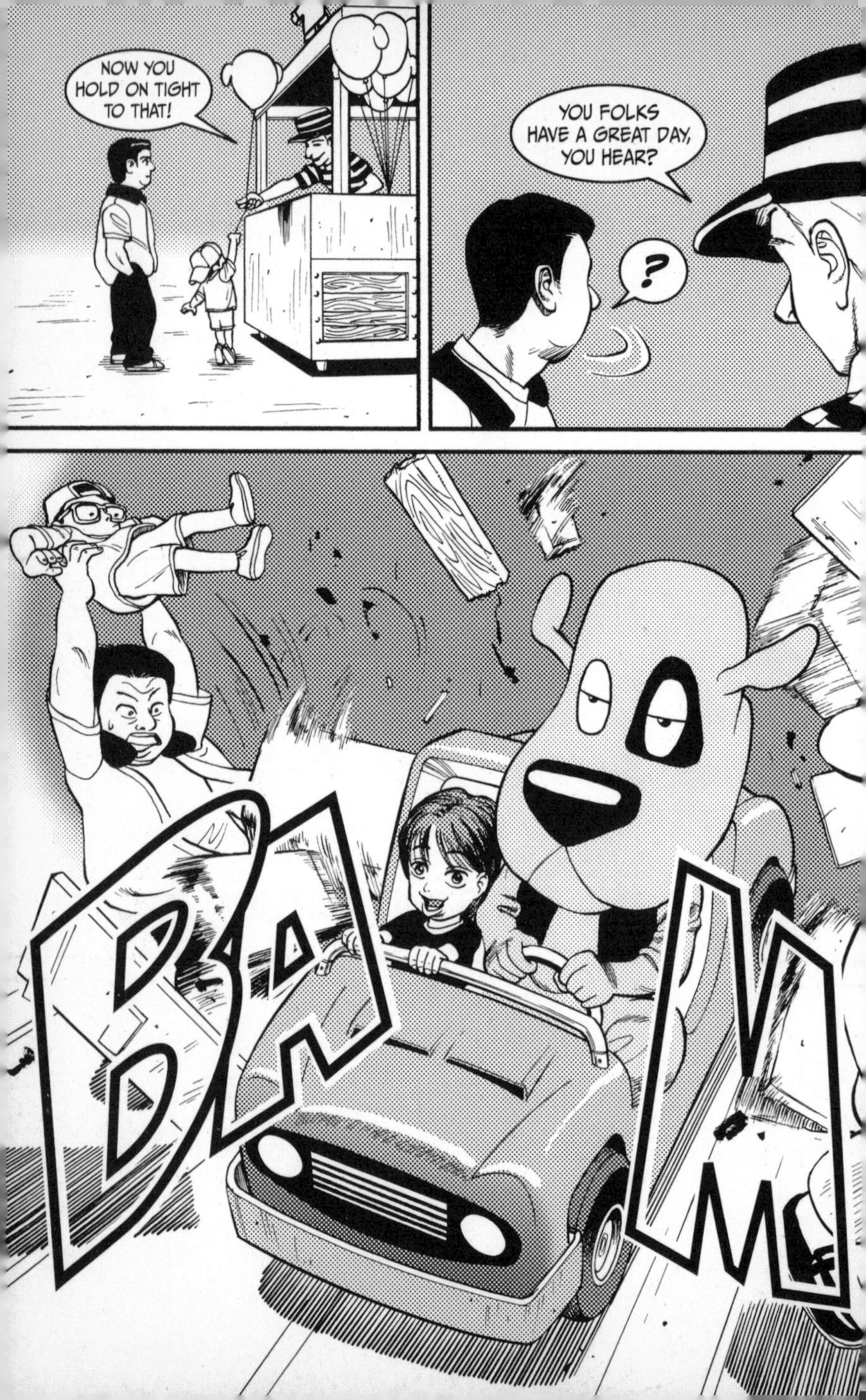
NOW YOU HOLD ON TIGHT TO THAT!
YOU FOLKS HAVE A GREAT DAY, YOU HEAR?
?
BAM

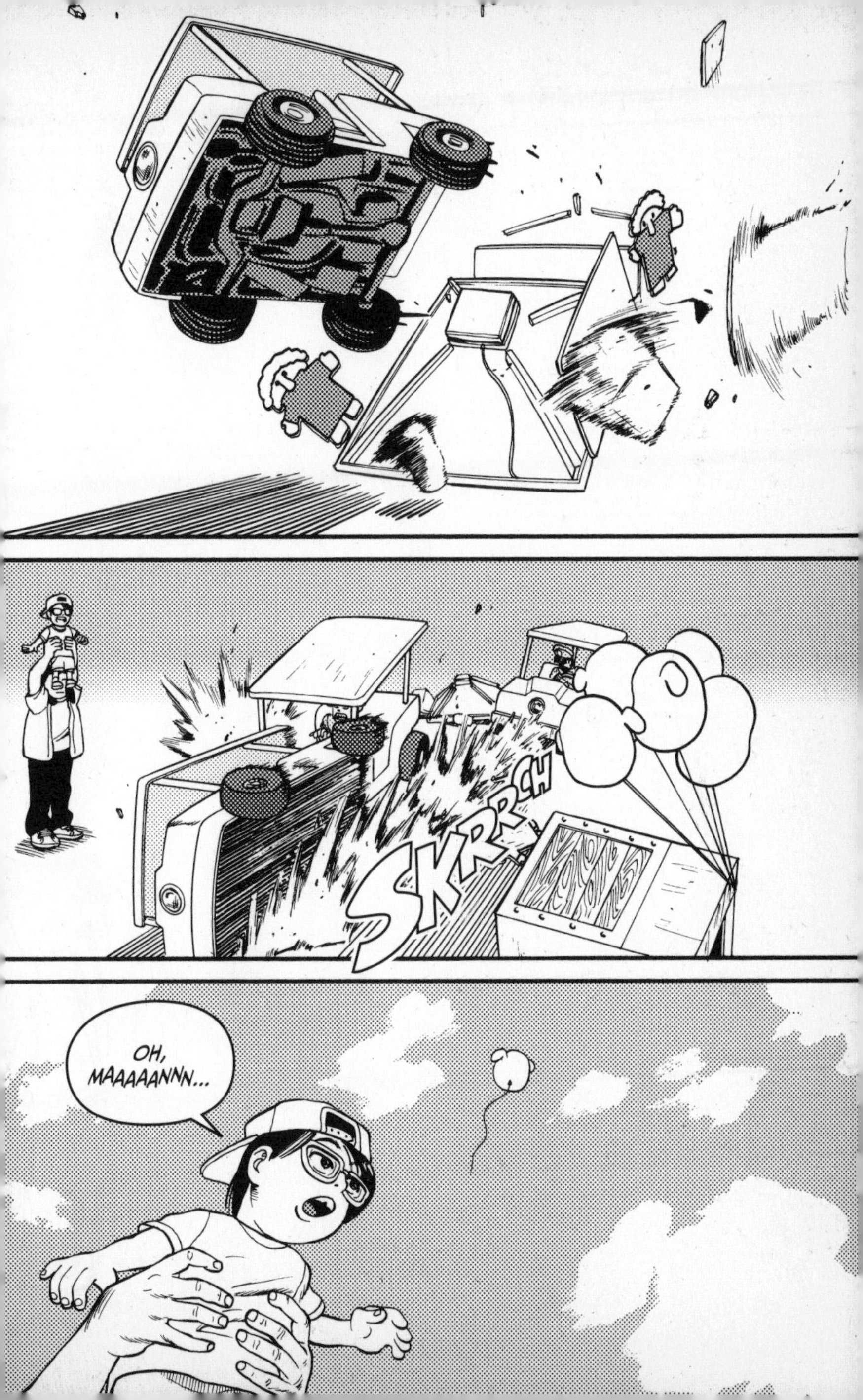
SKRRRCH
OH, MAAAAANNN...

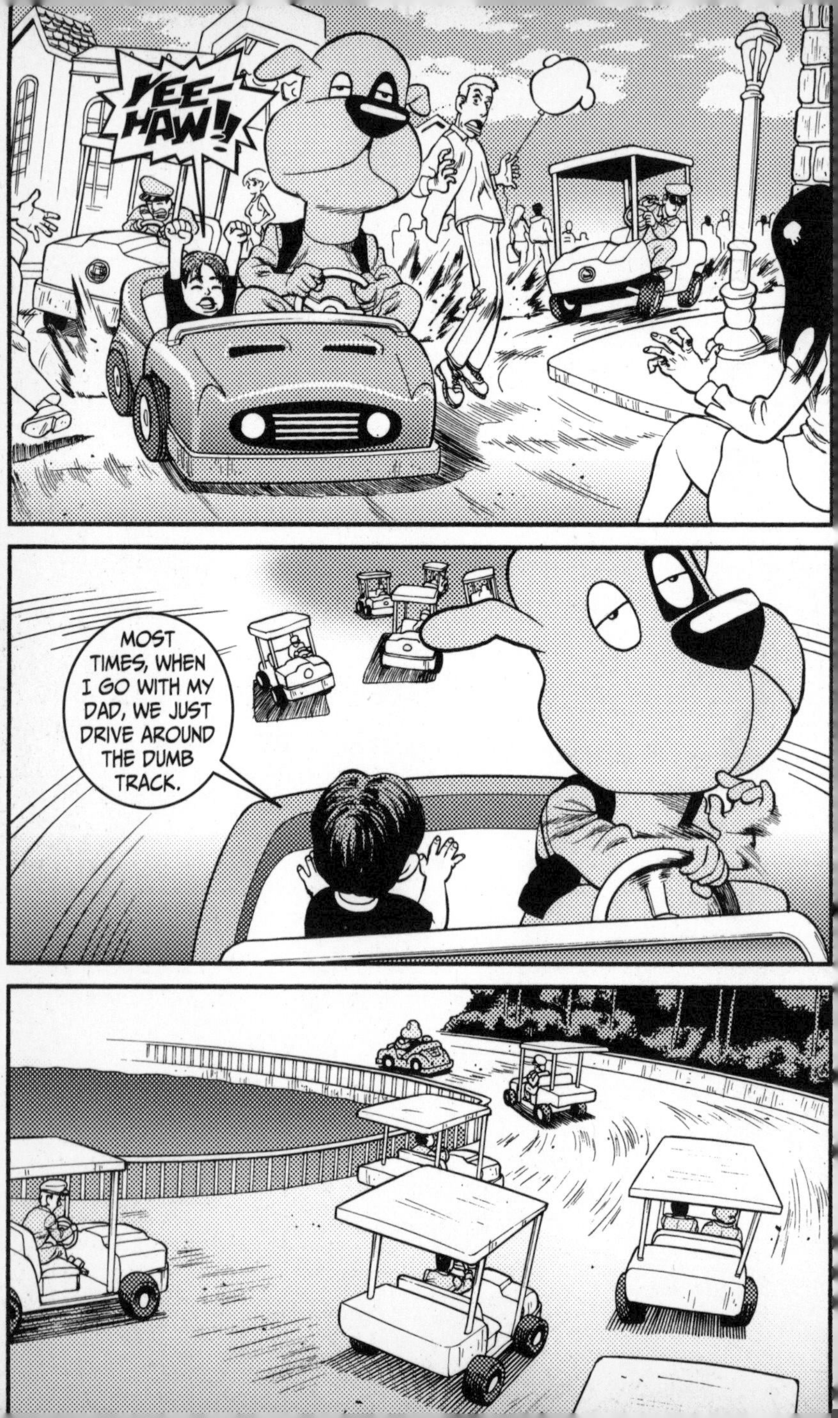
YEE-HAW!!
MOST TIMES, WHEN I GO WITH MY DAD, WE JUST DRIVE AROUND THE DUMB TRACK.

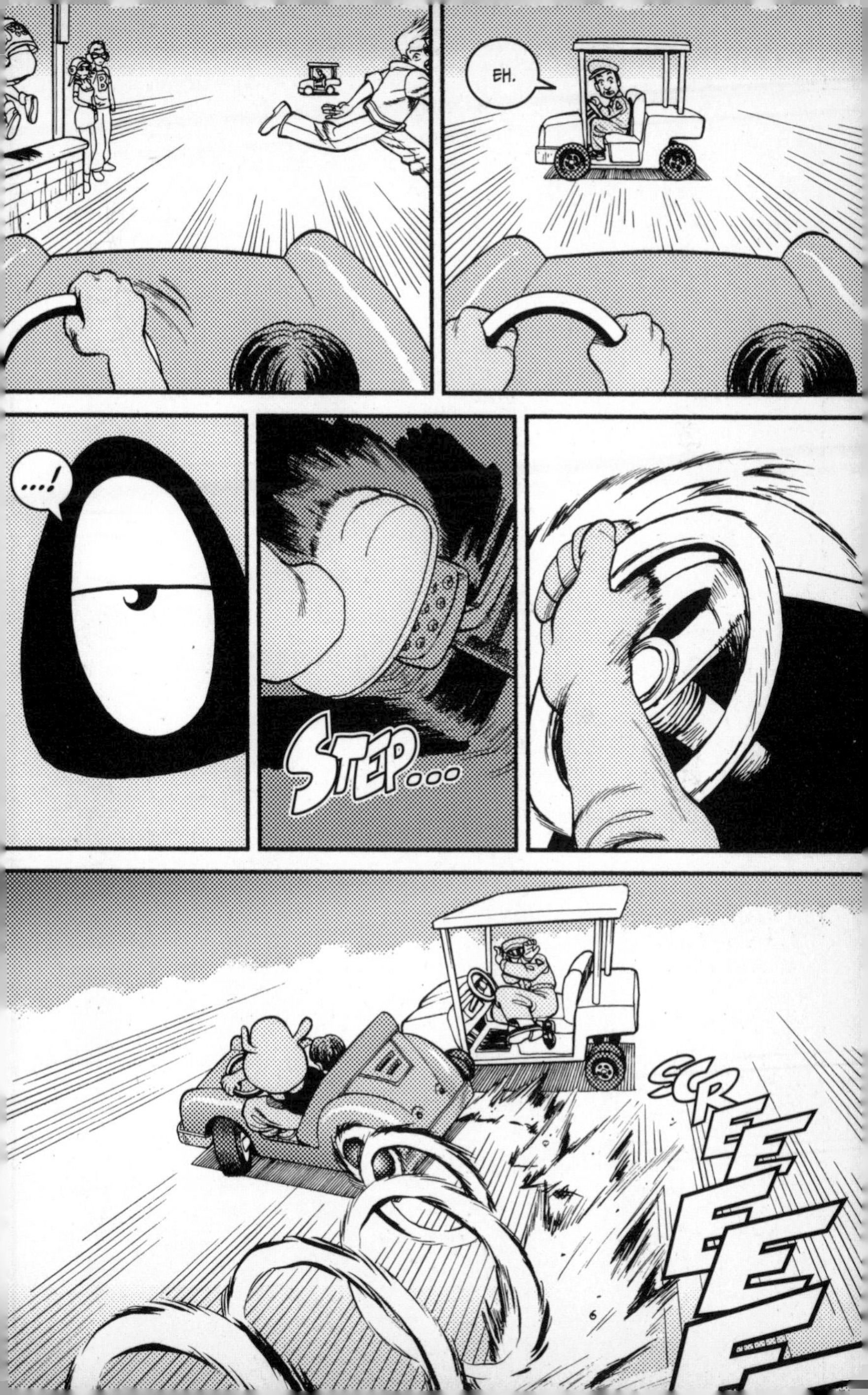
EH.
...!
STEP...
SCREEEEEE

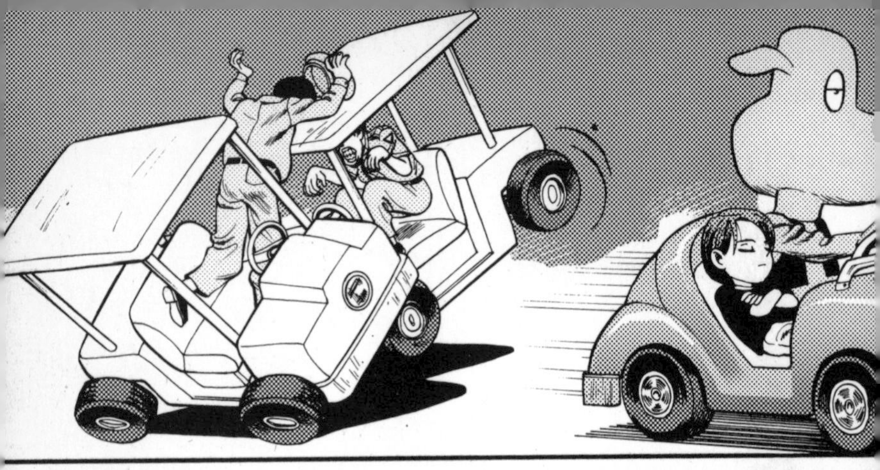
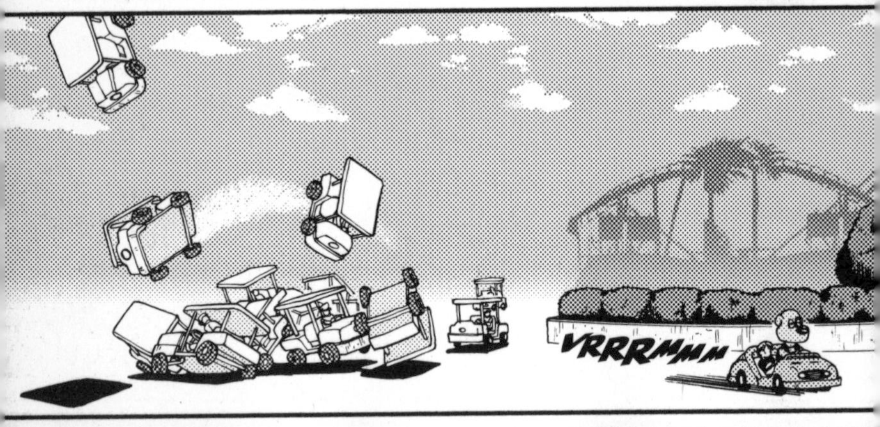
VRRRMMM
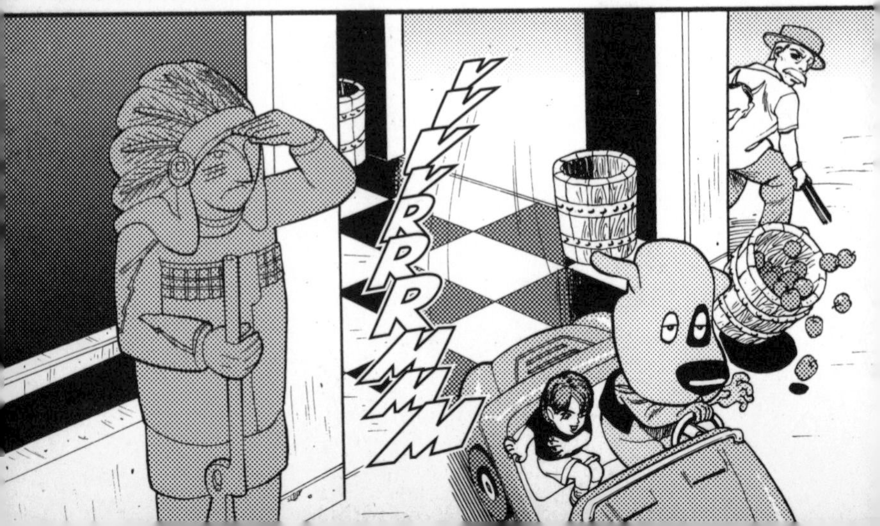
VVVVVRRRMMMM

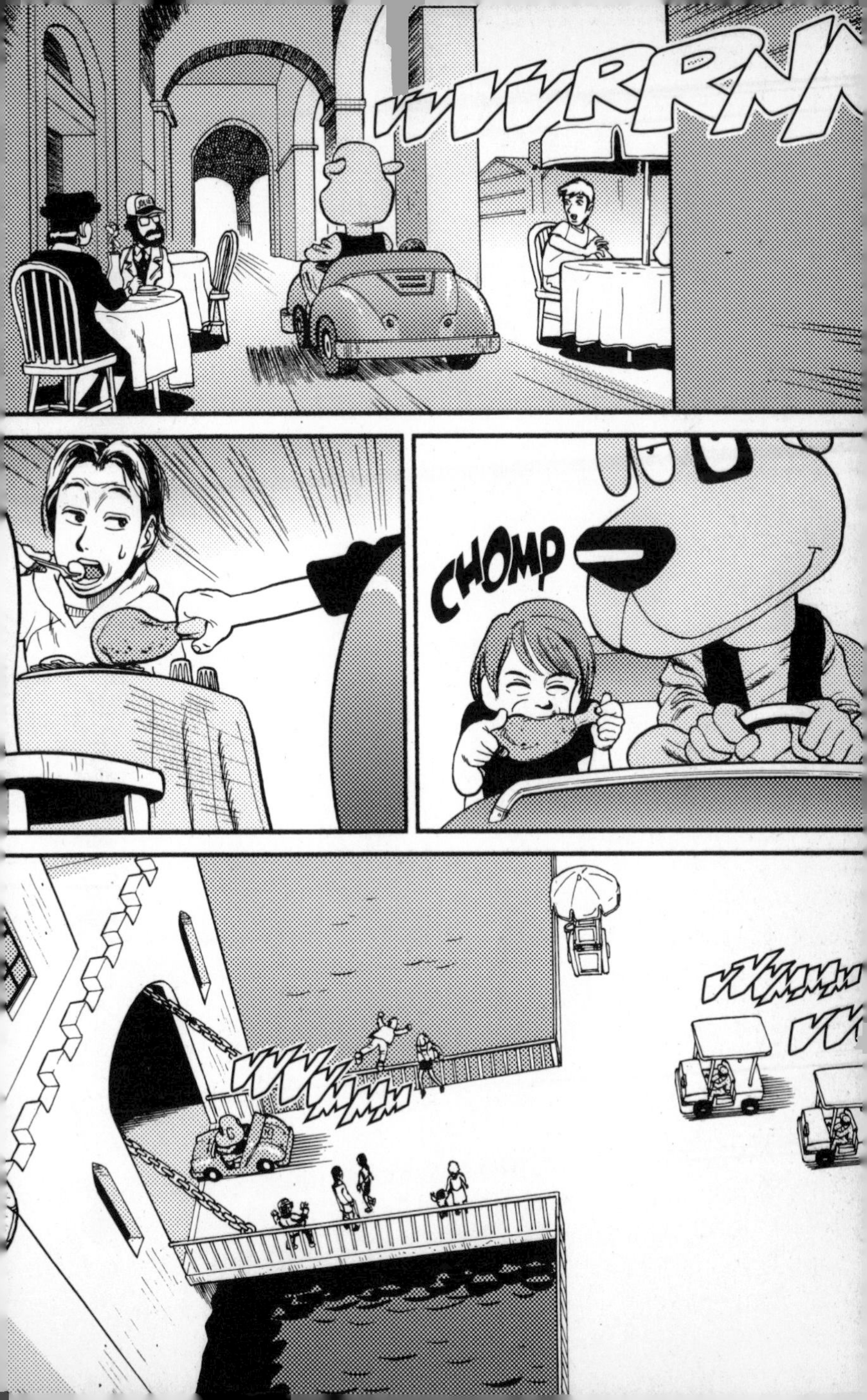
VVVVRRRNN
CHOMP
VVVMMMM
VVVMMMM
VVV

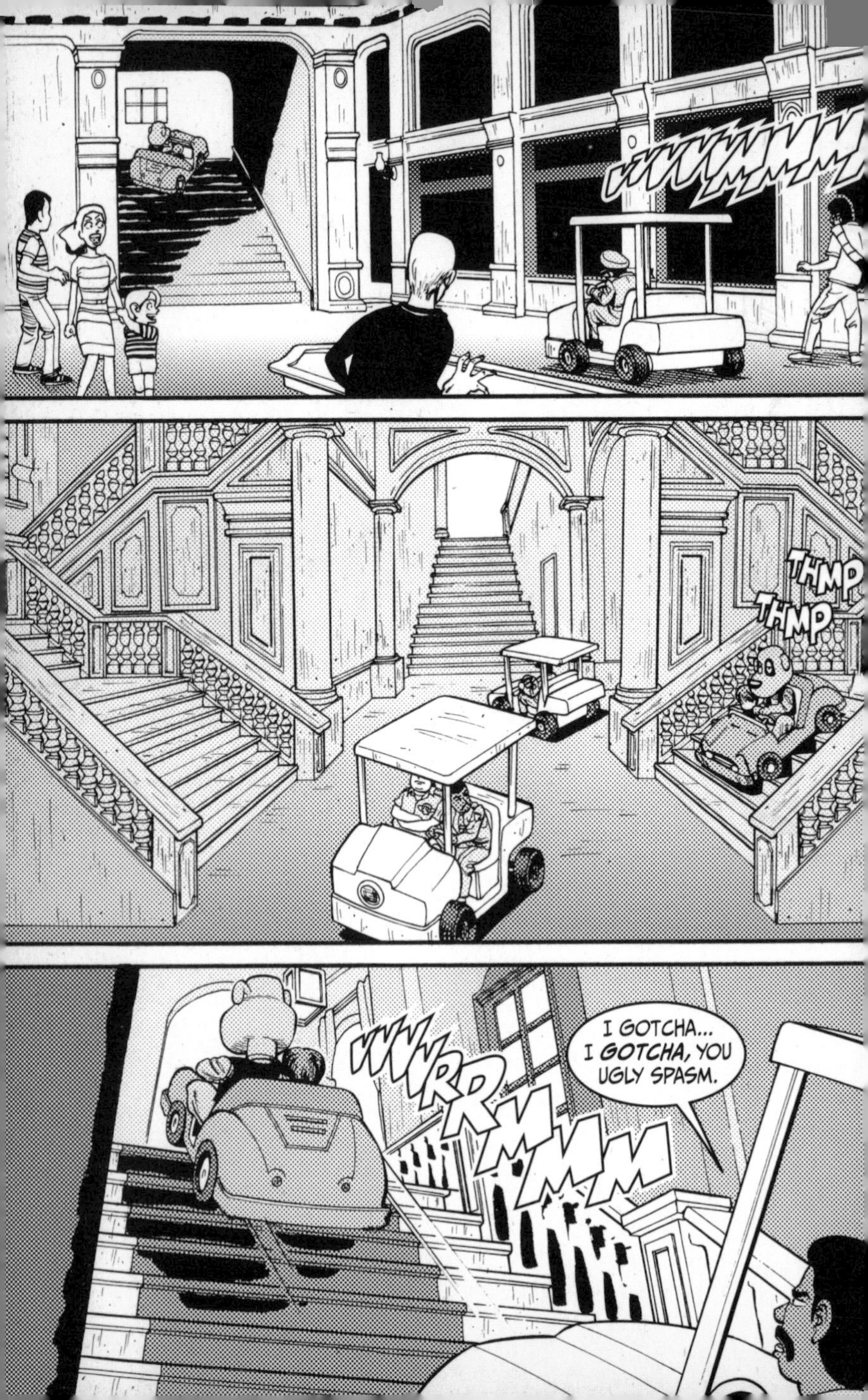
VVVVMMM
THMP
THMP
VVVRRMMM
I GOTCHA... I GOTCHA, YOU UGLY SPASM.

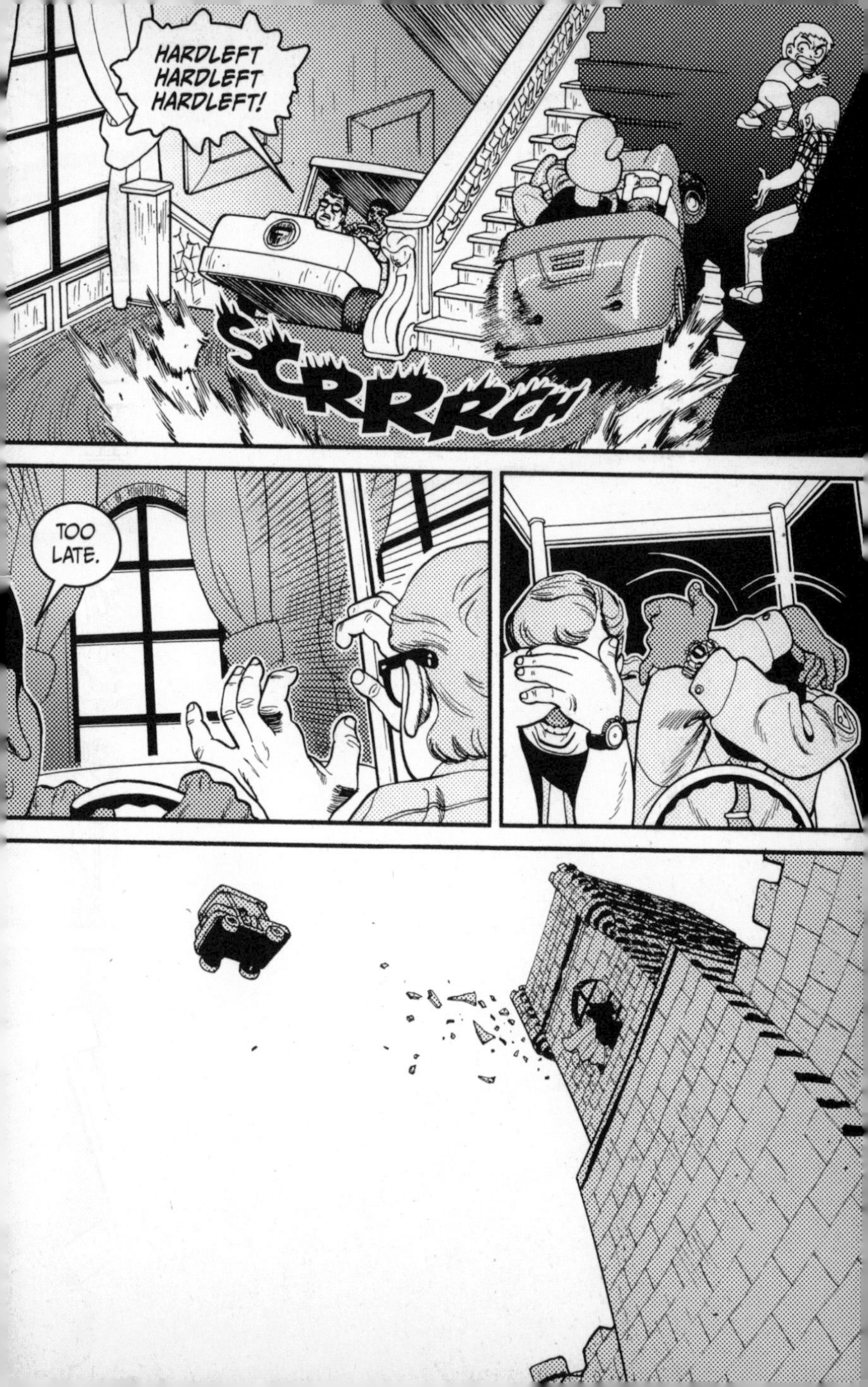
HARDLEFT HARDLEFT HARDLEFT!
SCRRRCH
TOO LATE.

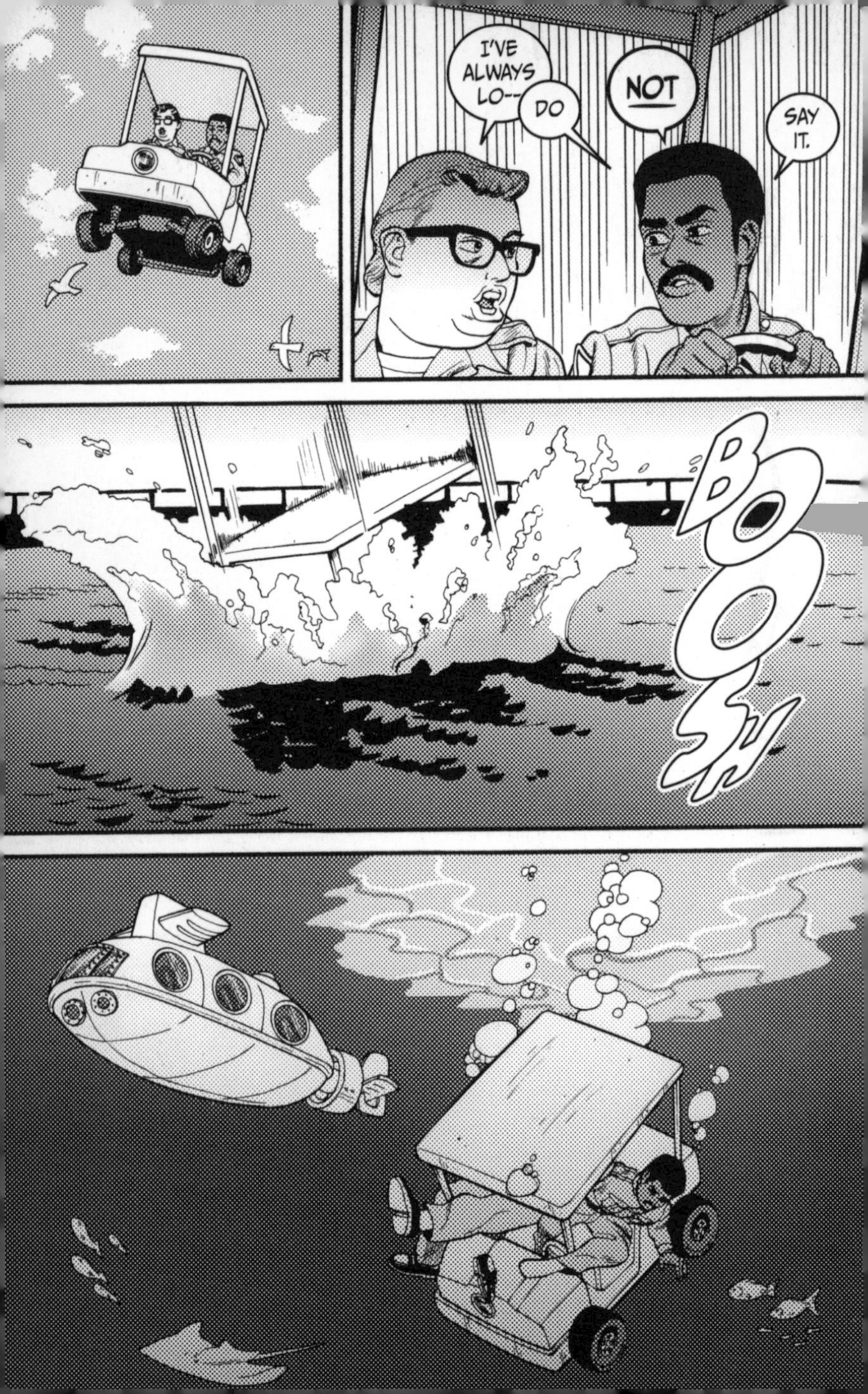
I'VE ALWAYS LO--
DO
NOT
SAY IT.
BOOOSH

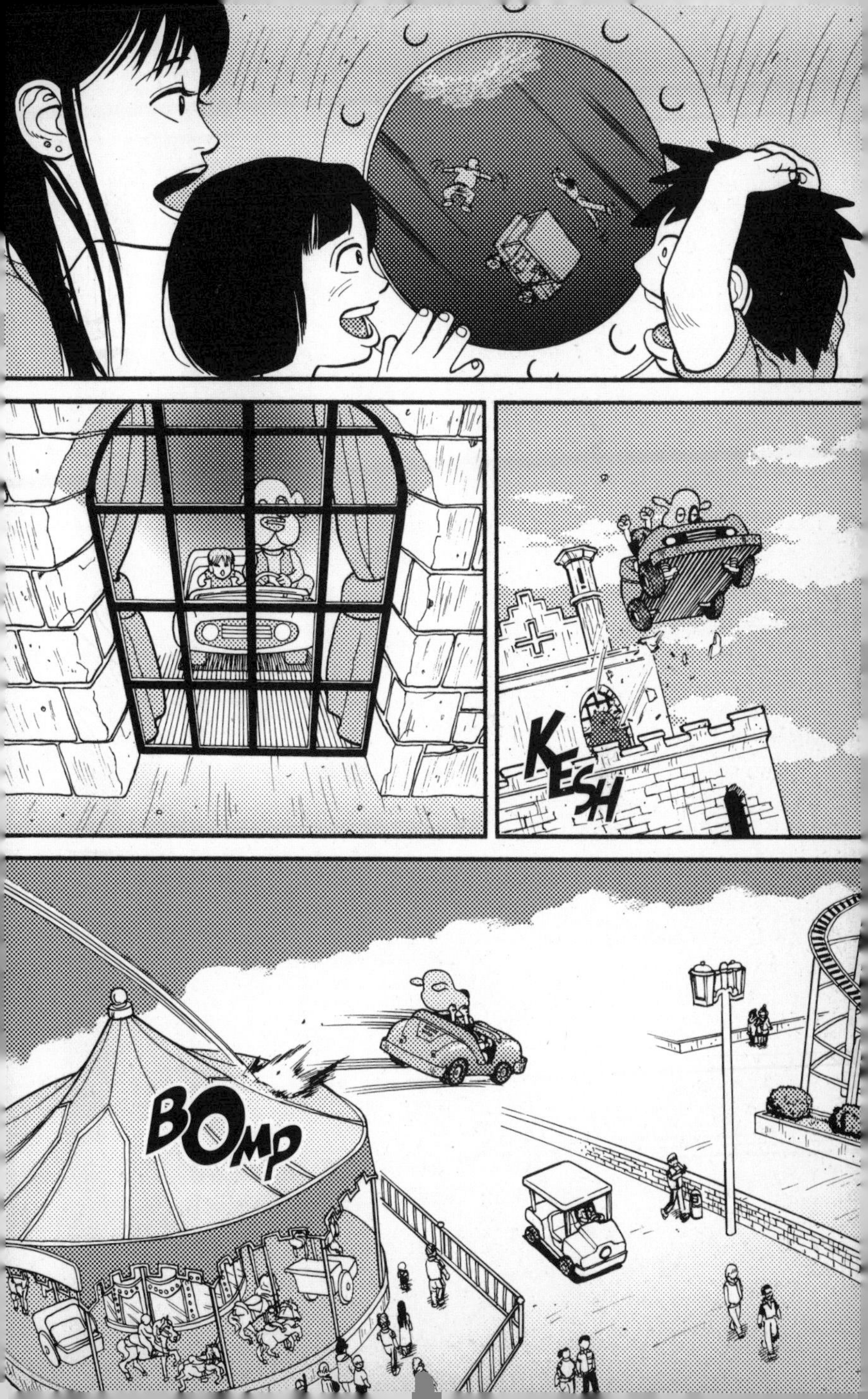
KESH
BOMP

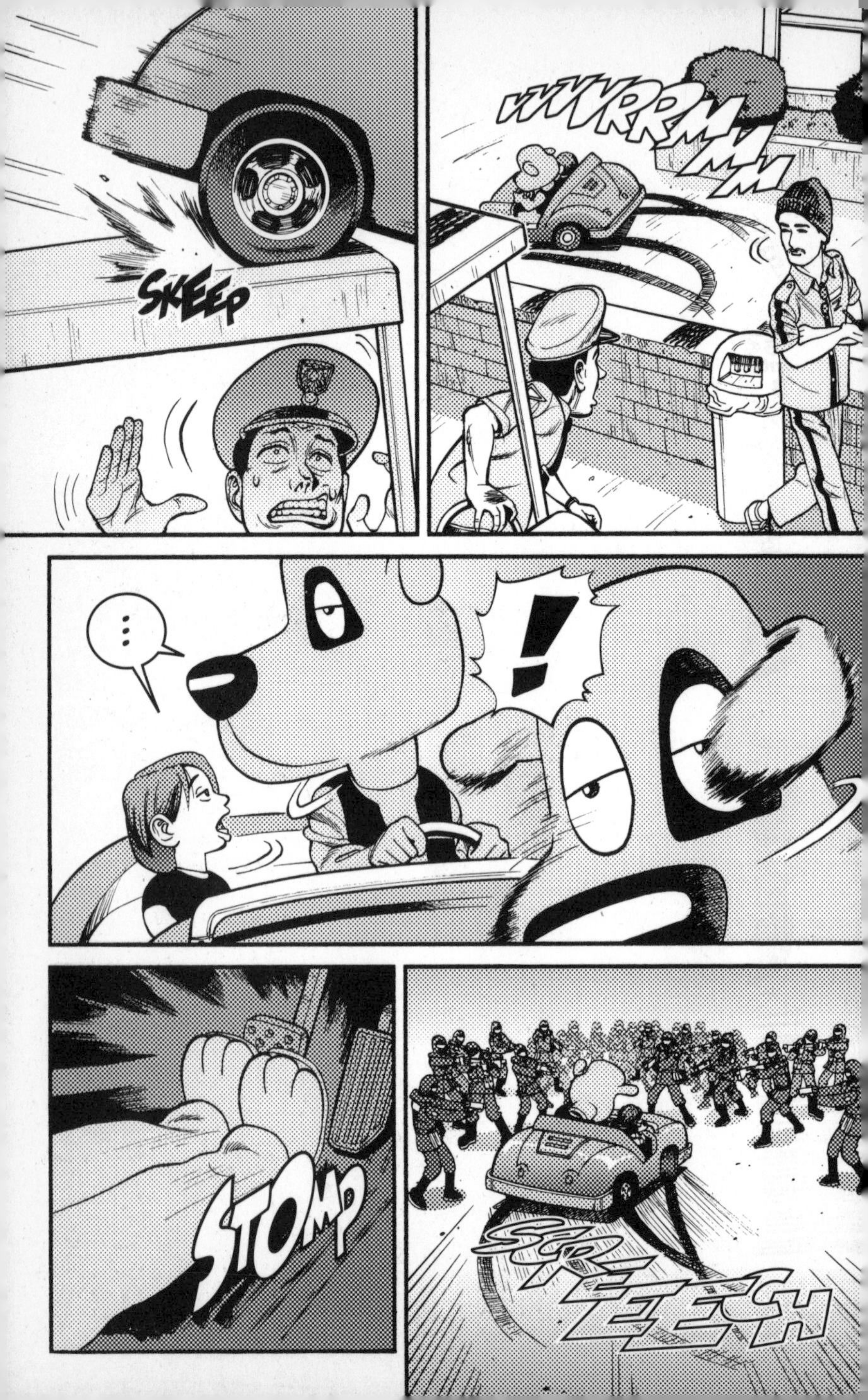
SKEEP
VVVVRRRMMMM
...
!
STOMP
SCREEECH

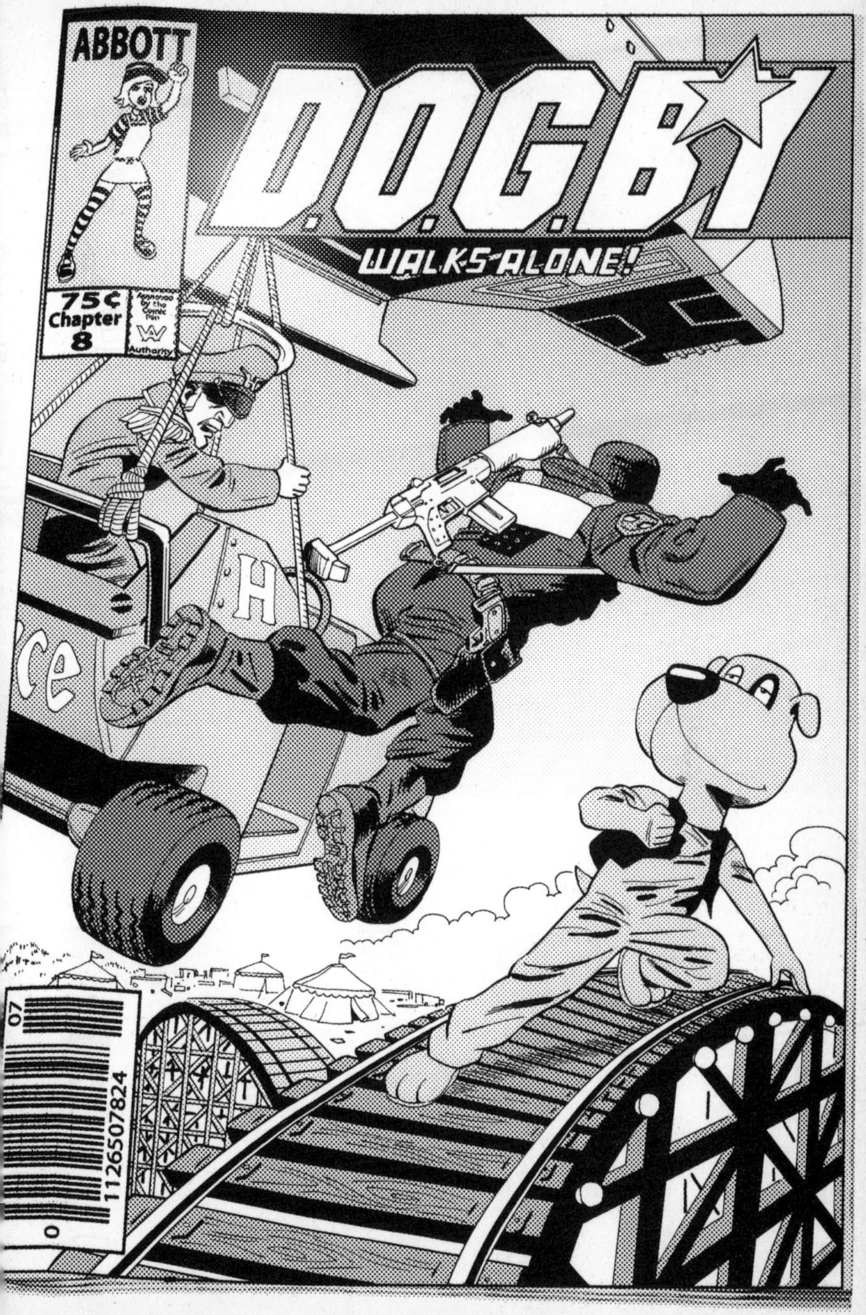
ABBOTT
D.O.G.B.I
WALKS ALONE!
75¢
Chapter
8
H

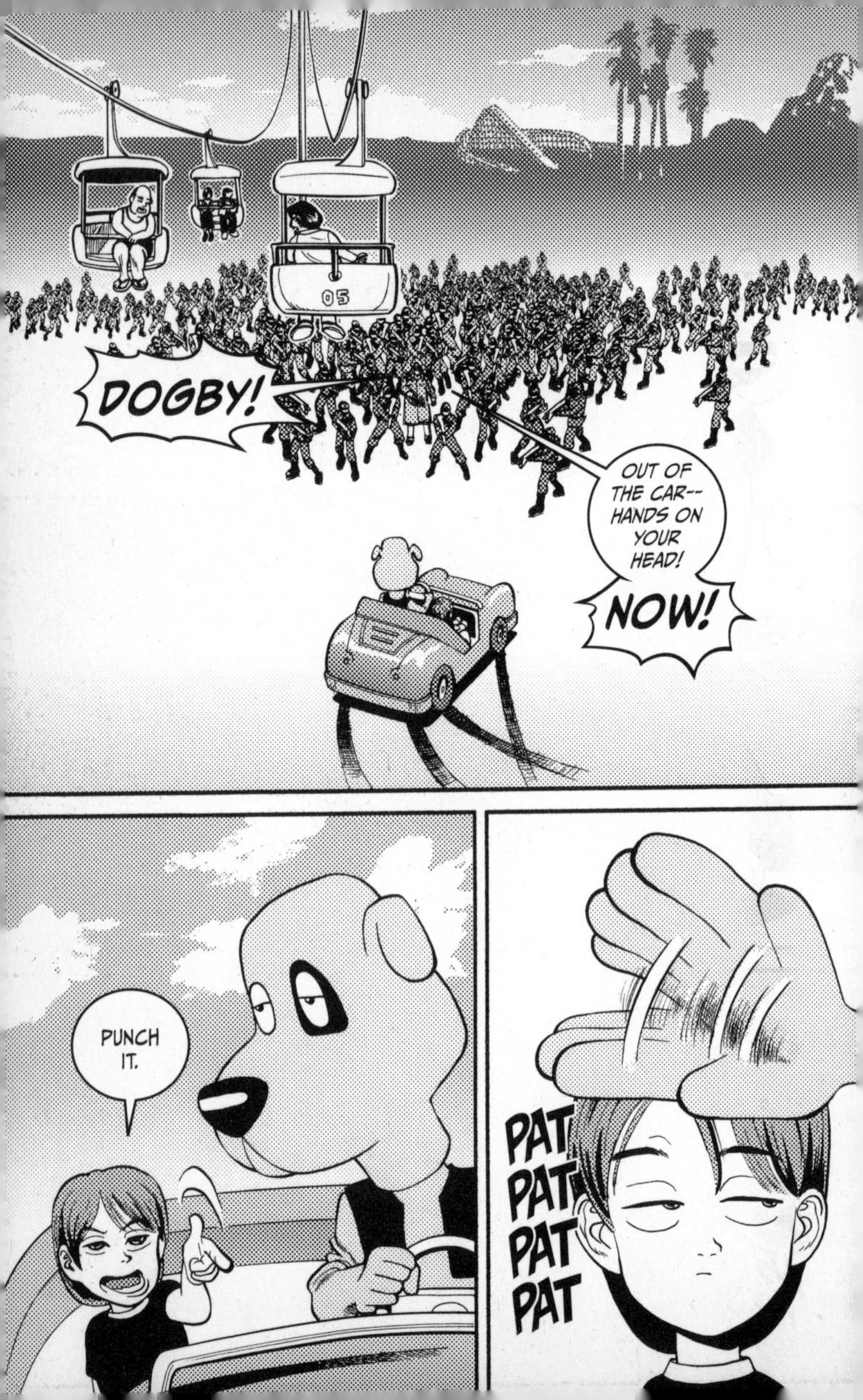
DOGBY!
OUT OF THE CAR-- HANDS ON YOUR HEAD!
NOW!
PUNCH IT.
PAT PAT PAT PAT

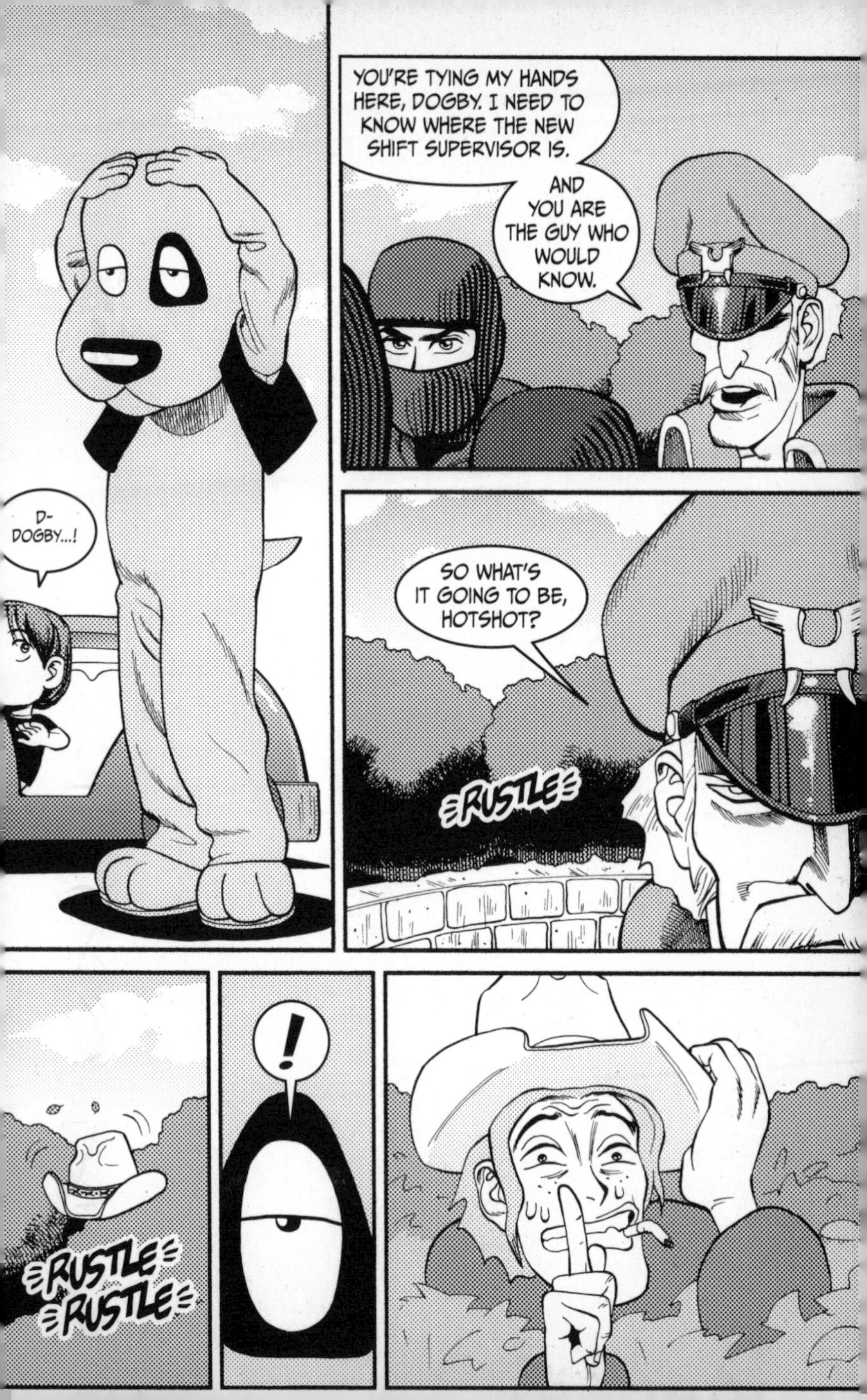
D-DOGBY...!
YOU'RE TYING MY HANDS HERE, DOGBY. I NEED TO KNOW WHERE THE NEW SHIFT SUPERVISOR IS.
AND YOU ARE THE GUY WHO WOULD KNOW.
SO WHAT'S IT GOING TO BE, HOTSHOT?
RUSTLE
RUSTLE RUSTLE
!

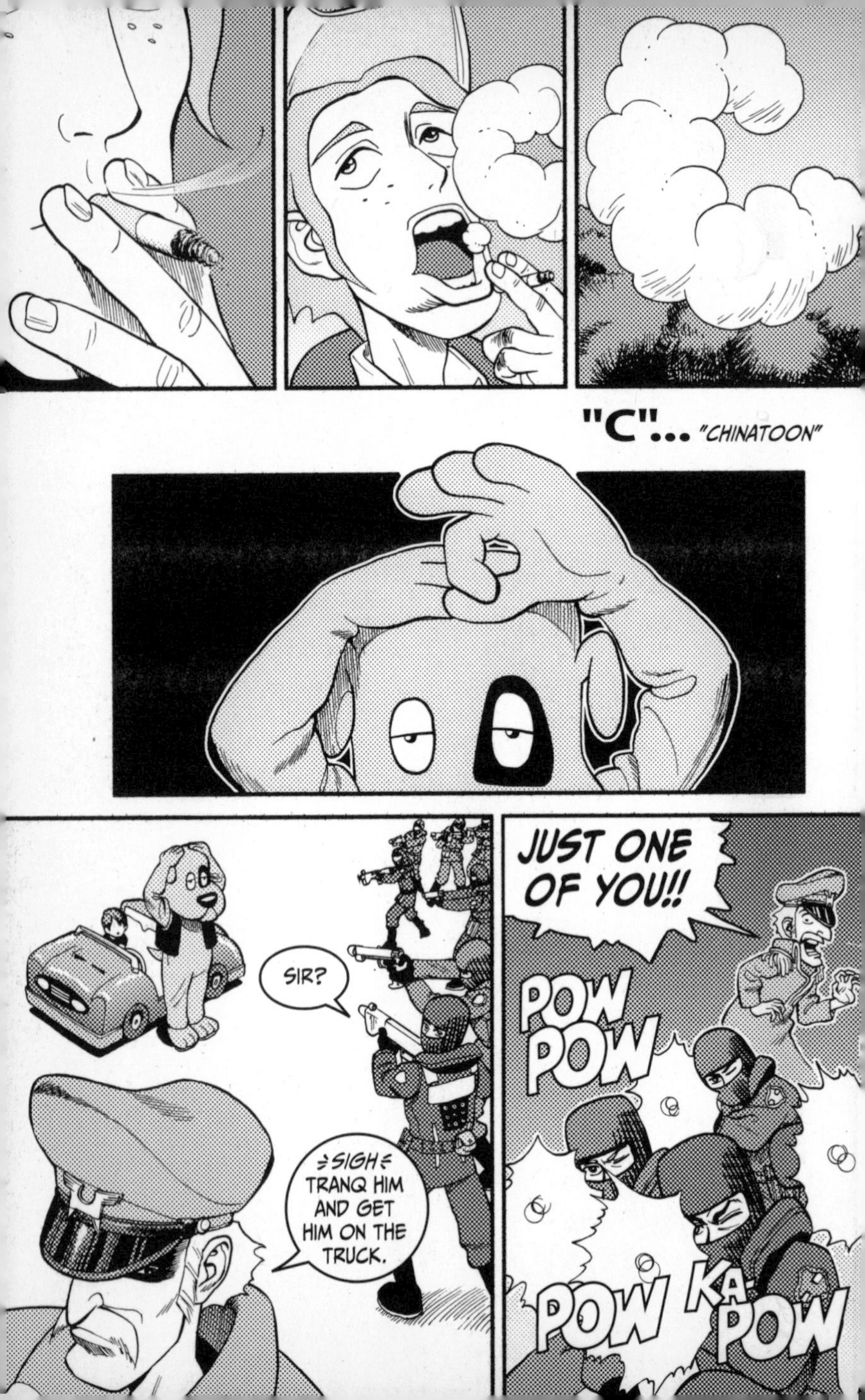
"C"... "CHINATOON"
SIR?
≶SIGH≷ TRANQ HIM AND GET HIM ON THE TRUCK.
JUST ONE OF YOU!!
POW POW
POW KA-POW

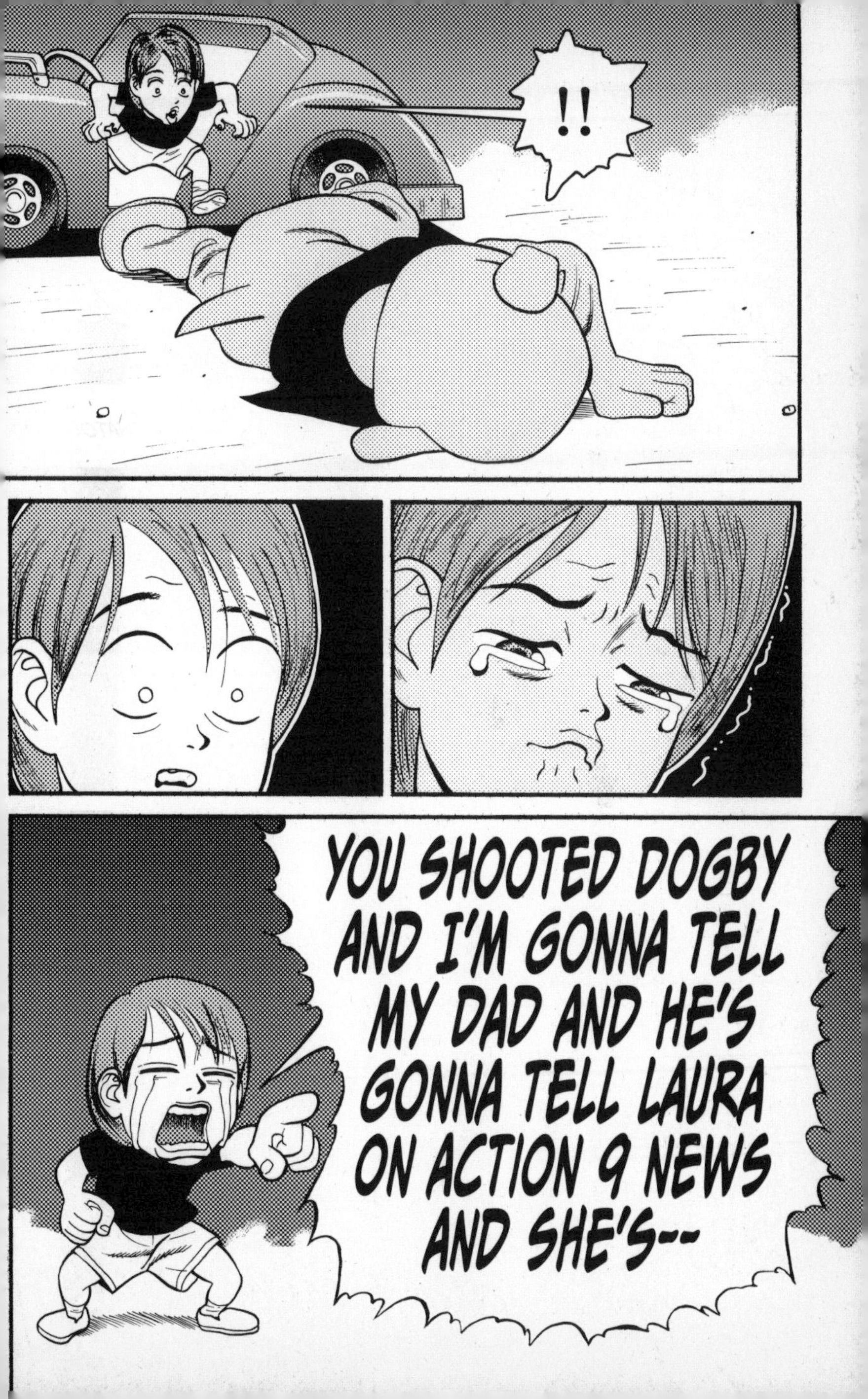
!!
YOU SHOOTED DOGBY AND I'M GONNA TELL MY DAD AND HE'S GONNA TELL LAURA ON ACTION 9 NEWS AND SHE'S--

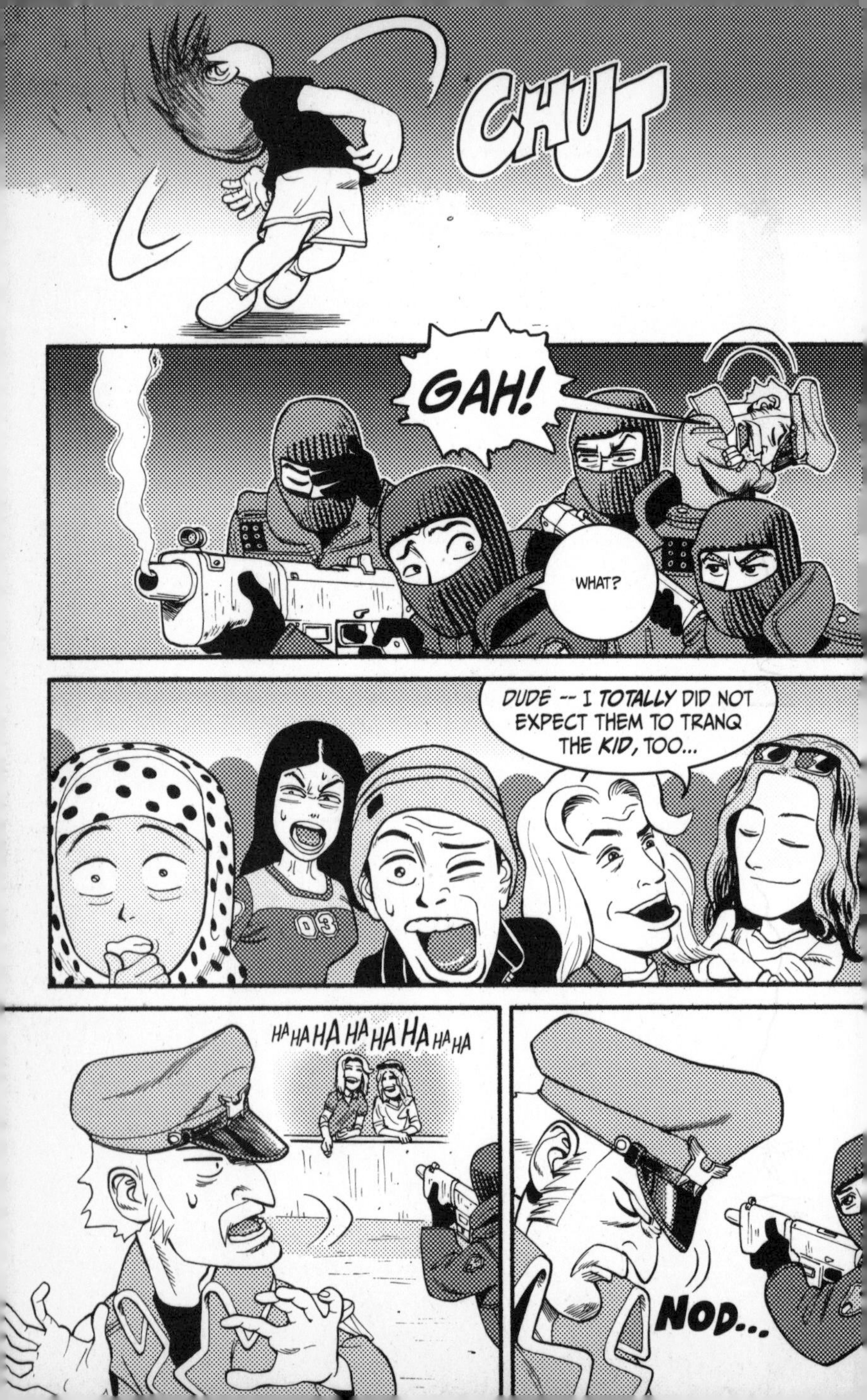
CHUT
GAH!
WHAT?
DUDE -- I *TOTALLY* DID NOT EXPECT THEM TO TRANQ THE *KID*, TOO...
HA HA HA HA HA HA HA HA
NOD...

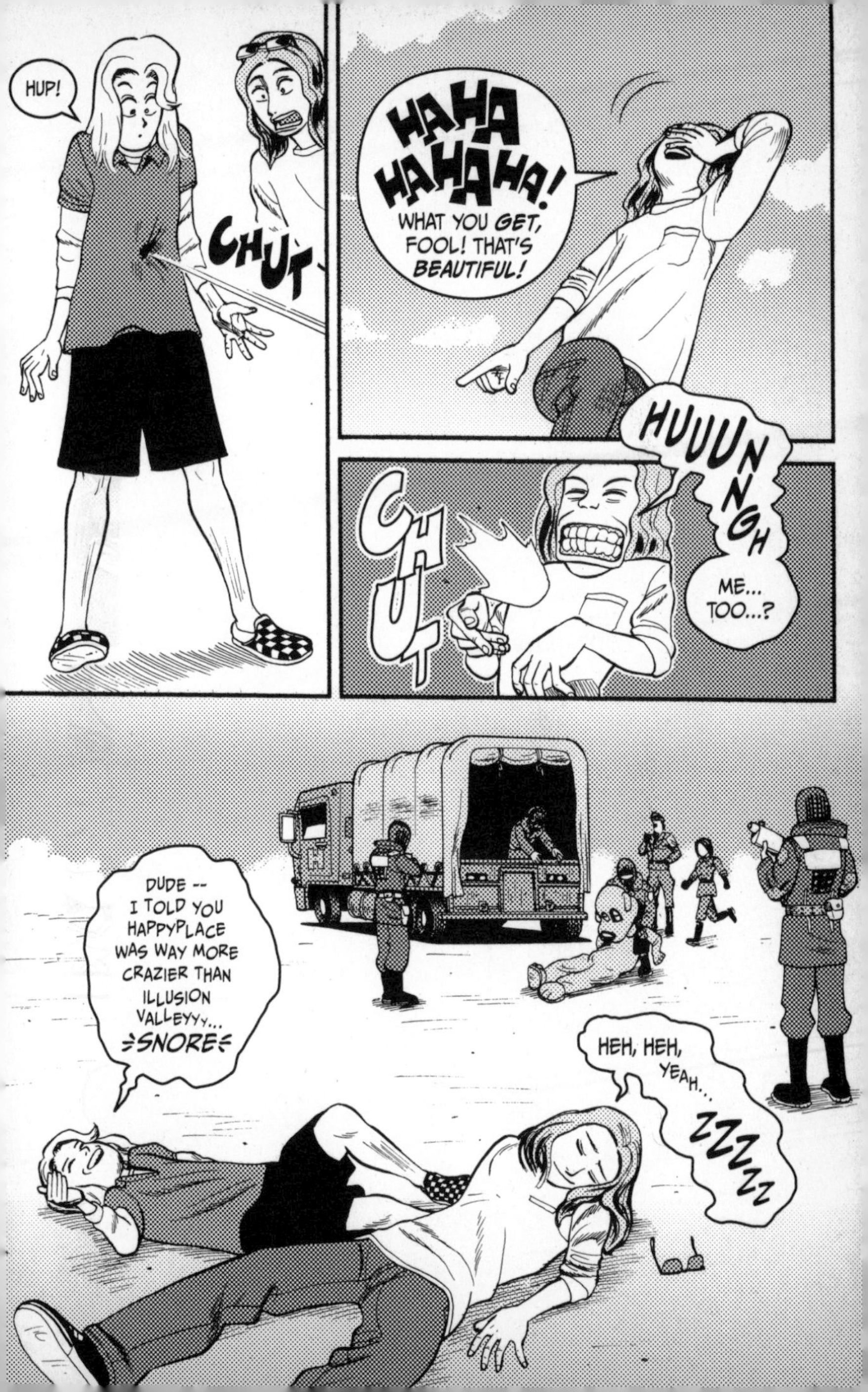
HUP!
CHUT
HAHA HAHAHA! WHAT YOU GET, FOOL! THAT'S BEAUTIFUL!
CHUT
HUUUNNNGH
ME... TOO...?
DUDE -- I TOLD YOU HAPPYPLACE WAS WAY MORE CRAZIER THAN ILLUSION VALLEYYY... SNORE
HEH, HEH, YEAH... ZZZZZ

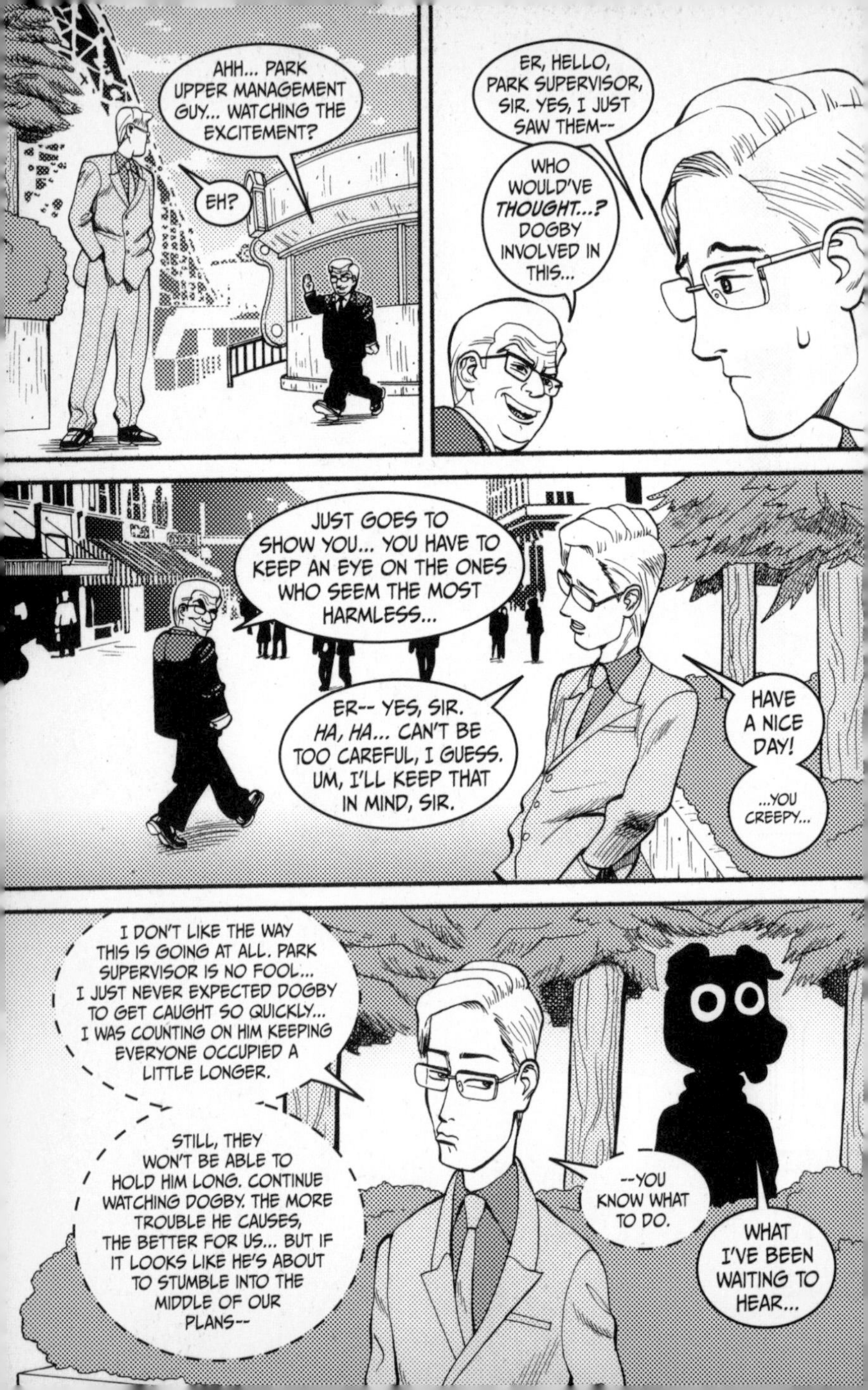
AHH... PARK UPPER MANAGEMENT GUY... WATCHING THE EXCITEMENT?
EH?
ER, HELLO, PARK SUPERVISOR, SIR. YES, I JUST SAW THEM--
WHO WOULD'VE *THOUGHT...?* DOGBY INVOLVED IN THIS...
JUST GOES TO SHOW YOU... YOU HAVE TO KEEP AN EYE ON THE ONES WHO SEEM THE MOST HARMLESS...
ER-- YES, SIR. *HA, HA...* CAN'T BE TOO CAREFUL, I GUESS. UM, I'LL KEEP THAT IN MIND, SIR.
HAVE A NICE DAY!
...YOU CREEPY...
I DON'T LIKE THE WAY THIS IS GOING AT ALL. PARK SUPERVISOR IS NO FOOL... I JUST NEVER EXPECTED DOGBY TO GET CAUGHT SO QUICKLY... I WAS COUNTING ON HIM KEEPING EVERYONE OCCUPIED A LITTLE LONGER.
STILL, THEY WON'T BE ABLE TO HOLD HIM LONG. CONTINUE WATCHING DOGBY. THE MORE TROUBLE HE CAUSES, THE BETTER FOR US... BUT IF IT LOOKS LIKE HE'S ABOUT TO STUMBLE INTO THE MIDDLE OF OUR PLANS--
--YOU KNOW WHAT TO DO.
WHAT I'VE BEEN WAITING TO HEAR...

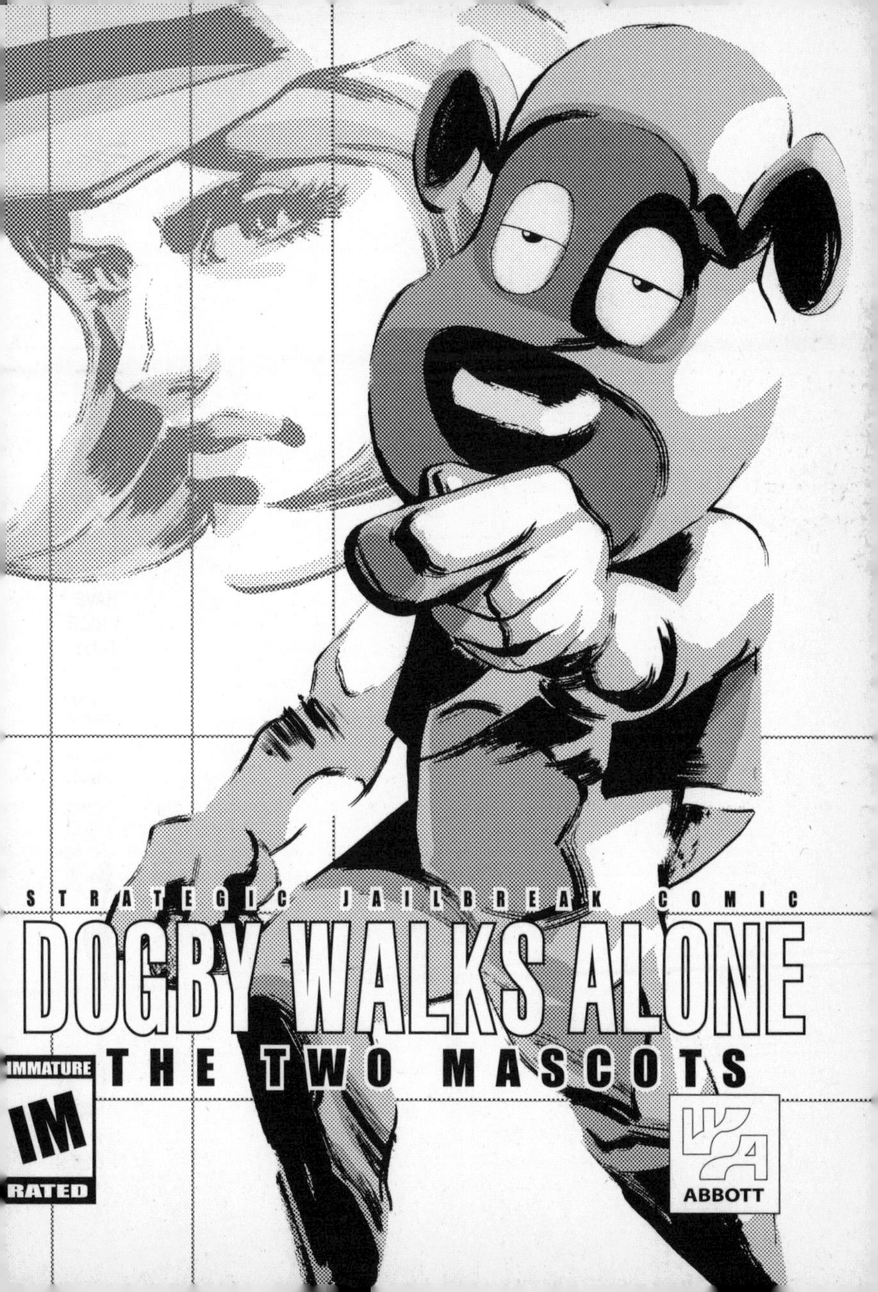
STRATEGIC JAILBREAK COMIC
DOGBY WALKS ALONE
THE TWO MASCOTS
IMMATURE
IM
RATED
ABBOTT

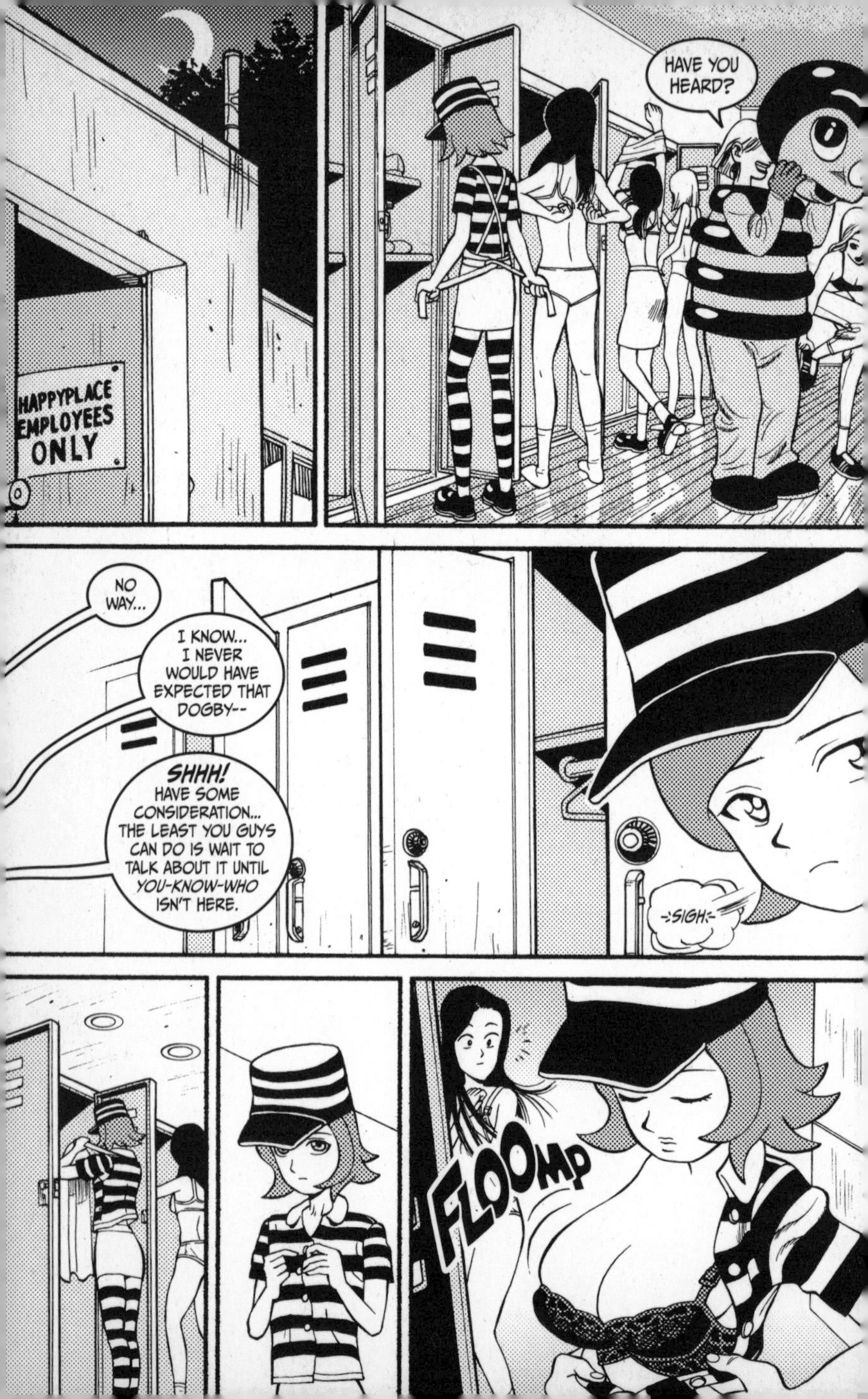
HAPPYPLACE EMPLOYEES ONLY
HAVE YOU HEARD?
NO WAY...
I KNOW... I NEVER WOULD HAVE EXPECTED THAT DOGBY--
SHHH! HAVE SOME CONSIDERATION... THE LEAST YOU GUYS CAN DO IS WAIT TO TALK ABOUT IT UNTIL YOU-KNOW-WHO ISN'T HERE.
-SIGH-
FLOOMP

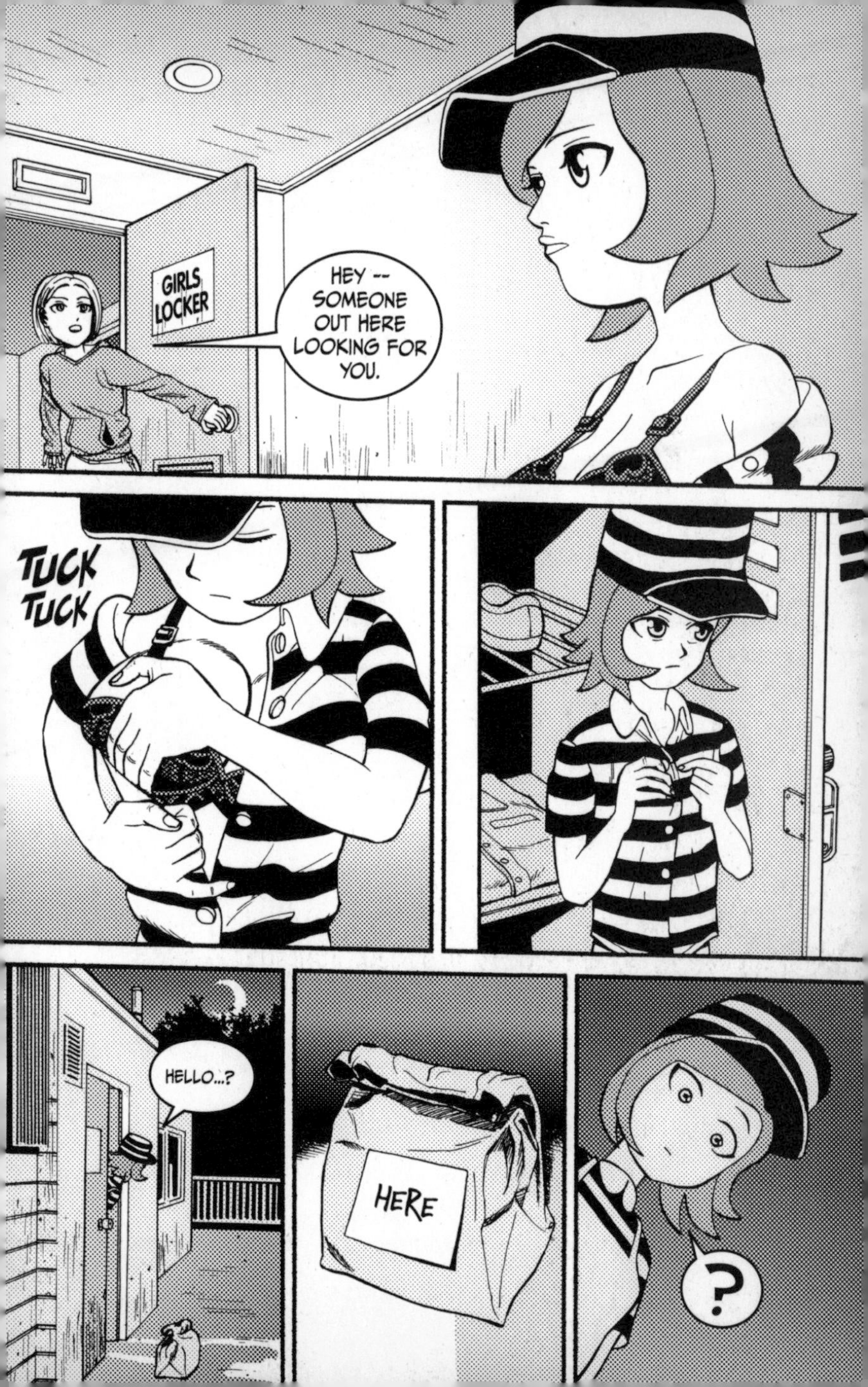
GIRLS LOCKER
HEY -- SOMEONE OUT HERE LOOKING FOR YOU.
TUCK TUCK
HELLO...?
HERE
?

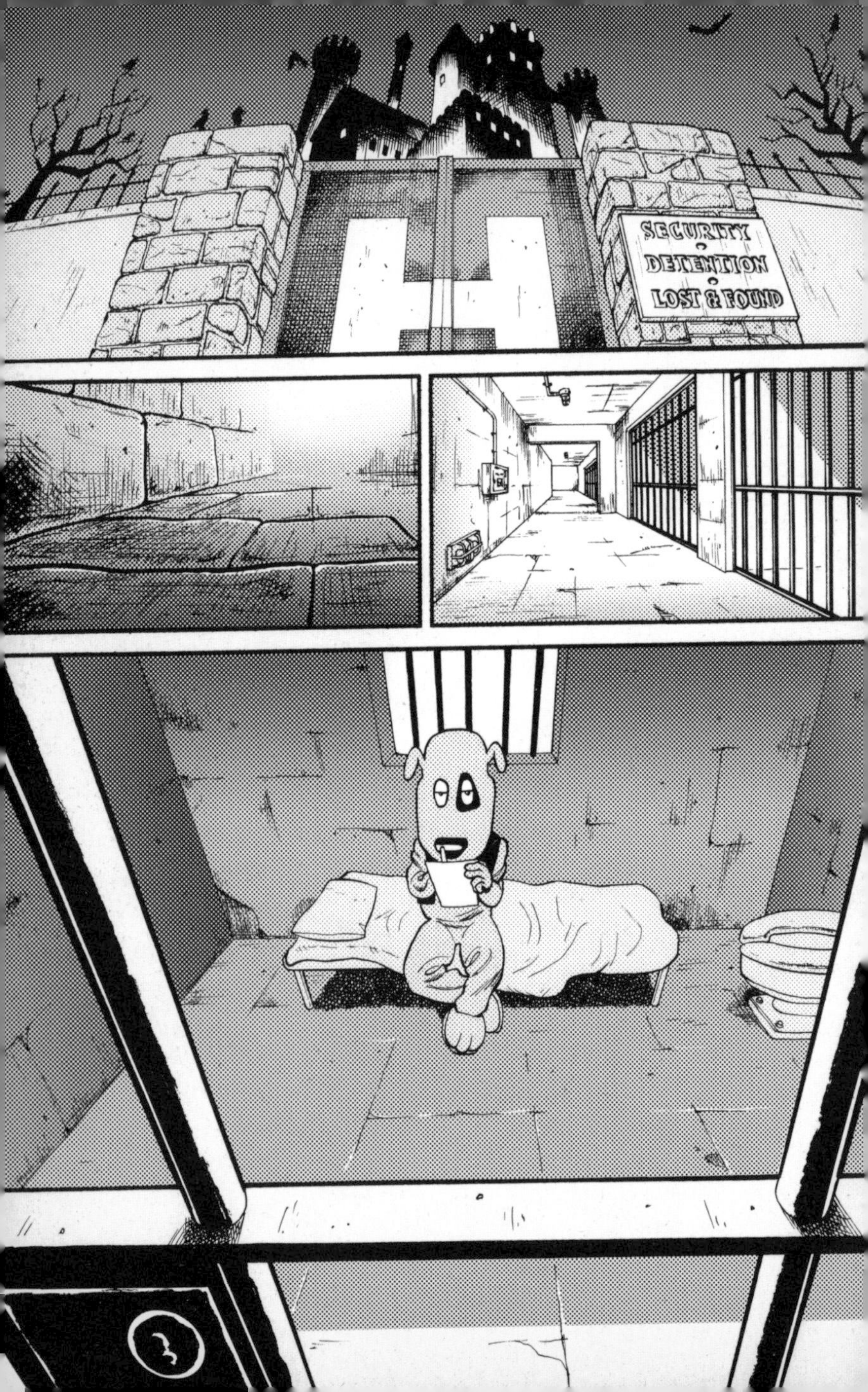
SECURITY
DETENTION
LOST & FOUND

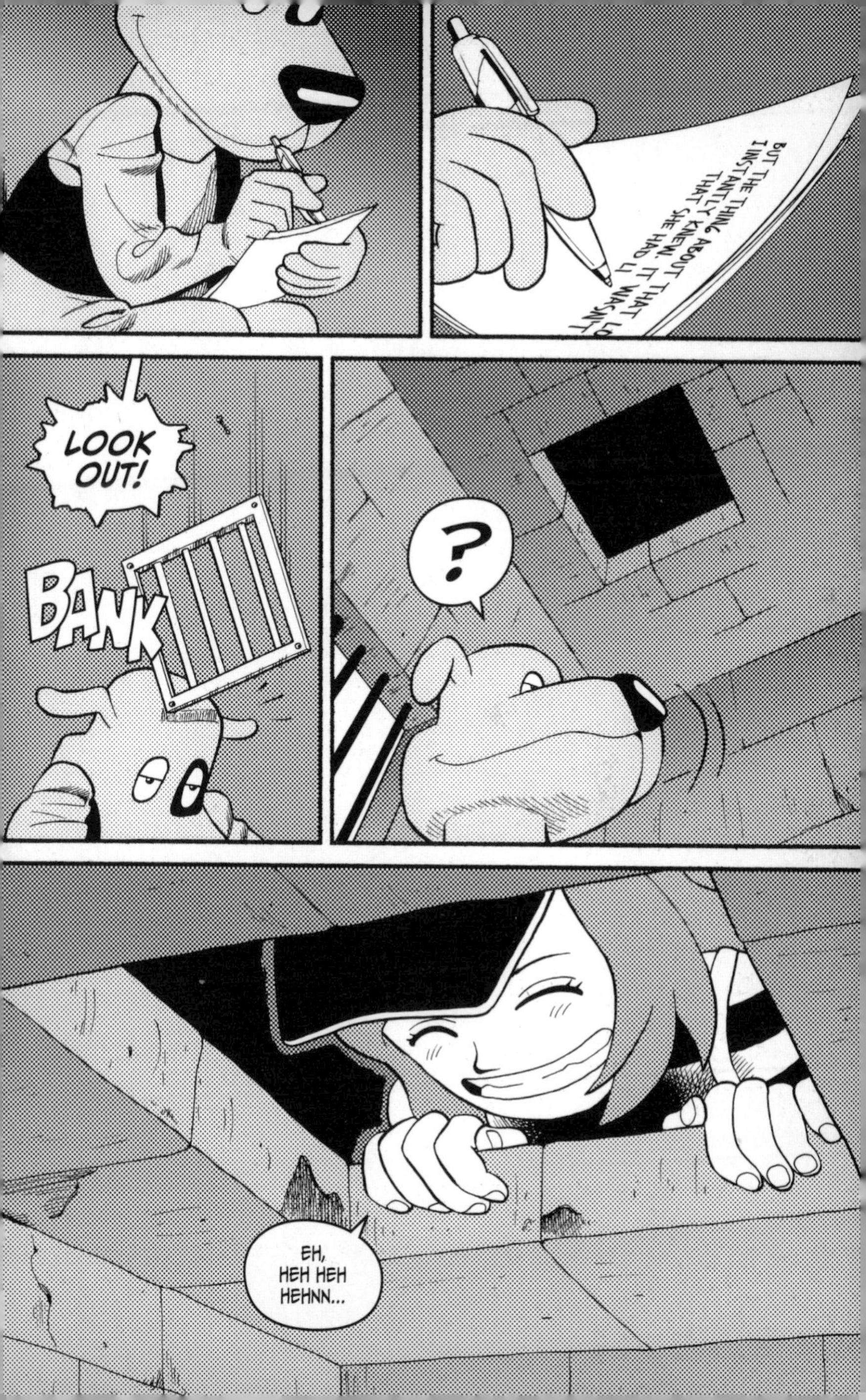
BUT THE THING ABOUT
IINSTANTLY KNEW. IT THAT LO
THAT SHE HAD LI WASN'T
LOOK OUT!
BANK
?
EH, HEH HEH HEHNN...

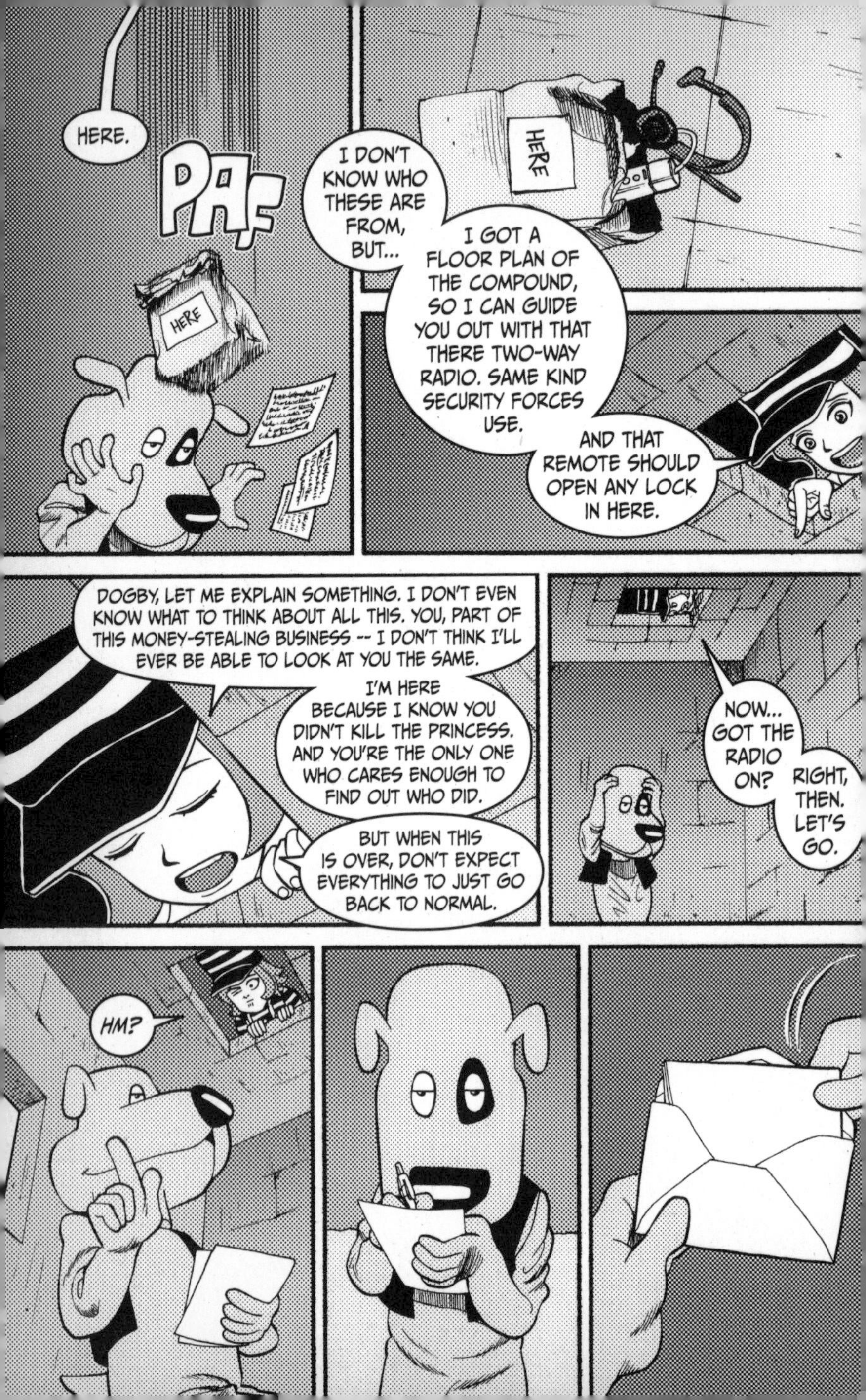
HERE.
PAF
HERE
HERE
I DON'T KNOW WHO THESE ARE FROM, BUT...
I GOT A FLOOR PLAN OF THE COMPOUND, SO I CAN GUIDE YOU OUT WITH THAT THERE TWO-WAY RADIO. SAME KIND SECURITY FORCES USE.
AND THAT REMOTE SHOULD OPEN ANY LOCK IN HERE.
DOGBY, LET ME EXPLAIN SOMETHING. I DON'T EVEN KNOW WHAT TO THINK ABOUT ALL THIS. YOU, PART OF THIS MONEY-STEALING BUSINESS -- I DON'T THINK I'LL EVER BE ABLE TO LOOK AT YOU THE SAME.
I'M HERE BECAUSE I KNOW YOU DIDN'T KILL THE PRINCESS. AND YOU'RE THE ONLY ONE WHO CARES ENOUGH TO FIND OUT WHO DID.
BUT WHEN THIS IS OVER, DON'T EXPECT EVERYTHING TO JUST GO BACK TO NORMAL.
NOW... GOT THE RADIO ON?
RIGHT, THEN. LET'S GO.
HM?

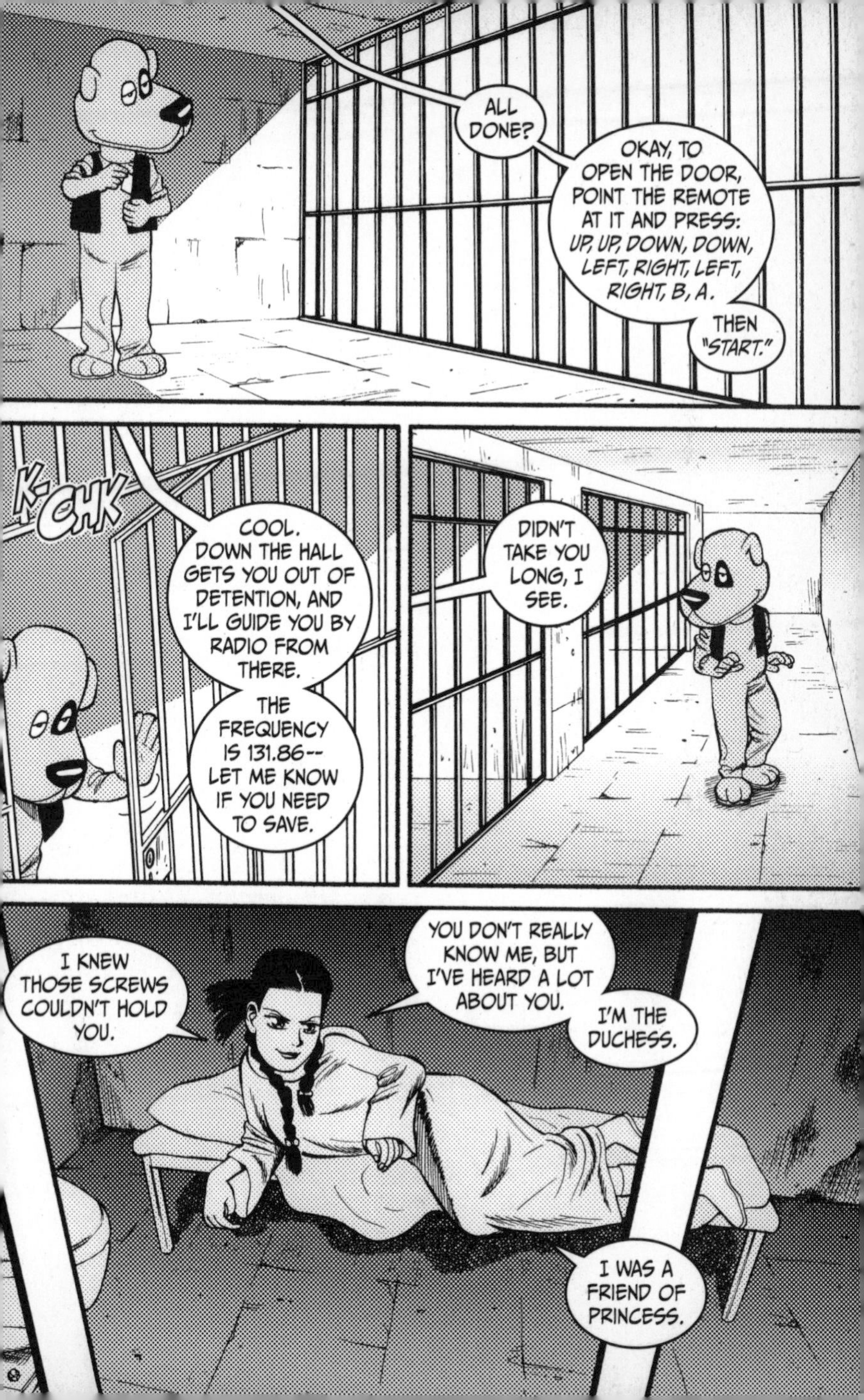
ALL DONE?
OKAY, TO OPEN THE DOOR, POINT THE REMOTE AT IT AND PRESS: UP, UP, DOWN, DOWN, LEFT, RIGHT, LEFT, RIGHT, B, A.
THEN "START."
K-CHK
COOL. DOWN THE HALL GETS YOU OUT OF DETENTION, AND I'LL GUIDE YOU BY RADIO FROM THERE.
THE FREQUENCY IS 131.86-- LET ME KNOW IF YOU NEED TO SAVE.
DIDN'T TAKE YOU LONG, I SEE.
I KNEW THOSE SCREWS COULDN'T HOLD YOU.
YOU DON'T REALLY KNOW ME, BUT I'VE HEARD A LOT ABOUT YOU.
I'M THE DUCHESS.
I WAS A FRIEND OF PRINCESS.

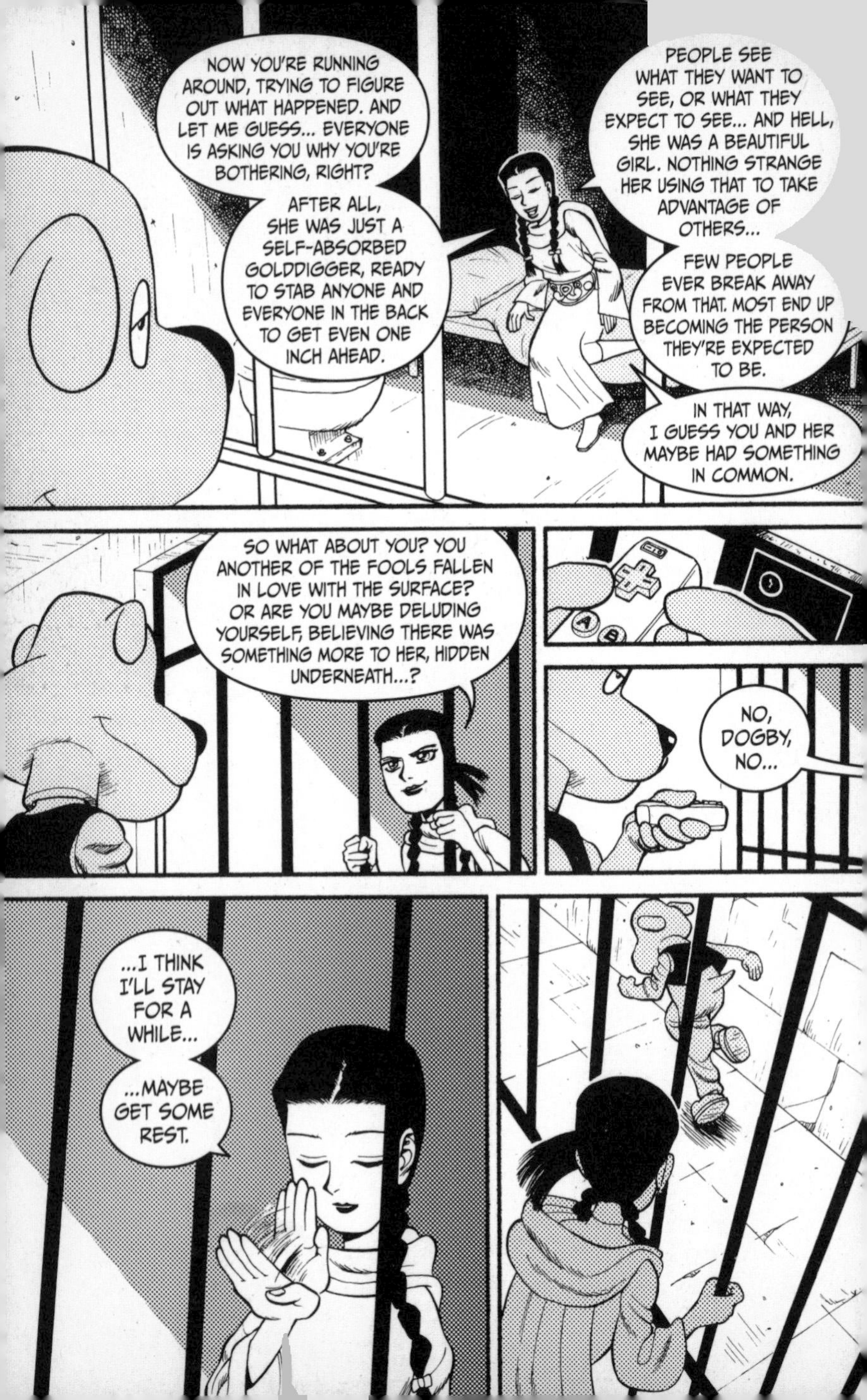
NOW YOU'RE RUNNING AROUND, TRYING TO FIGURE OUT WHAT HAPPENED. AND LET ME GUESS... EVERYONE IS ASKING YOU WHY YOU'RE BOTHERING, RIGHT?
AFTER ALL, SHE WAS JUST A SELF-ABSORBED GOLDDIGGER, READY TO STAB ANYONE AND EVERYONE IN THE BACK TO GET EVEN ONE INCH AHEAD.
PEOPLE SEE WHAT THEY WANT TO SEE, OR WHAT THEY EXPECT TO SEE... AND HELL, SHE WAS A BEAUTIFUL GIRL. NOTHING STRANGE HER USING THAT TO TAKE ADVANTAGE OF OTHERS...
FEW PEOPLE EVER BREAK AWAY FROM THAT. MOST END UP BECOMING THE PERSON THEY'RE EXPECTED TO BE.
IN THAT WAY, I GUESS YOU AND HER MAYBE HAD SOMETHING IN COMMON.
SO WHAT ABOUT YOU? YOU ANOTHER OF THE FOOLS FALLEN IN LOVE WITH THE SURFACE? OR ARE YOU MAYBE DELUDING YOURSELF, BELIEVING THERE WAS SOMETHING MORE TO HER, HIDDEN UNDERNEATH...?
NO, DOGBY, NO...
...I THINK I'LL STAY FOR A WHILE...
...MAYBE GET SOME REST.

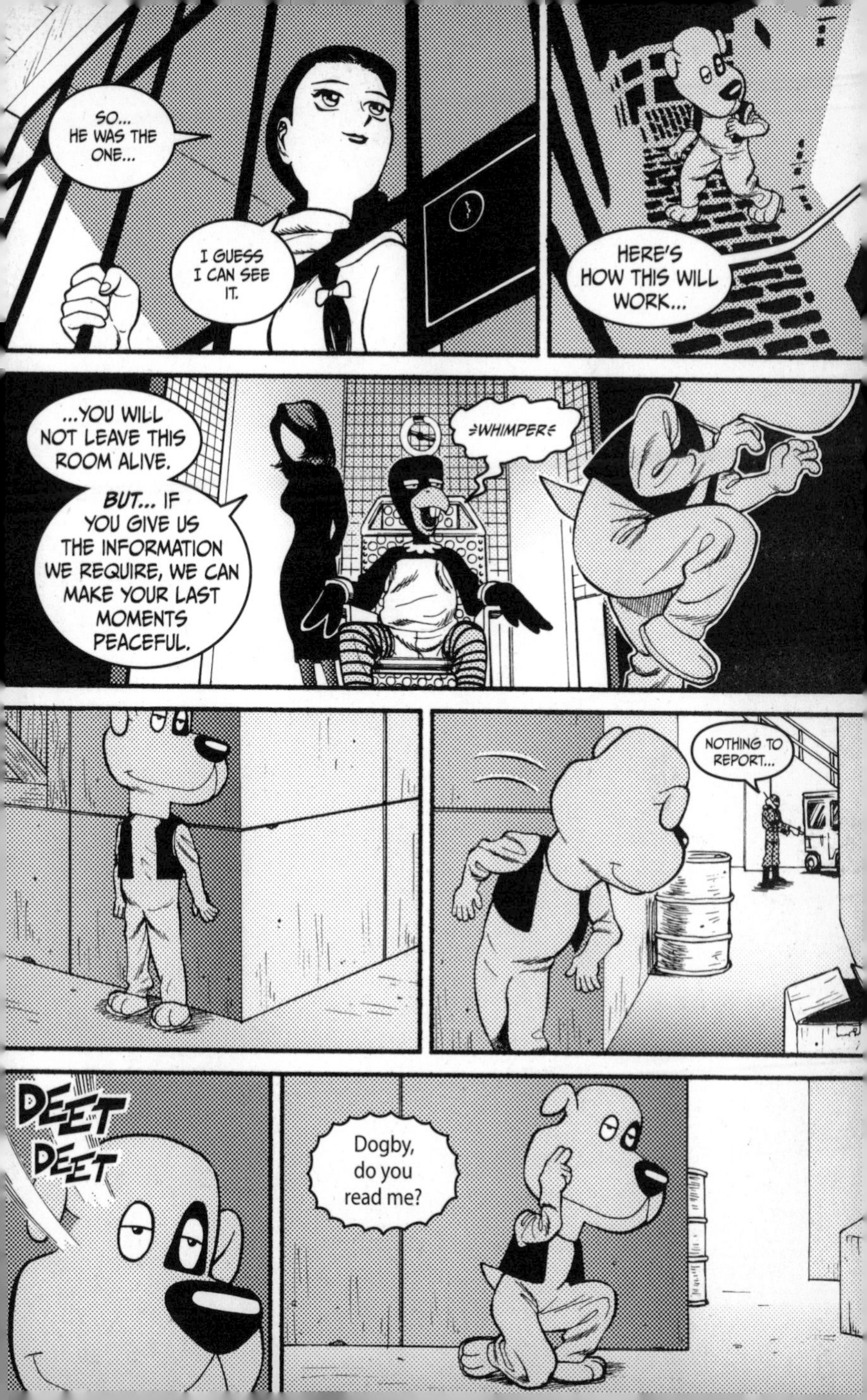
SO... HE WAS THE ONE...
I GUESS I CAN SEE IT.
HERE'S HOW THIS WILL WORK...
...YOU WILL NOT LEAVE THIS ROOM ALIVE.
BUT... IF YOU GIVE US THE INFORMATION WE REQUIRE, WE CAN MAKE YOUR LAST MOMENTS PEACEFUL.
WHIMPER
NOTHING TO REPORT...
DEET DEET
Dogby, do you read me?

Kept me waiting, huh? Are you at the sneak point?

....

You'll need to procure any weapons on site. Don't forget-- Happyplace Security forces are made up of ex-Russian Mafia... Be careful.

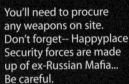

There's a set of stairs

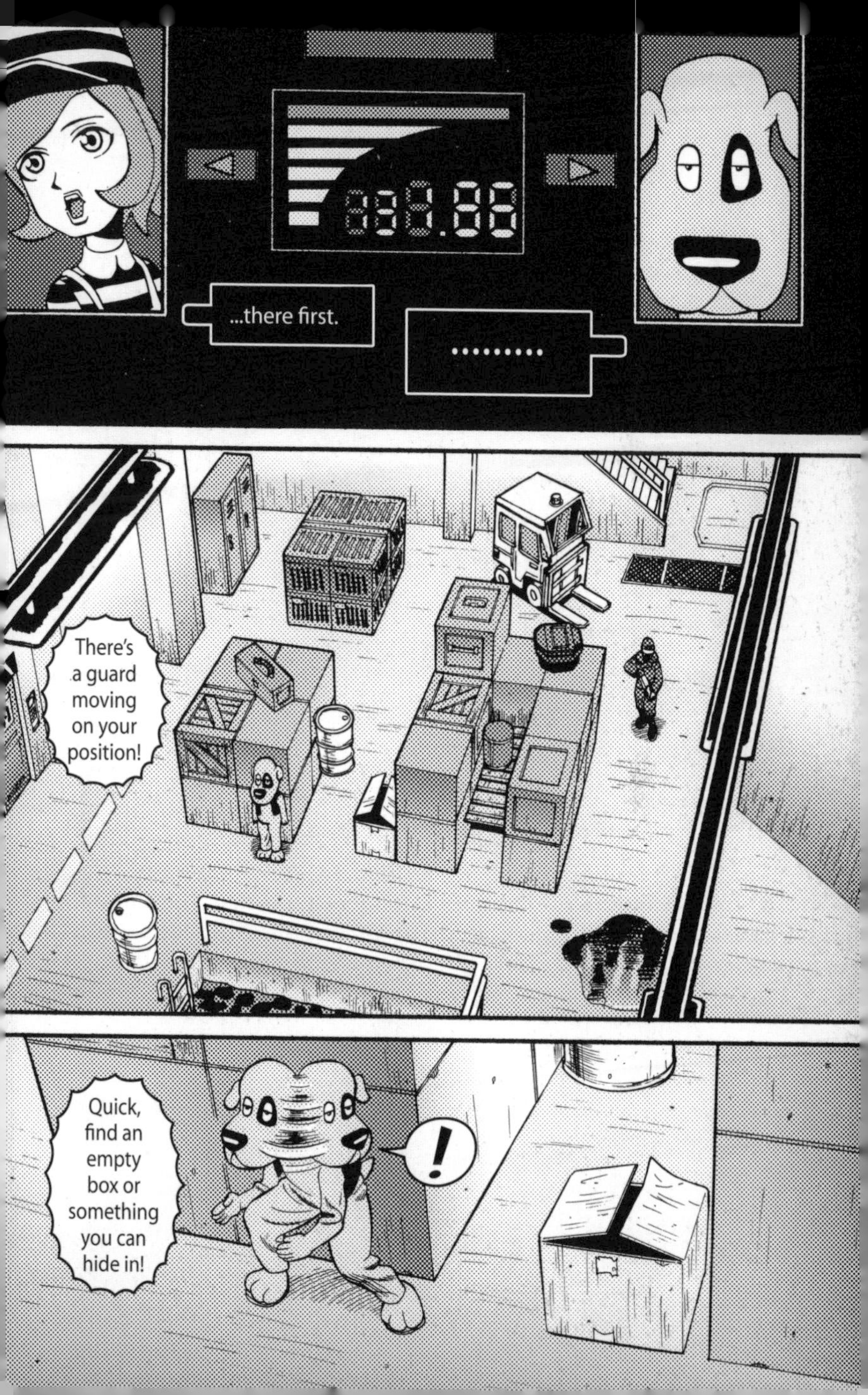
...there first.
....
There's a guard moving on your position!
Quick, find an empty box or something you can hide in!
!

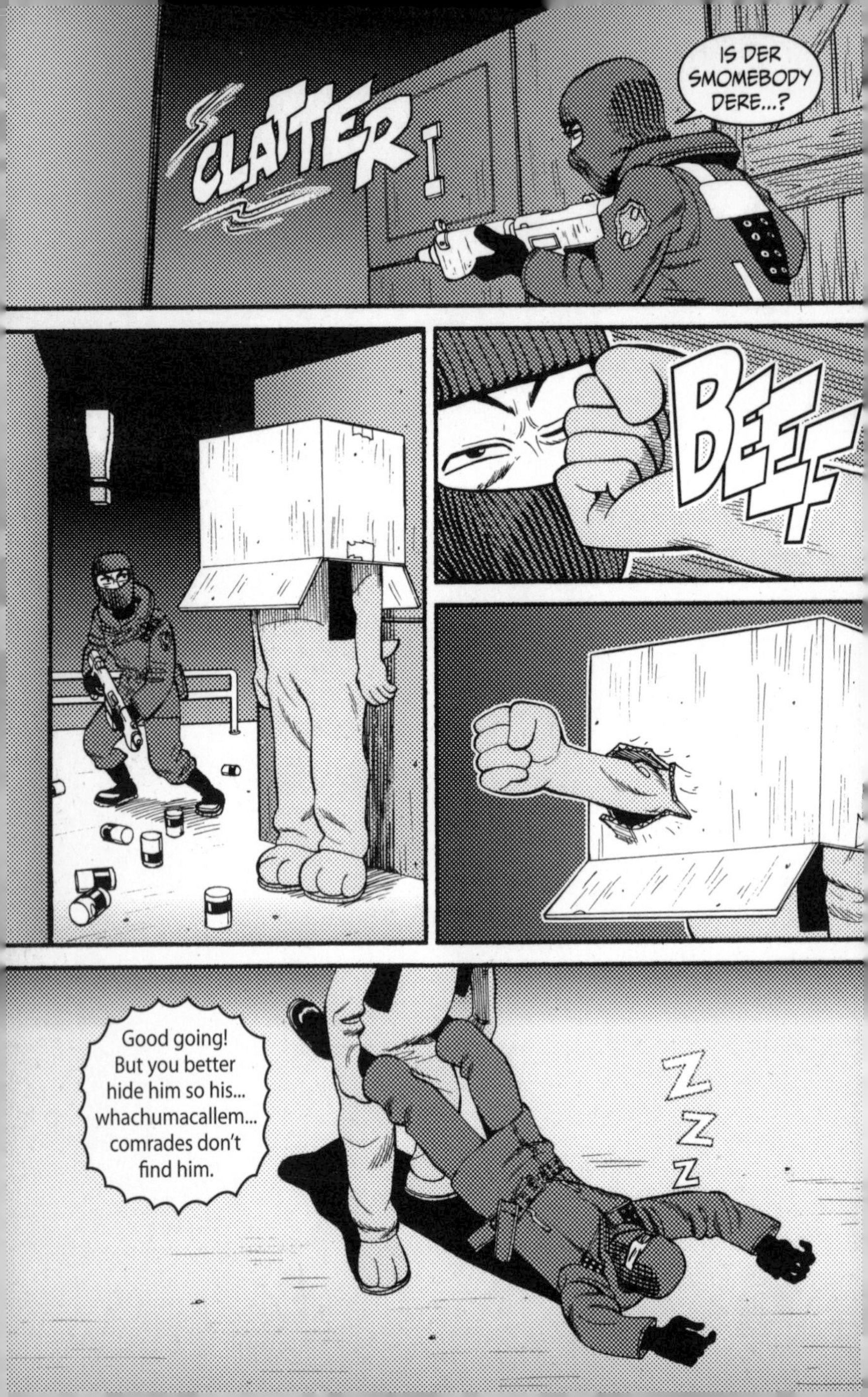
CLATTER
IS DER SMOMEBODY DERE...?
!
BEEF
Good going! But you better hide him so his... whachumacallem... comrades don't find him.
Z Z Z

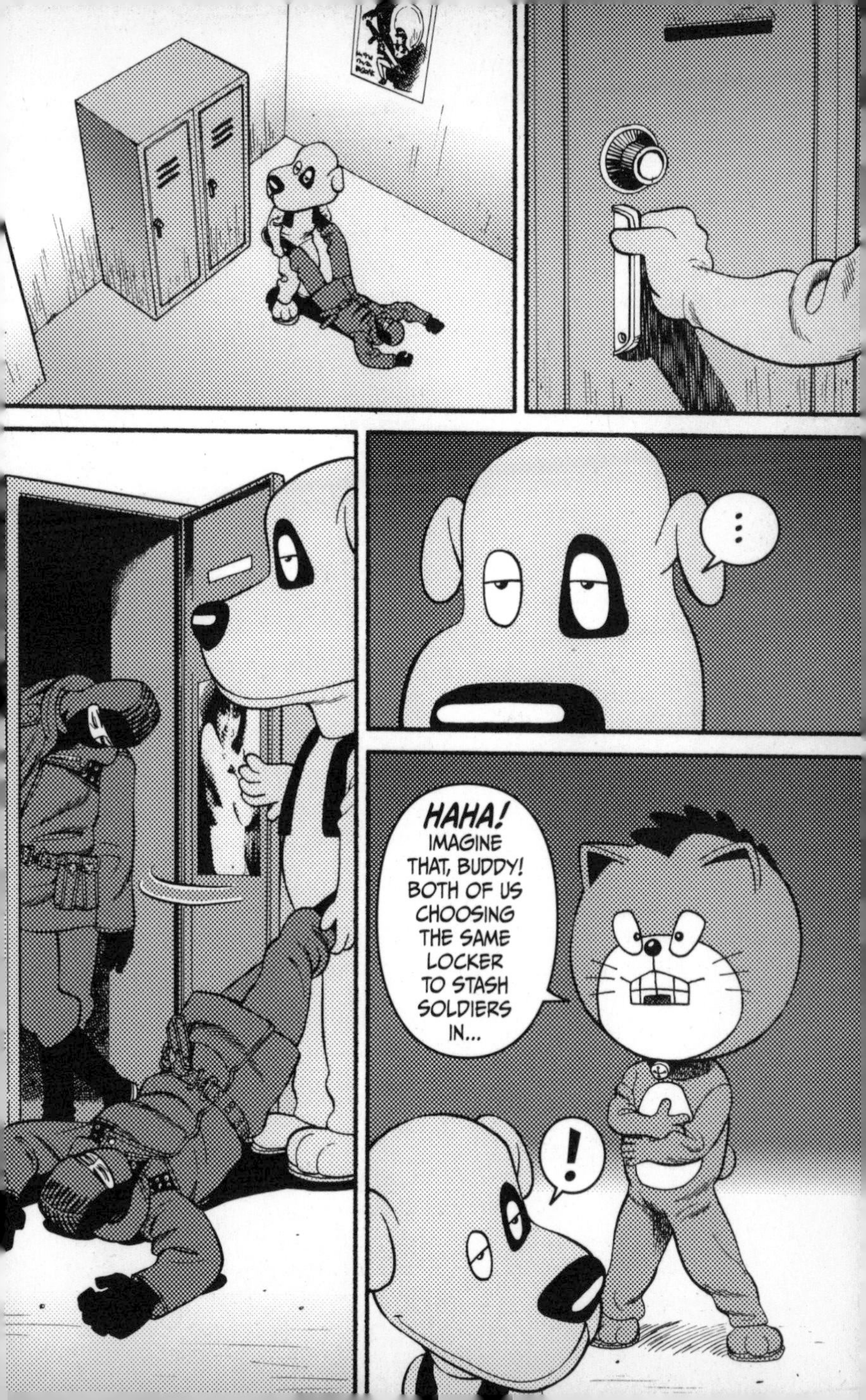
...
HAHA! IMAGINE THAT, BUDDY! BOTH OF US CHOOSING THE SAME LOCKER TO STASH SOLDIERS IN...
!

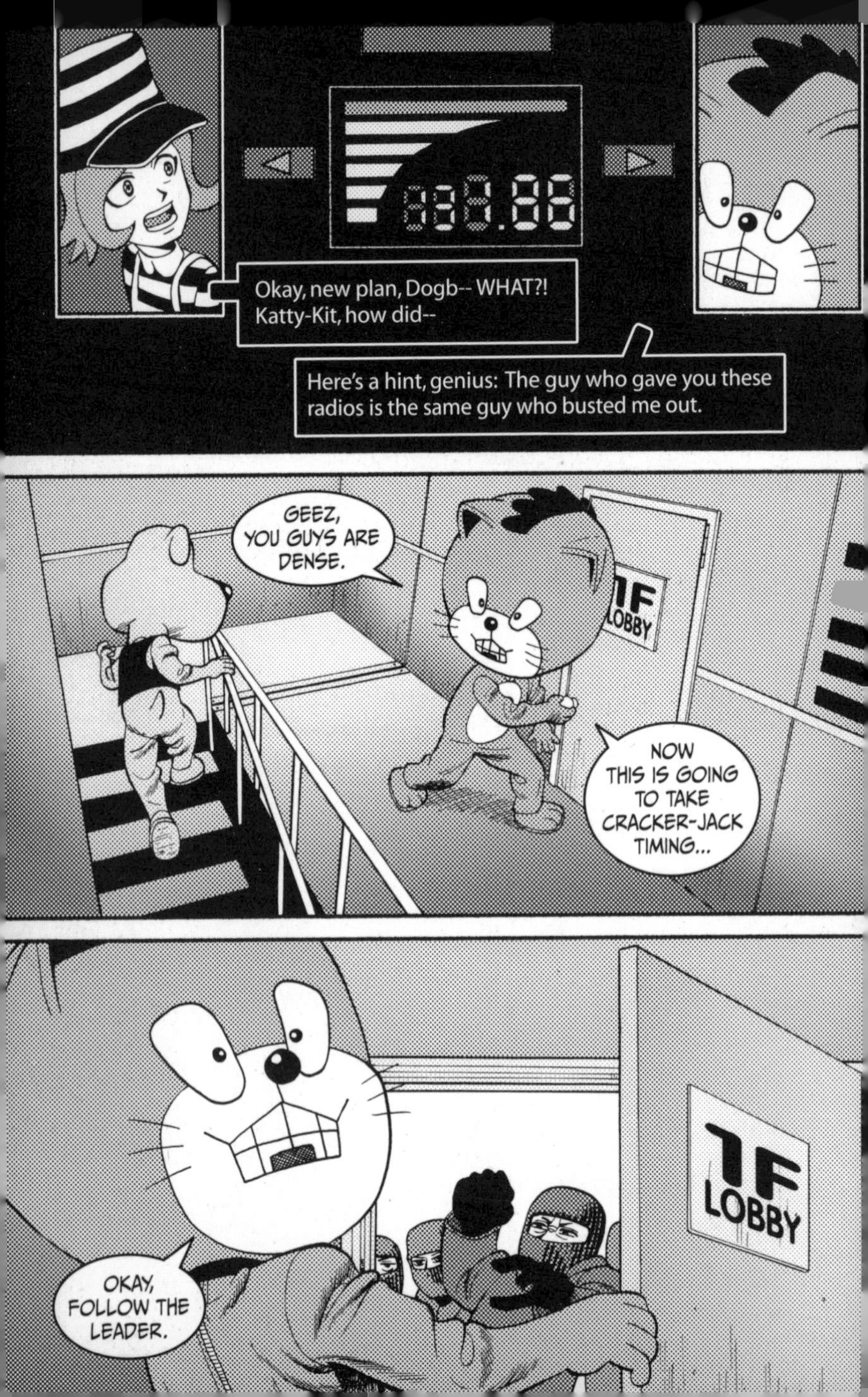
888.88
Okay, new plan, Dogb-- WHAT?! Katty-Kit, how did--
Here's a hint, genius: The guy who gave you these radios is the same guy who busted me out.
GEEZ, YOU GUYS ARE DENSE.
1F LOBBY
NOW THIS IS GOING TO TAKE CRACKER-JACK TIMING...
OKAY, FOLLOW THE LEADER.
1F LOBBY

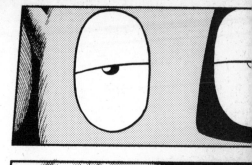

THE DOG
THE CAT
AND THE
LAW

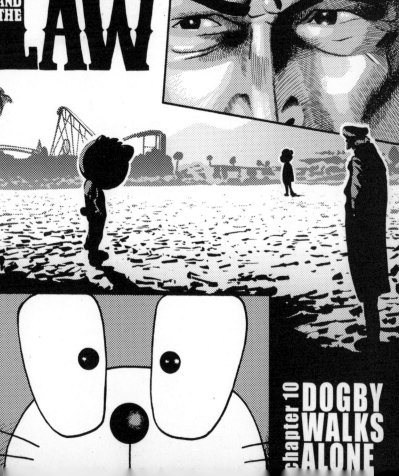

chapter 10 DOGBY WALKS ALONE

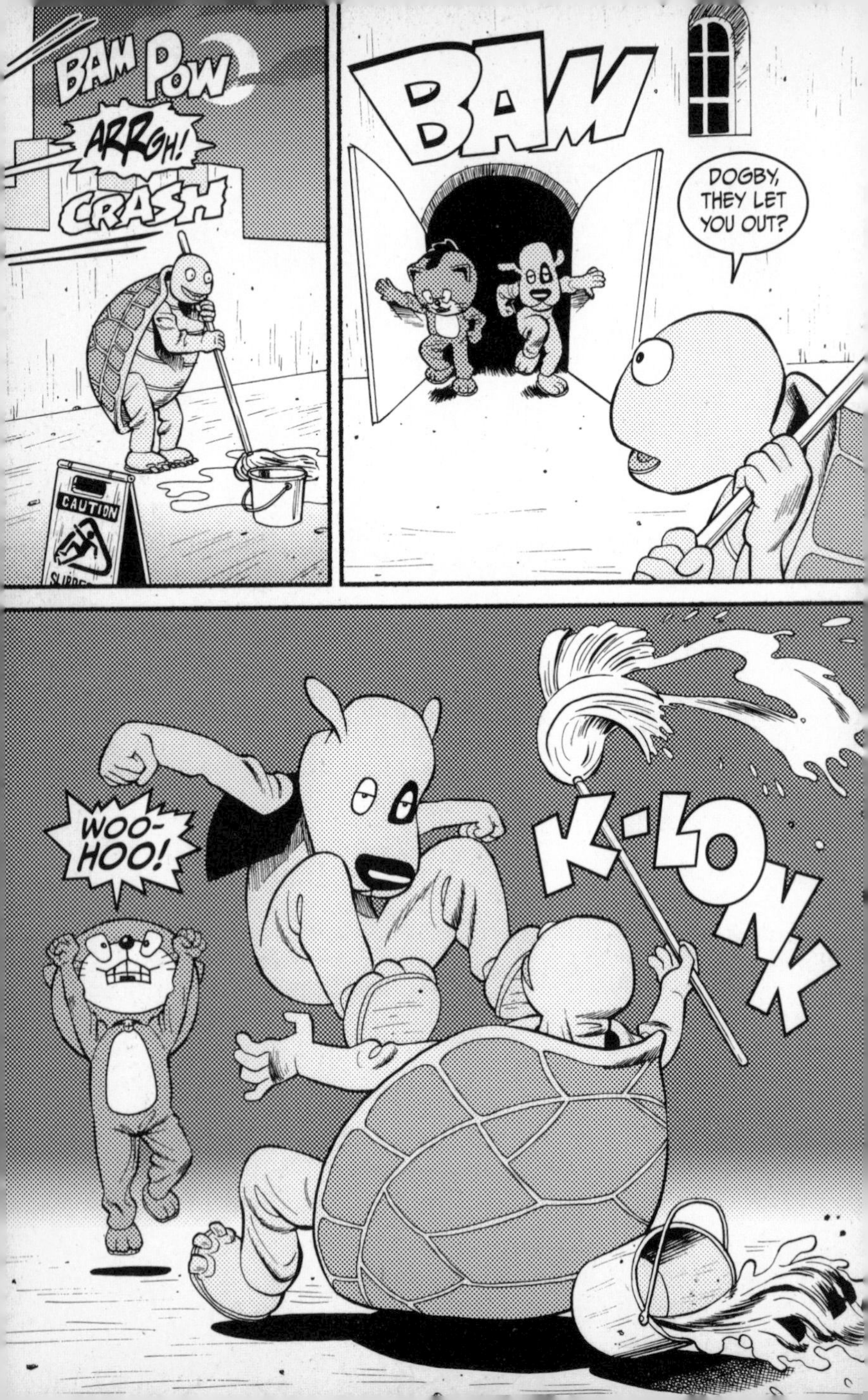
BAM POW
ARRGH!
CRASH
CAUTION
BAM
DOGBY, THEY LET YOU OUT?
WOO-HOO!
K-LONK

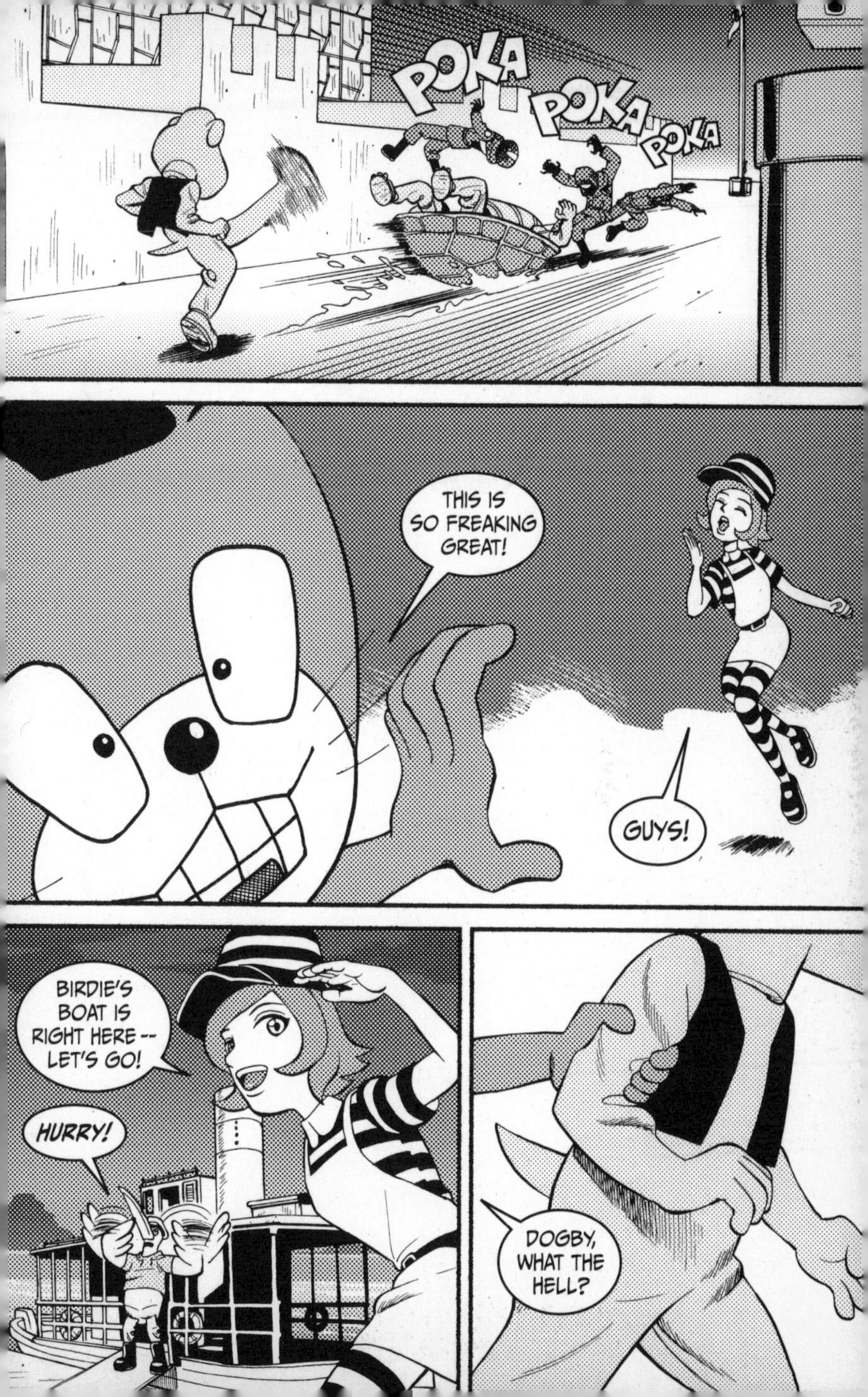
POKA
POKA
POKA
THIS IS SO FREAKING GREAT!
GUYS!
BIRDIE'S BOAT IS RIGHT HERE -- LET'S GO!
HURRY!
DOGBY, WHAT THE HELL?

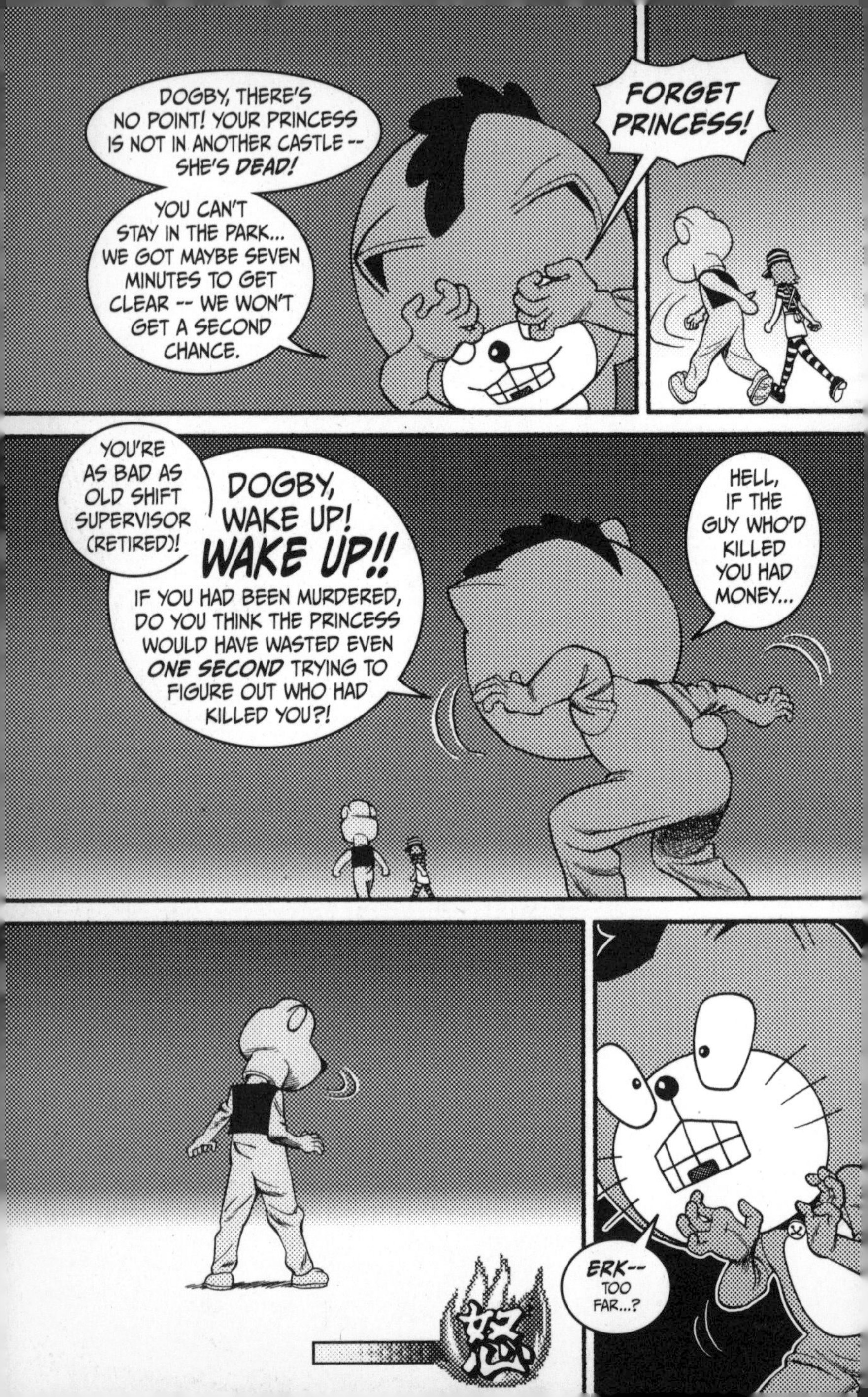
DOGBY, THERE'S NO POINT! YOUR PRINCESS IS NOT IN ANOTHER CASTLE -- SHE'S *DEAD!*
YOU CAN'T STAY IN THE PARK... WE GOT MAYBE SEVEN MINUTES TO GET CLEAR -- WE WON'T GET A SECOND CHANCE.
FORGET PRINCESS!
YOU'RE AS BAD AS OLD SHIFT SUPERVISOR (RETIRED)!
DOGBY, WAKE UP! **WAKE UP!!**
IF YOU HAD BEEN MURDERED, DO YOU THINK THE PRINCESS WOULD HAVE WASTED EVEN ***ONE SECOND*** TRYING TO FIGURE OUT WHO HAD KILLED YOU?!
HELL, IF THE GUY WHO'D KILLED YOU HAD MONEY...
怒
ERK-- TOO FAR...?

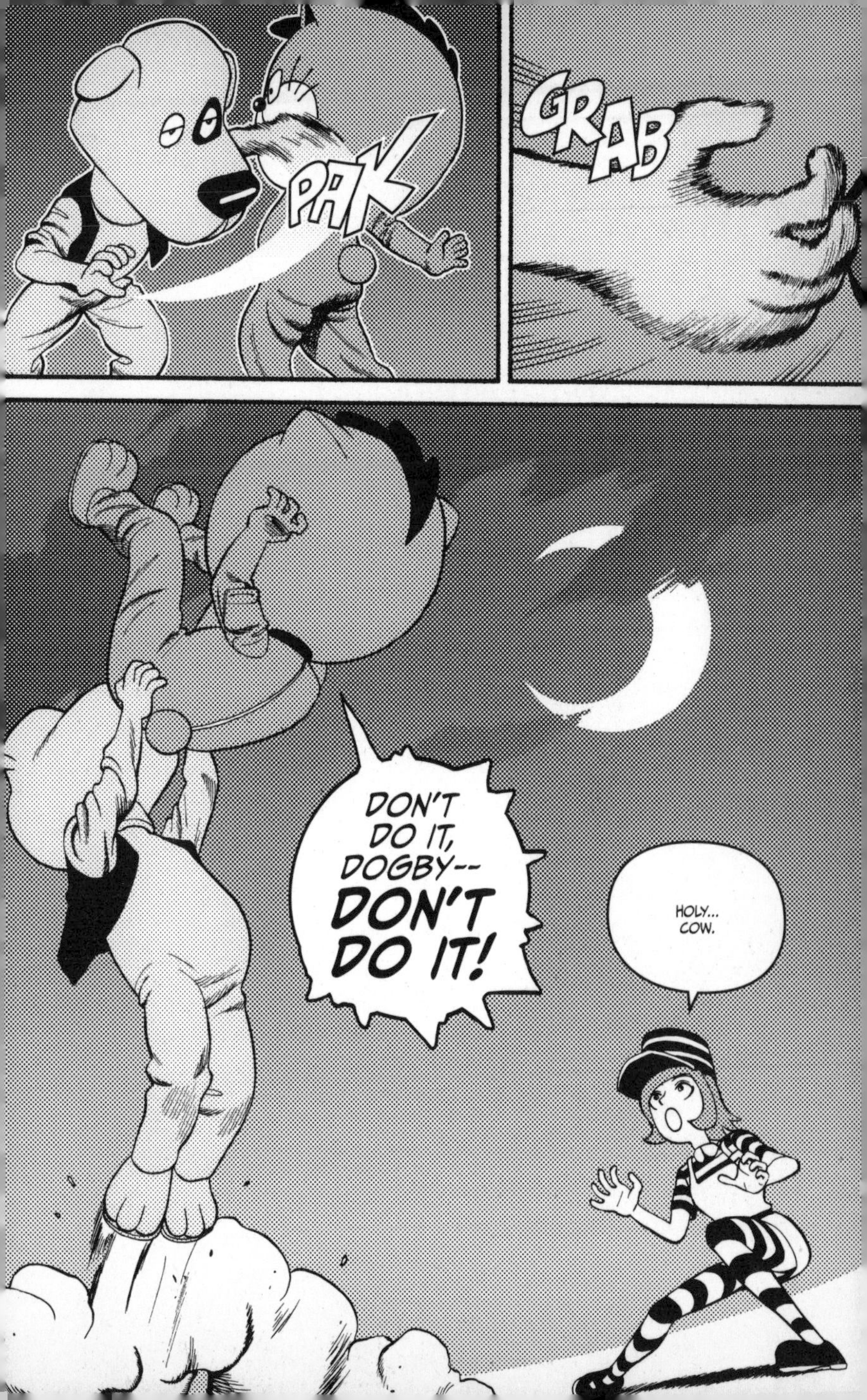
PAK
GRAB
DON'T DO IT, DOGBY-- DON'T DO IT!
HOLY... COW.

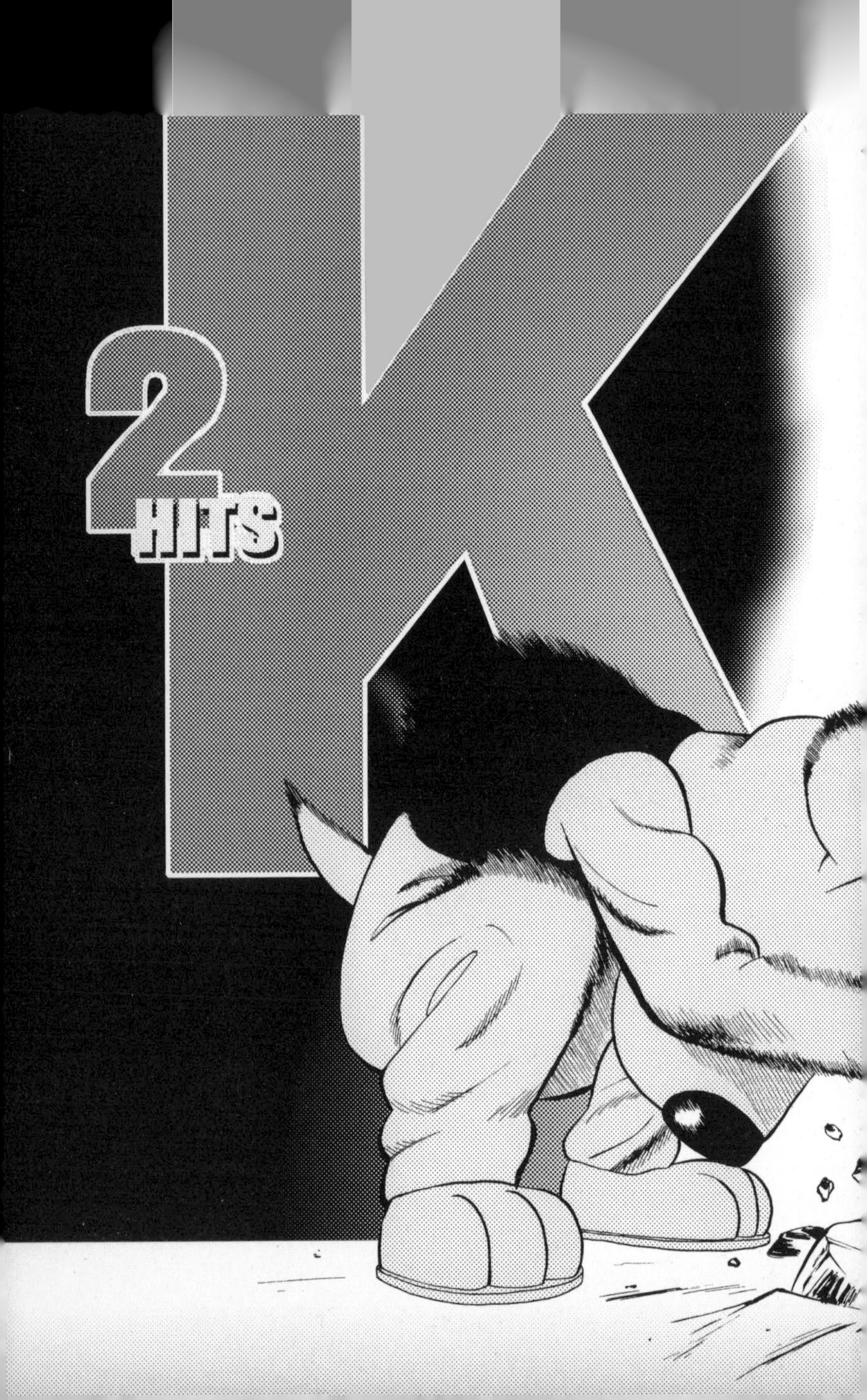
K
2
HITS

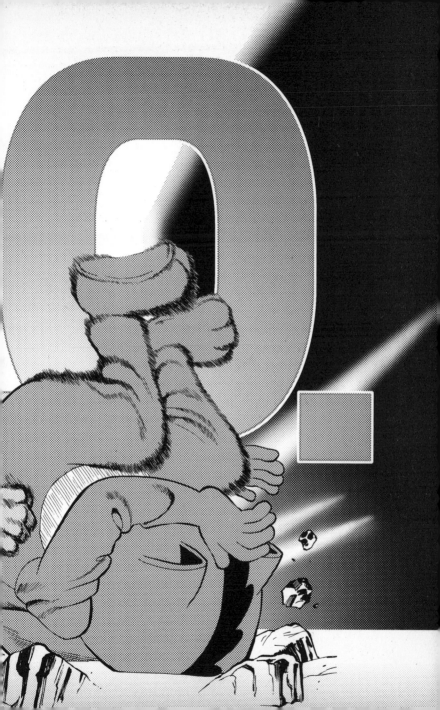

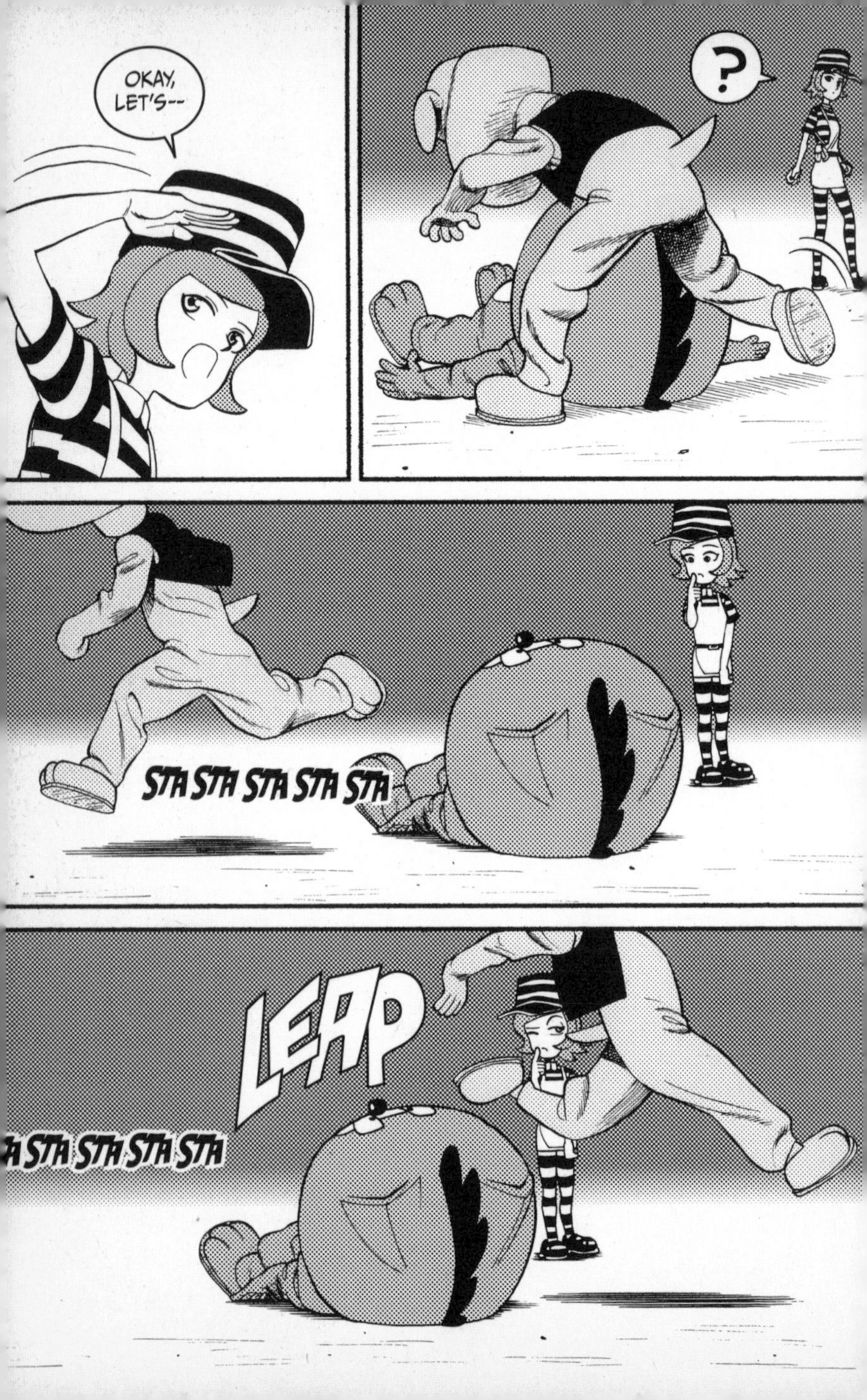
OKAY, LET'S--
?
STA STA STA STA STA
LEAP
STA STA STA STA STA

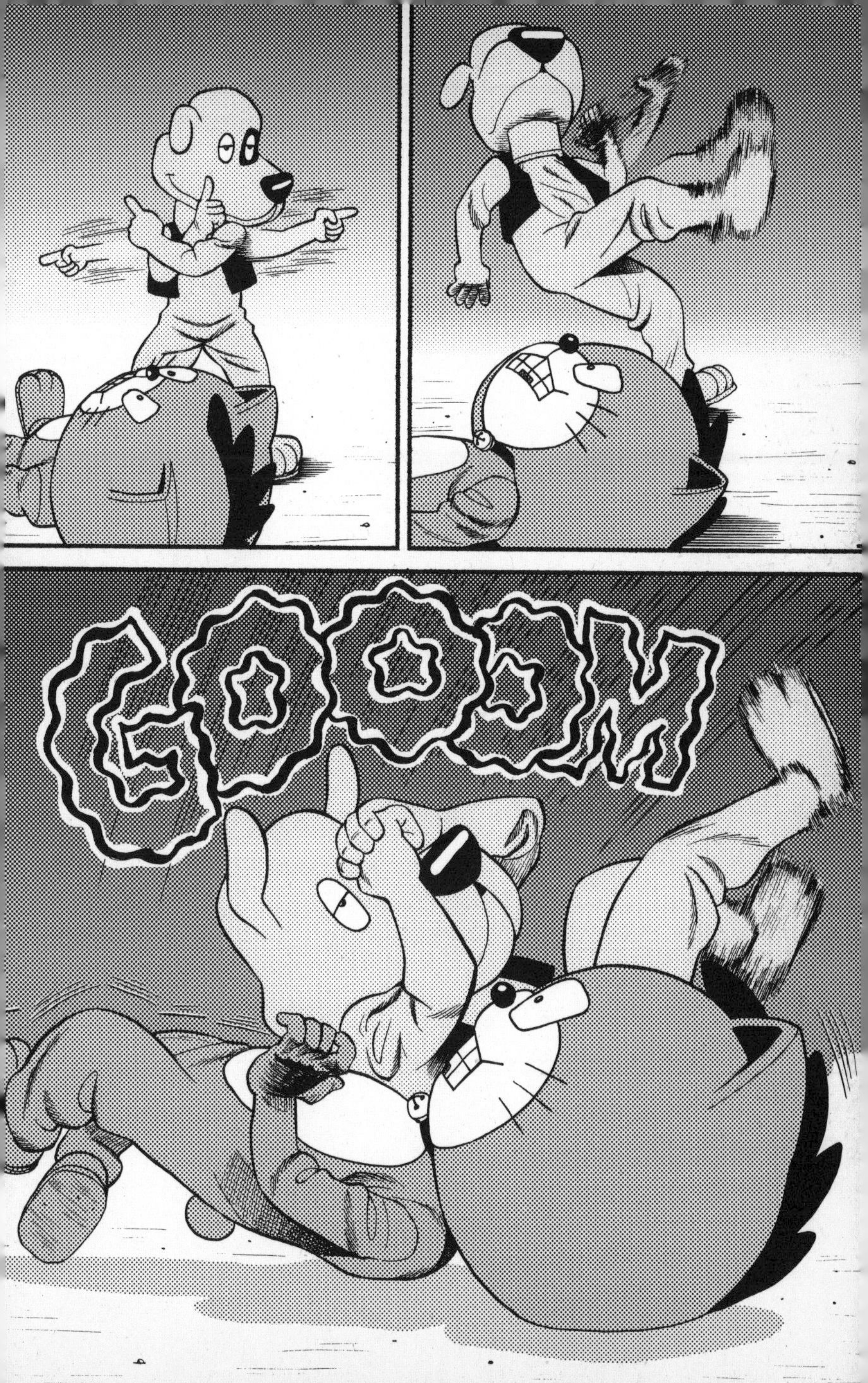
GOOOM

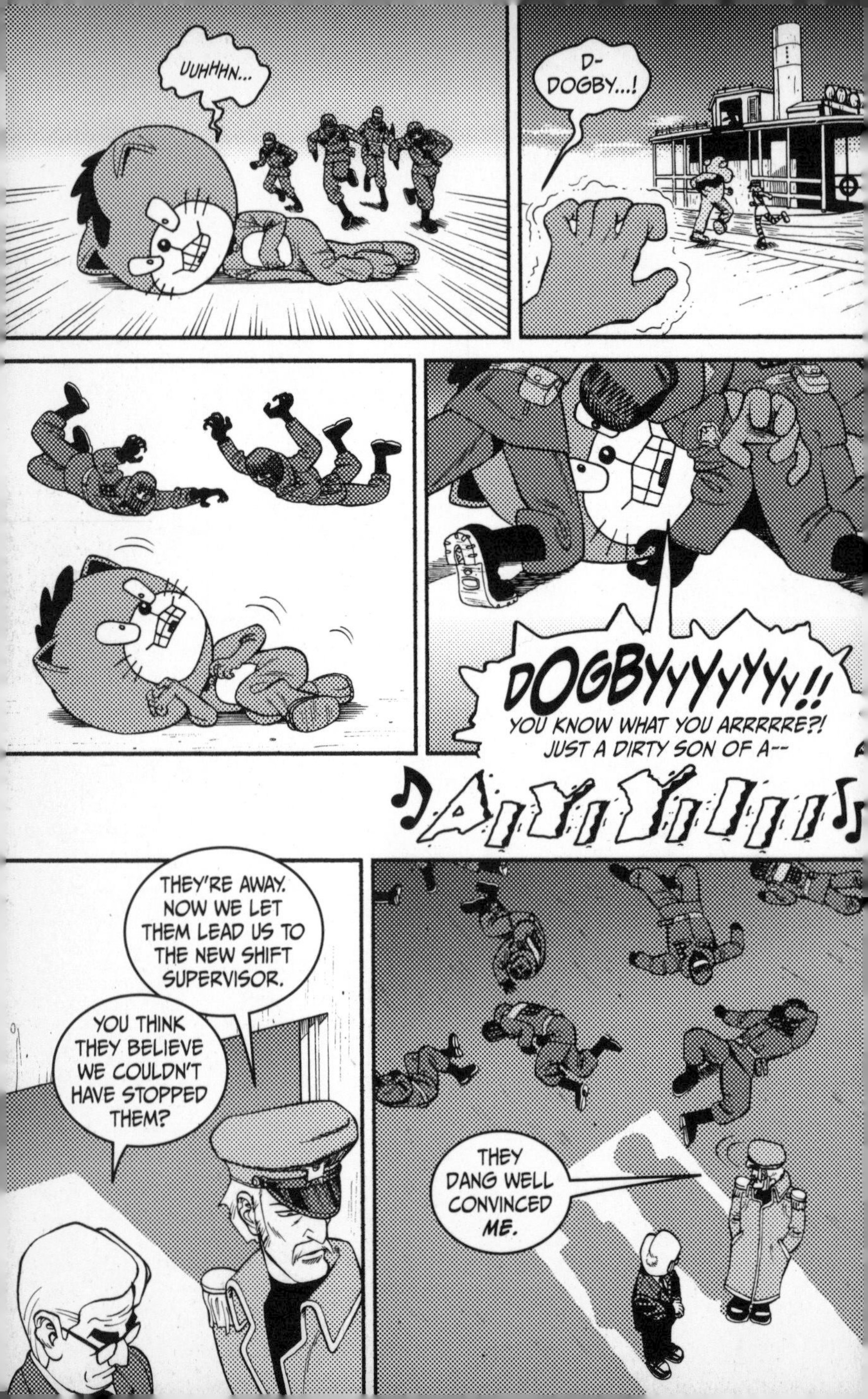
UUHHHN...
D-
DOGBY...!
DOGBYYYYYYY!!
YOU KNOW WHAT YOU ARRRRRE?!
JUST A DIRTY SON OF A--
AIYIYIIIII
THEY'RE AWAY. NOW WE LET THEM LEAD US TO THE NEW SHIFT SUPERVISOR.
YOU THINK THEY BELIEVE WE COULDN'T HAVE STOPPED THEM?
THEY DANG WELL CONVINCED *ME.*

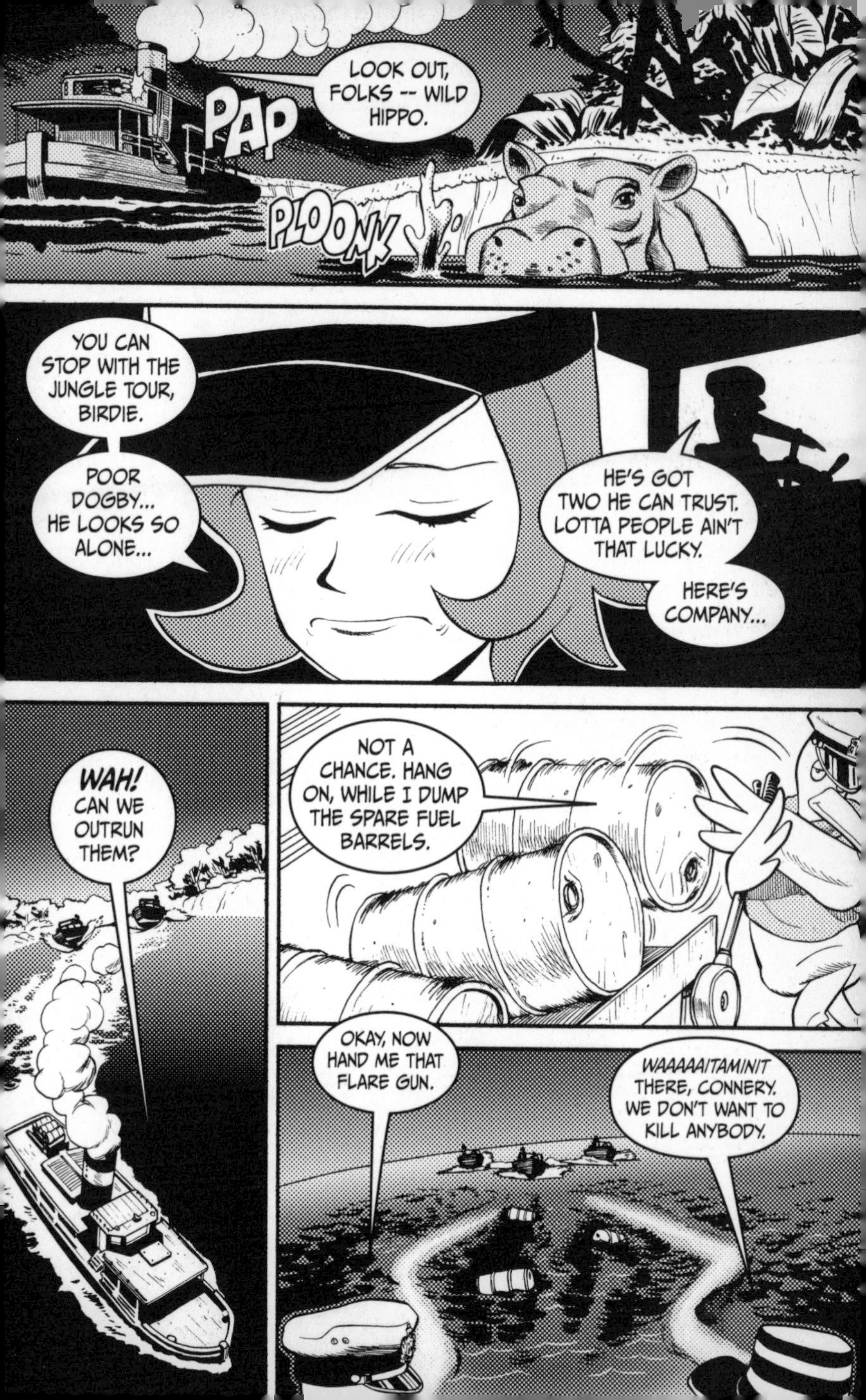
LOOK OUT, FOLKS -- WILD HIPPO.
PAP
PLOONK
YOU CAN STOP WITH THE JUNGLE TOUR, BIRDIE.
POOR DOGBY... HE LOOKS SO ALONE...
HE'S GOT TWO HE CAN TRUST. LOTTA PEOPLE AIN'T THAT LUCKY.
HERE'S COMPANY...
WAH! CAN WE OUTRUN THEM?
NOT A CHANCE. HANG ON, WHILE I DUMP THE SPARE FUEL BARRELS.
OKAY, NOW HAND ME THAT FLARE GUN.
WAAAAAITAMINIT THERE, CONNERY. WE DON'T WANT TO KILL ANYBODY.

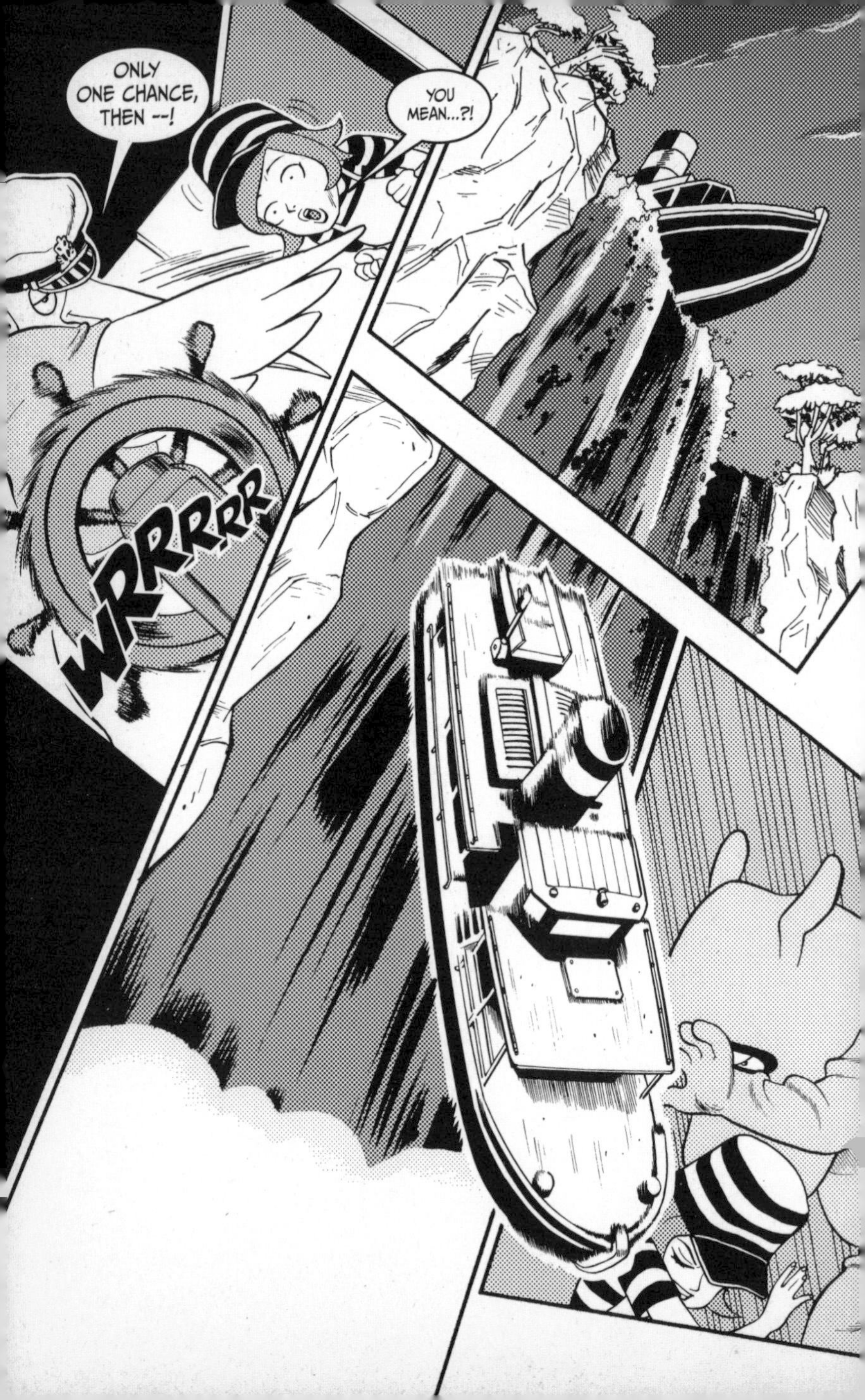
ONLY ONE CHANCE, THEN --!
YOU MEAN...?!
WRRRRR

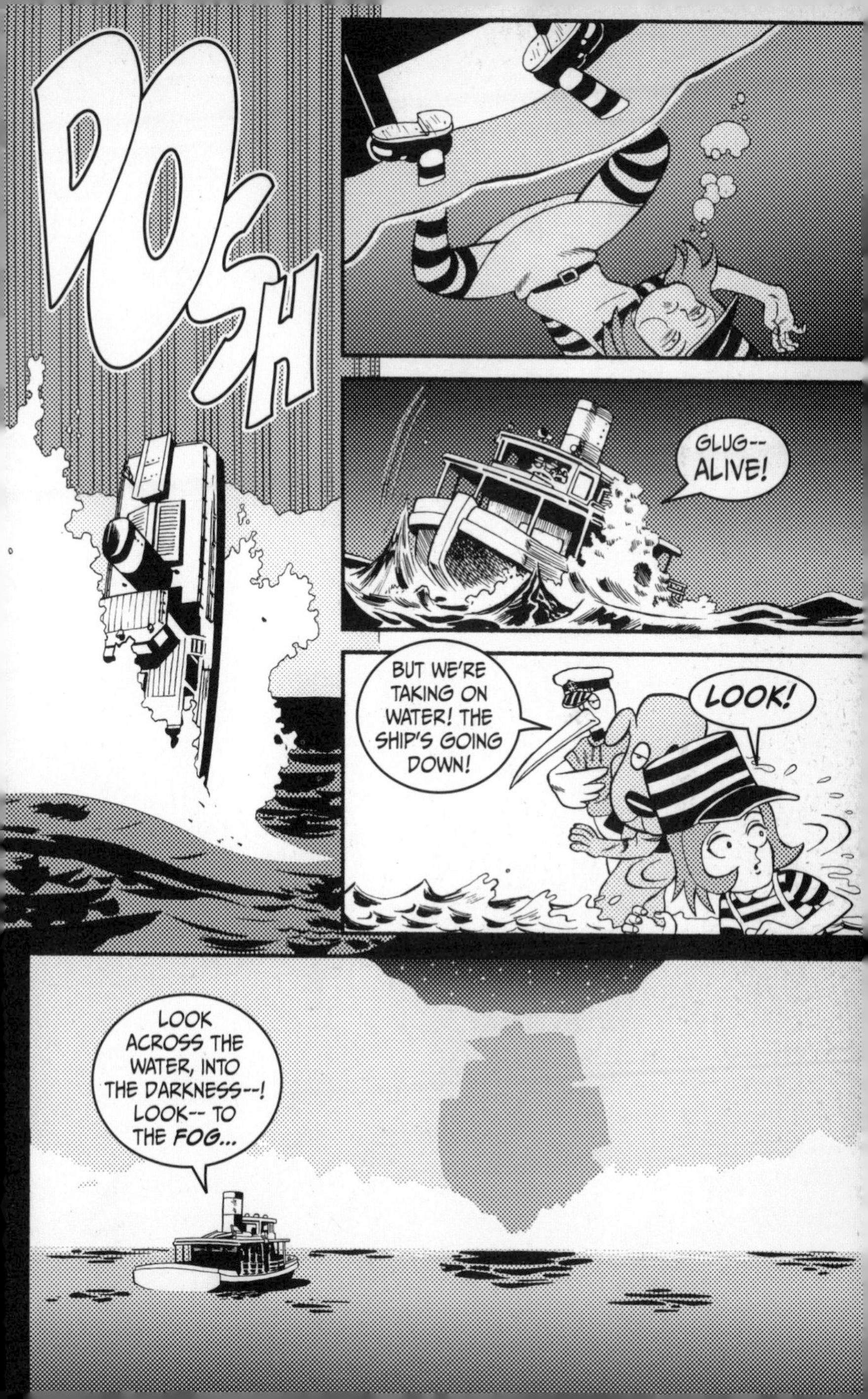
POOSH
GLUG-- ALIVE!
BUT WE'RE TAKING ON WATER! THE SHIP'S GOING DOWN!
LOOK!
LOOK ACROSS THE WATER, INTO THE DARKNESS--! LOOK-- TO THE FOG...

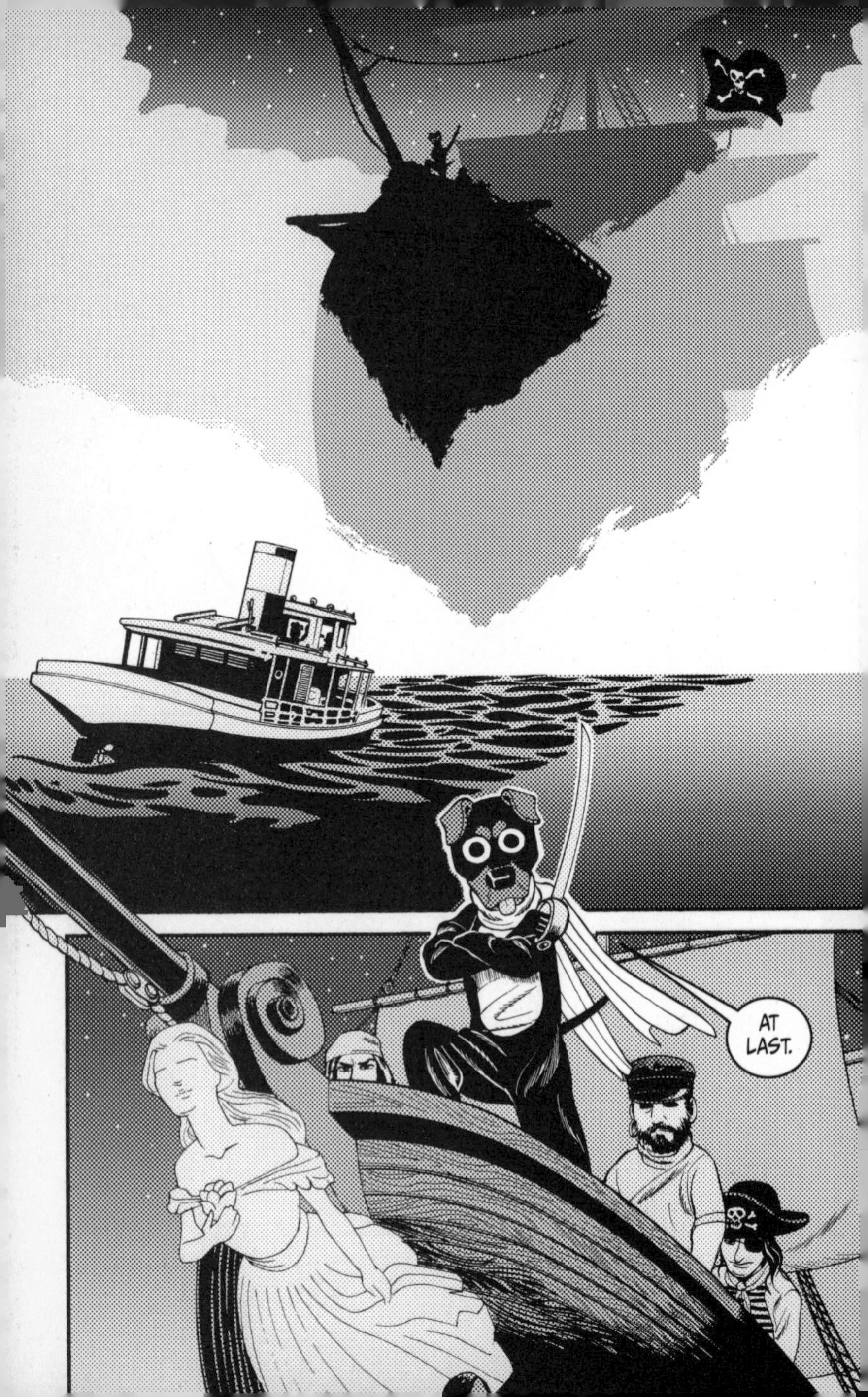
AT LAST.

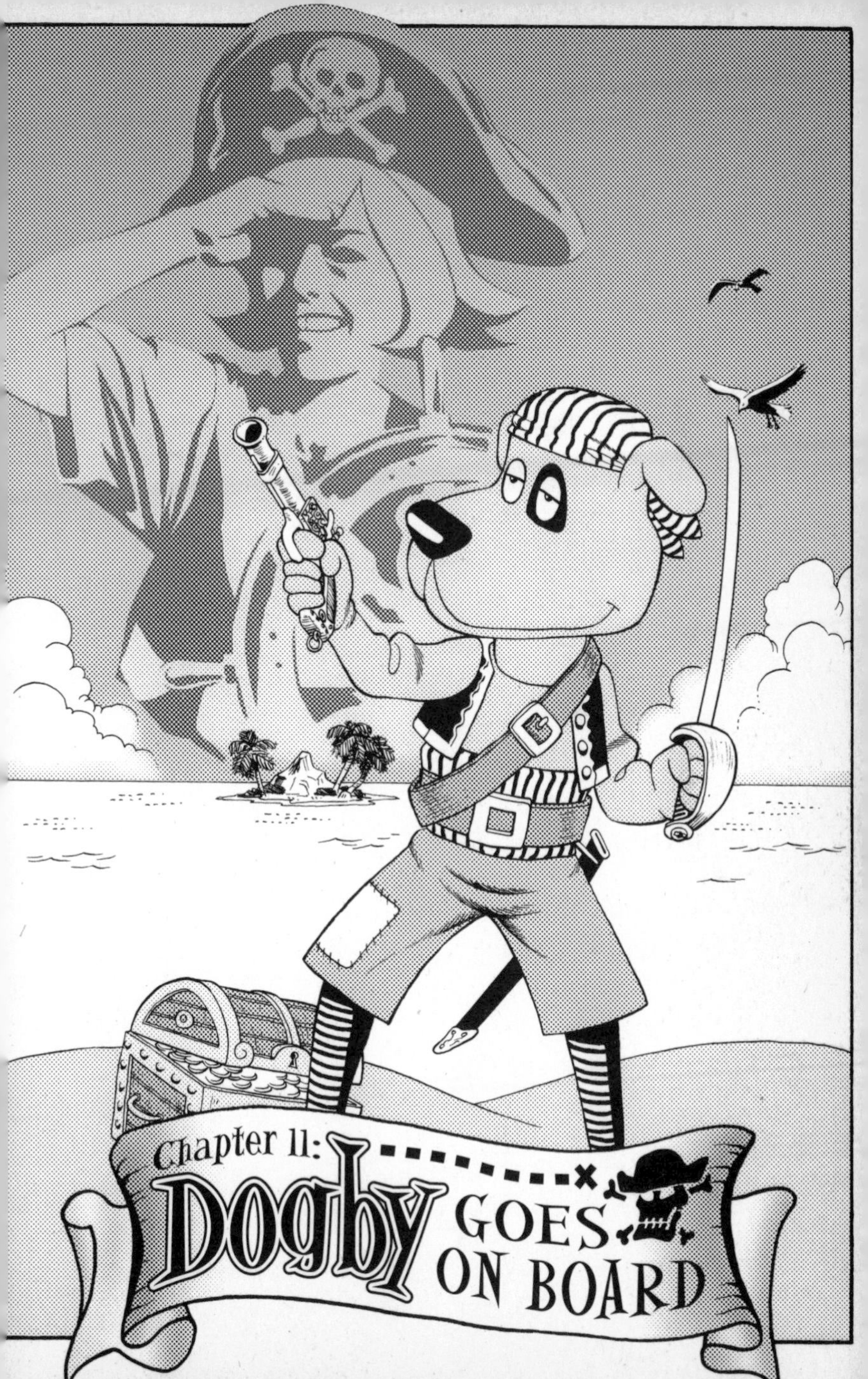
Chapter 11:
Dogby GOES ON BOARD

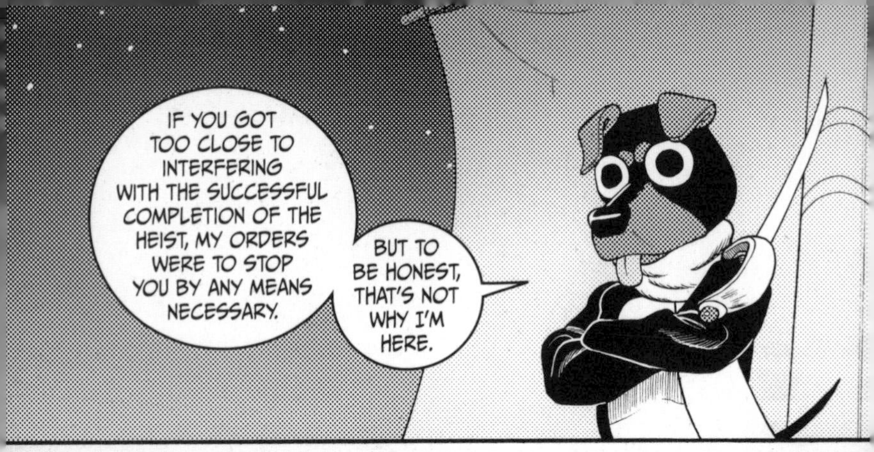
IF YOU GOT TOO CLOSE TO INTERFERING WITH THE SUCCESSFUL COMPLETION OF THE HEIST, MY ORDERS WERE TO STOP YOU BY ANY MEANS NECESSARY.
BUT TO BE HONEST, THAT'S NOT WHY I'M HERE.

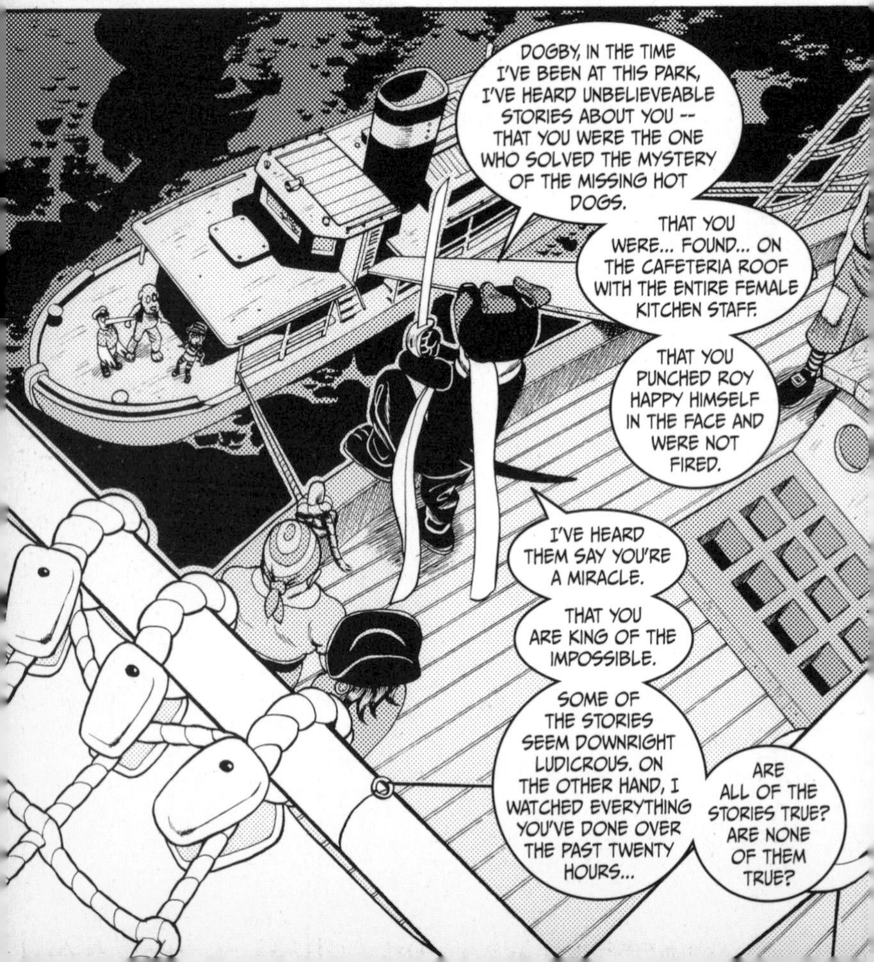
DOGBY, IN THE TIME I'VE BEEN AT THIS PARK, I'VE HEARD UNBELIEVEABLE STORIES ABOUT YOU -- THAT YOU WERE THE ONE WHO SOLVED THE MYSTERY OF THE MISSING HOT DOGS.
THAT YOU WERE... FOUND... ON THE CAFETERIA ROOF WITH THE ENTIRE FEMALE KITCHEN STAFF.
THAT YOU PUNCHED ROY HAPPY HIMSELF IN THE FACE AND WERE NOT FIRED.
I'VE HEARD THEM SAY YOU'RE A MIRACLE.
THAT YOU ARE KING OF THE IMPOSSIBLE.
SOME OF THE STORIES SEEM DOWNRIGHT LUDICROUS. ON THE OTHER HAND, I WATCHED EVERYTHING YOU'VE DONE OVER THE PAST TWENTY HOURS...
ARE ALL OF THE STORIES TRUE? ARE NONE OF THEM TRUE?

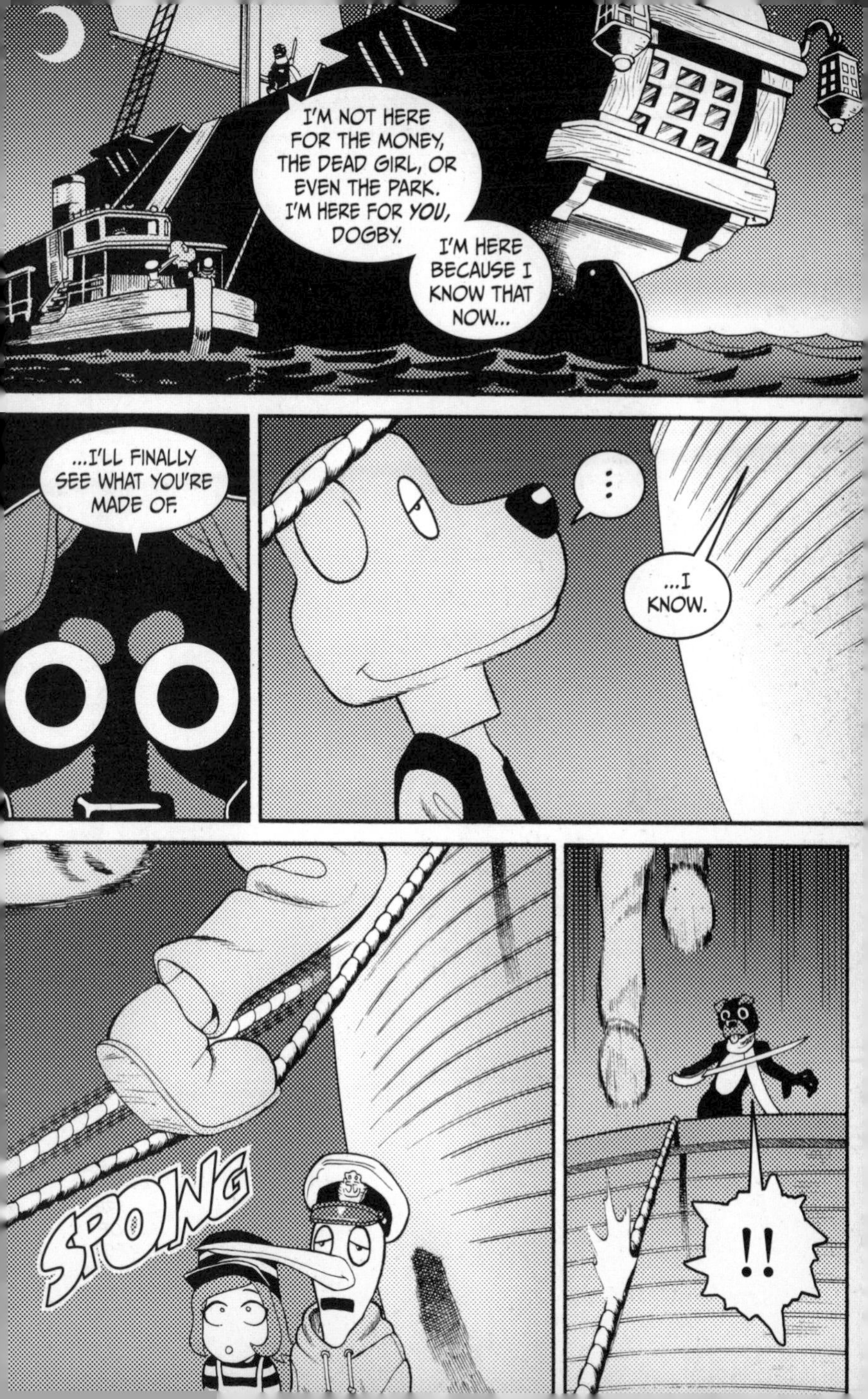
I'M NOT HERE FOR THE MONEY, THE DEAD GIRL, OR EVEN THE PARK. I'M HERE FOR *YOU*, DOGBY.
I'M HERE BECAUSE I KNOW THAT NOW...
...I'LL FINALLY SEE WHAT YOU'RE MADE OF.
...
...I KNOW.
SPOING
!!

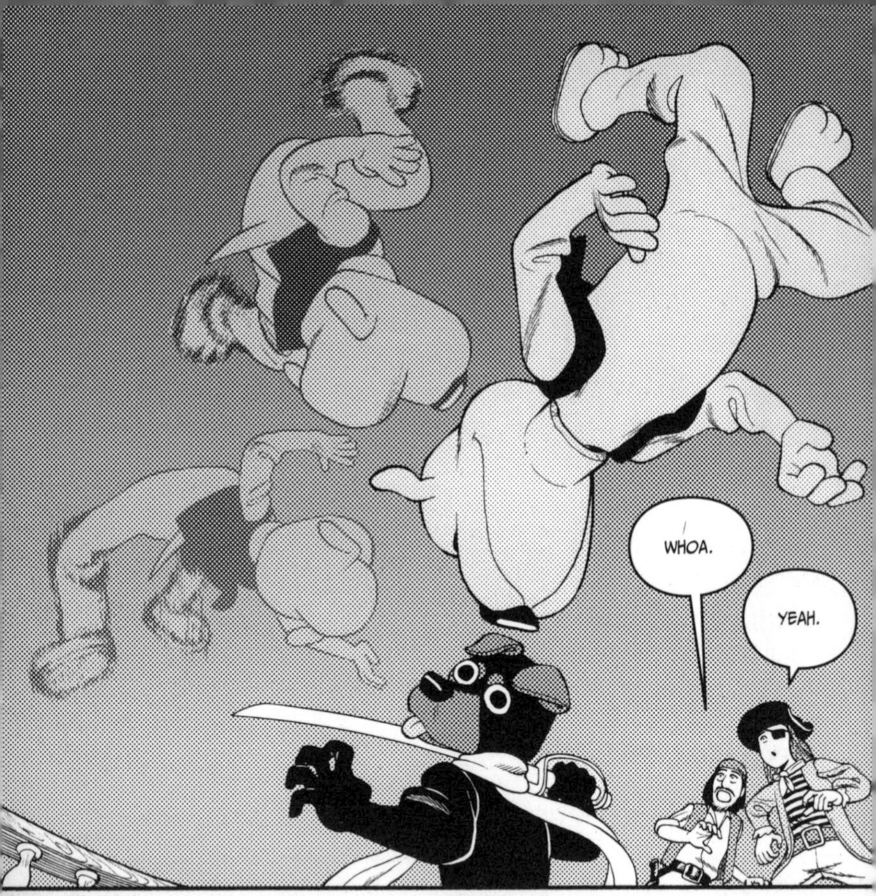
WHOA.
YEAH.
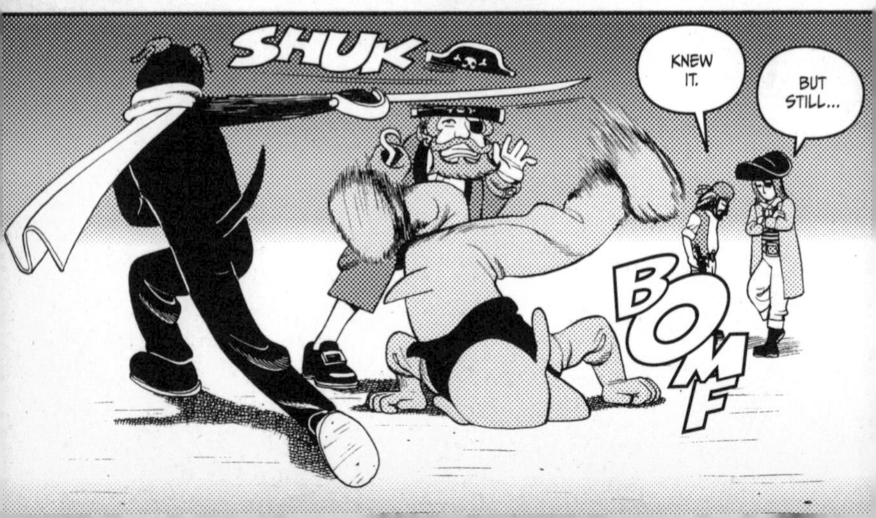
SHUK
KNEW IT.
BUT STILL...
BOMF

MY... HAT...

MMF SWORMMF!

HAVE AT YE, DOGBY--!

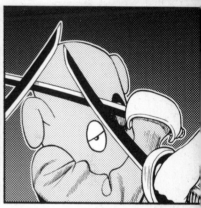

CLANG

BAF

I KNOW WE'RE SUPPOSED TO BE ROOTING AGAINST DOGBY, BUT...

YEAH, I'M RIGHT THERE WITH YOU...

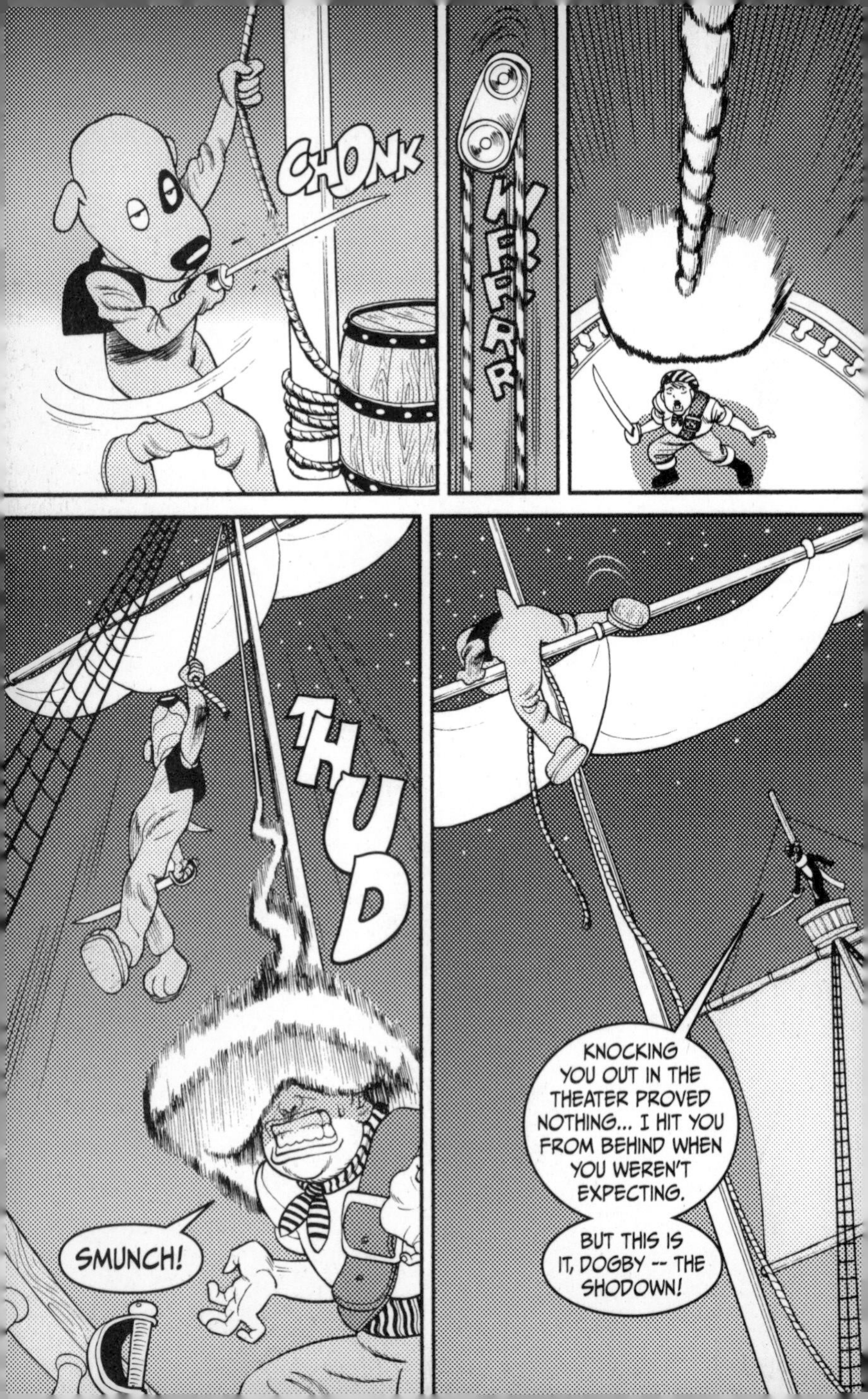
CHONK
WFFRR
THUD
SMUNCH!
KNOCKING YOU OUT IN THE THEATER PROVED NOTHING... I HIT YOU FROM BEHIND WHEN YOU WEREN'T EXPECTING.
BUT THIS IS IT, DOGBY -- THE SHODOWN!

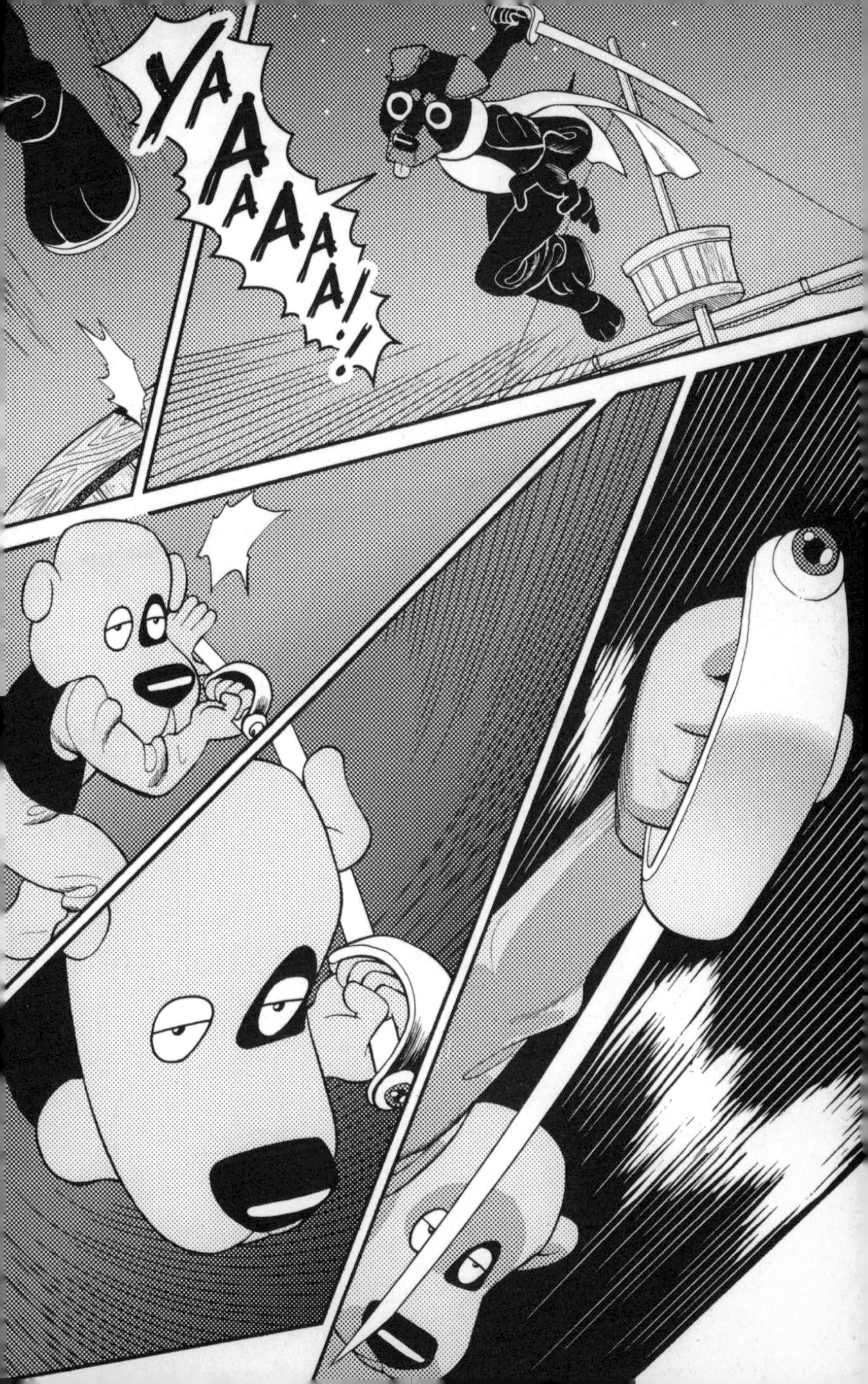
YAAAAAAA!!

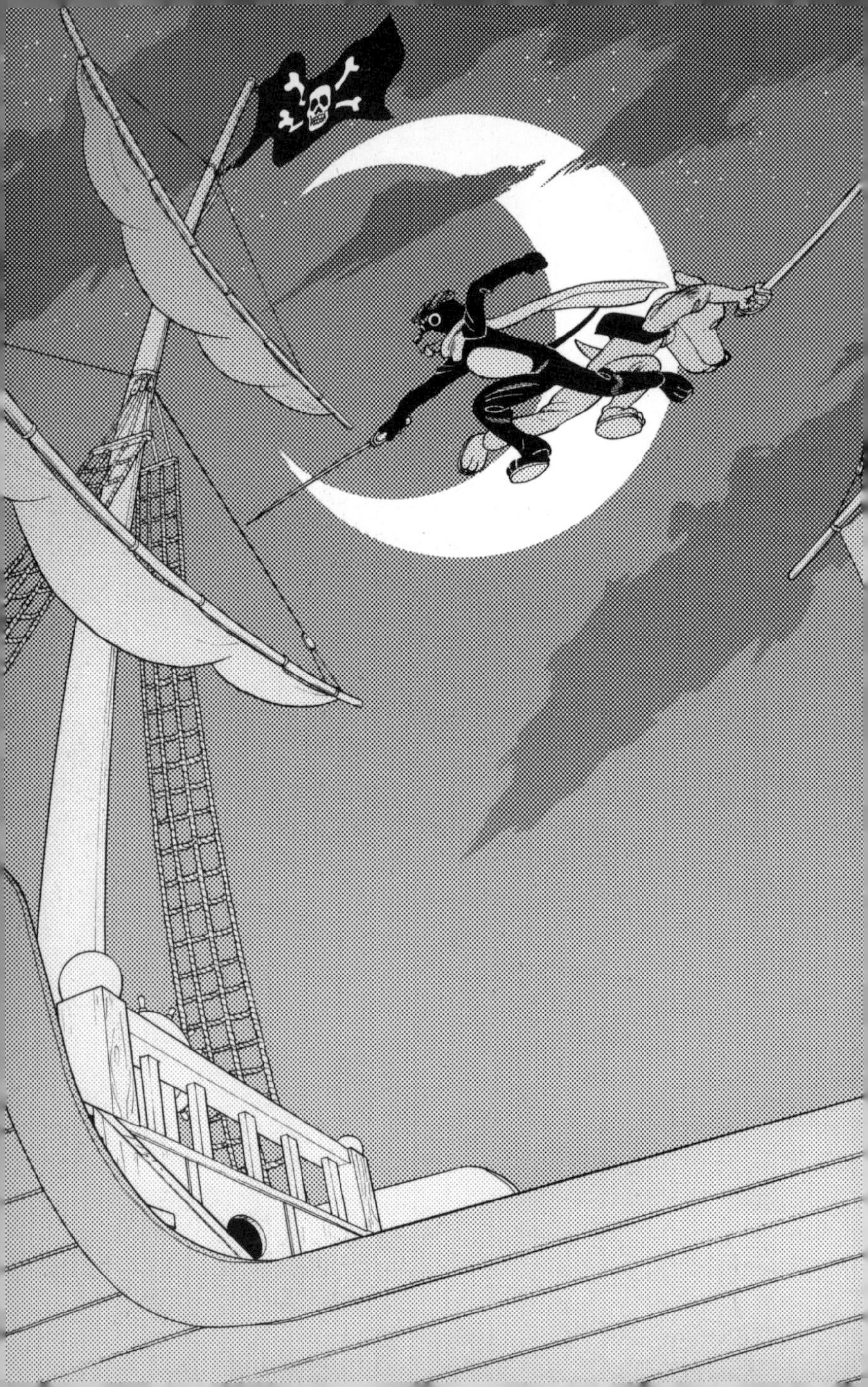

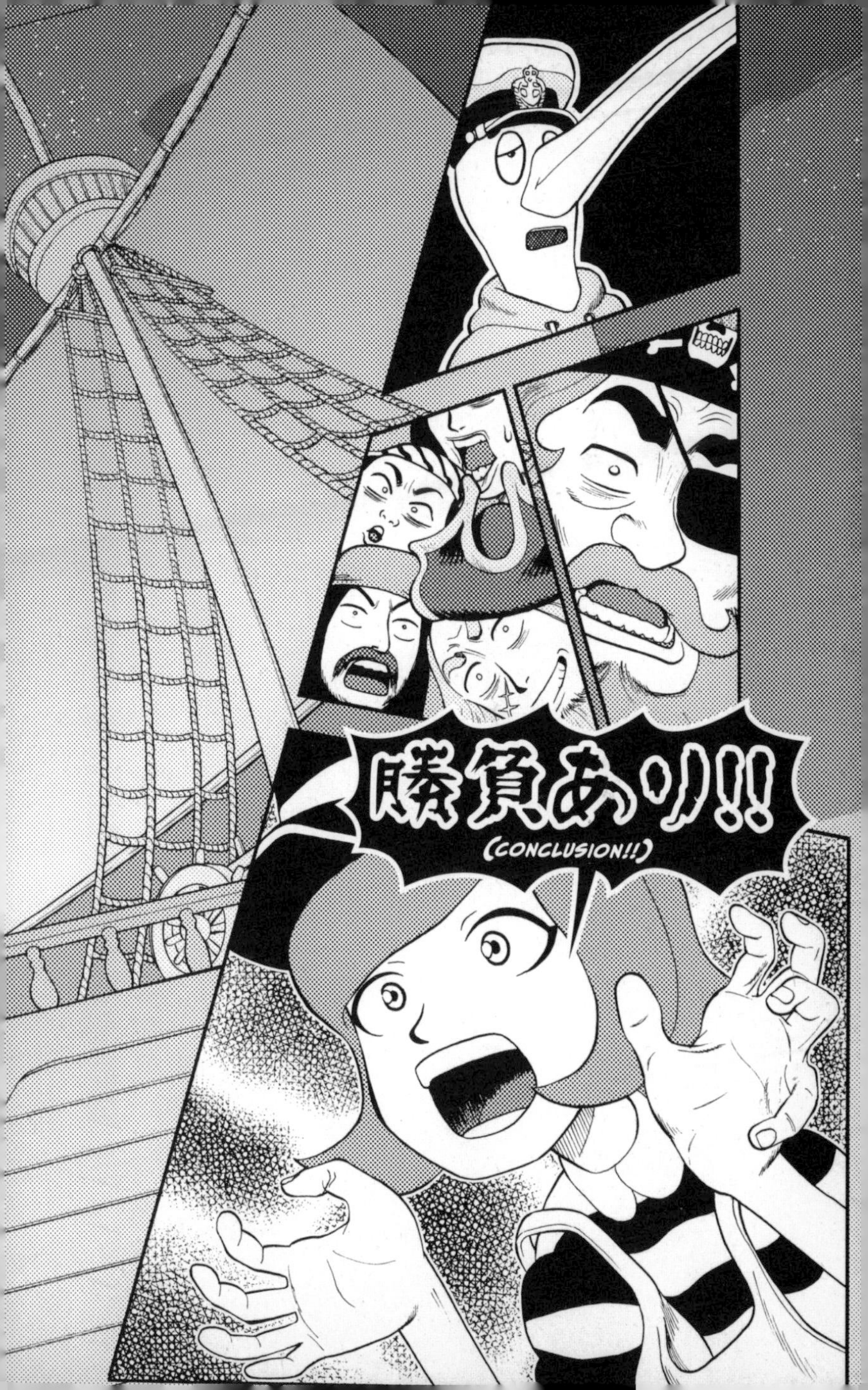
勝負あり!!
(CONCLUSION!!)

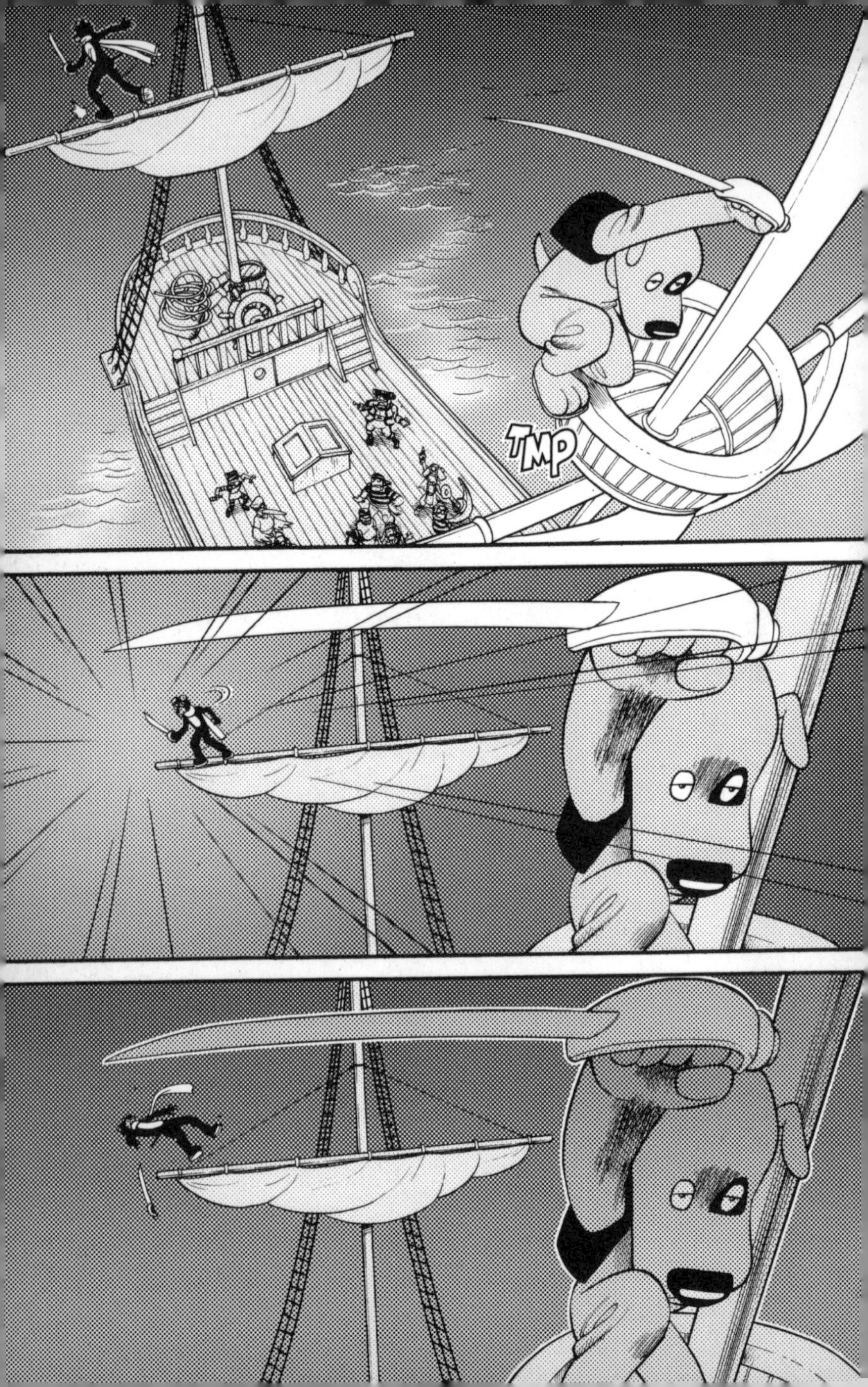
TMP

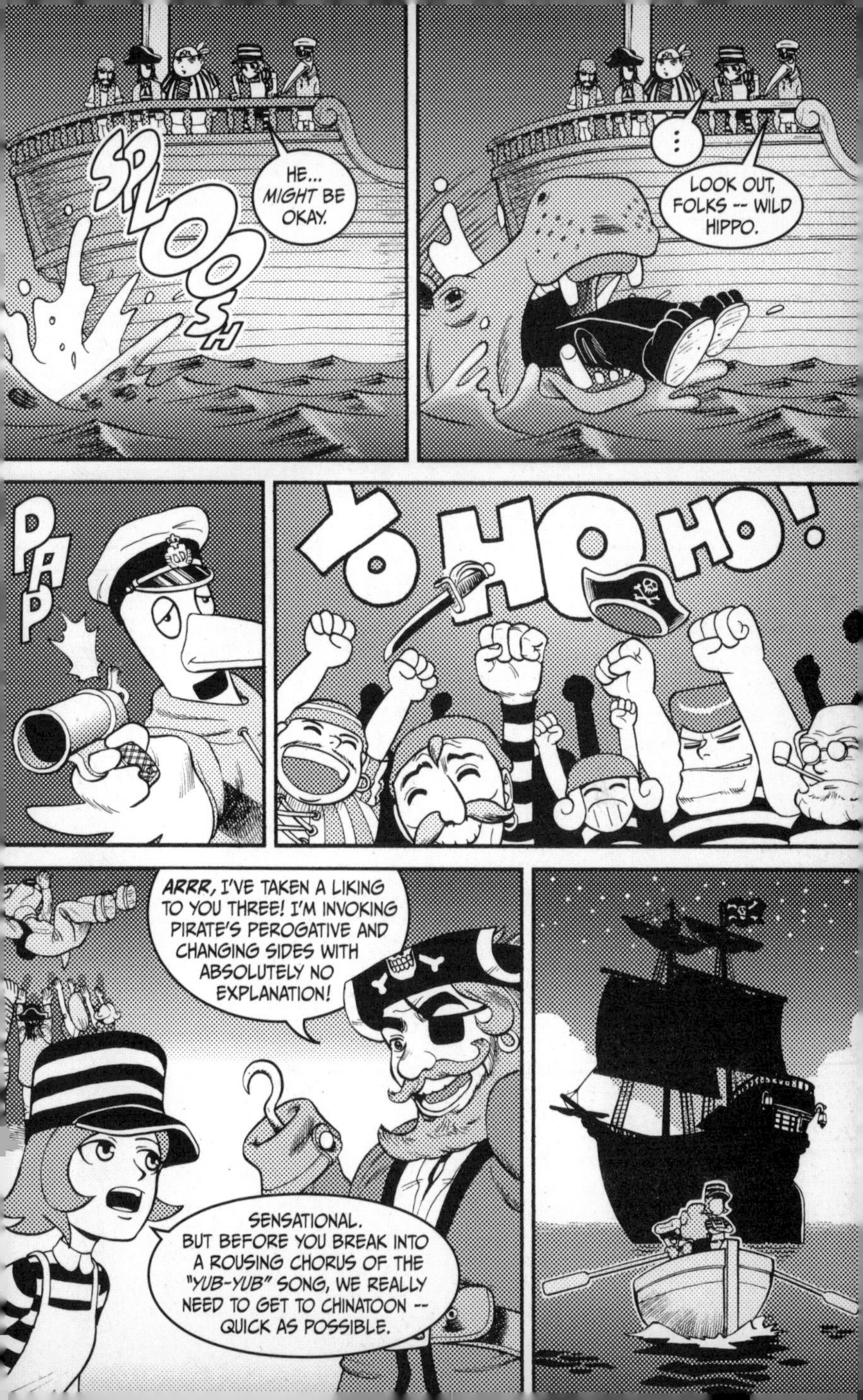
SPLOOOOSH
HE... MIGHT BE OKAY.
...
LOOK OUT, FOLKS -- WILD HIPPO.
PAP
YO HO HO!
ARRR, I'VE TAKEN A LIKING TO YOU THREE! I'M INVOKING PIRATE'S PEROGATIVE AND CHANGING SIDES WITH ABSOLUTELY NO EXPLANATION!
SENSATIONAL. BUT BEFORE YOU BREAK INTO A ROUSING CHORUS OF THE "YUB-YUB" SONG, WE REALLY NEED TO GET TO CHINATOON -- QUICK AS POSSIBLE.

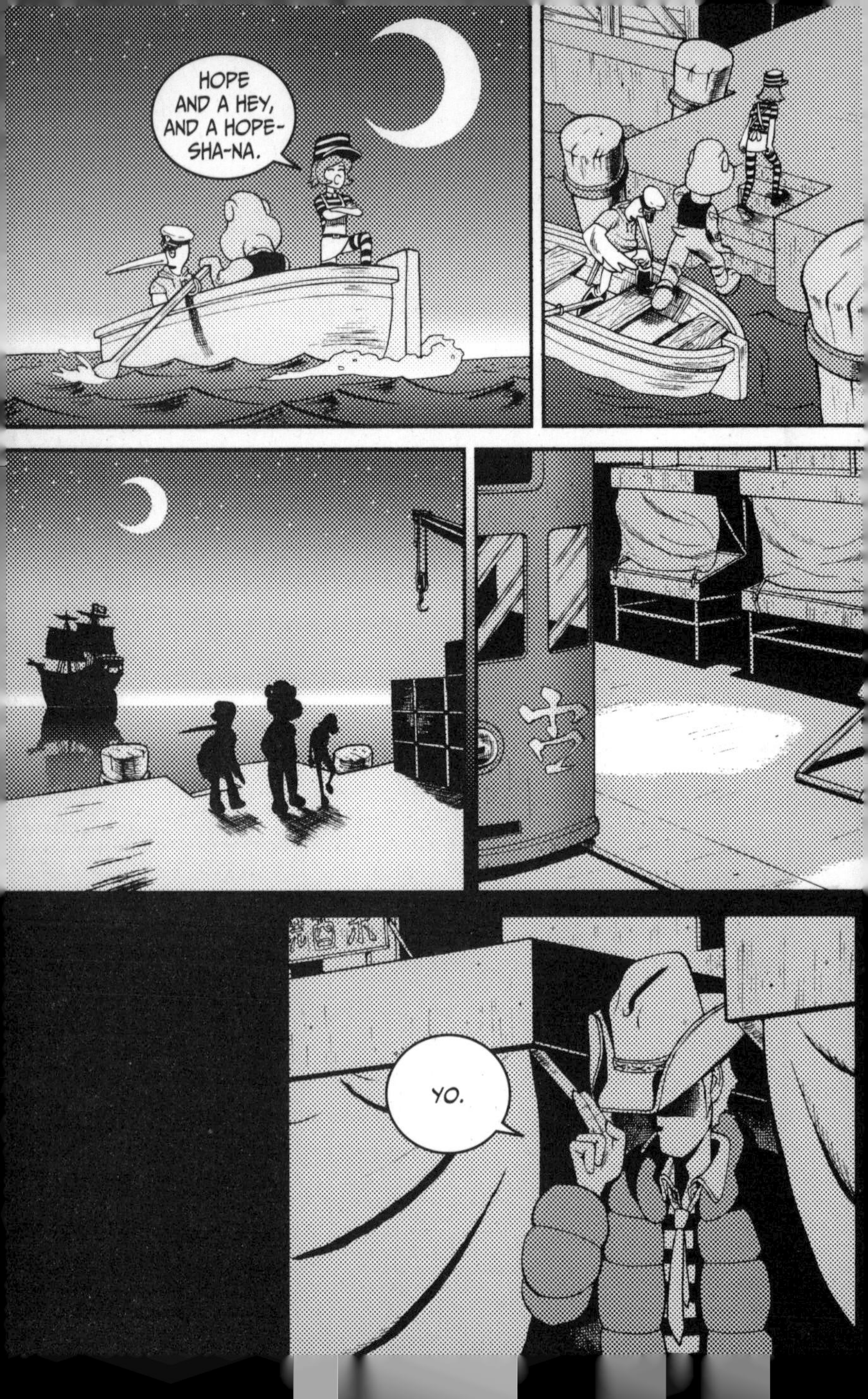
HOPE AND A HEY, AND A HOPE-SHA-NA.
YO.

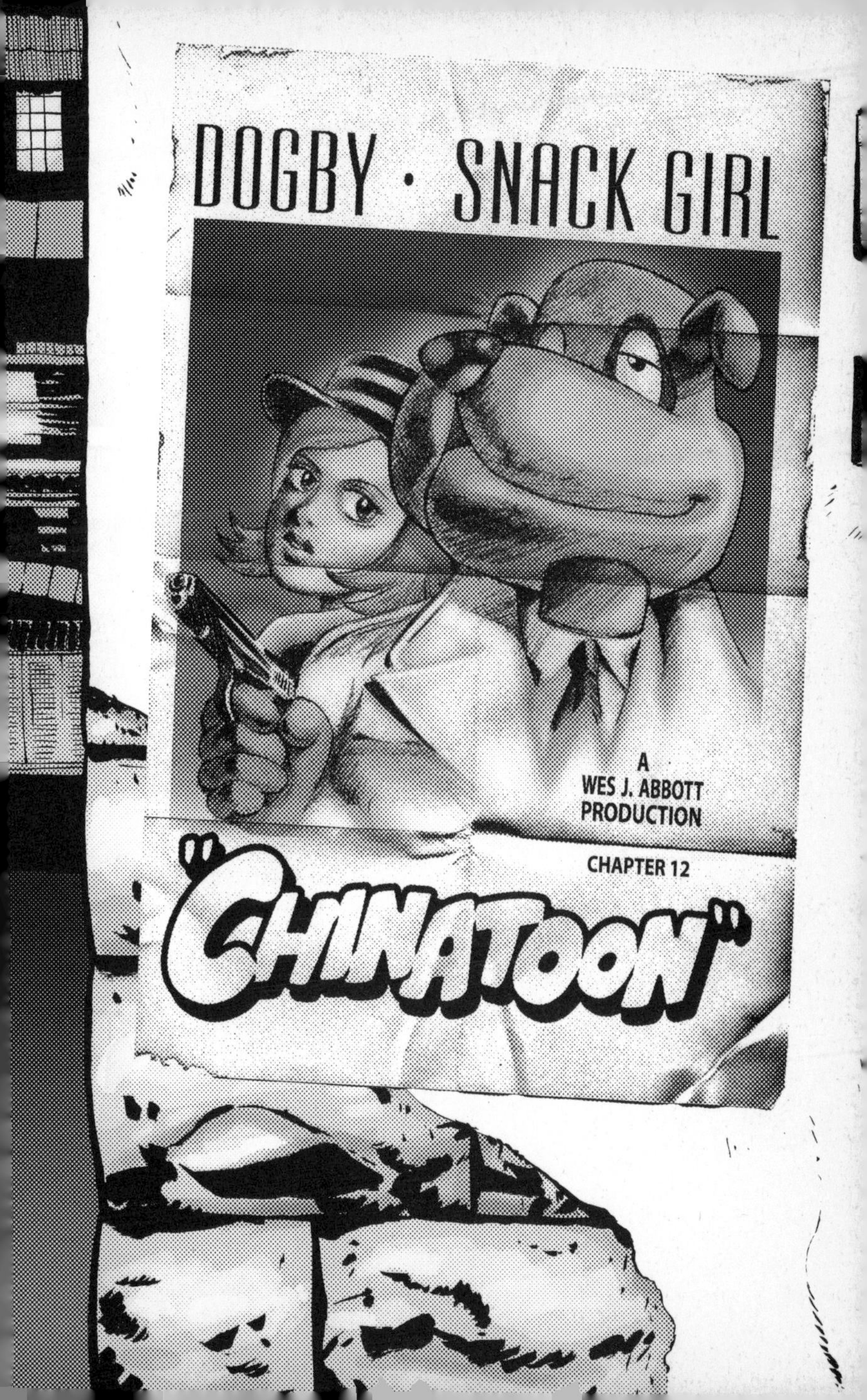
DOGBY · SNACK GIRL
A
WES J. ABBOTT
PRODUCTION
CHAPTER 12
"CHINATOON"

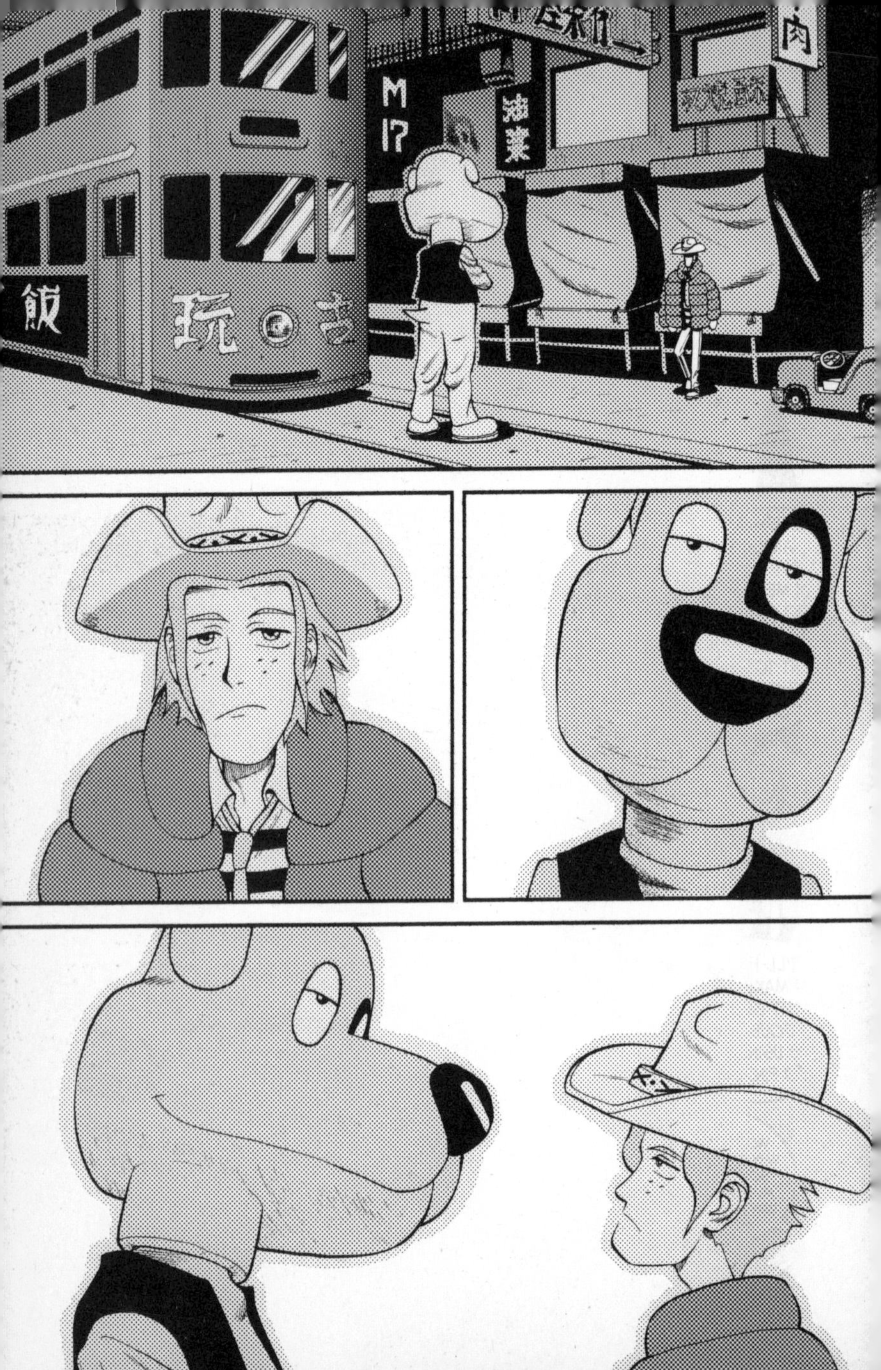
M
17
肉
飯
玩

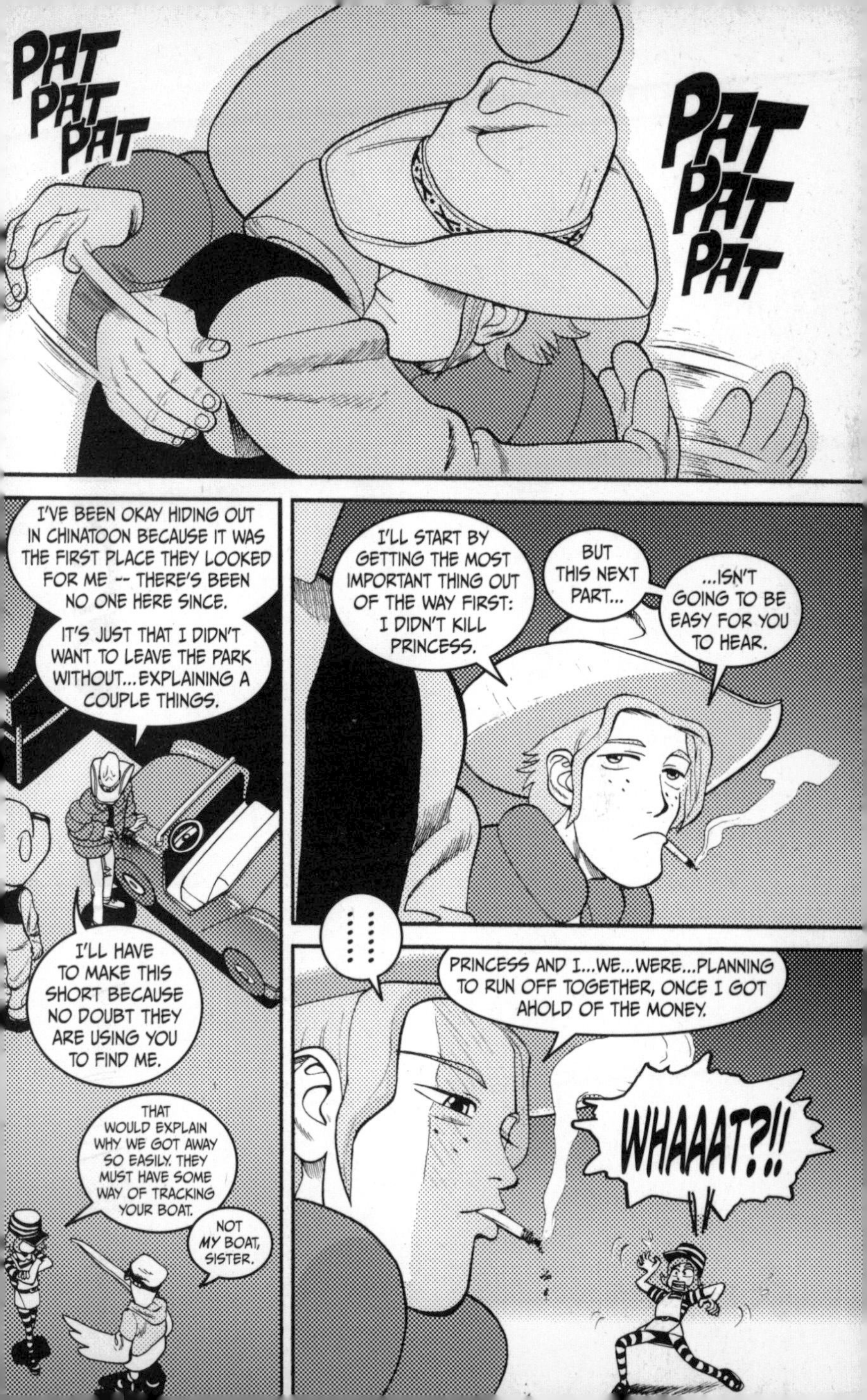
PAT PAT PAT
PAT PAT PAT
I'VE BEEN OKAY HIDING OUT IN CHINATOON BECAUSE IT WAS THE FIRST PLACE THEY LOOKED FOR ME -- THERE'S BEEN NO ONE HERE SINCE.
IT'S JUST THAT I DIDN'T WANT TO LEAVE THE PARK WITHOUT...EXPLAINING A COUPLE THINGS.
I'LL HAVE TO MAKE THIS SHORT BECAUSE NO DOUBT THEY ARE USING YOU TO FIND ME.
THAT WOULD EXPLAIN WHY WE GOT AWAY SO EASILY. THEY MUST HAVE SOME WAY OF TRACKING YOUR BOAT.
NOT MY BOAT, SISTER.
I'LL START BY GETTING THE MOST IMPORTANT THING OUT OF THE WAY FIRST: I DIDN'T KILL PRINCESS.
BUT THIS NEXT PART...
...ISN'T GOING TO BE EASY FOR YOU TO HEAR.
...
PRINCESS AND I...WE...WERE...PLANNING TO RUN OFF TOGETHER, ONCE I GOT AHOLD OF THE MONEY.
WHAAAT?!!

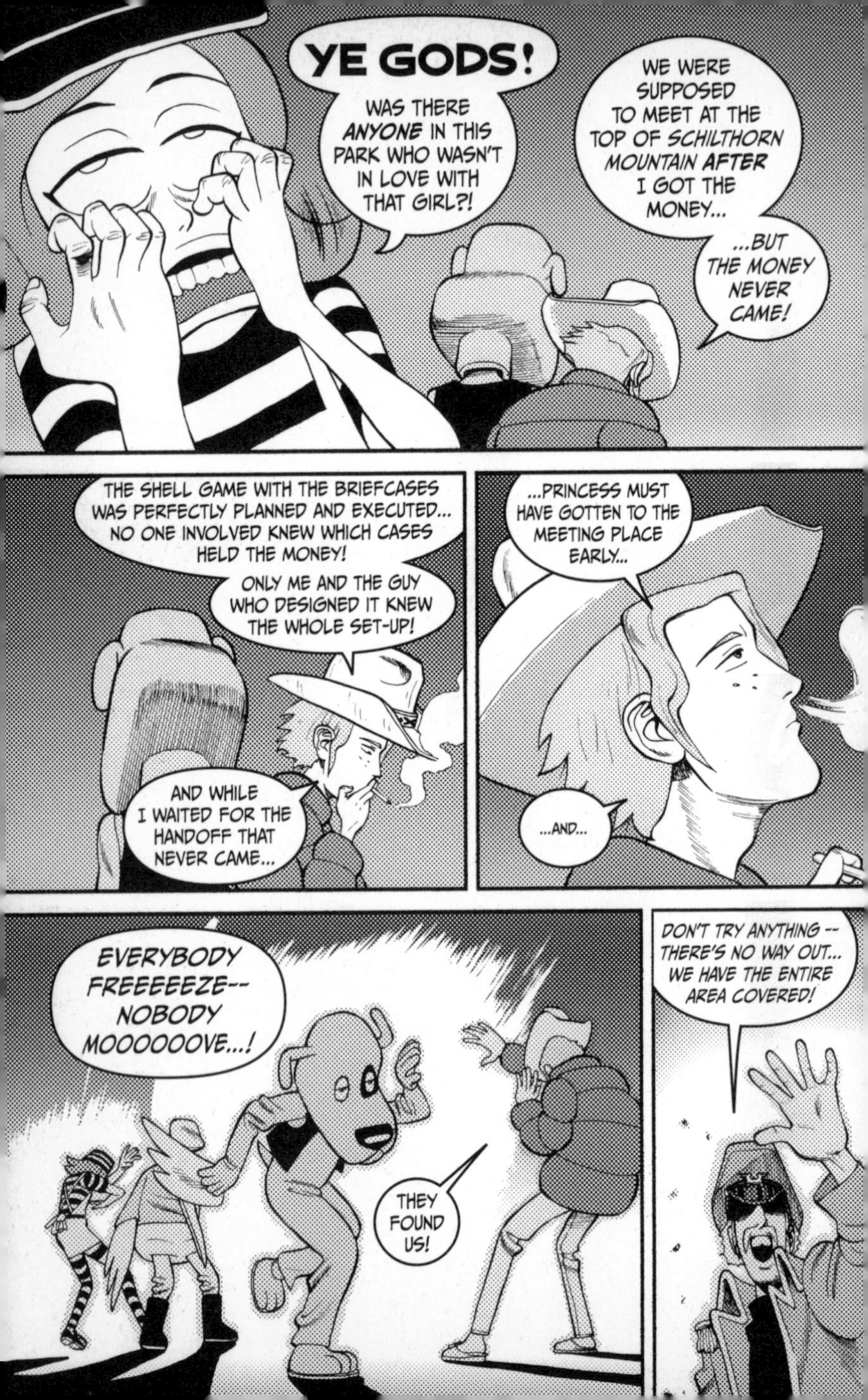
YE GODS!
WAS THERE ANYONE IN THIS PARK WHO WASN'T IN LOVE WITH THAT GIRL?!
WE WERE SUPPOSED TO MEET AT THE TOP OF SCHILTHORN MOUNTAIN AFTER I GOT THE MONEY...
...BUT THE MONEY NEVER CAME!
THE SHELL GAME WITH THE BRIEFCASES WAS PERFECTLY PLANNED AND EXECUTED... NO ONE INVOLVED KNEW WHICH CASES HELD THE MONEY!
ONLY ME AND THE GUY WHO DESIGNED IT KNEW THE WHOLE SET-UP!
AND WHILE I WAITED FOR THE HANDOFF THAT NEVER CAME...
...PRINCESS MUST HAVE GOTTEN TO THE MEETING PLACE EARLY...
...AND...
EVERYBODY FREEEEEZE-- NOBODY MOOOOOOVE...!
THEY FOUND US!
DON'T TRY ANYTHING -- THERE'S NO WAY OUT... WE HAVE THE ENTIRE AREA COVERED!

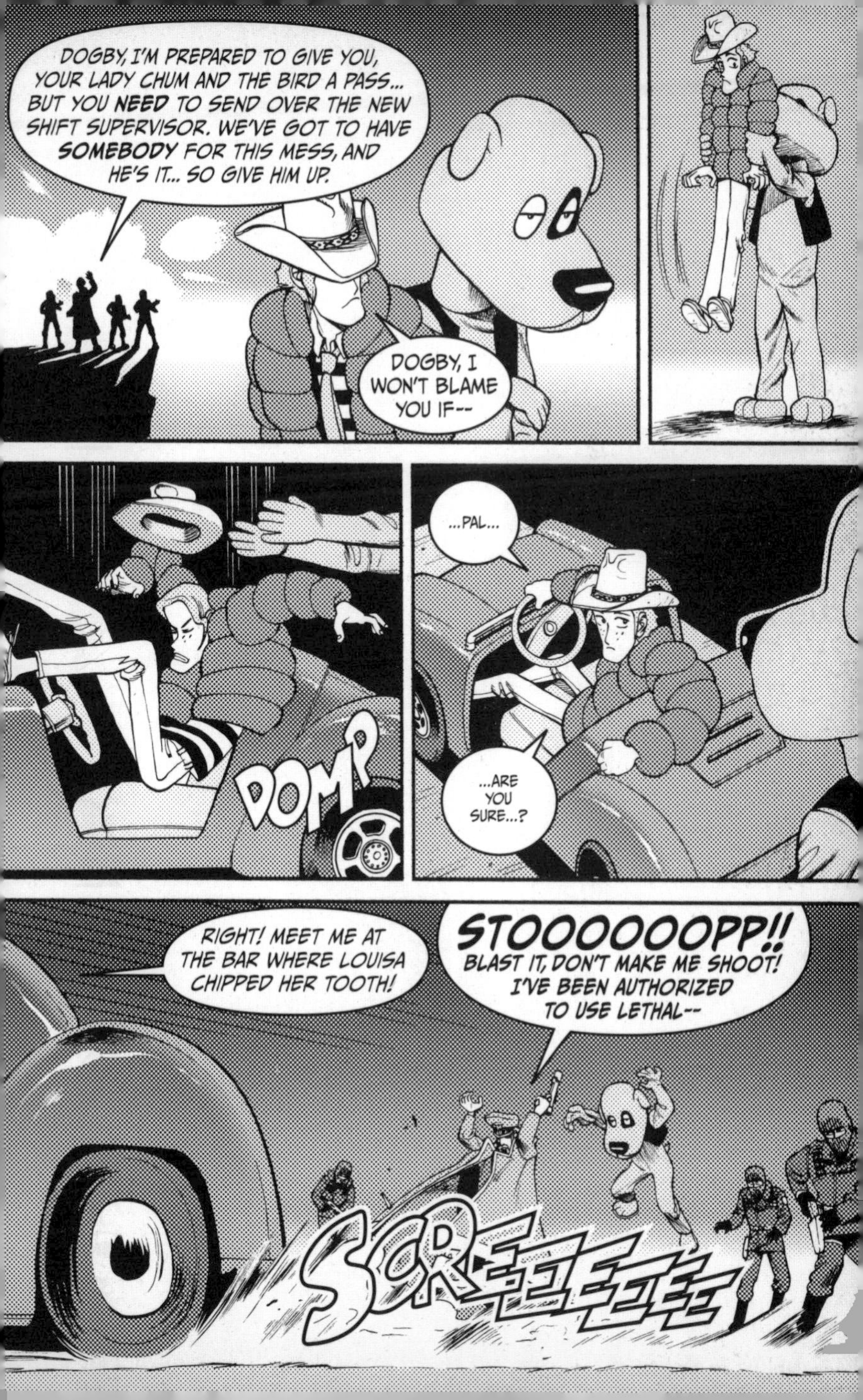
DOGBY, I'M PREPARED TO GIVE YOU, YOUR LADY CHUM AND THE BIRD A PASS... BUT YOU NEED TO SEND OVER THE NEW SHIFT SUPERVISOR. WE'VE GOT TO HAVE SOMEBODY FOR THIS MESS, AND HE'S IT... SO GIVE HIM UP.
DOGBY, I WON'T BLAME YOU IF--
DOMP
...PAL...
...ARE YOU SURE...?
RIGHT! MEET ME AT THE BAR WHERE LOUISA CHIPPED HER TOOTH!
STOOOOOOPP!! BLAST IT, DON'T MAKE ME SHOOT! I'VE BEEN AUTHORIZED TO USE LETHAL--
SCREEEEEEE

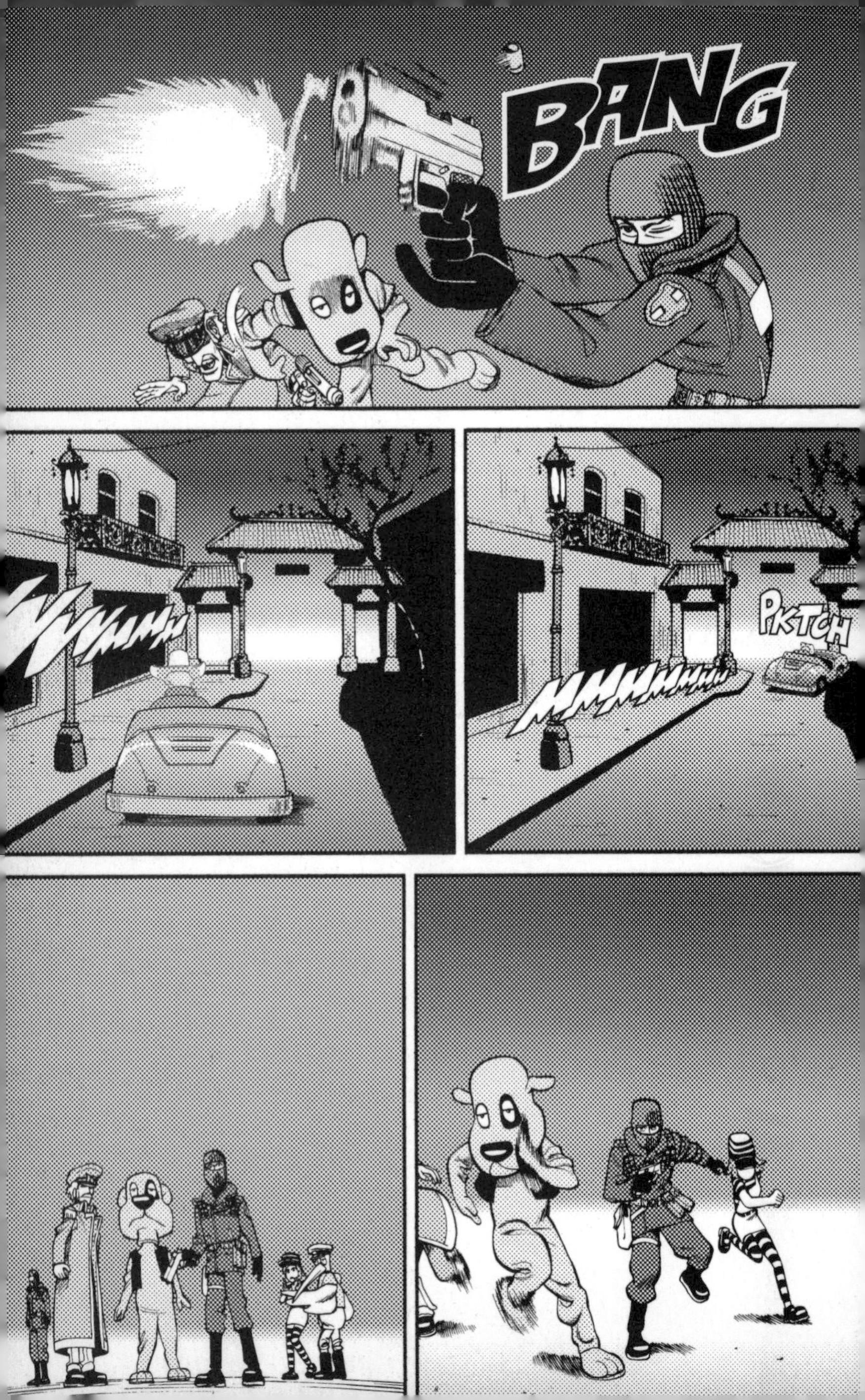
BANG
VVVMMMM
PKTCH
MMMMMMM

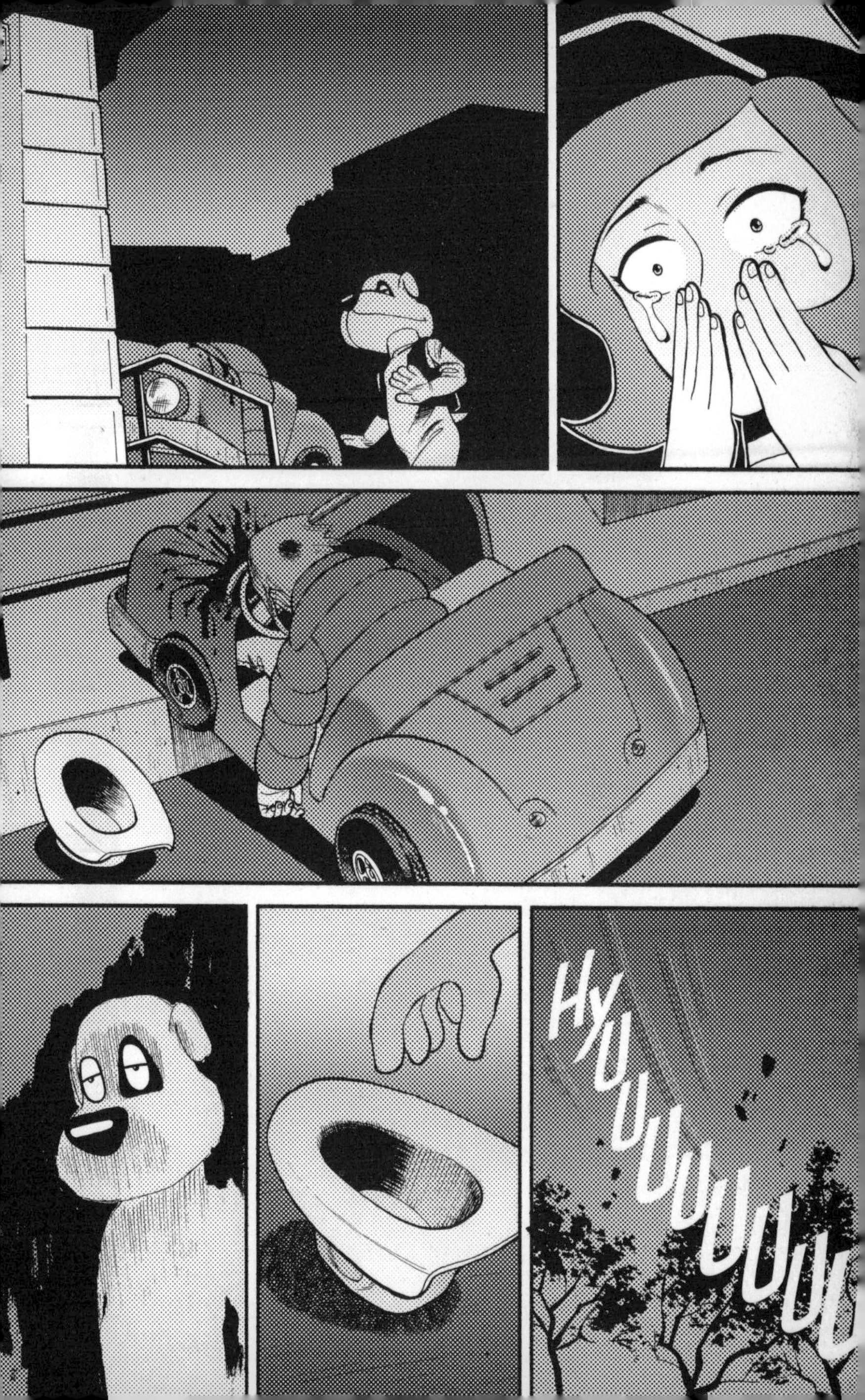
HYUUUUUUUUUU

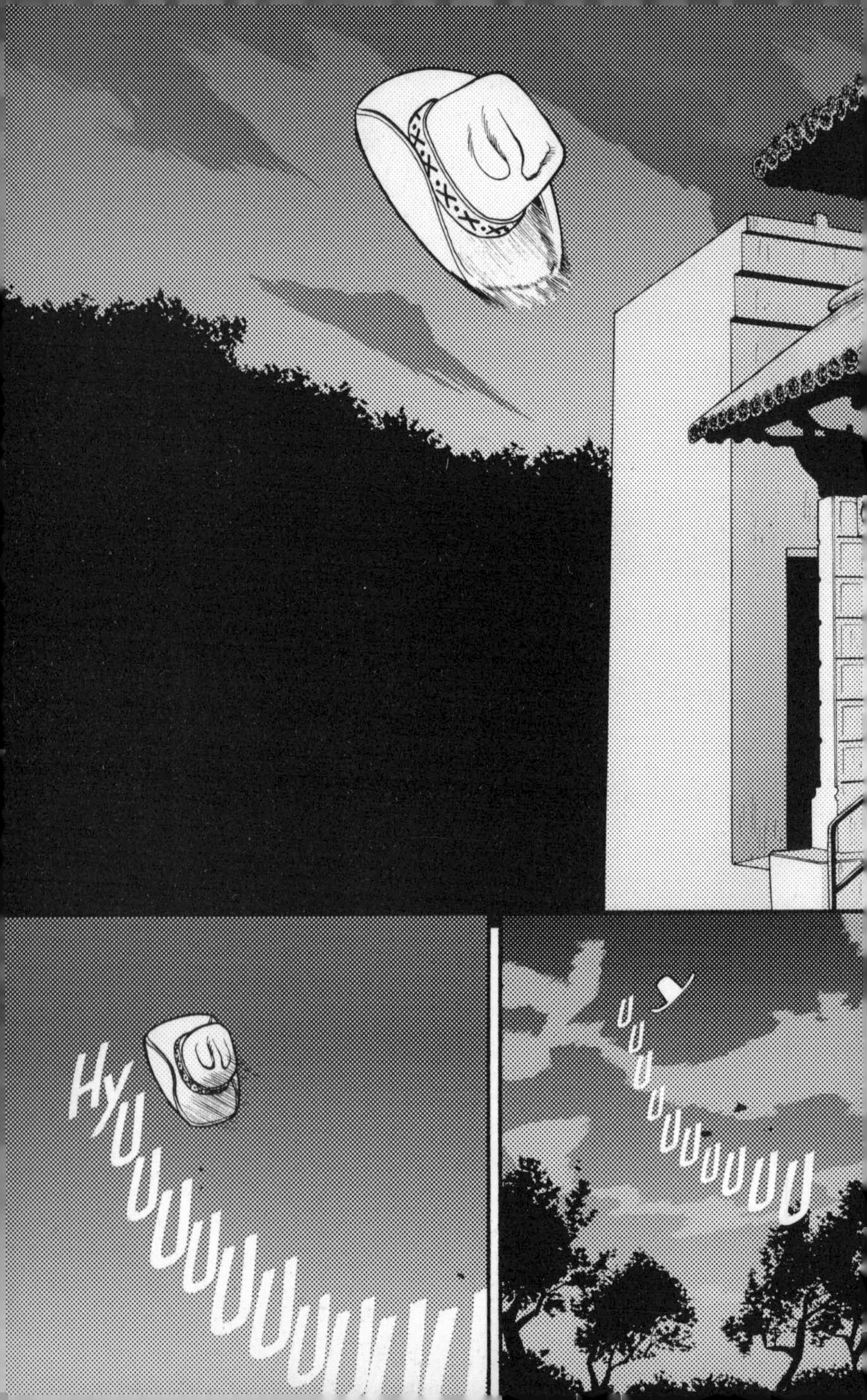
HyUUUUUUUUU
UUUUUUUUUUU

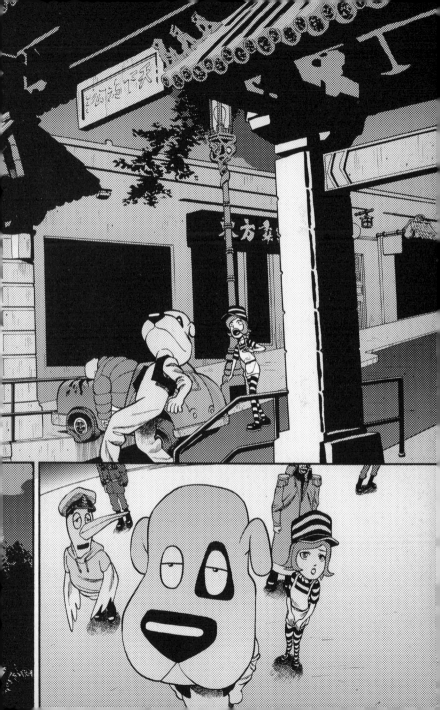

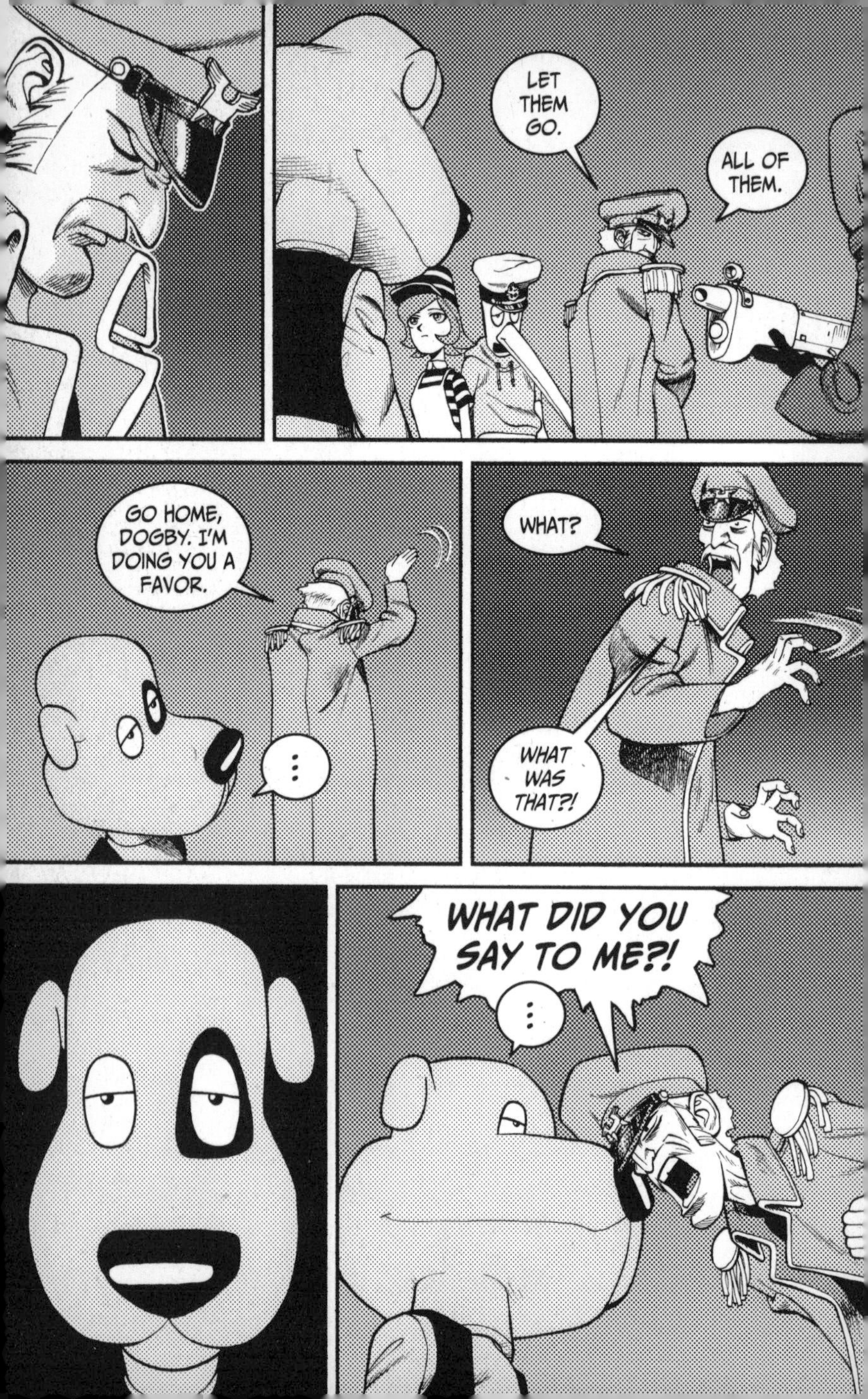
LET THEM GO.
ALL OF THEM.
GO HOME, DOGBY. I'M DOING YOU A FAVOR.
...
WHAT?
WHAT WAS THAT?!
WHAT DID YOU SAY TO ME?!
...

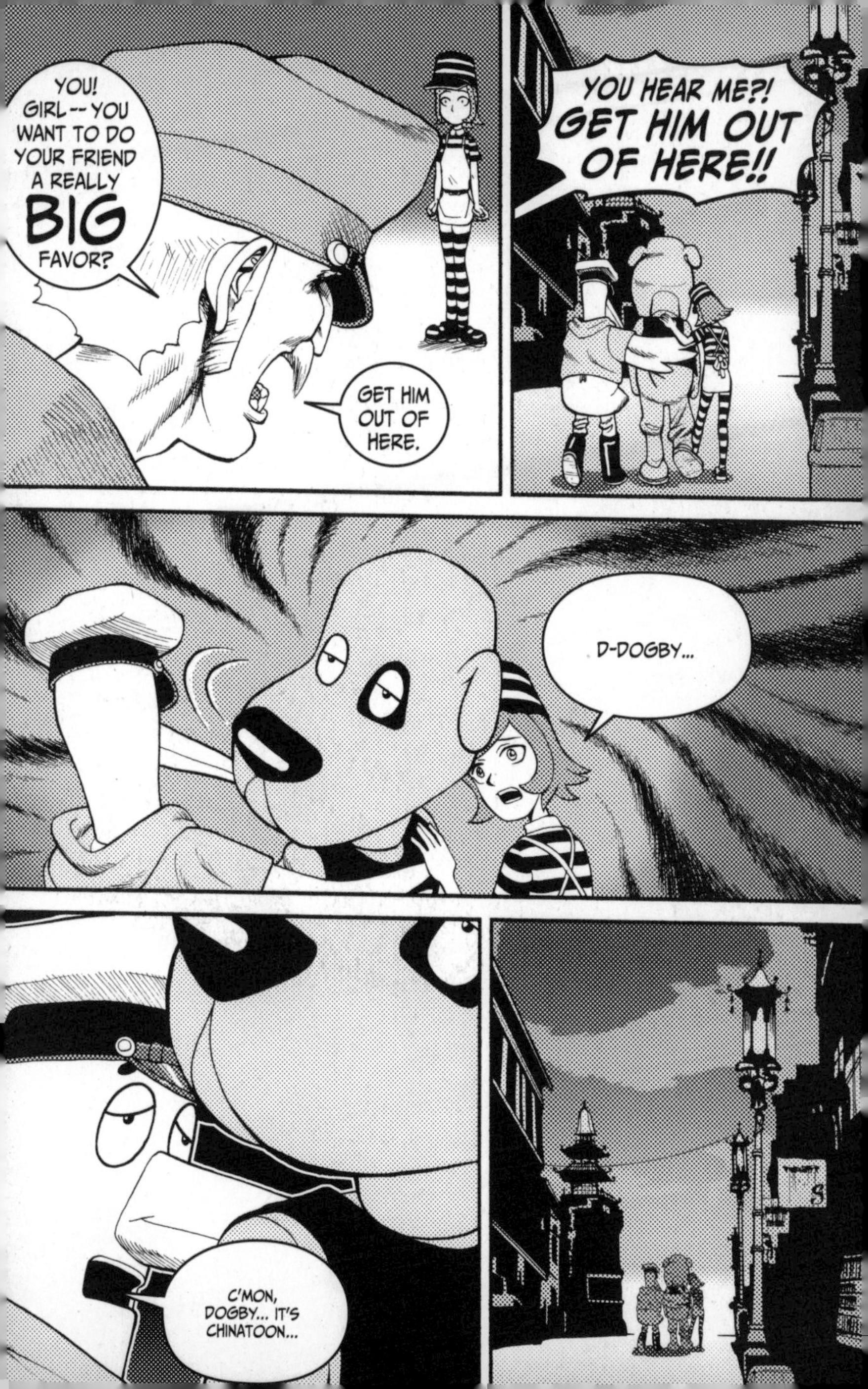
YOU! GIRL-- YOU WANT TO DO YOUR FRIEND A REALLY BIG FAVOR?
GET HIM OUT OF HERE.
YOU HEAR ME?! GET HIM OUT OF HERE!!
D-DOGBY...
C'MON, DOGBY... IT'S CHINATOON...

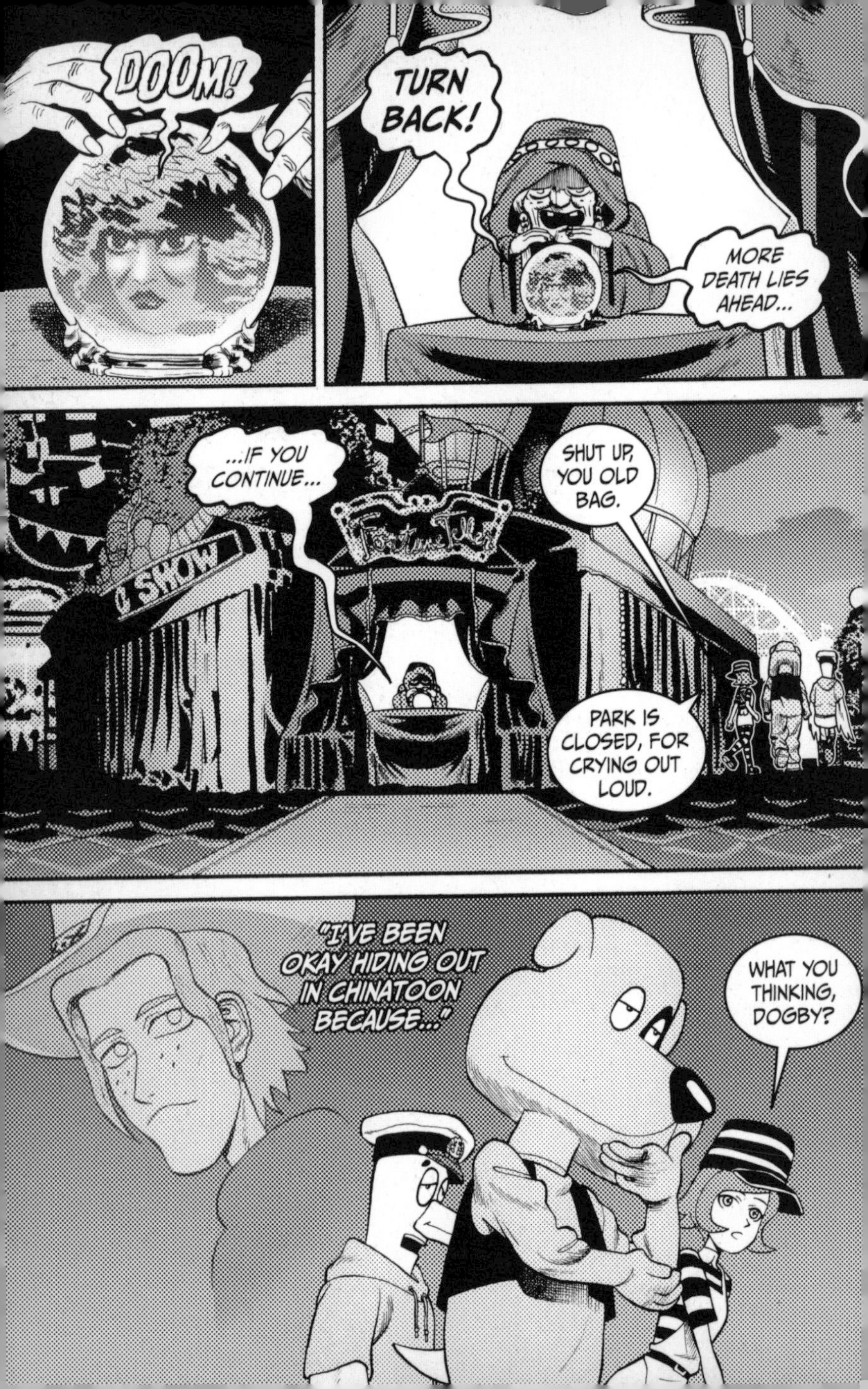
DOOM!
TURN BACK!
MORE DEATH LIES AHEAD...
...IF YOU CONTINUE...
SHOW
SHUT UP, YOU OLD BAG.
PARK IS CLOSED, FOR CRYING OUT LOUD.
"I'VE BEEN OKAY HIDING OUT IN CHINATOON BECAUSE..."
WHAT YOU THINKING, DOGBY?

?

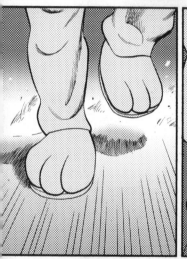

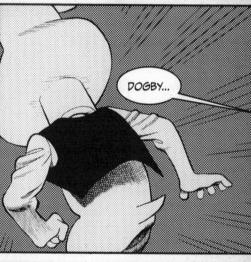

DOGBY...

YOU KNOW I'M WITH YOU ONE HUNDRED PERCENT, BUT MY AGE IS CATCHING UP WITH ME HERE.

I JUST CAN'T GO OVER A WATERFALL THEN RUN A MILE THE WAY I COULD FIVE YEARS AGO.

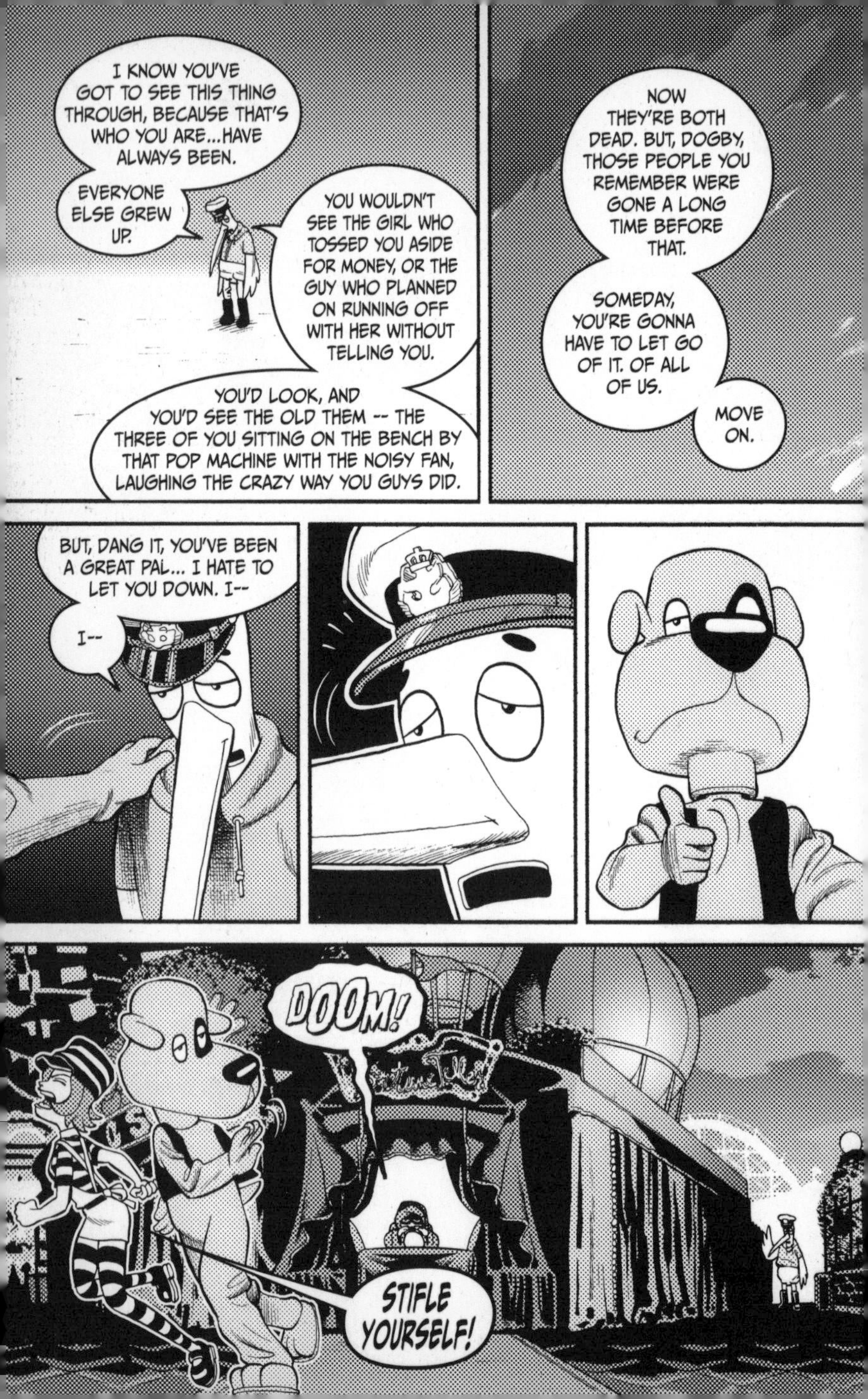
I KNOW YOU'VE GOT TO SEE THIS THING THROUGH, BECAUSE THAT'S WHO YOU ARE...HAVE ALWAYS BEEN.
EVERYONE ELSE GREW UP.
YOU WOULDN'T SEE THE GIRL WHO TOSSED YOU ASIDE FOR MONEY, OR THE GUY WHO PLANNED ON RUNNING OFF WITH HER WITHOUT TELLING YOU.
YOU'D LOOK, AND YOU'D SEE THE OLD THEM -- THE THREE OF YOU SITTING ON THE BENCH BY THAT POP MACHINE WITH THE NOISY FAN, LAUGHING THE CRAZY WAY YOU GUYS DID.
NOW THEY'RE BOTH DEAD. BUT, DOGBY, THOSE PEOPLE YOU REMEMBER WERE GONE A LONG TIME BEFORE THAT.
SOMEDAY, YOU'RE GONNA HAVE TO LET GO OF IT. OF ALL OF US.
MOVE ON.
BUT, DANG IT, YOU'VE BEEN A GREAT PAL... I HATE TO LET YOU DOWN. I--
I--
DOOM!
STIFLE YOURSELF!

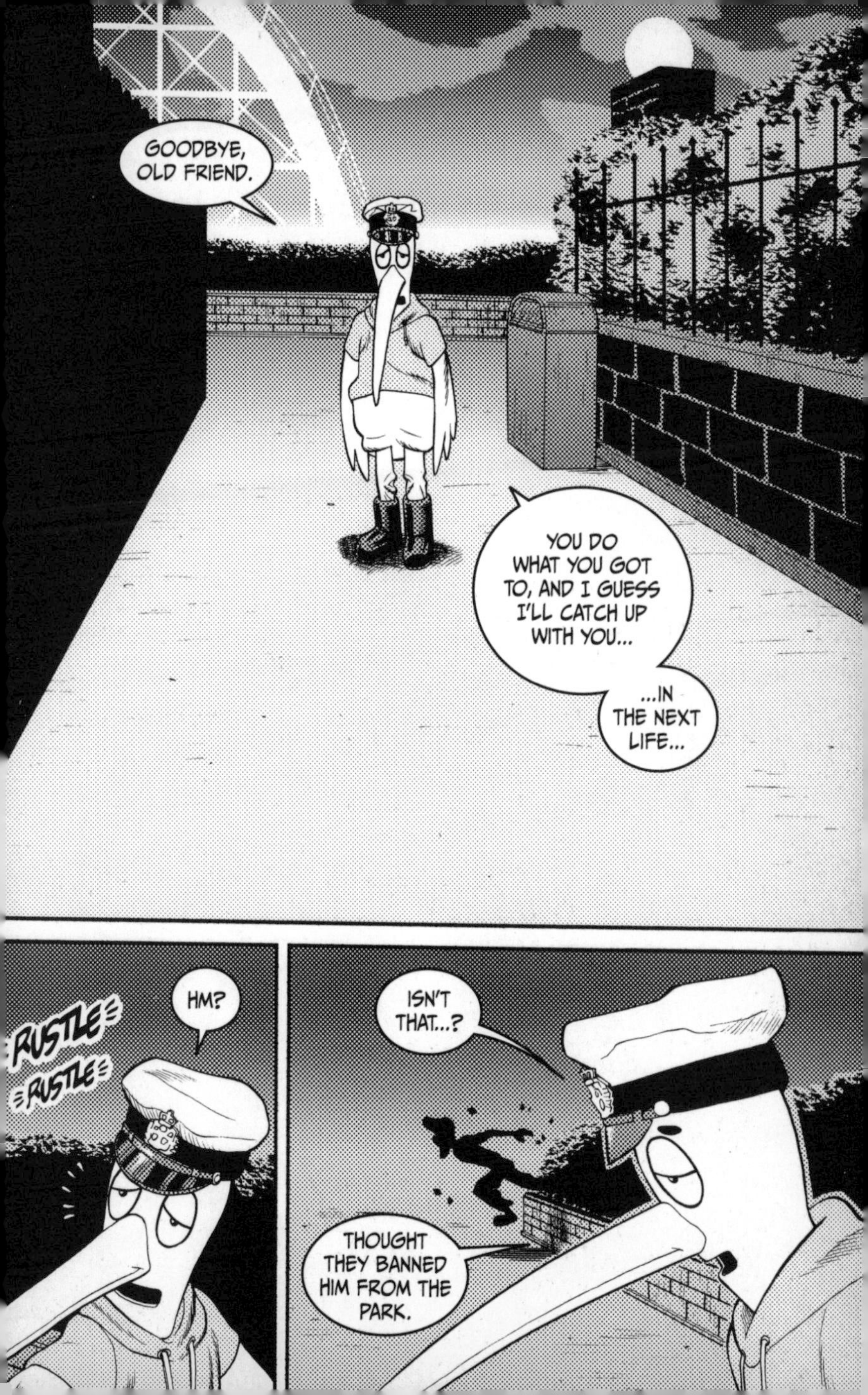
GOODBYE, OLD FRIEND.
YOU DO WHAT YOU GOT TO, AND I GUESS I'LL CATCH UP WITH YOU...
...IN THE NEXT LIFE...
RUSTLE
RUSTLE
HM?
ISN'T THAT...?
THOUGHT THEY BANNED HIM FROM THE PARK.

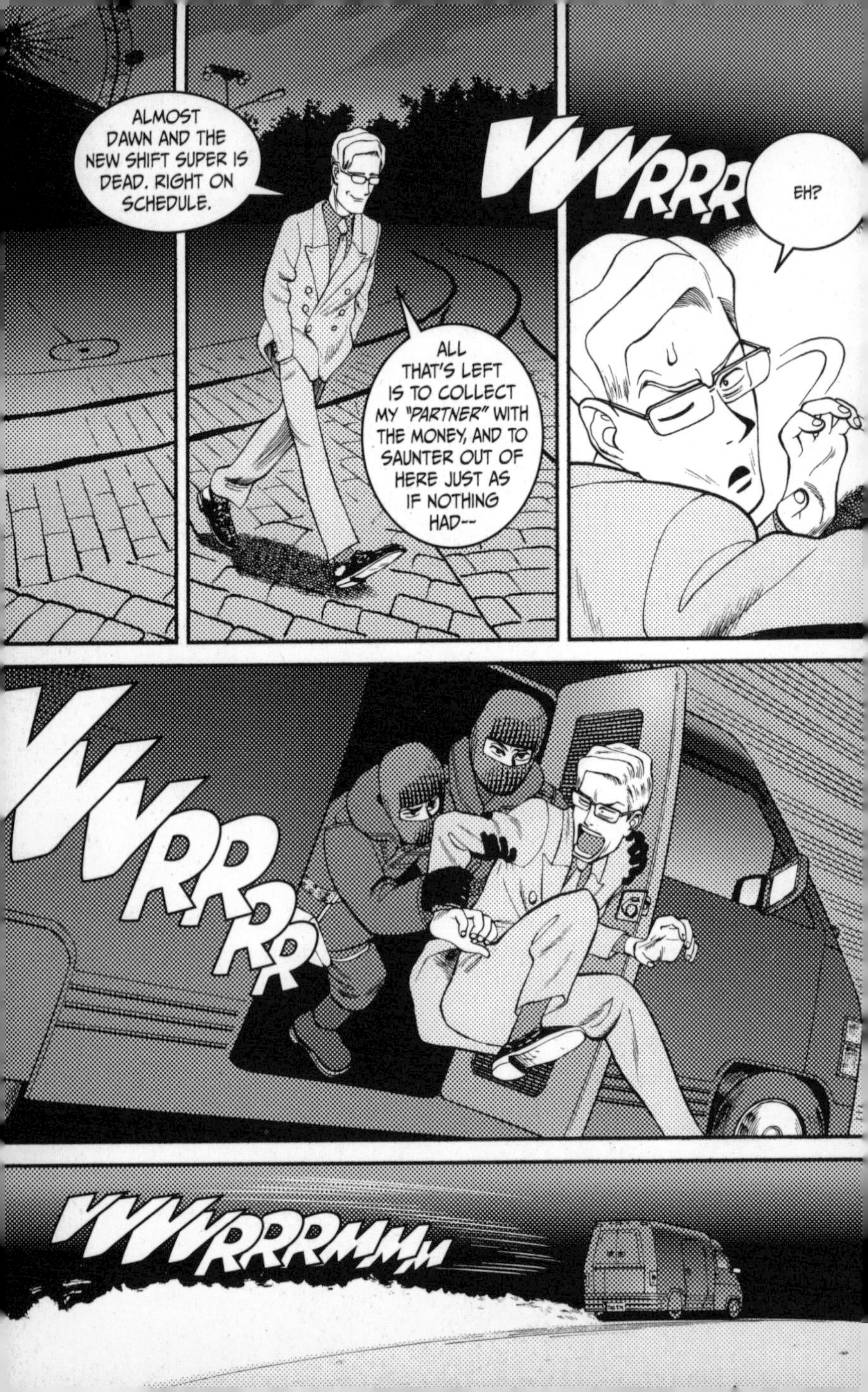
ALMOST DAWN AND THE NEW SHIFT SUPER IS DEAD. RIGHT ON SCHEDULE.
ALL THAT'S LEFT IS TO COLLECT MY "PARTNER" WITH THE MONEY, AND TO SAUNTER OUT OF HERE JUST AS IF NOTHING HAD--
VVVRRR
EH?
VVVRRRRR
VVVRRRMMMM

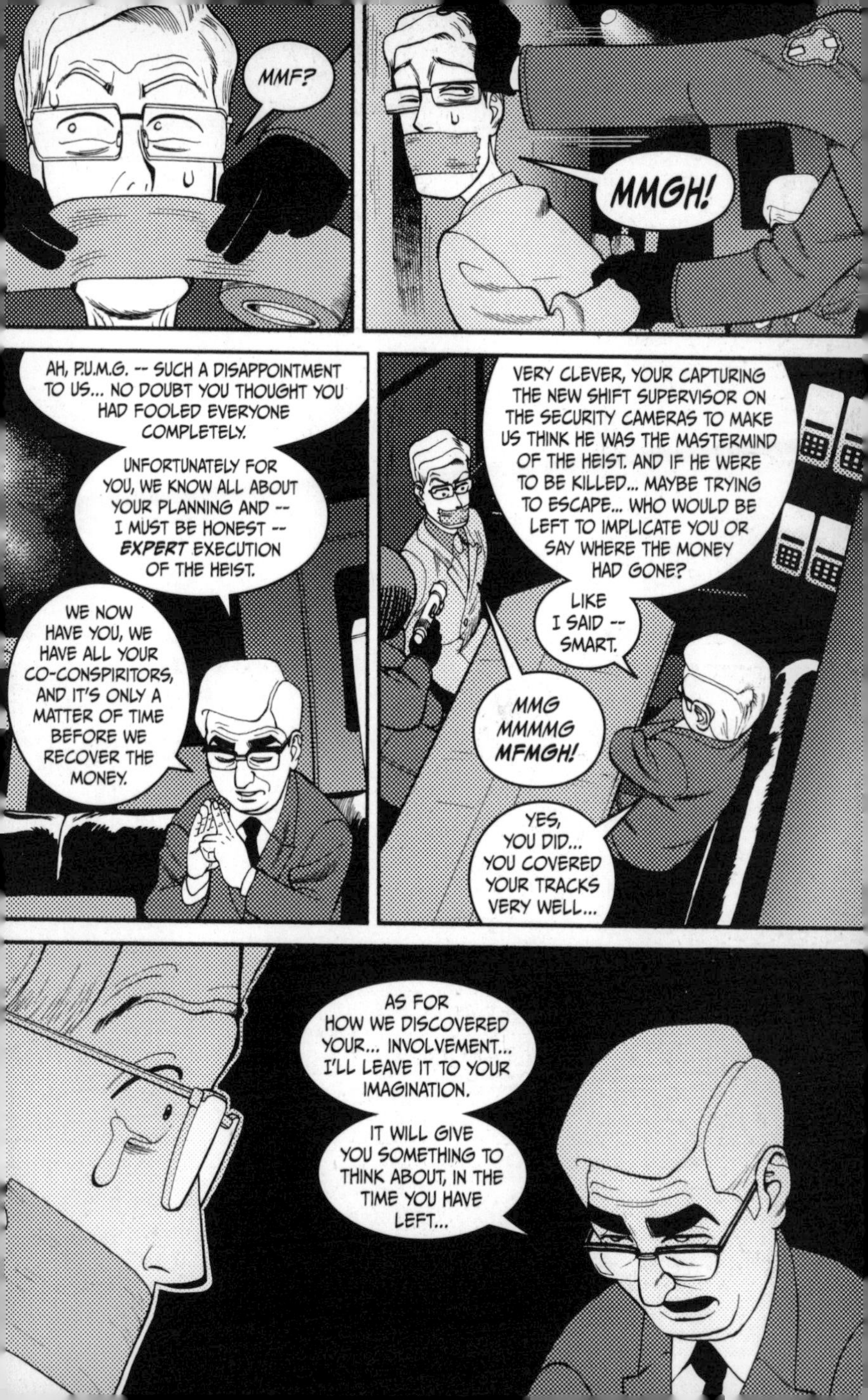
MMF?
MMGH!
AH, P.U.M.G. -- SUCH A DISAPPOINTMENT TO US... NO DOUBT YOU THOUGHT YOU HAD FOOLED EVERYONE COMPLETELY.
UNFORTUNATELY FOR YOU, WE KNOW ALL ABOUT YOUR PLANNING AND -- I MUST BE HONEST -- EXPERT EXECUTION OF THE HEIST.
WE NOW HAVE YOU, WE HAVE ALL YOUR CO-CONSPIRITORS, AND IT'S ONLY A MATTER OF TIME BEFORE WE RECOVER THE MONEY.
VERY CLEVER, YOUR CAPTURING THE NEW SHIFT SUPERVISOR ON THE SECURITY CAMERAS TO MAKE US THINK HE WAS THE MASTERMIND OF THE HEIST. AND IF HE WERE TO BE KILLED... MAYBE TRYING TO ESCAPE... WHO WOULD BE LEFT TO IMPLICATE YOU OR SAY WHERE THE MONEY HAD GONE?
LIKE I SAID -- SMART.
MMG MMMMG MFMGH!
YES, YOU DID... YOU COVERED YOUR TRACKS VERY WELL...
AS FOR HOW WE DISCOVERED YOUR... INVOLVEMENT... I'LL LEAVE IT TO YOUR IMAGINATION.
IT WILL GIVE YOU SOMETHING TO THINK ABOUT, IN THE TIME YOU HAVE LEFT...

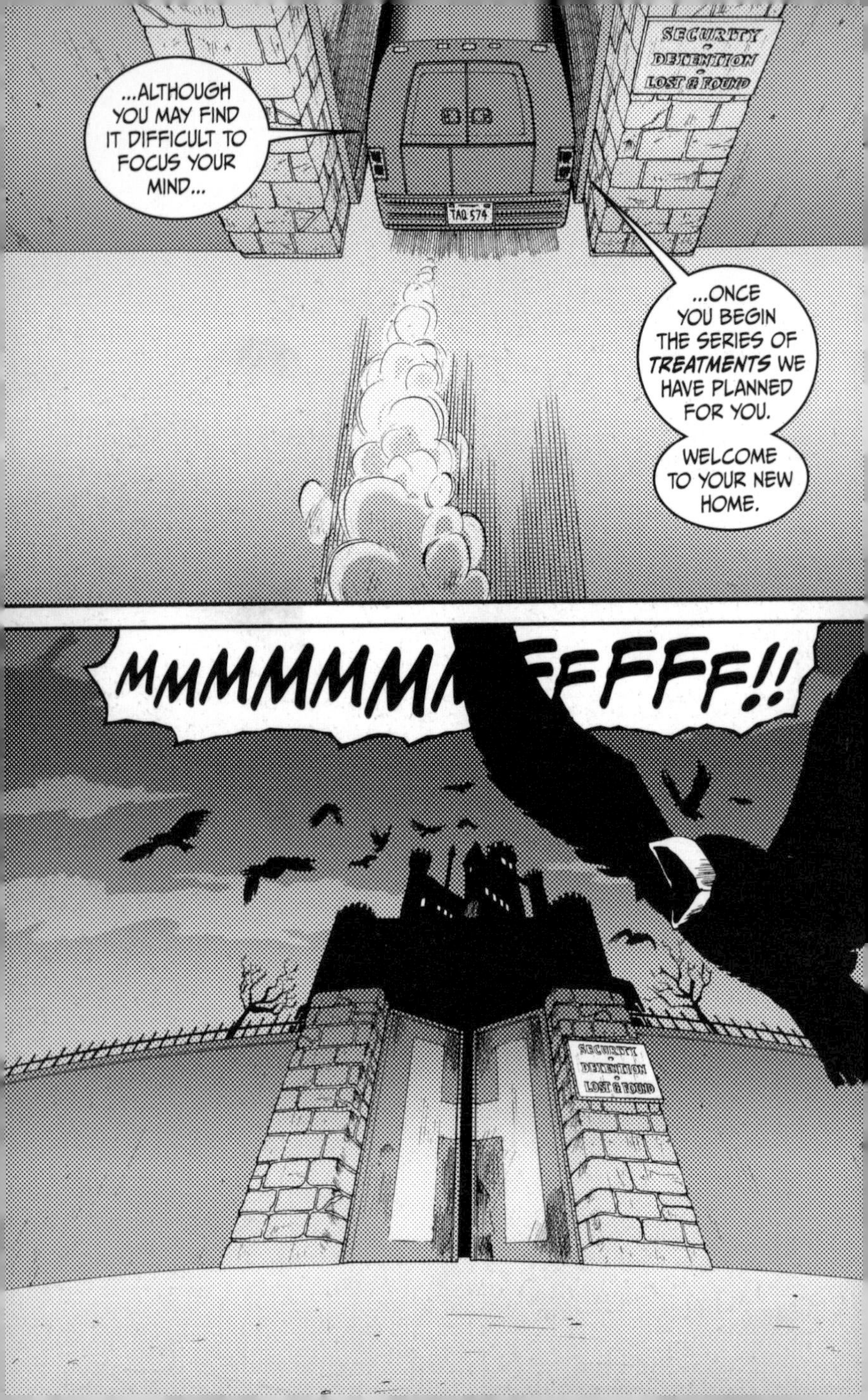
SECURITY
DETENTION
LOST & FOUND
...ALTHOUGH YOU MAY FIND IT DIFFICULT TO FOCUS YOUR MIND...
...ONCE YOU BEGIN THE SERIES OF *TREATMENTS* WE HAVE PLANNED FOR YOU.
WELCOME TO YOUR NEW HOME.
MMMMMM FFFFF!!
SECURITY
DETENTION
LOST & FOUND

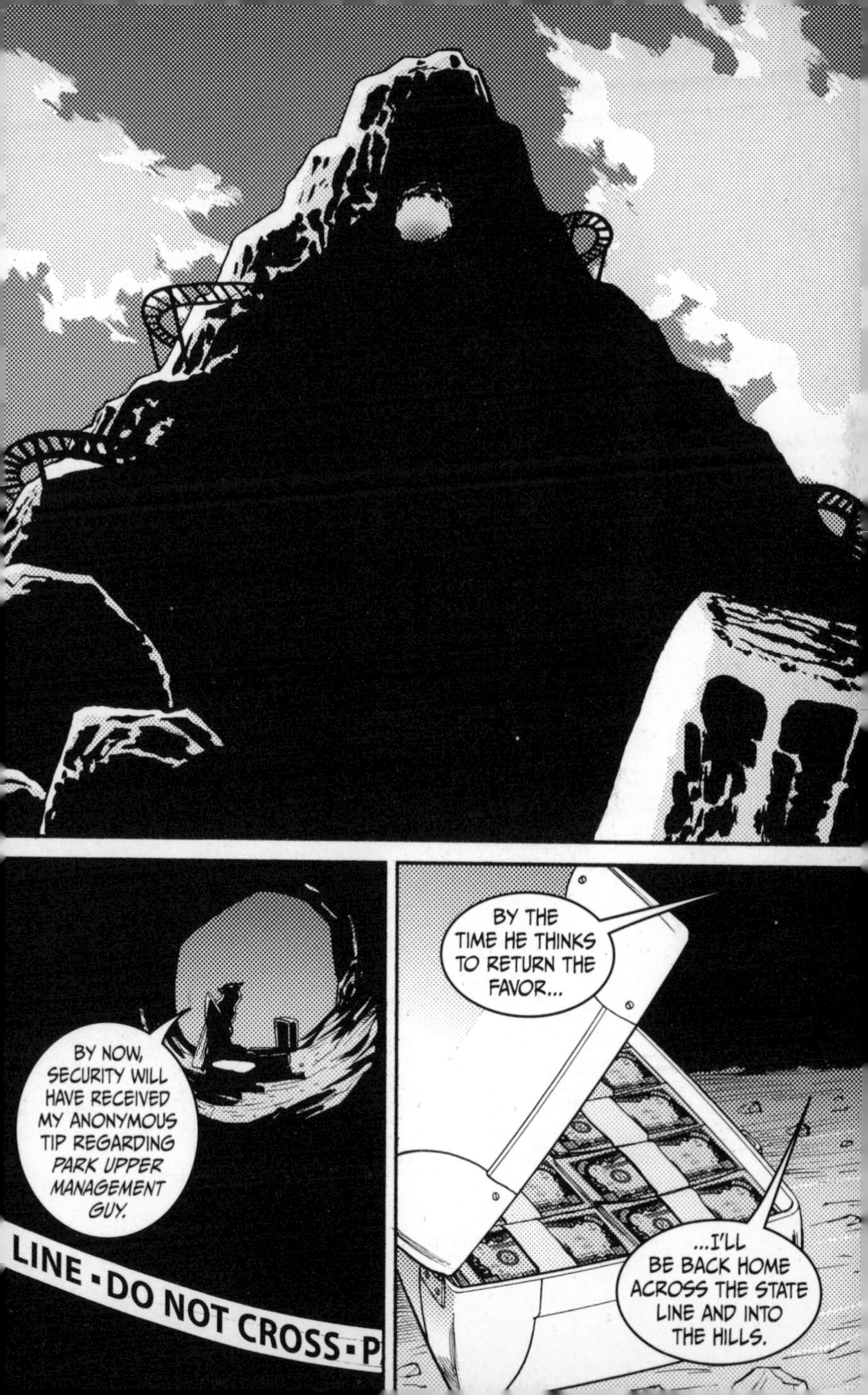
BY NOW, SECURITY WILL HAVE RECEIVED MY ANONYMOUS TIP REGARDING *PARK UPPER MANAGEMENT GUY.*
LINE - DO NOT CROSS - P
BY THE TIME HE THINKS TO RETURN THE FAVOR...
...I'LL BE BACK HOME ACROSS THE STATE LINE AND INTO THE HILLS.

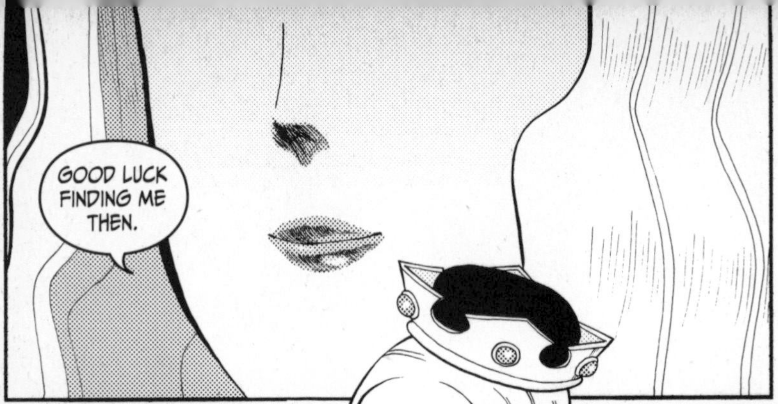
GOOD LUCK FINDING ME THEN.
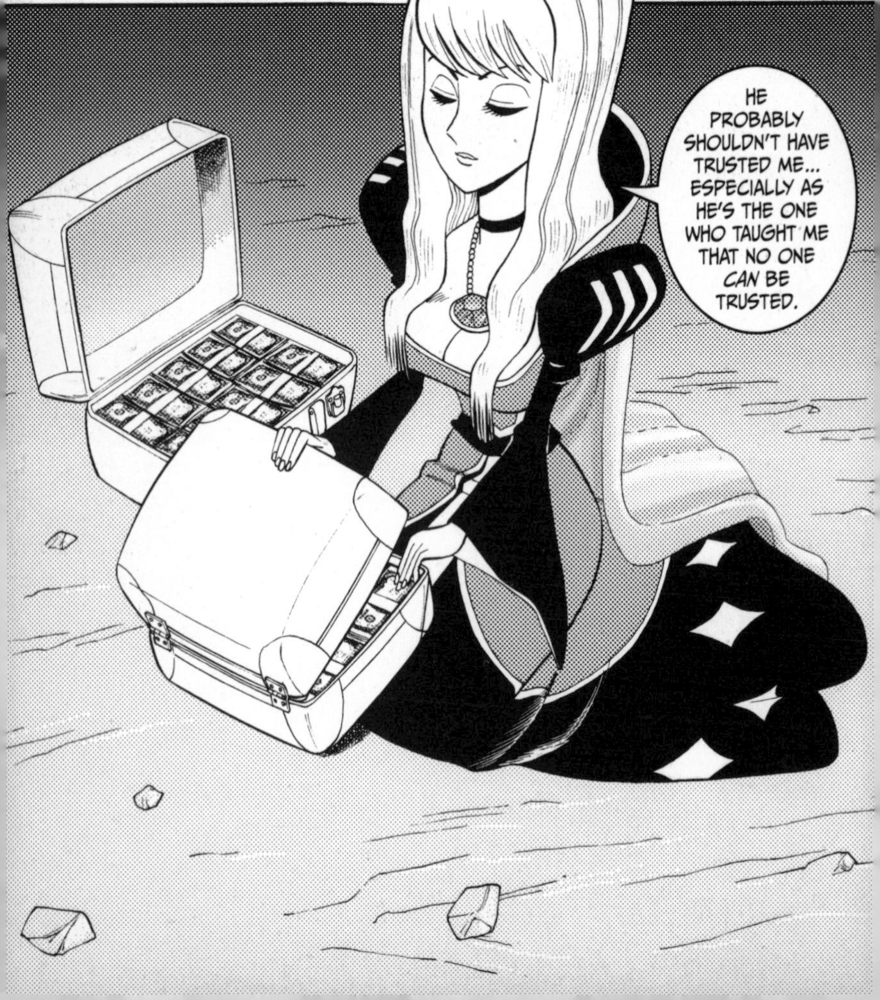
HE PROBABLY SHOULDN'T HAVE TRUSTED ME... ESPECIALLY AS HE'S THE ONE WHO TAUGHT ME THAT NO ONE CAN BE TRUSTED.

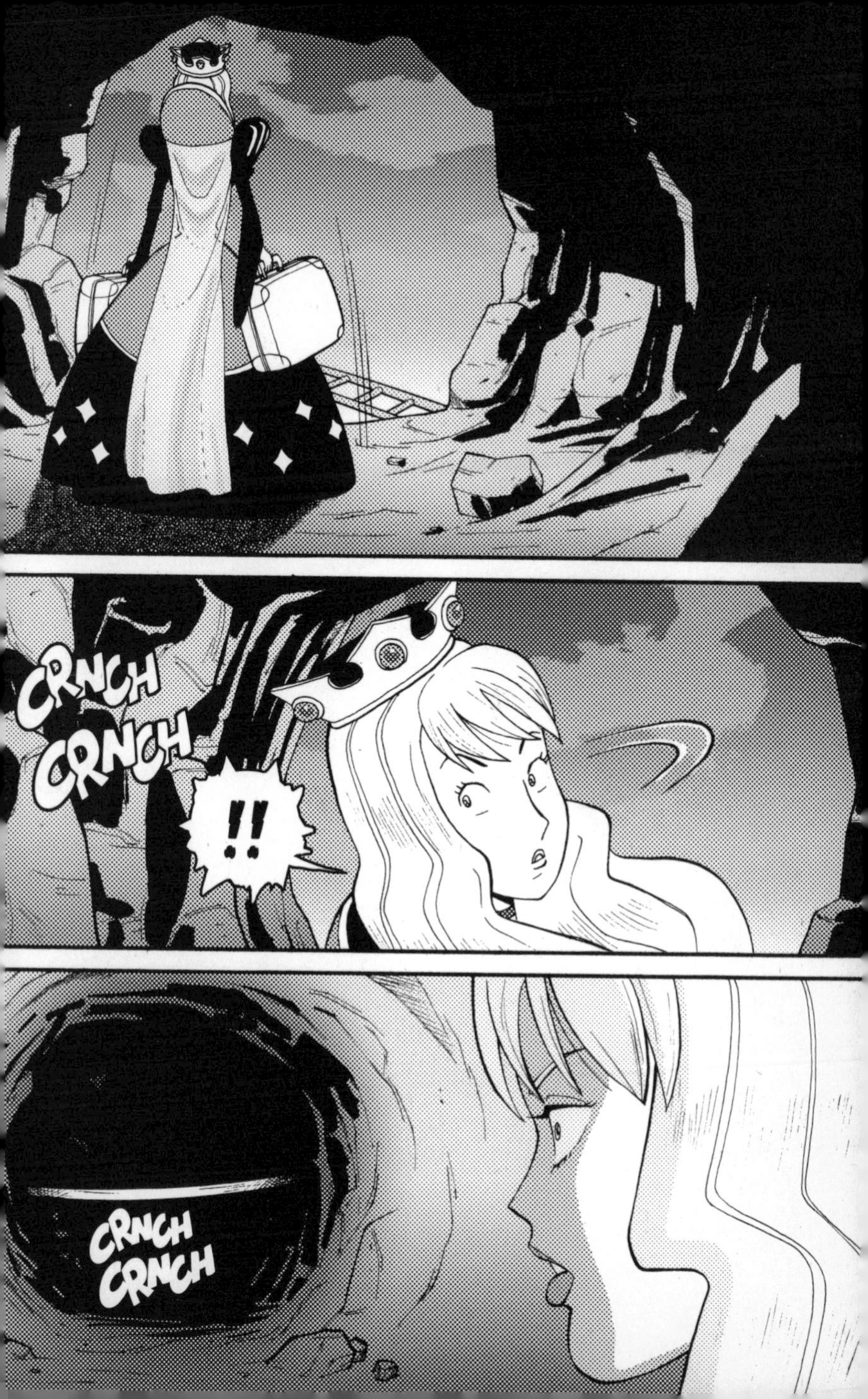
CRNCH CRNCH
!!
CRNCH CRNCH

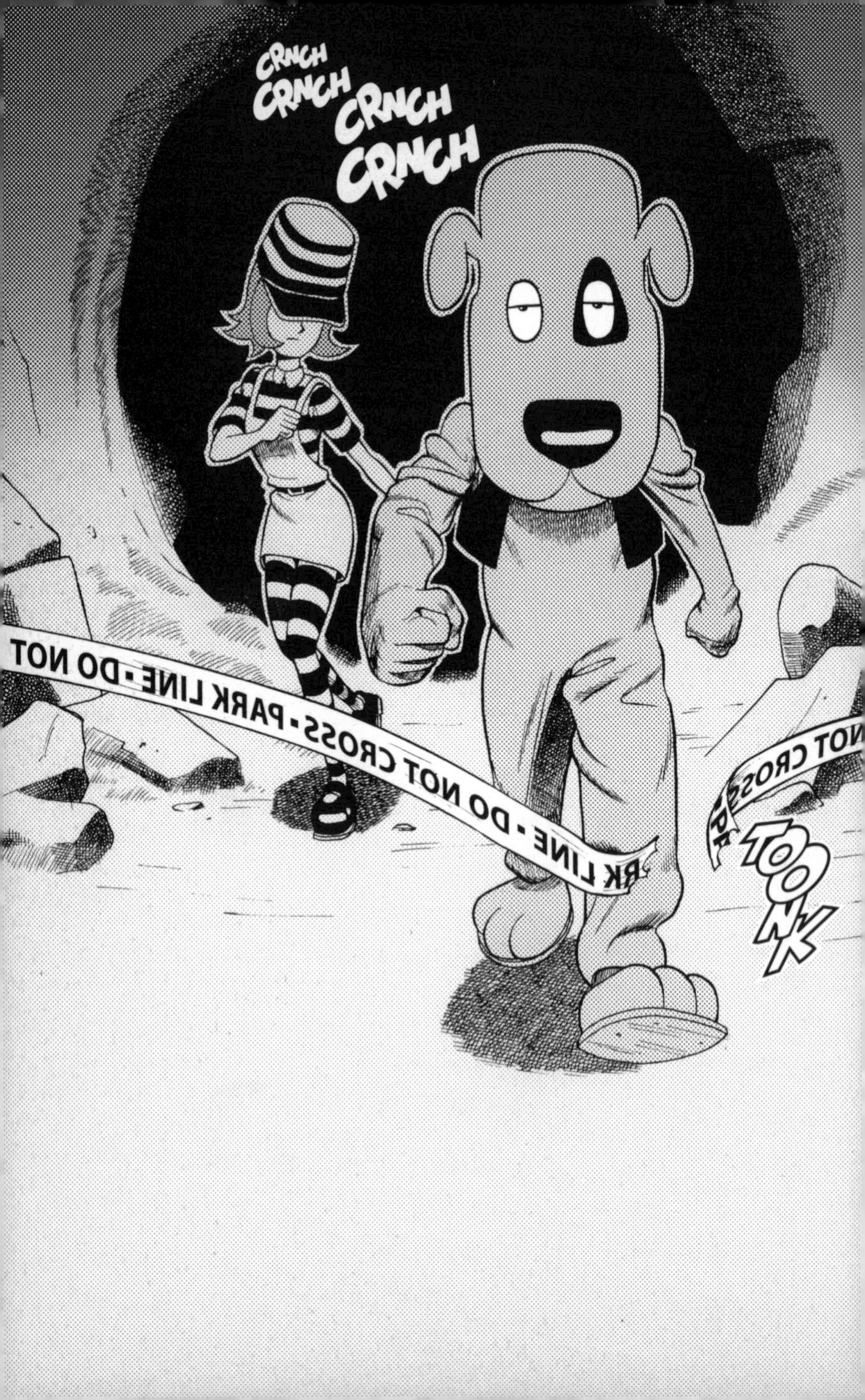
CRNCH
CRNCH
CRNCH
CRNCH
DO NOT CROSS • PARK LINE • DO NOT
RK LINE • DO NOT CROSS
PA CROSS NOT
TOONK

chapter 13: Lyin' Eyes

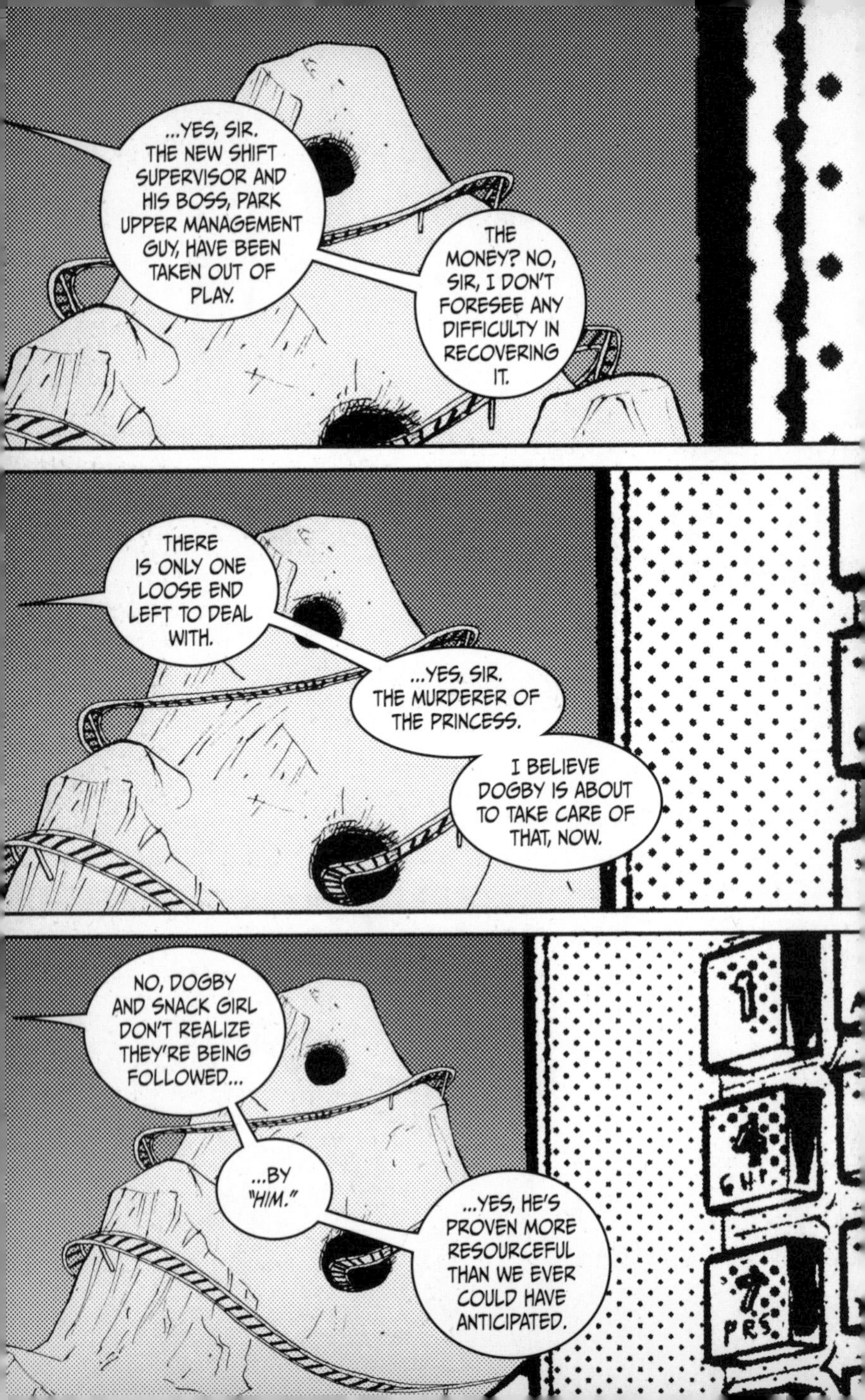
...YES, SIR. THE NEW SHIFT SUPERVISOR AND HIS BOSS, PARK UPPER MANAGEMENT GUY, HAVE BEEN TAKEN OUT OF PLAY.
THE MONEY? NO, SIR, I DON'T FORESEE ANY DIFFICULTY IN RECOVERING IT.
THERE IS ONLY ONE LOOSE END LEFT TO DEAL WITH.
...YES, SIR. THE MURDERER OF THE PRINCESS.
I BELIEVE DOGBY IS ABOUT TO TAKE CARE OF THAT, NOW.
NO, DOGBY AND SNACK GIRL DON'T REALIZE THEY'RE BEING FOLLOWED...
...BY *"HIM."*
...YES, HE'S PROVEN MORE RESOURCEFUL THAN WE EVER COULD HAVE ANTICIPATED.

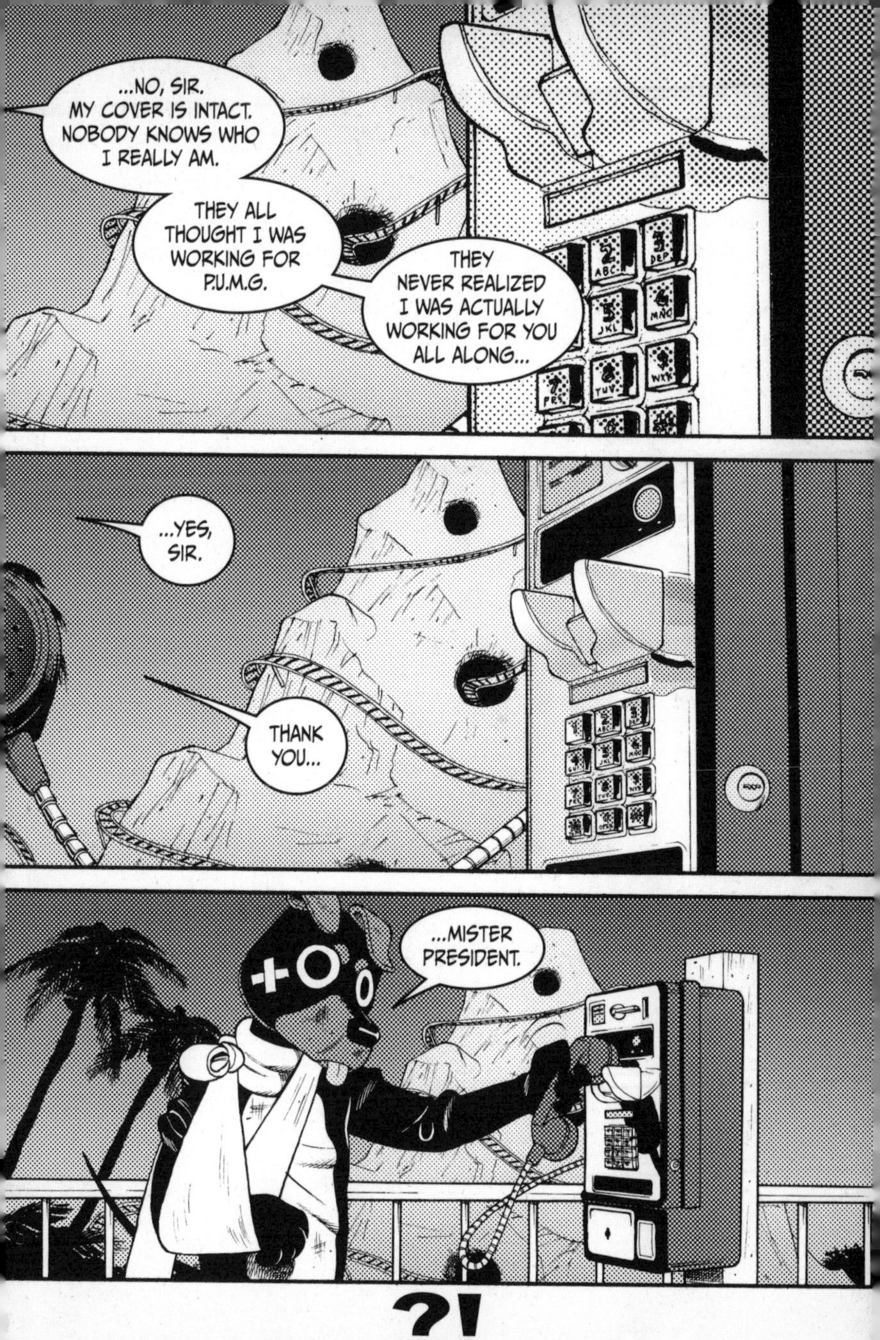
...NO, SIR. MY COVER IS INTACT. NOBODY KNOWS WHO I REALLY AM.
THEY ALL THOUGHT I WAS WORKING FOR P.U.M.G.
THEY NEVER REALIZED I WAS ACTUALLY WORKING FOR YOU ALL ALONG...
...YES, SIR.
THANK YOU...
...MISTER PRESIDENT.
?!

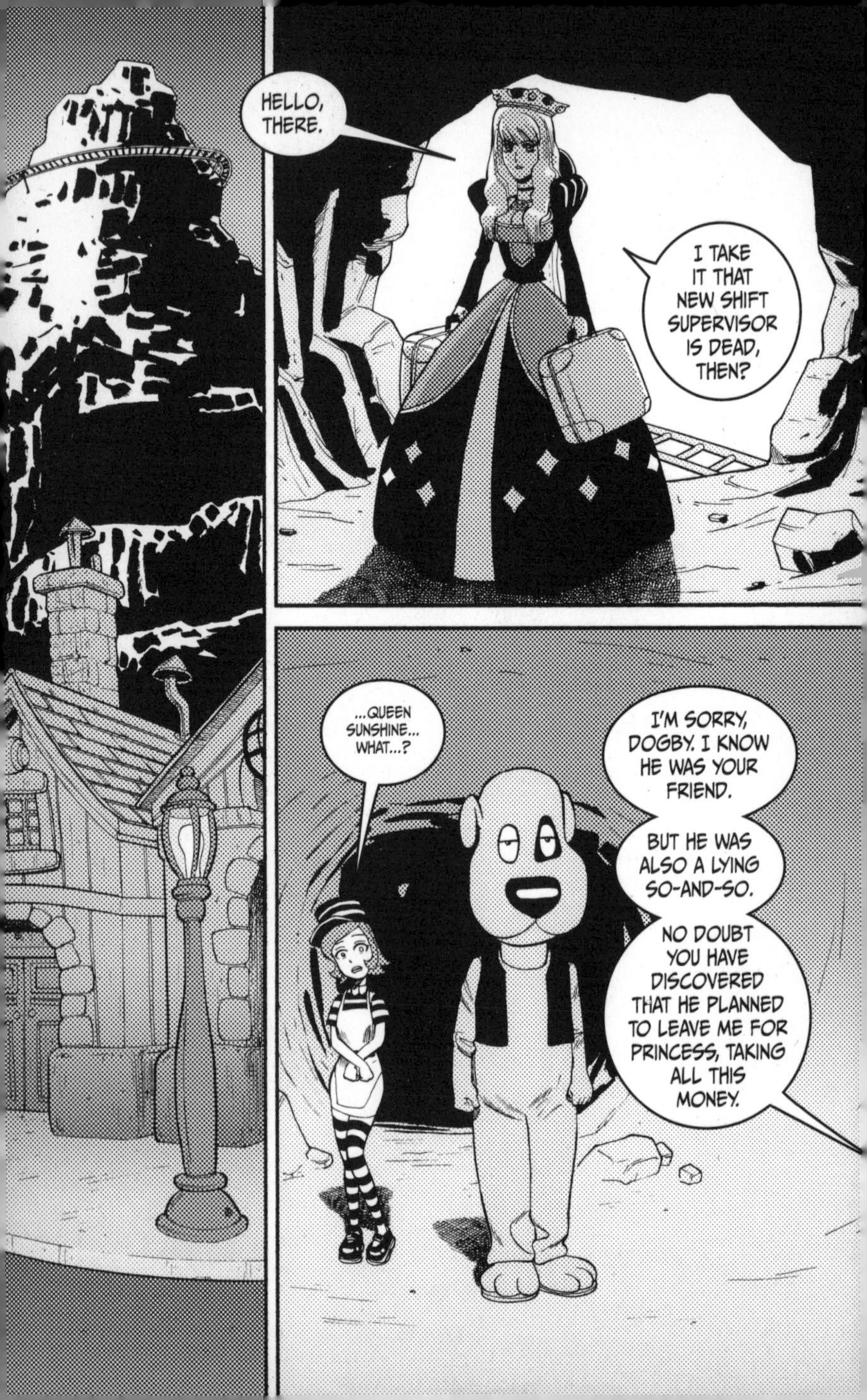
HELLO, THERE.
I TAKE IT THAT NEW SHIFT SUPERVISOR IS DEAD, THEN?
...QUEEN SUNSHINE... WHAT...?
I'M SORRY, DOGBY. I KNOW HE WAS YOUR FRIEND.
BUT HE WAS ALSO A LYING SO-AND-SO.
NO DOUBT YOU HAVE DISCOVERED THAT HE PLANNED TO LEAVE ME FOR PRINCESS, TAKING ALL THIS MONEY.

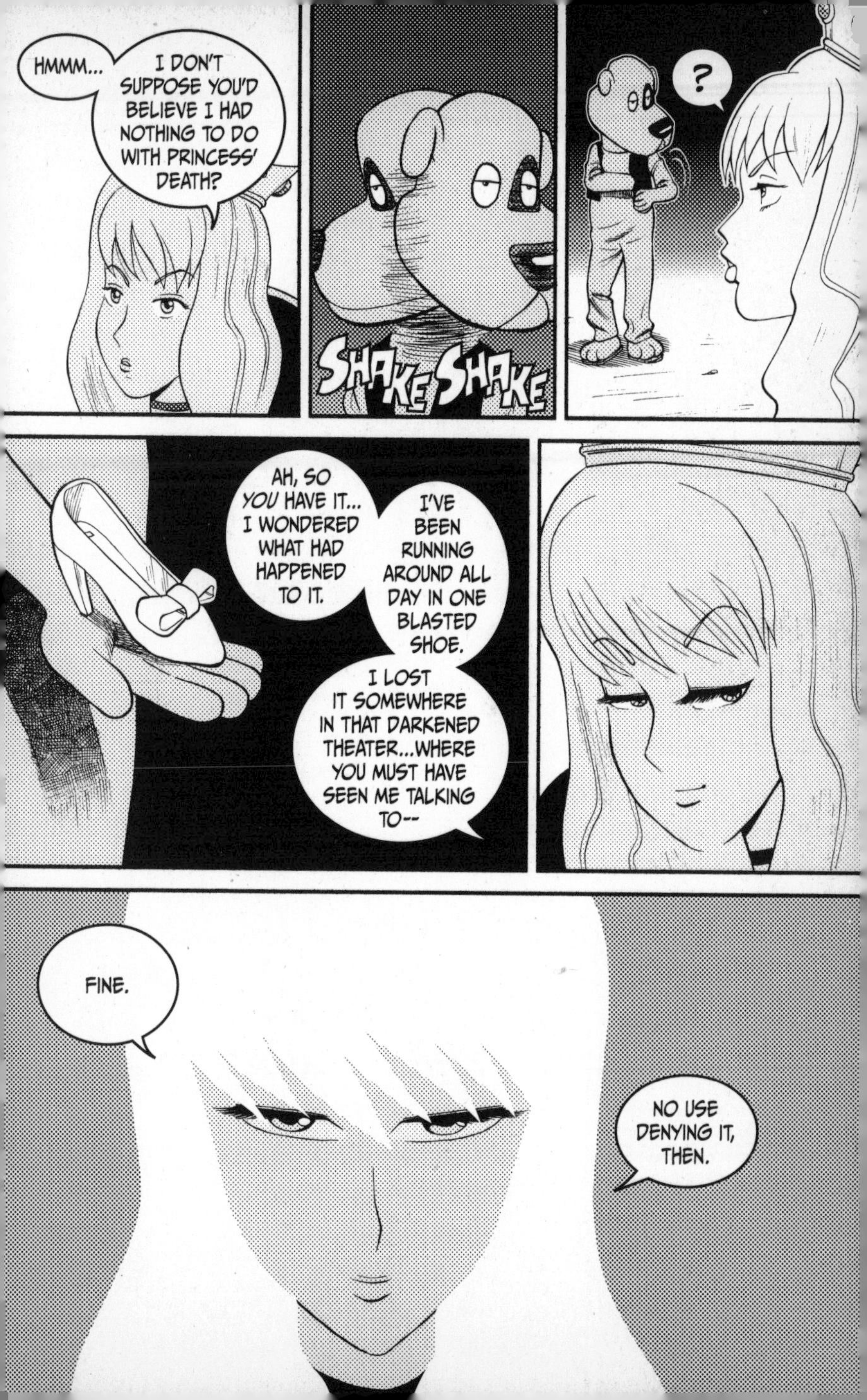
HMMM...
I DON'T SUPPOSE YOU'D BELIEVE I HAD NOTHING TO DO WITH PRINCESS' DEATH?
SHAKE SHAKE
?
AH, SO *YOU* HAVE IT... I WONDERED WHAT HAD HAPPENED TO IT.
I'VE BEEN RUNNING AROUND ALL DAY IN ONE BLASTED SHOE.
I LOST IT SOMEWHERE IN THAT DARKENED THEATER...WHERE YOU MUST HAVE SEEN ME TALKING TO--
FINE.
NO USE DENYING IT, THEN.

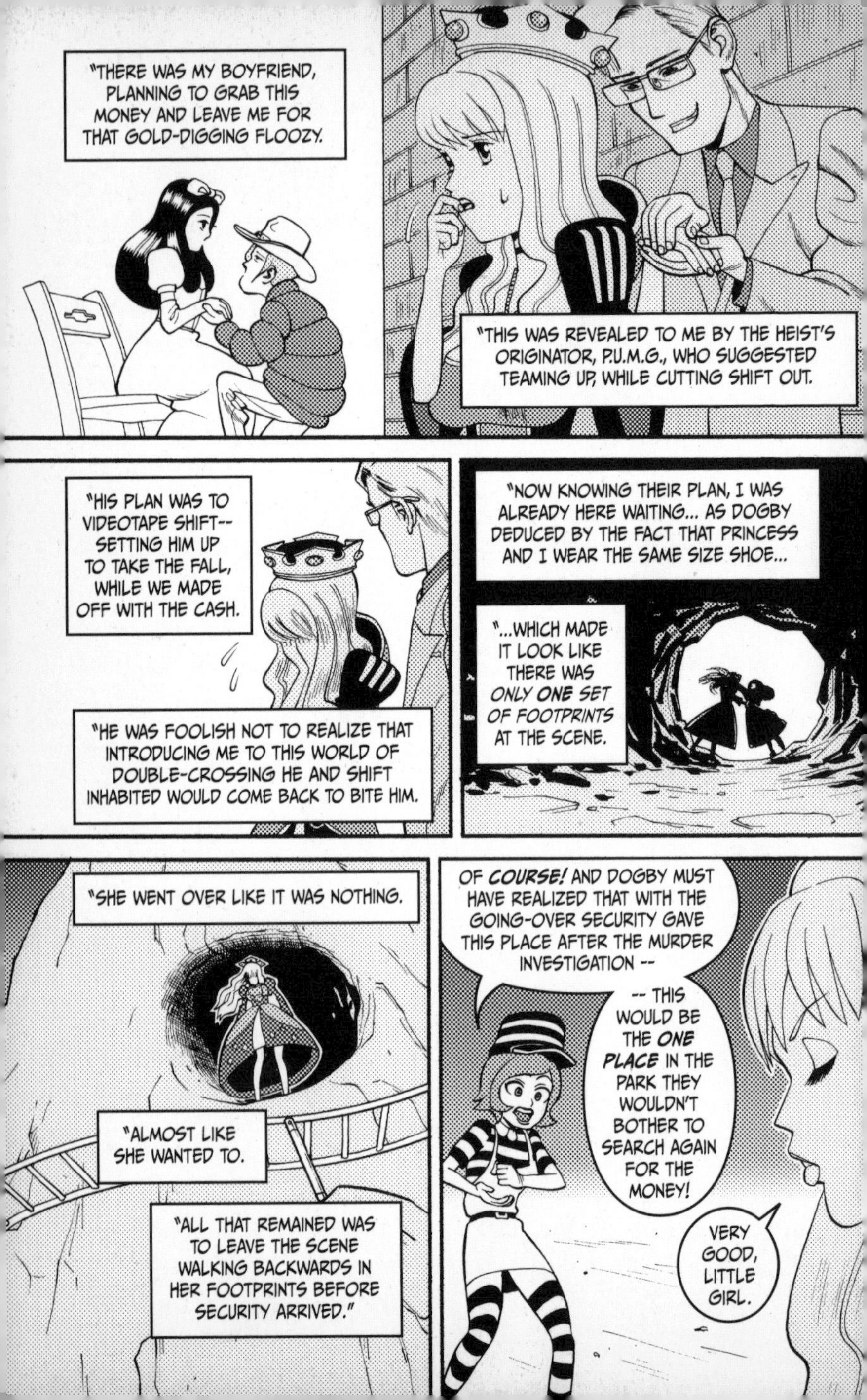
"THERE WAS MY BOYFRIEND, PLANNING TO GRAB THIS MONEY AND LEAVE ME FOR THAT GOLD-DIGGING FLOOZY.
"THIS WAS REVEALED TO ME BY THE HEIST'S ORIGINATOR, P.U.M.G., WHO SUGGESTED TEAMING UP, WHILE CUTTING SHIFT OUT.
"HIS PLAN WAS TO VIDEOTAPE SHIFT-- SETTING HIM UP TO TAKE THE FALL, WHILE WE MADE OFF WITH THE CASH.
"HE WAS FOOLISH NOT TO REALIZE THAT INTRODUCING ME TO THIS WORLD OF DOUBLE-CROSSING HE AND SHIFT INHABITED WOULD COME BACK TO BITE HIM.
"NOW KNOWING THEIR PLAN, I WAS ALREADY HERE WAITING... AS DOGBY DEDUCED BY THE FACT THAT PRINCESS AND I WEAR THE SAME SIZE SHOE...
"...WHICH MADE IT LOOK LIKE THERE WAS *ONLY **ONE** SET OF FOOTPRINTS* AT THE SCENE.
"SHE WENT OVER LIKE IT WAS NOTHING.
"ALMOST LIKE SHE WANTED TO.
"ALL THAT REMAINED WAS TO LEAVE THE SCENE WALKING BACKWARDS IN HER FOOTPRINTS BEFORE SECURITY ARRIVED."
OF ***COURSE!*** AND DOGBY MUST HAVE REALIZED THAT WITH THE GOING-OVER SECURITY GAVE THIS PLACE AFTER THE MURDER INVESTIGATION --
-- THIS WOULD BE THE ***ONE PLACE*** IN THE PARK THEY WOULDN'T BOTHER TO SEARCH AGAIN FOR THE MONEY!
VERY GOOD, LITTLE GIRL.

WHOA! DO THAT AGAIN!

I DON'T WANT TO KILL YOU, DOGBY. YOU'RE LIKE ME -- ABANDONED BY THE ONE YOU SACRIFICED EVERYTHING FOR. WE WERE TOO GOOD FOR THEM... DON'T MAKE ME SHOOT YOU.

YOU COULD COME WITH ME...

WE COULD GO ANYWHERE WITH THIS MONEY. WITH YOU, MAYBE I WOULD REMEMBER AGAIN WHAT IT FELT LIKE TO TRUST SOMEONE.

COME ON, DOGBY -- MAYBE IT ISN'T TOO LATE TO BRING ME BACK TO LIFE.

YOU GIVE YOURSELF AWAY TO THESE PEOPLE WHO TOSS YOU ASIDE WHEN THEY'RE DONE WITH YOU... AREN'T I A THING WORTH SAVING?

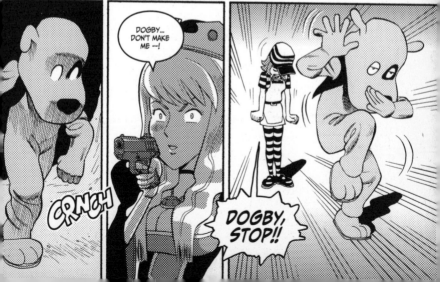

DOGBY... DON'T MAKE ME --!

CRNCH

DOGBY, STOP!!

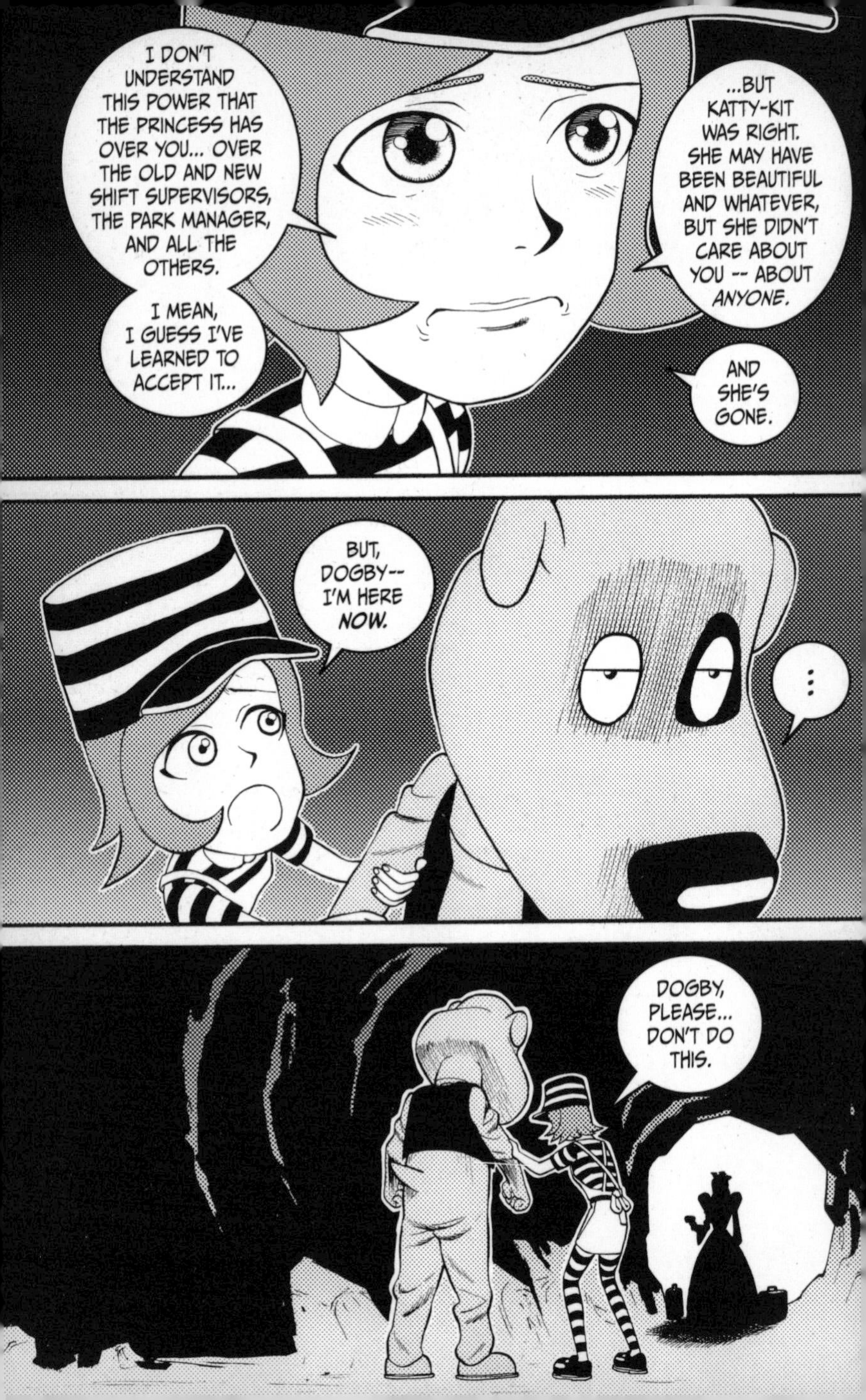
I DON'T UNDERSTAND THIS POWER THAT THE PRINCESS HAS OVER YOU... OVER THE OLD AND NEW SHIFT SUPERVISORS, THE PARK MANAGER, AND ALL THE OTHERS.
I MEAN, I GUESS I'VE LEARNED TO ACCEPT IT...
...BUT KATTY-KIT WAS RIGHT. SHE MAY HAVE BEEN BEAUTIFUL AND WHATEVER, BUT SHE DIDN'T CARE ABOUT YOU -- ABOUT *ANYONE*.
AND SHE'S GONE.
BUT, DOGBY-- I'M HERE *NOW.*
...
DOGBY, PLEASE... DON'T DO THIS.

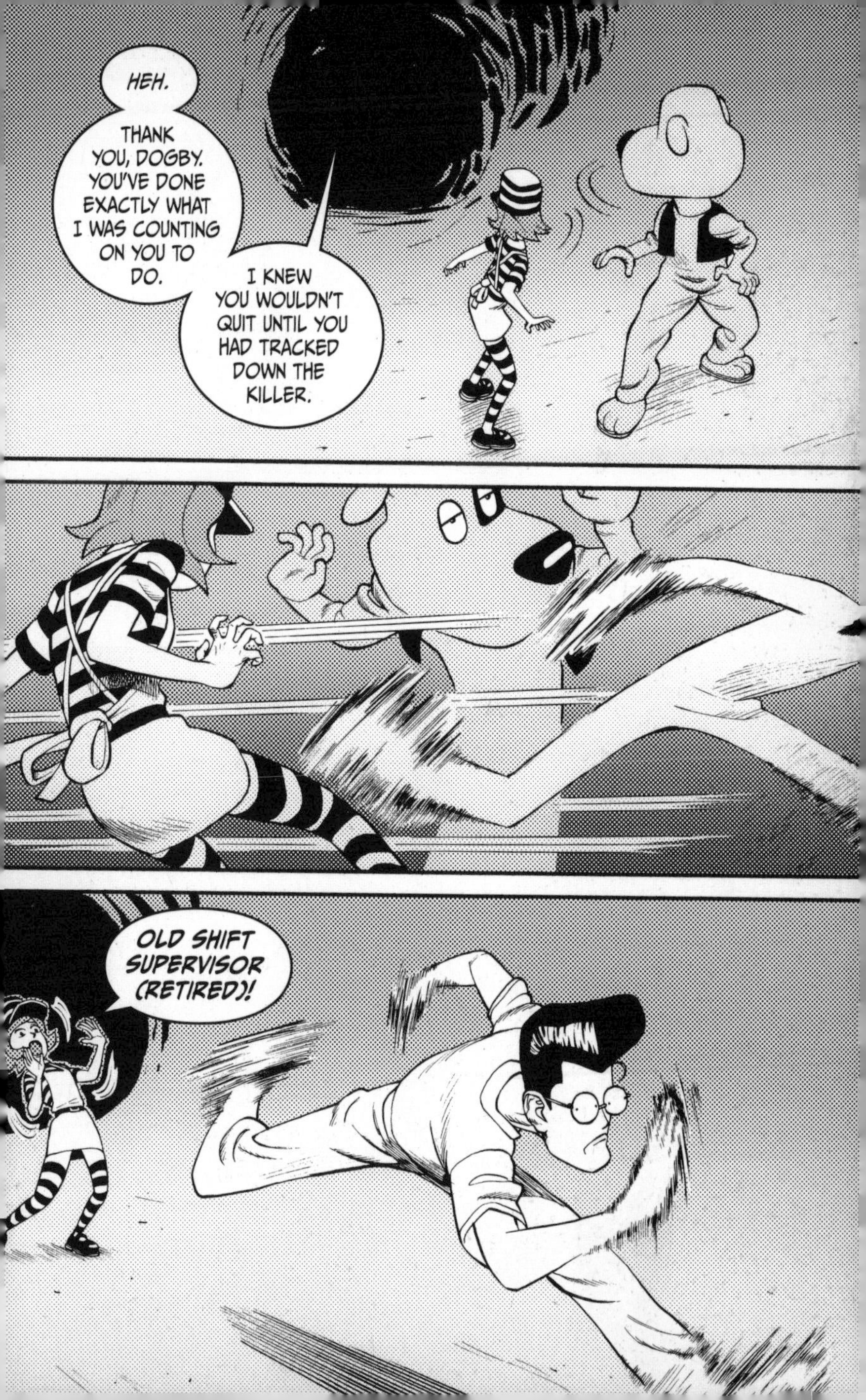
HEH.
THANK YOU, DOGBY. YOU'VE DONE EXACTLY WHAT I WAS COUNTING ON YOU TO DO.
I KNEW YOU WOULDN'T QUIT UNTIL YOU HAD TRACKED DOWN THE KILLER.
OLD SHIFT SUPERVISOR (RETIRED)!

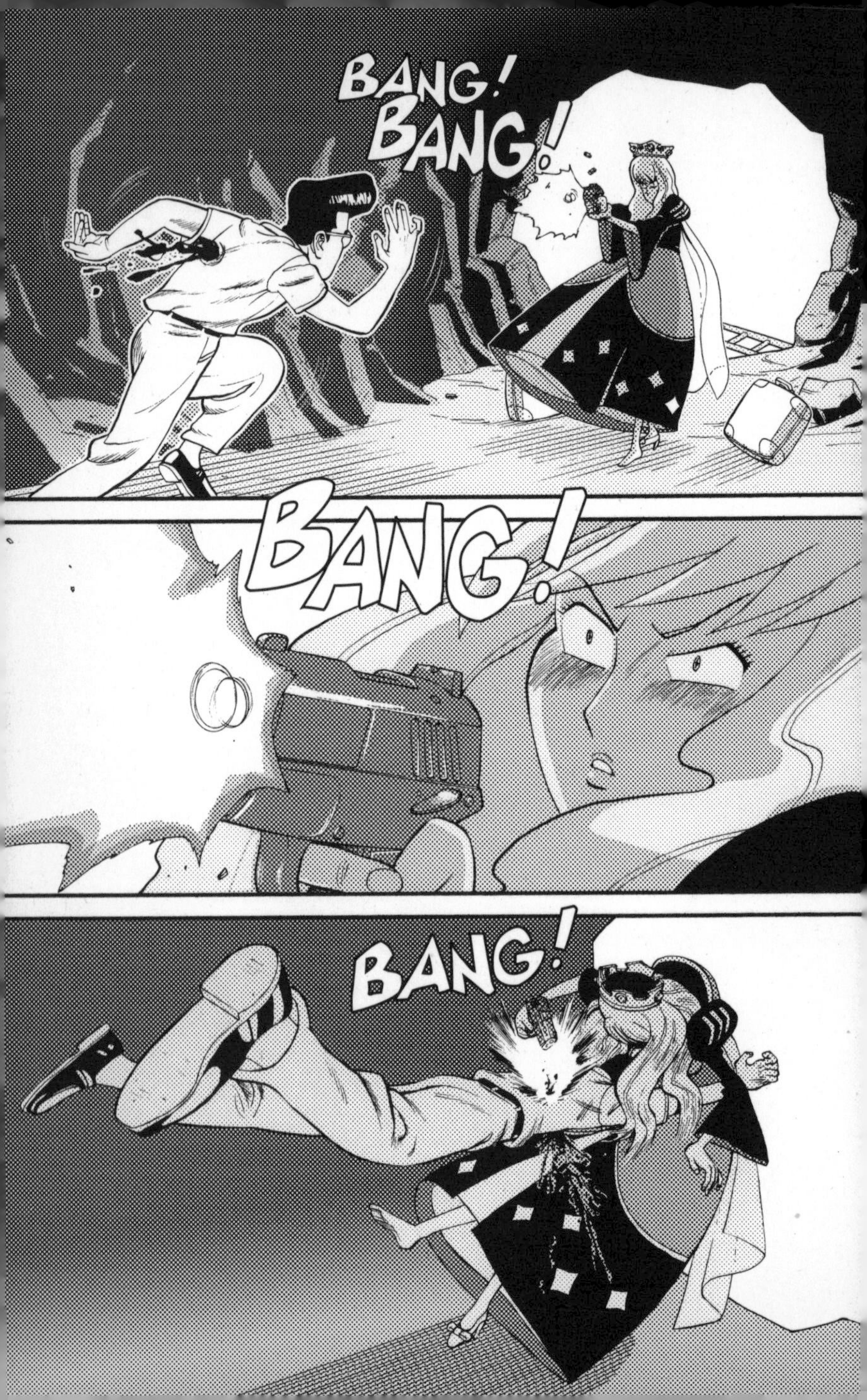
BANG! BANG!
BANG!
BANG!

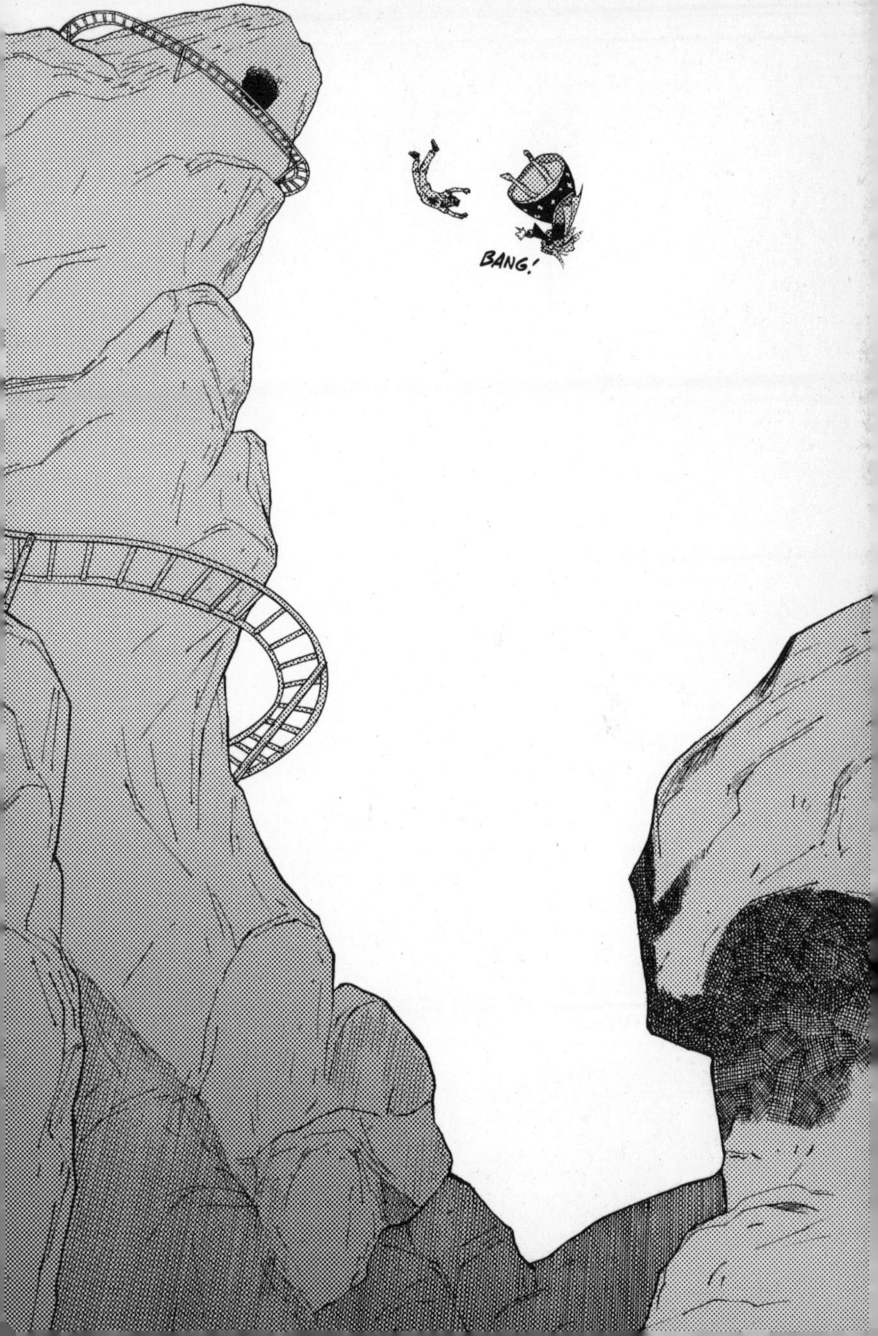
BANG!

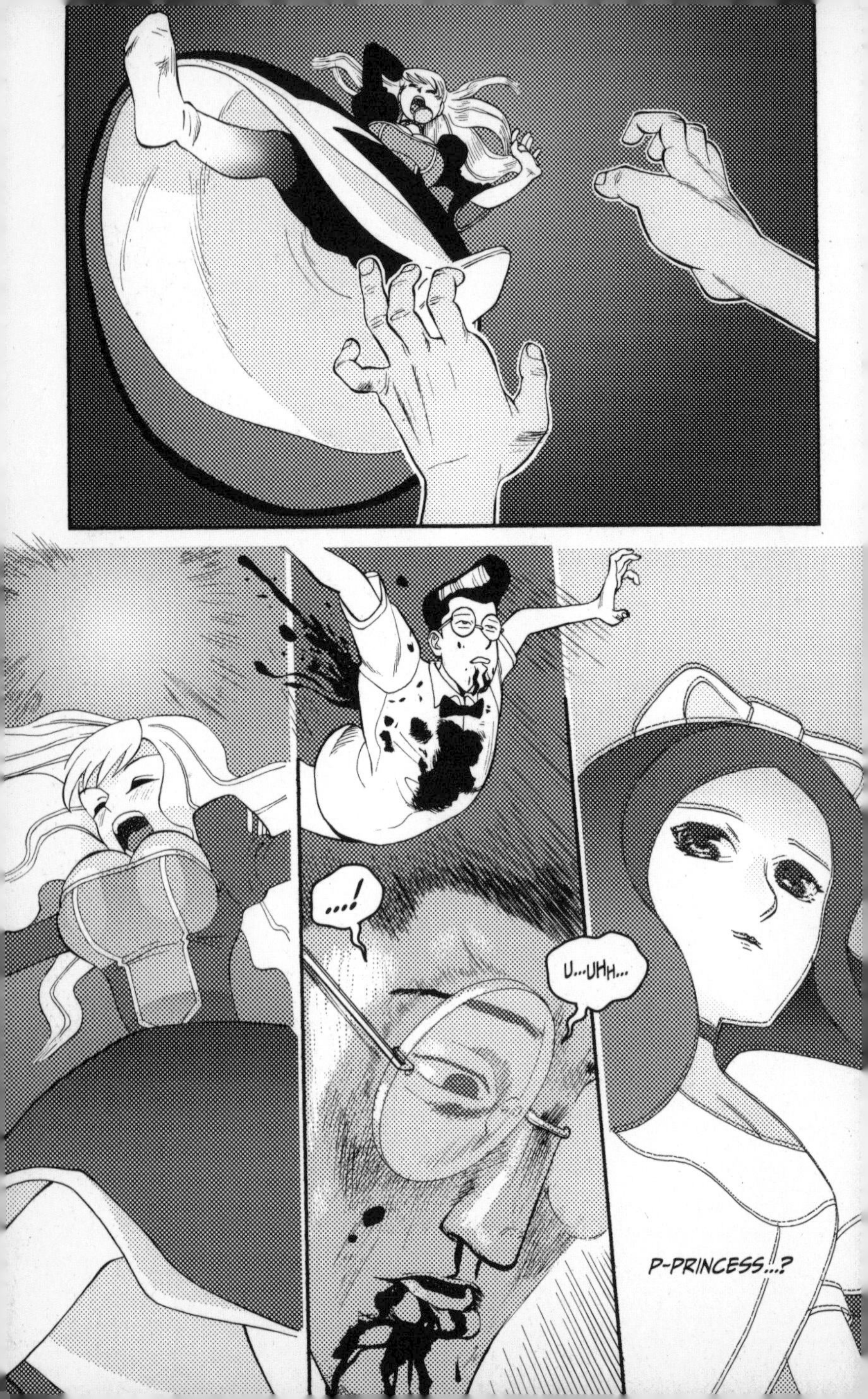
...!
U...UHH...
P-PRINCESS...?

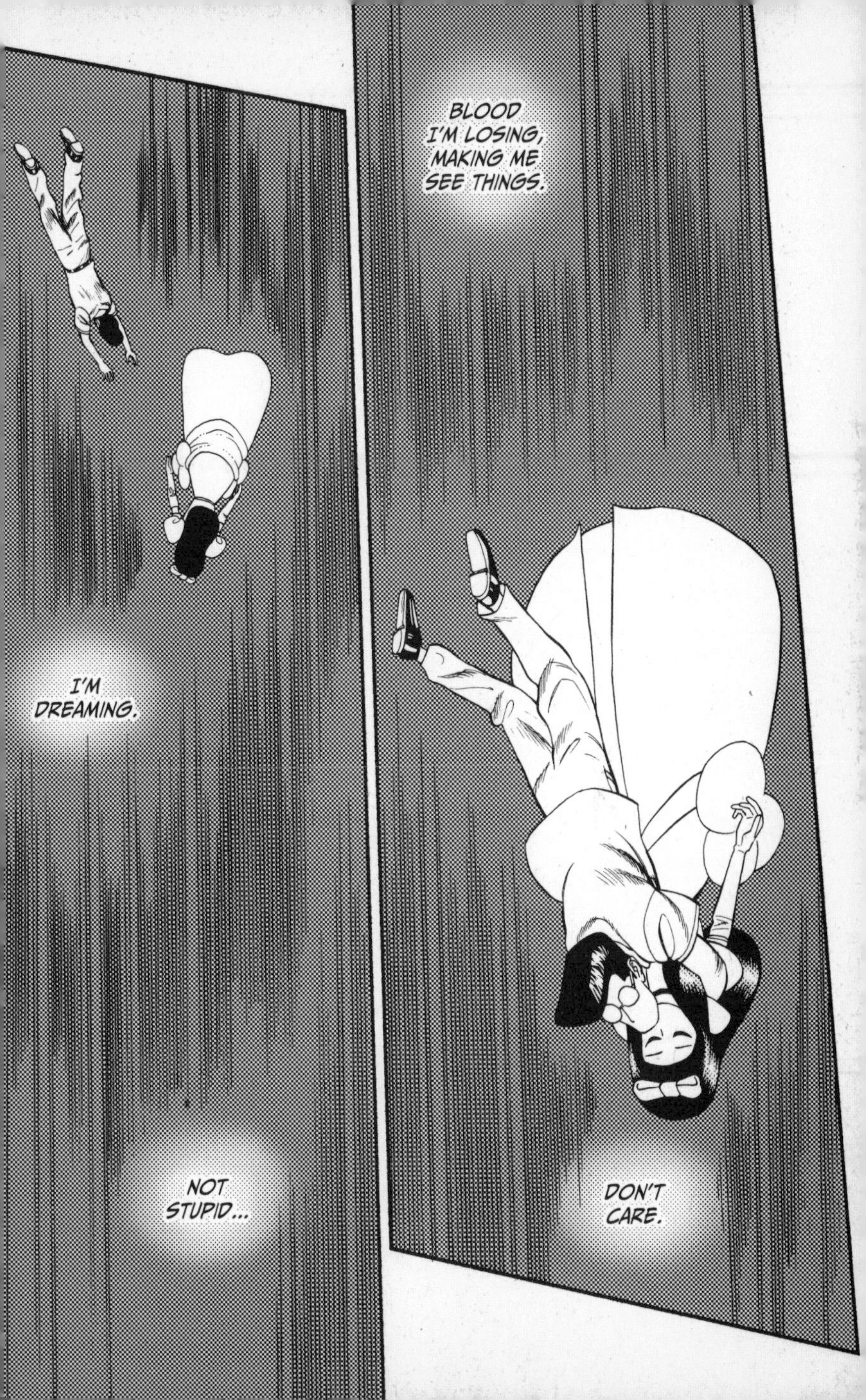
I'M DREAMING.
NOT STUPID...
BLOOD I'M LOSING, MAKING ME SEE THINGS.
DON'T CARE.

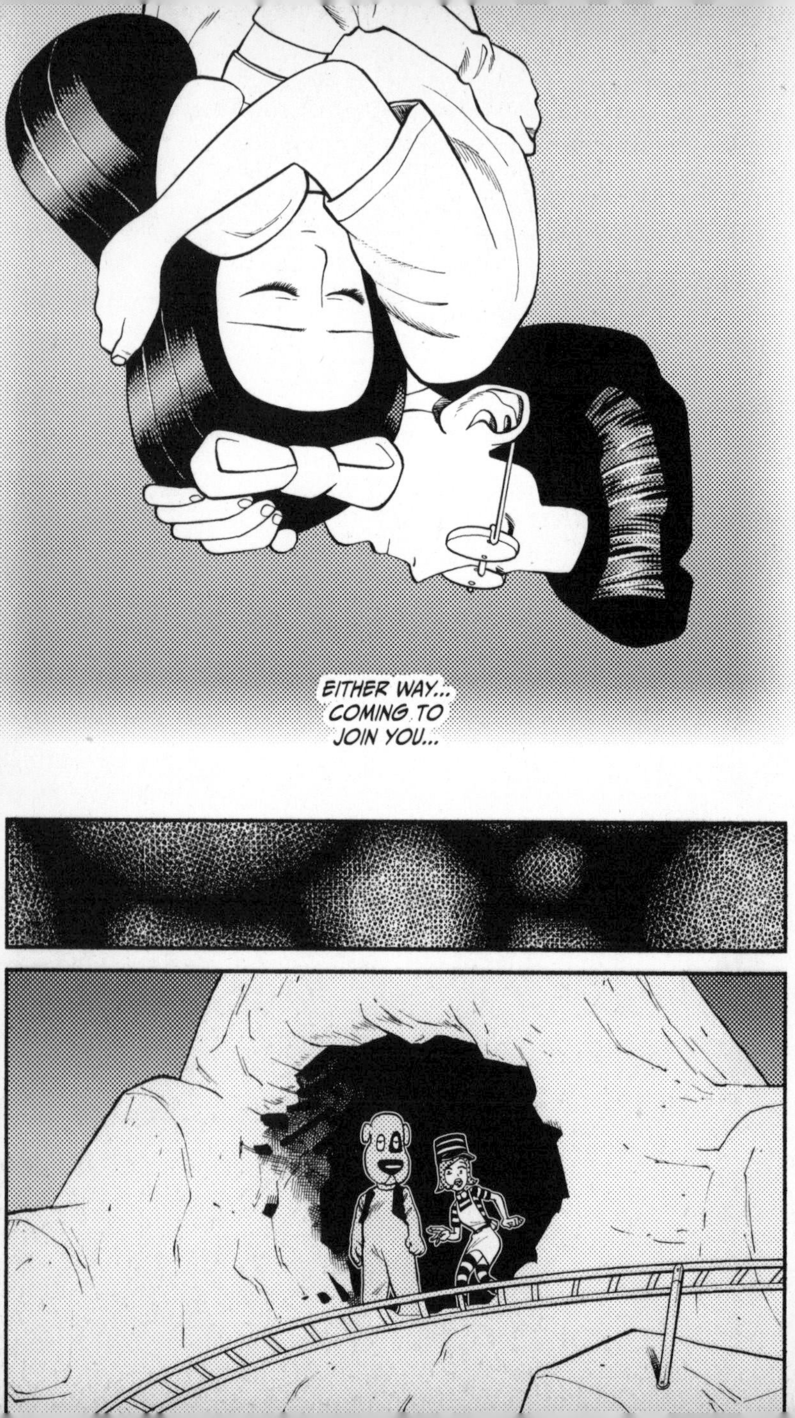
EITHER WAY... COMING TO JOIN YOU...

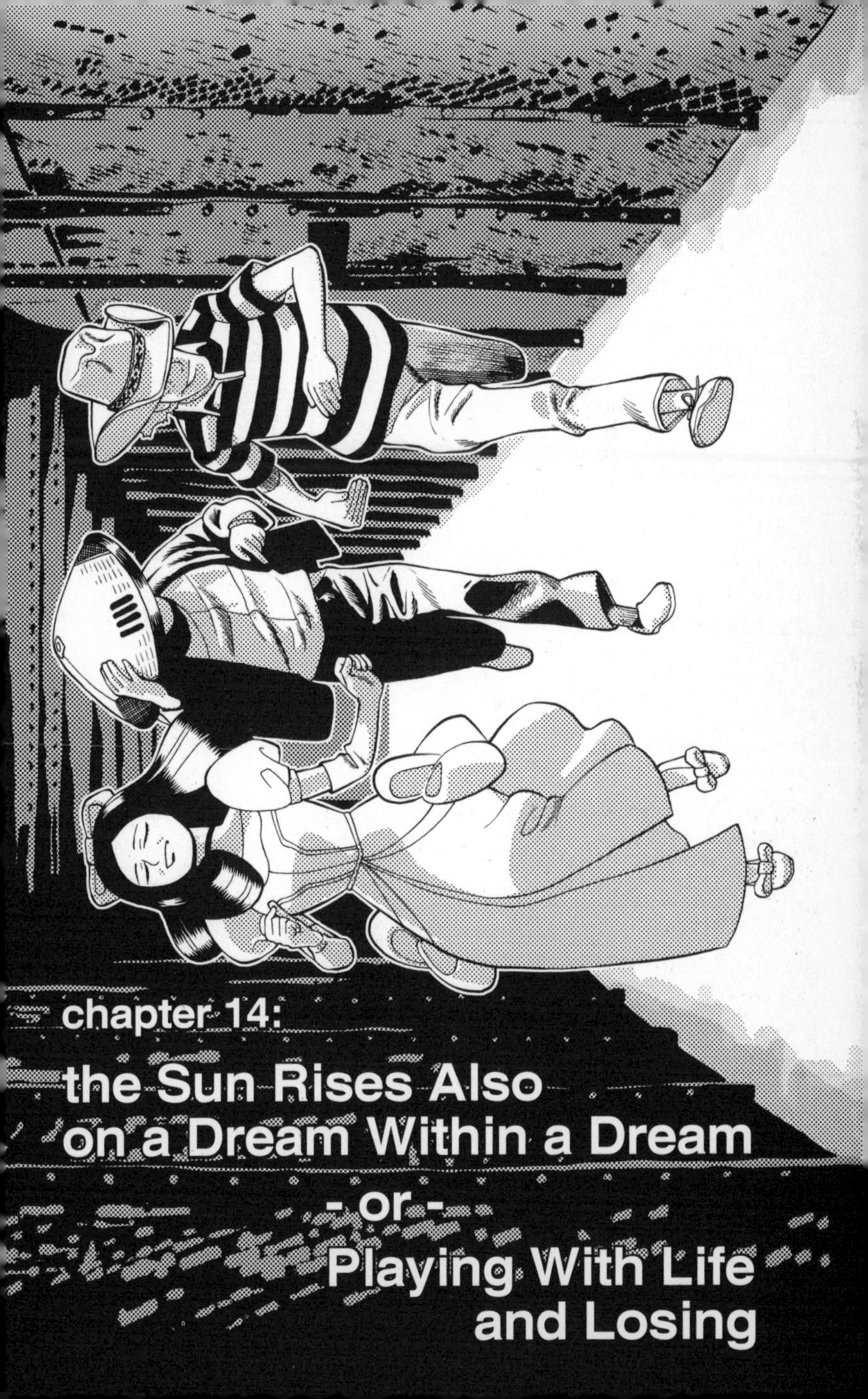

chapter 14:

the Sun Rises Also on a Dream Within a Dream
- or -
Playing With Life and Losing

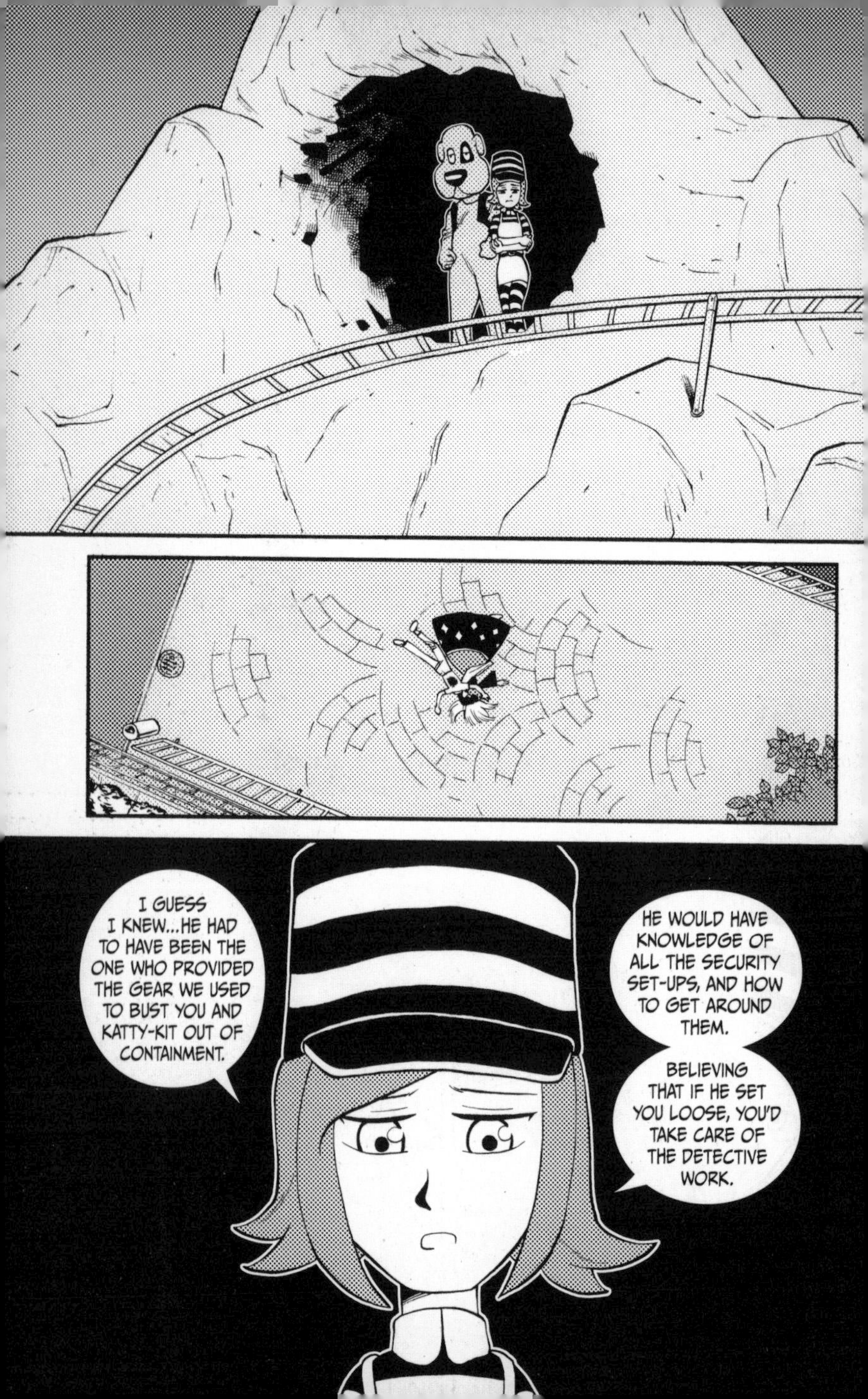
I GUESS I KNEW...HE HAD TO HAVE BEEN THE ONE WHO PROVIDED THE GEAR WE USED TO BUST YOU AND KATTY-KIT OUT OF CONTAINMENT.
HE WOULD HAVE KNOWLEDGE OF ALL THE SECURITY SET-UPS, AND HOW TO GET AROUND THEM.
BELIEVING THAT IF HE SET YOU LOOSE, YOU'D TAKE CARE OF THE DETECTIVE WORK.

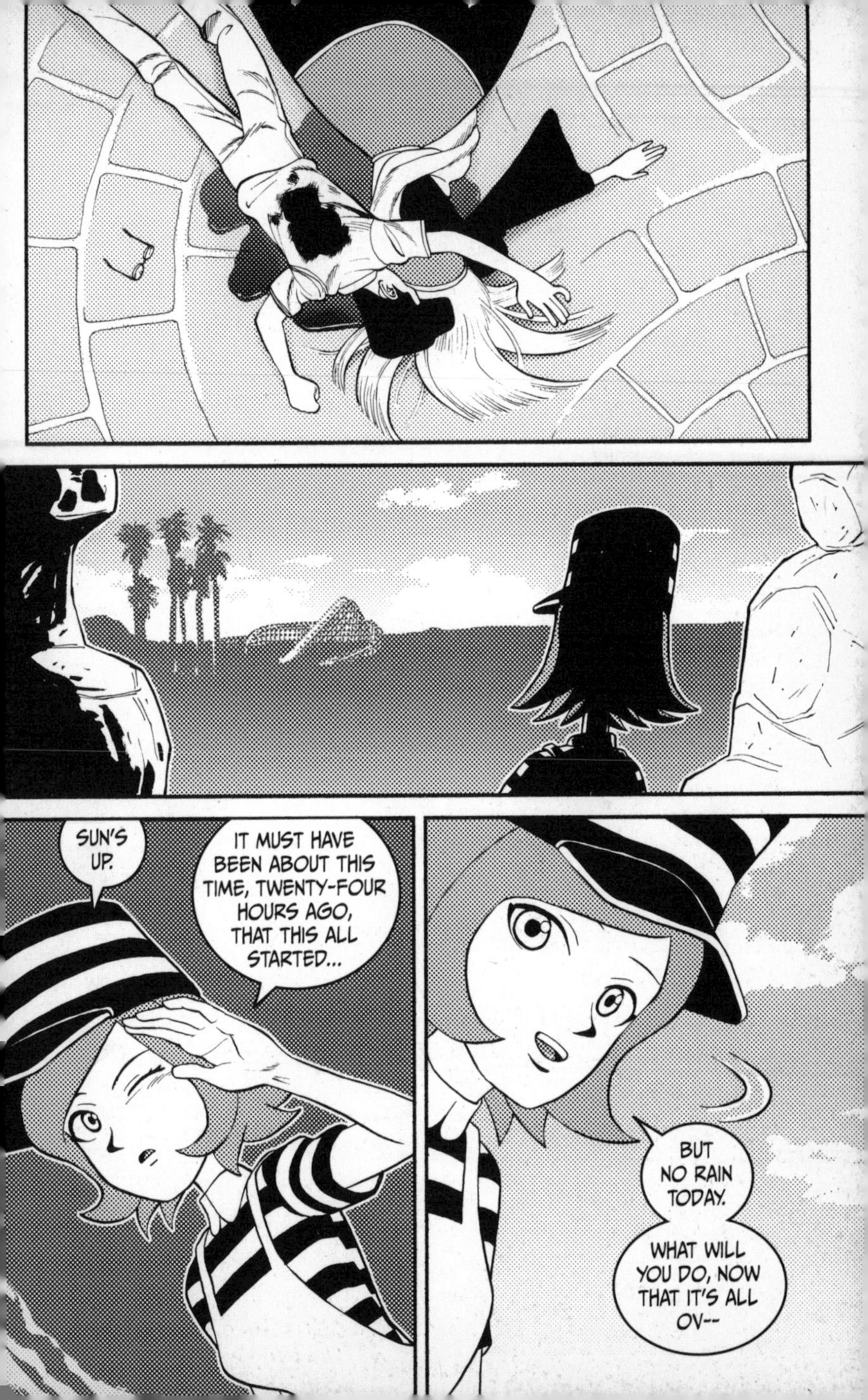
SUN'S UP.
IT MUST HAVE BEEN ABOUT THIS TIME, TWENTY-FOUR HOURS AGO, THAT THIS ALL STARTED...
BUT NO RAIN TODAY.
WHAT WILL YOU DO, NOW THAT IT'S ALL OV--

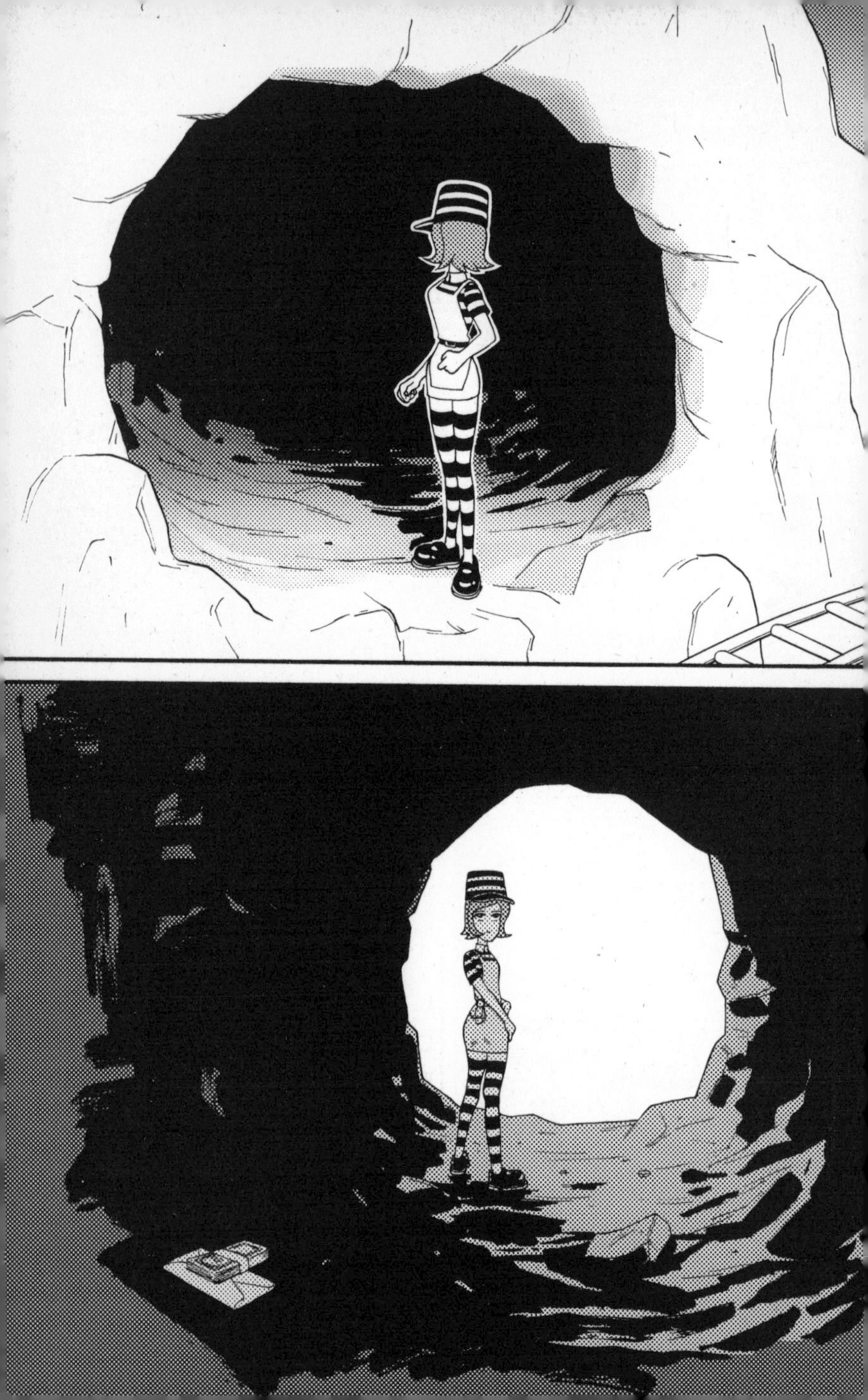

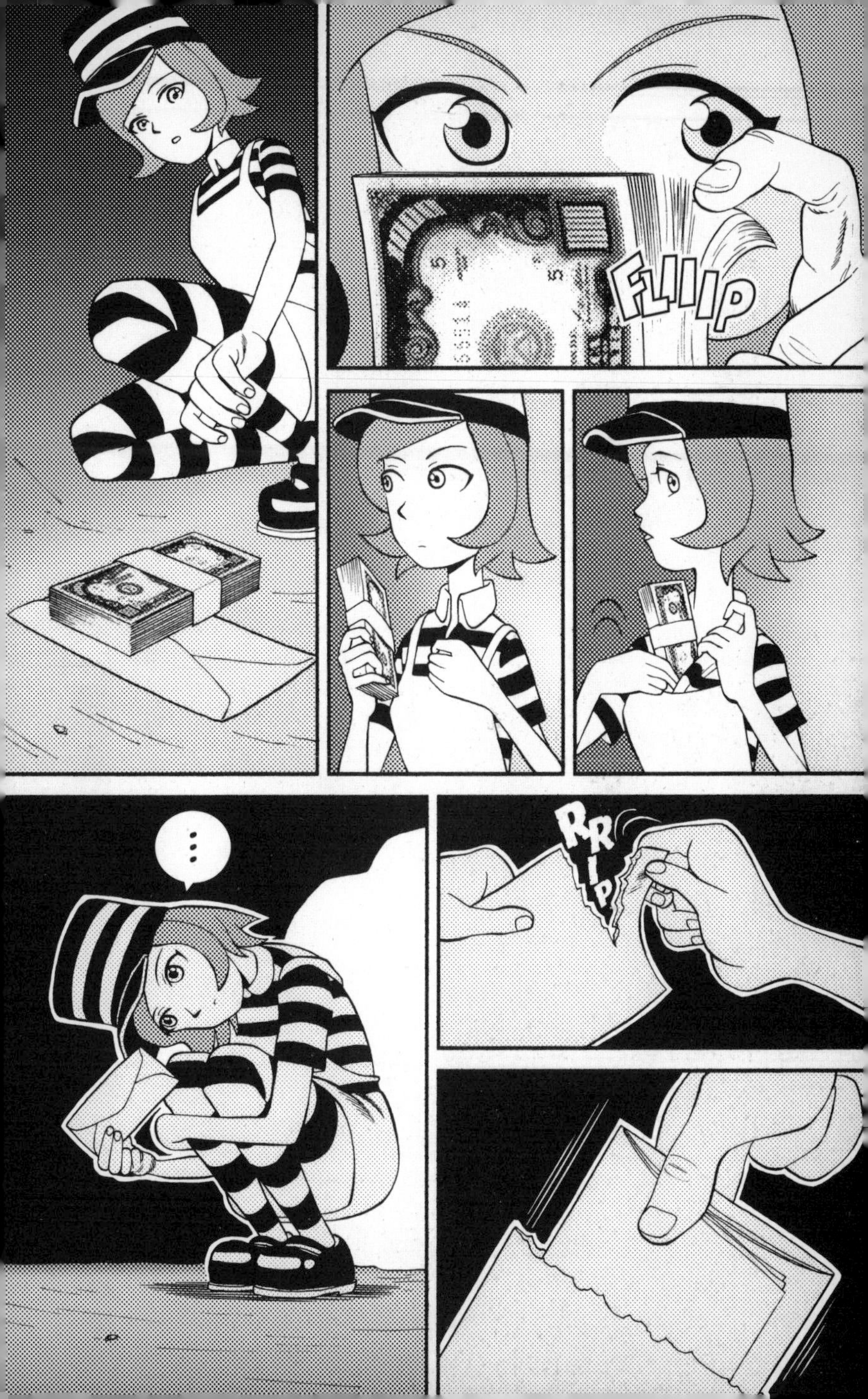
FLIIIP
...
RRIP

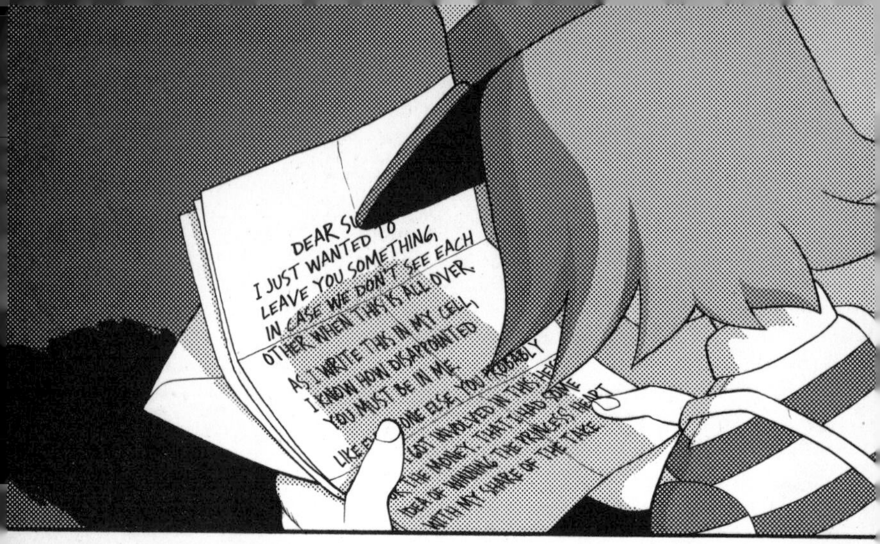
I JUST WANTED TO
LEAVE YOU SOMETHING,
IN CASE WE DON'T SEE EACH
OTHER WHEN THIS IS ALL OVER.
AS I WRITE THIS IN MY CELL,
I KNOW HOW DISAPPOINTED
YOU MUST BE IN ME

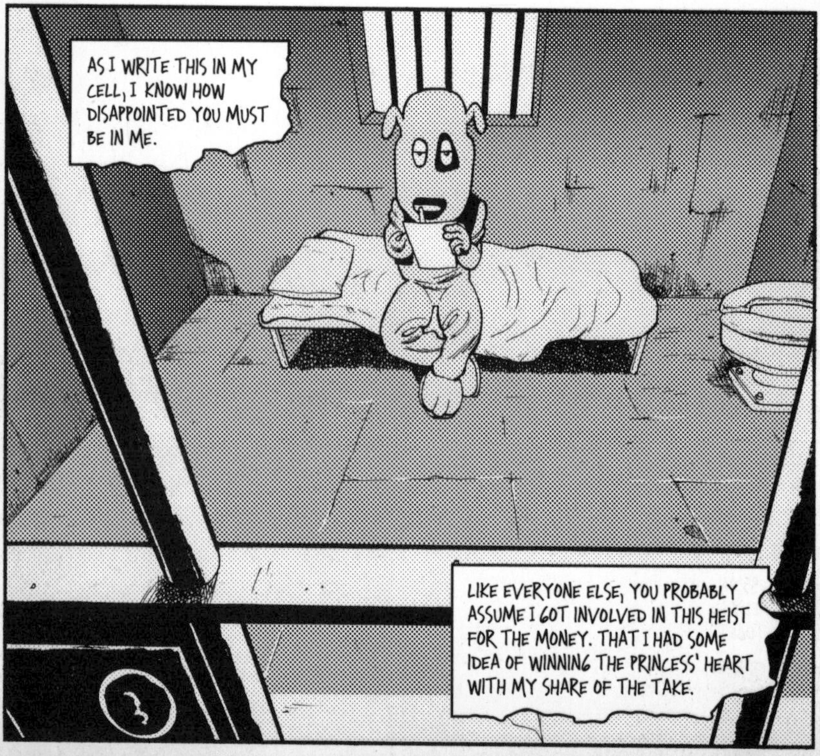
AS I WRITE THIS IN MY CELL, I KNOW HOW DISAPPOINTED YOU MUST BE IN ME.
LIKE EVERYONE ELSE, YOU PROBABLY ASSUME I GOT INVOLVED IN THIS HEIST FOR THE MONEY. THAT I HAD SOME IDEA OF WINNING THE PRINCESS' HEART WITH MY SHARE OF THE TAKE.

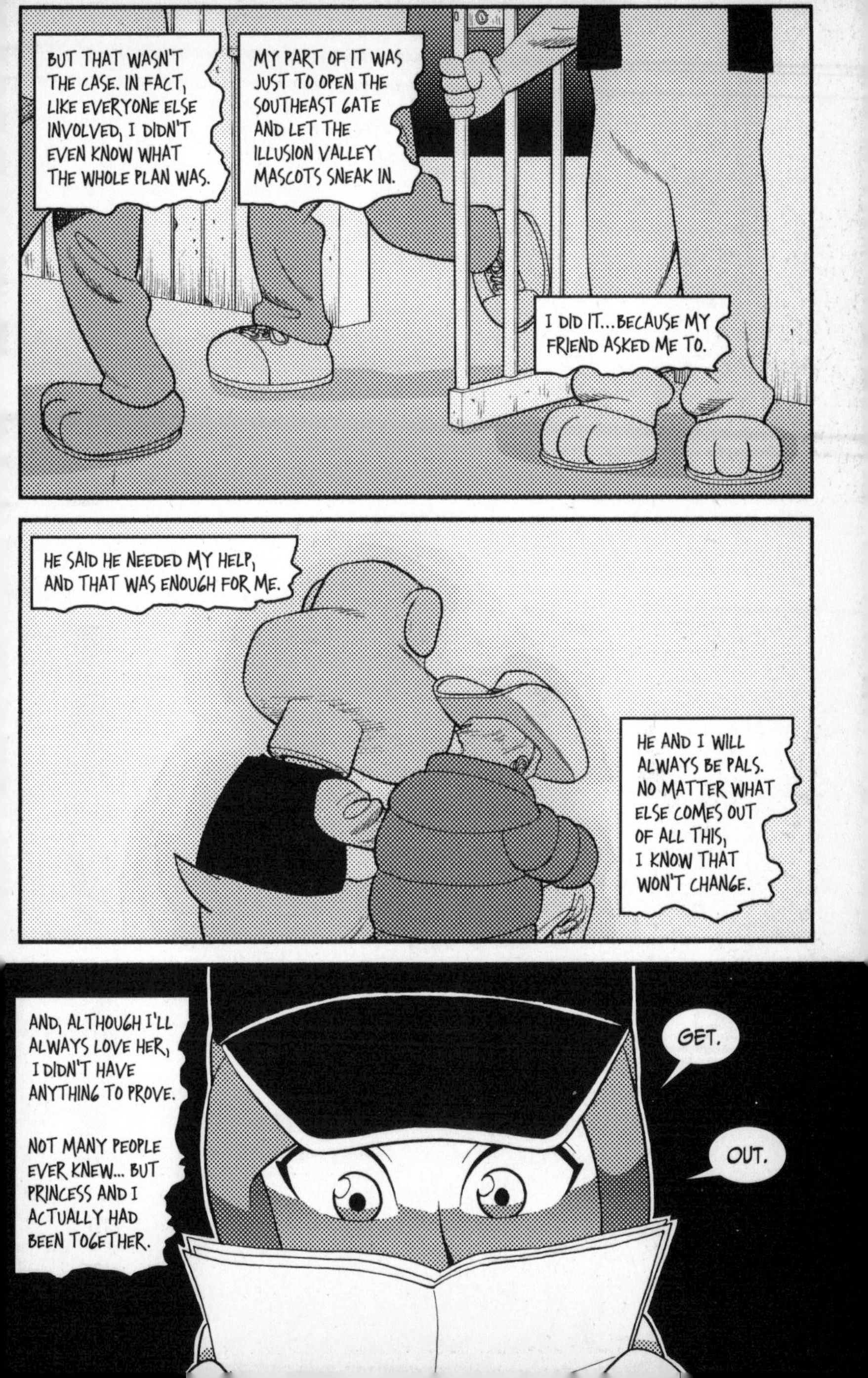
BUT THAT WASN'T THE CASE. IN FACT, LIKE EVERYONE ELSE INVOLVED, I DIDN'T EVEN KNOW WHAT THE WHOLE PLAN WAS.
MY PART OF IT WAS JUST TO OPEN THE SOUTHEAST GATE AND LET THE ILLUSION VALLEY MASCOTS SNEAK IN.
I DID IT...BECAUSE MY FRIEND ASKED ME TO.
HE SAID HE NEEDED MY HELP, AND THAT WAS ENOUGH FOR ME.
HE AND I WILL ALWAYS BE PALS. NO MATTER WHAT ELSE COMES OUT OF ALL THIS, I KNOW THAT WON'T CHANGE.
AND, ALTHOUGH I'LL ALWAYS LOVE HER, I DIDN'T HAVE ANYTHING TO PROVE.
NOT MANY PEOPLE EVER KNEW... BUT PRINCESS AND I ACTUALLY HAD BEEN TOGETHER.
GET.
OUT.

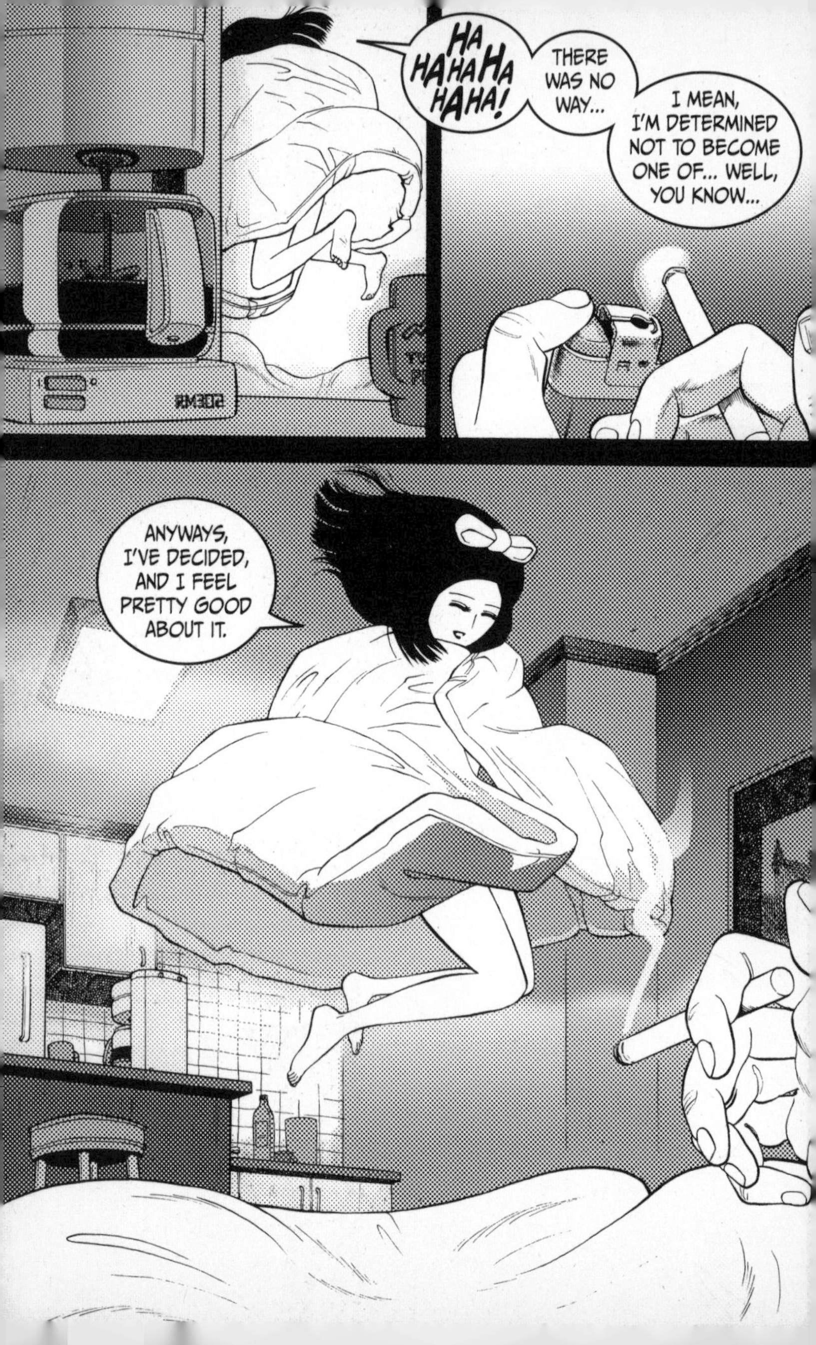
HA HAHAHA HAHA!
THERE WAS NO WAY...
I MEAN, I'M DETERMINED NOT TO BECOME ONE OF... WELL, YOU KNOW...
ANYWAYS, I'VE DECIDED, AND I FEEL PRETTY GOOD ABOUT IT.

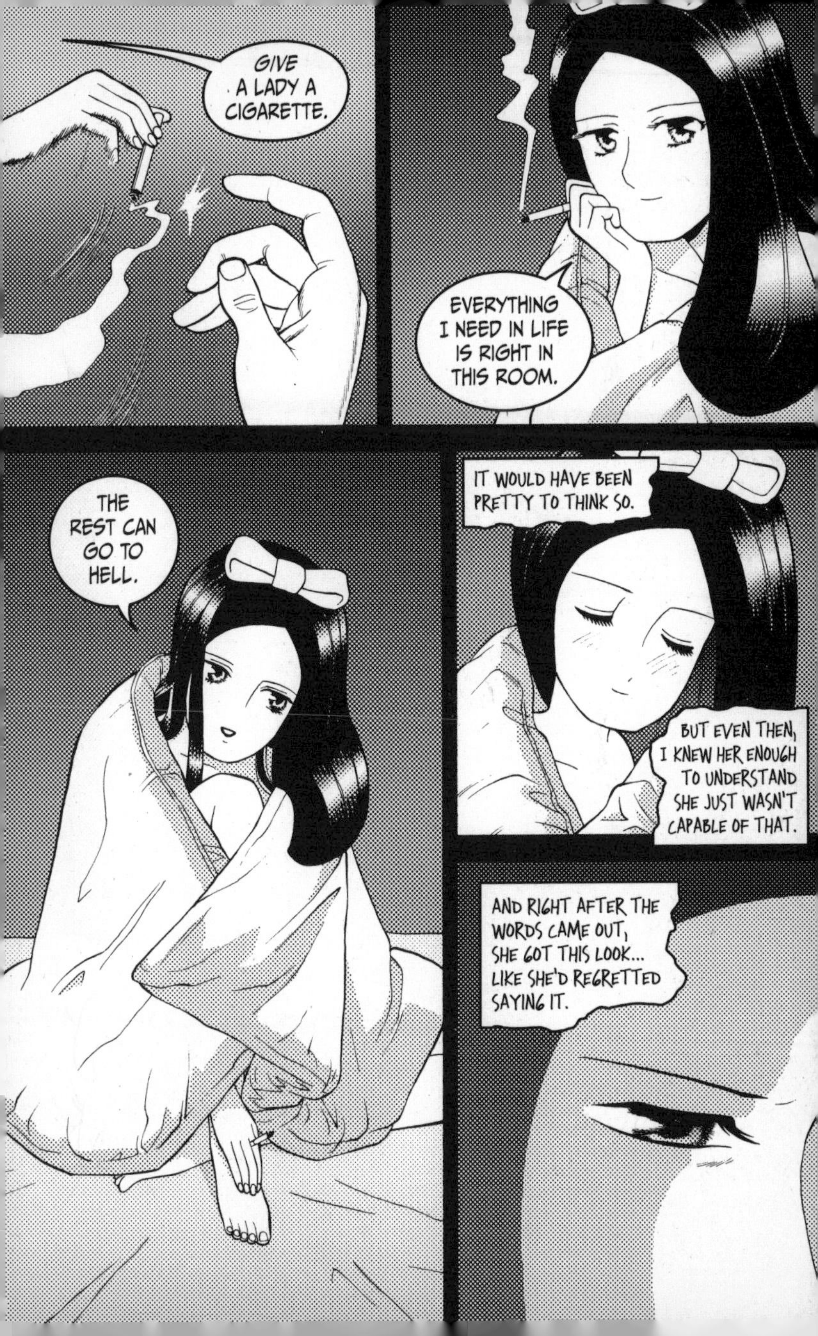
GIVE A LADY A CIGARETTE.
EVERYTHING I NEED IN LIFE IS RIGHT IN THIS ROOM.
THE REST CAN GO TO HELL.
IT WOULD HAVE BEEN PRETTY TO THINK SO.
BUT EVEN THEN, I KNEW HER ENOUGH TO UNDERSTAND SHE JUST WASN'T CAPABLE OF THAT.
AND RIGHT AFTER THE WORDS CAME OUT, SHE GOT THIS LOOK... LIKE SHE'D REGRETTED SAYING IT.

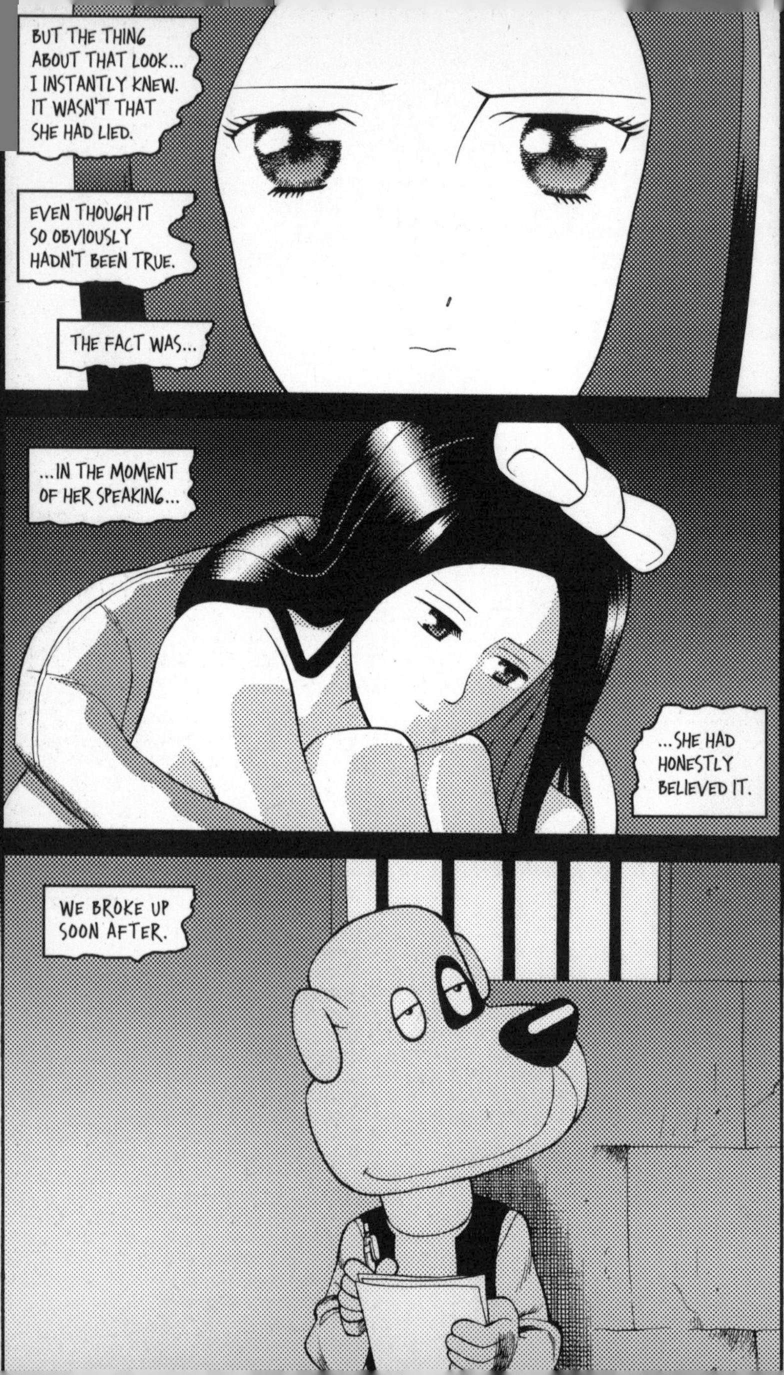
BUT THE THING ABOUT THAT LOOK... I INSTANTLY KNEW. IT WASN'T THAT SHE HAD LIED.
EVEN THOUGH IT SO OBVIOUSLY HADN'T BEEN TRUE.
THE FACT WAS...
...IN THE MOMENT OF HER SPEAKING...
...SHE HAD HONESTLY BELIEVED IT.
WE BROKE UP SOON AFTER.

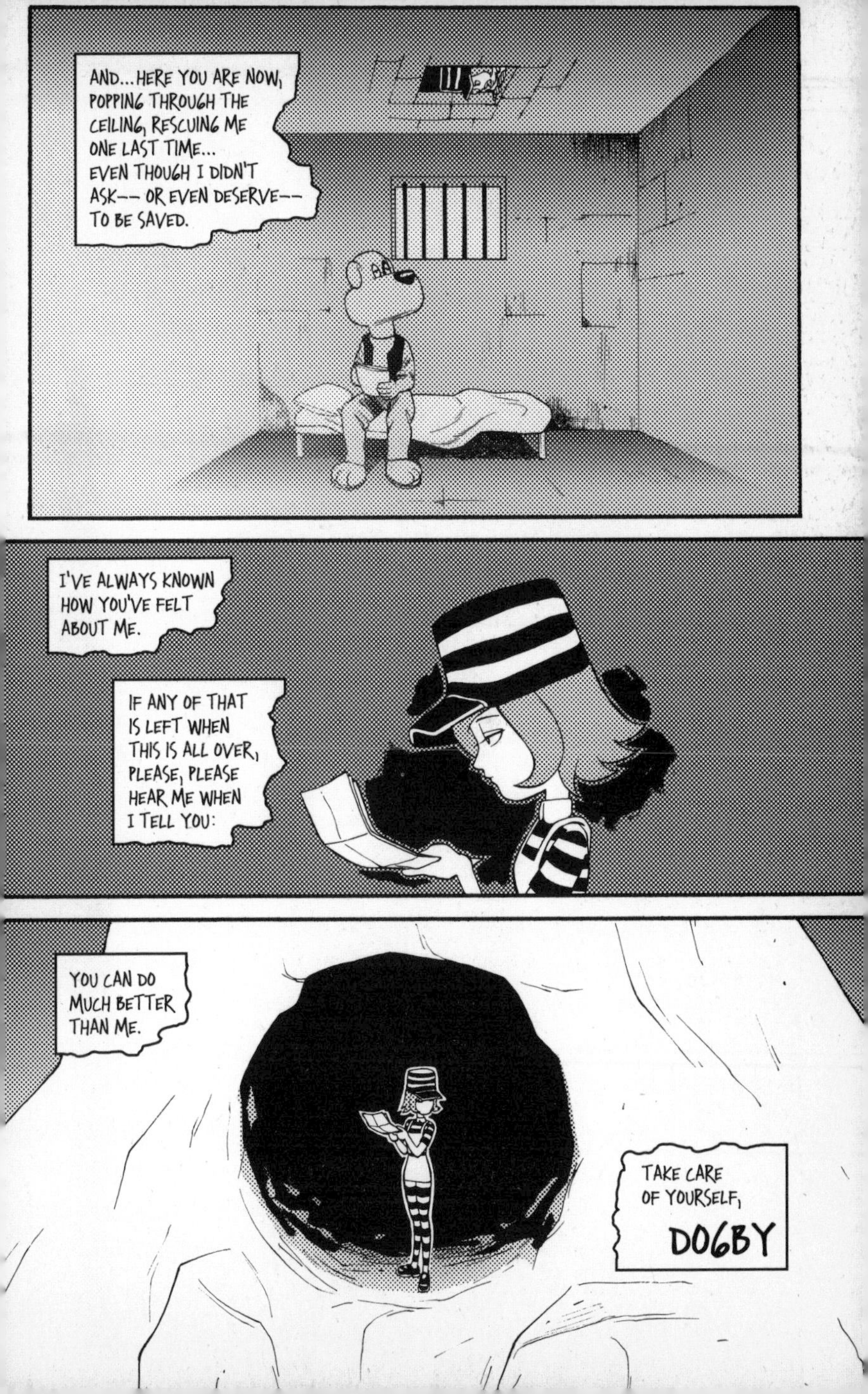
AND...HERE YOU ARE NOW, POPPING THROUGH THE CEILING, RESCUING ME ONE LAST TIME... EVEN THOUGH I DIDN'T ASK-- OR EVEN DESERVE-- TO BE SAVED.
I'VE ALWAYS KNOWN HOW YOU'VE FELT ABOUT ME.
IF ANY OF THAT IS LEFT WHEN THIS IS ALL OVER, PLEASE, PLEASE HEAR ME WHEN I TELL YOU:
YOU CAN DO MUCH BETTER THAN ME.
TAKE CARE OF YOURSELF,
DOGBY

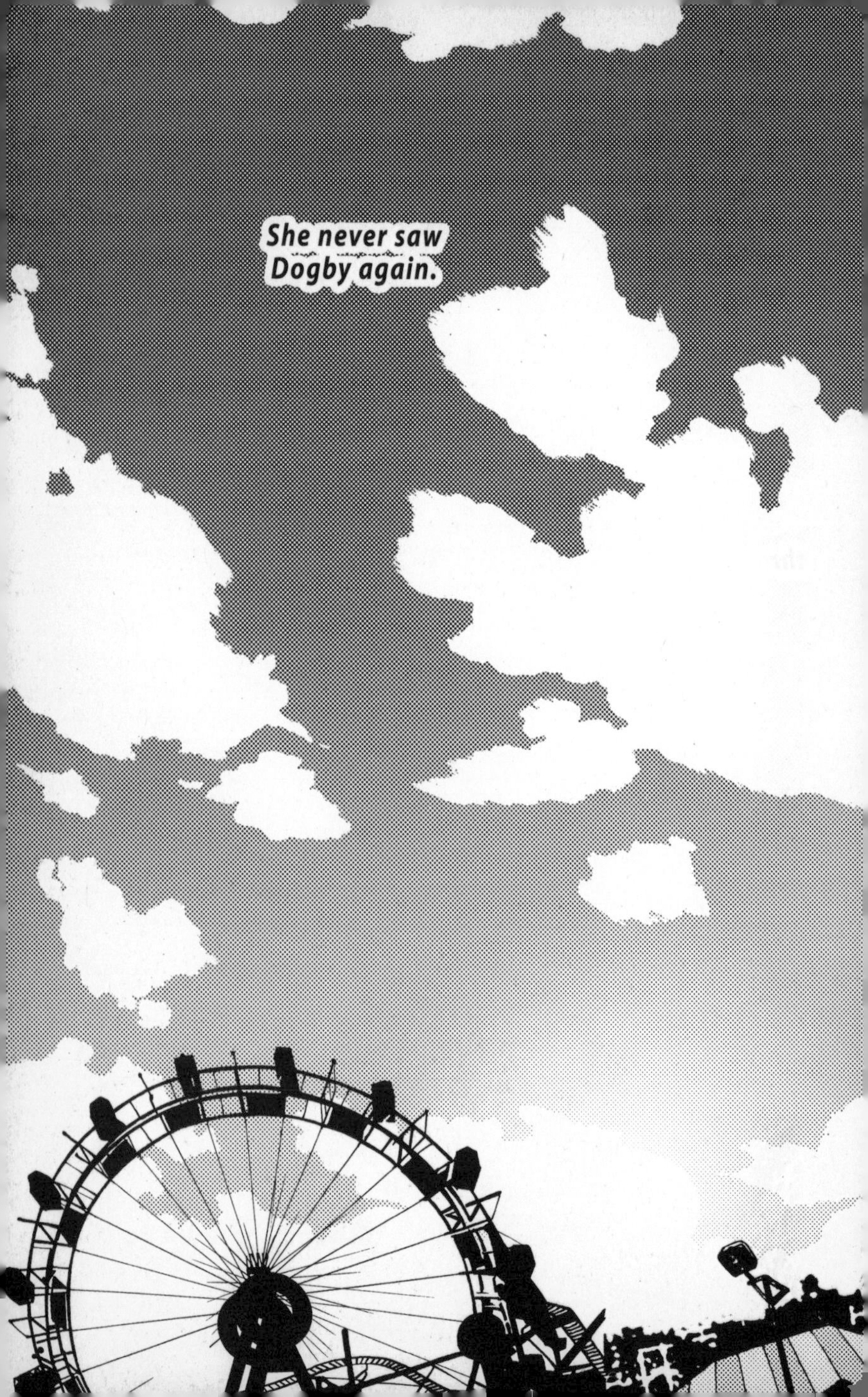
She never saw Dogby again.

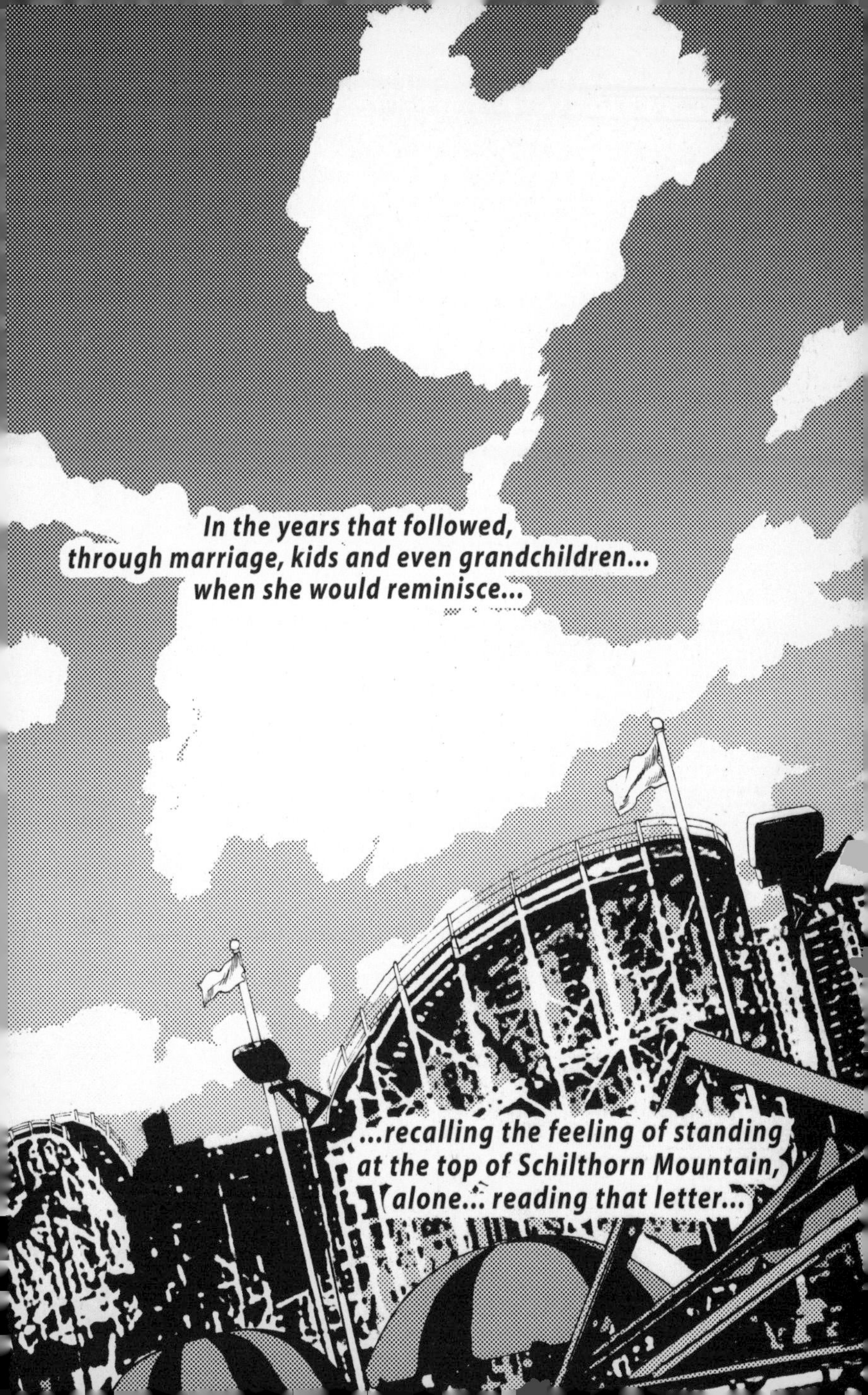
In the years that followed, through marriage, kids and even grandchildren... when she would reminisce...
...recalling the feeling of standing at the top of Schilthorn Mountain, alone... reading that letter...

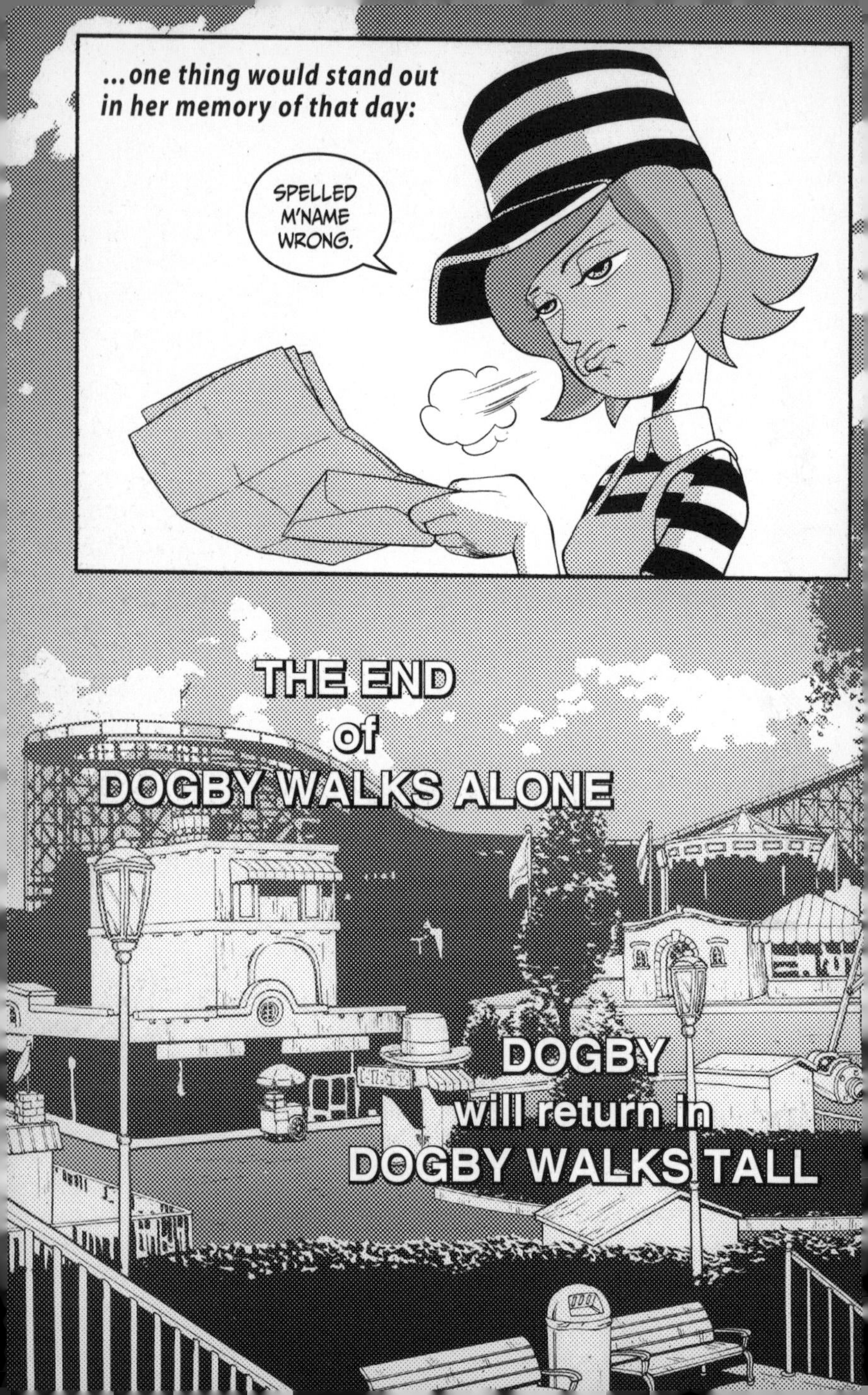
...one thing would stand out in her memory of that day:
SPELLED M'NAME WRONG.
THE END of DOGBY WALKS ALONE
DOGBY will return in DOGBY WALKS TALL

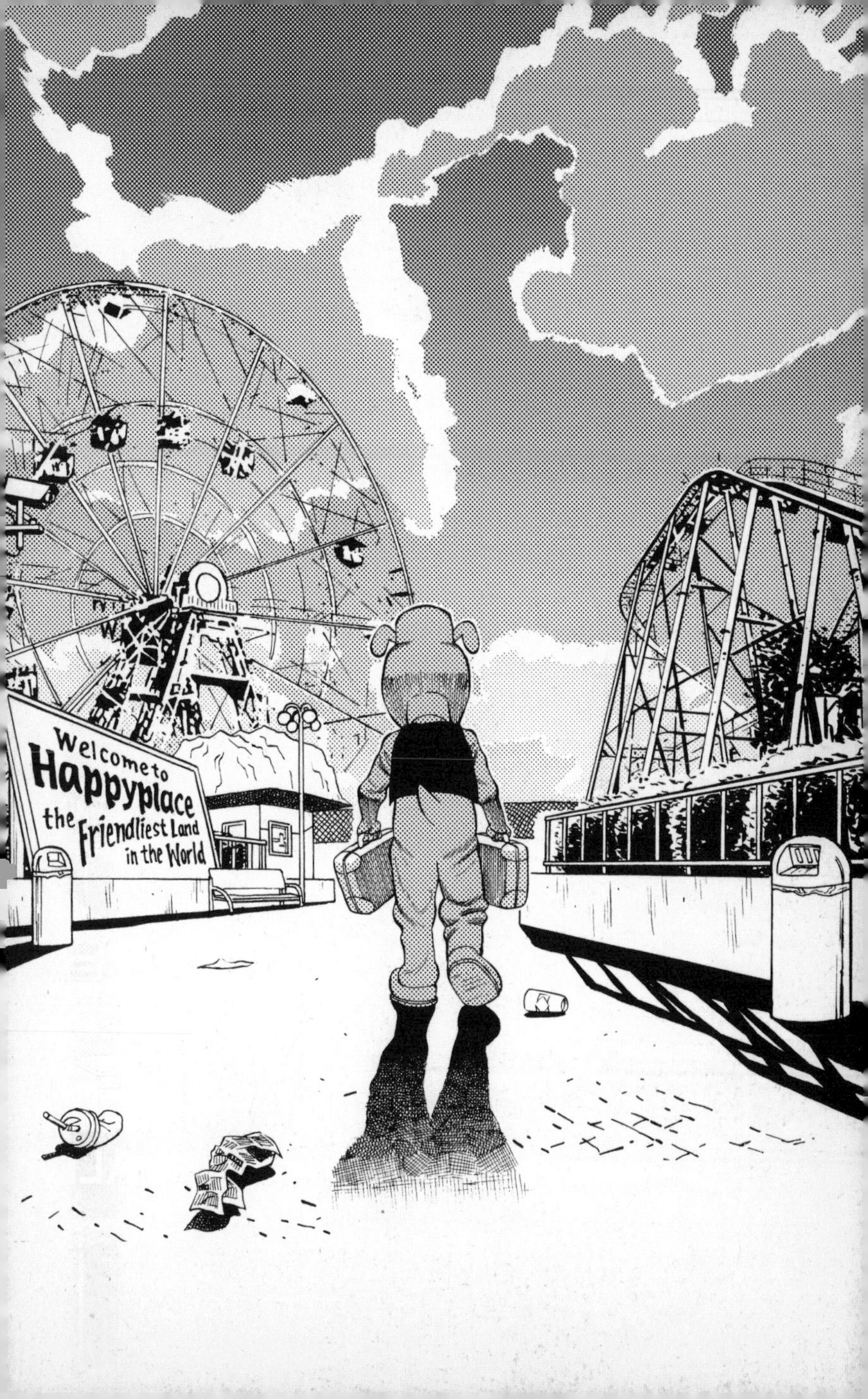
Welcome to
Happyplace
the Friendliest Land
in the World

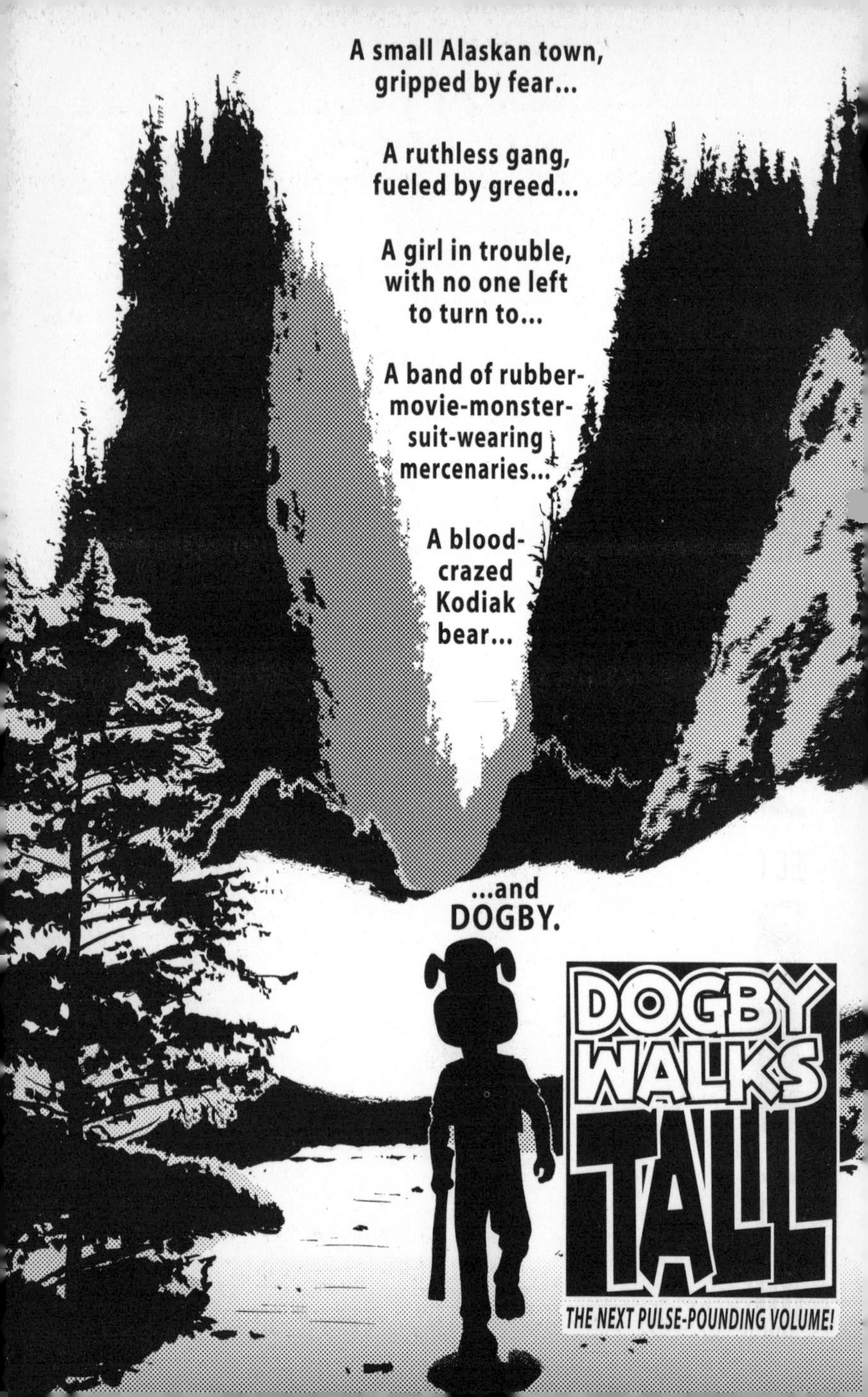
A small Alaskan town, gripped by fear...
A ruthless gang, fueled by greed...
A girl in trouble, with no one left to turn to...
A band of rubber-movie-monster-suit-wearing mercenaries...
A blood-crazed Kodiak bear...
...and DOGBY.
DOGBY WALKS TALL
THE NEXT PULSE-POUNDING VOLUME!

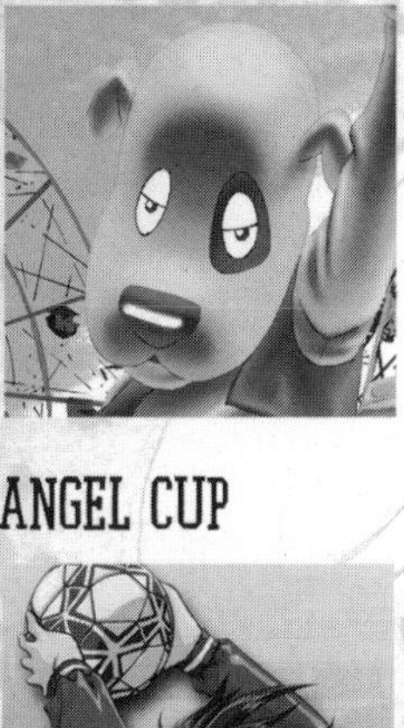

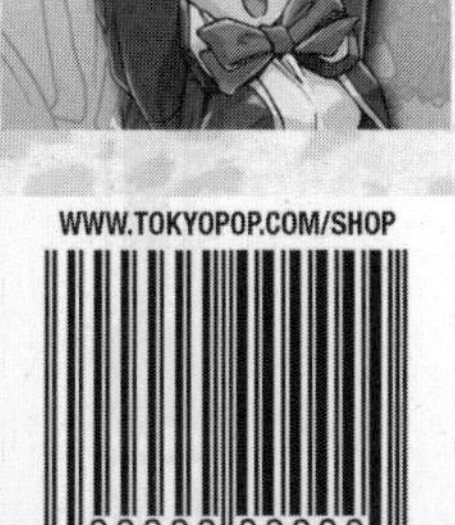

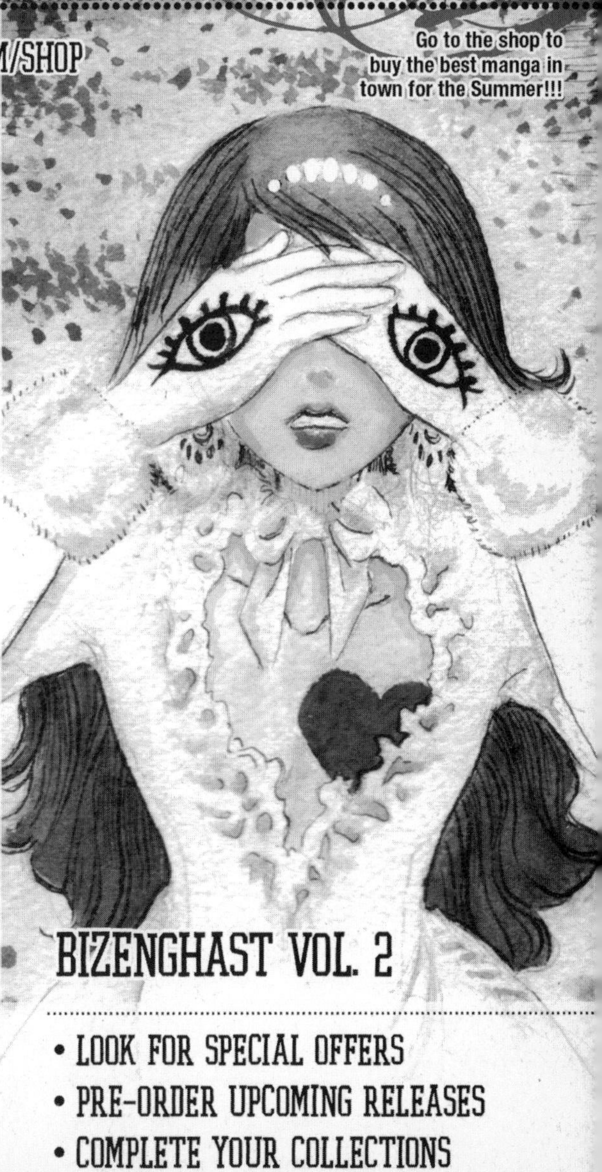

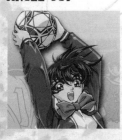

DRAMACON™

Sometimes even two's a crowd.

When Christie settles in the Artist Alley of her first-ever anime convention, she only sees it as an opportunity to promote the comic she has started with her boyfriend. But conventions are never what you expect, and soon a whirlwind of events sweeps Christie off her feet and changes her life. Who is the mysterious cosplayer who won't even take off his sunglasses indoors? What do you do when you fall in love with a guy who is going to be miles away from you in just a couple of days?

CREATED BY SVETLANA CHMAKOVA!
"YOU CAN'T AVOID FALLING UNDER ITS CHARM." -IGN.COM

READ AN ENTIRE CHAPTER ONLINE FOR FREE:
WWW.TOKYOPOP.COM/MANGAONLINE

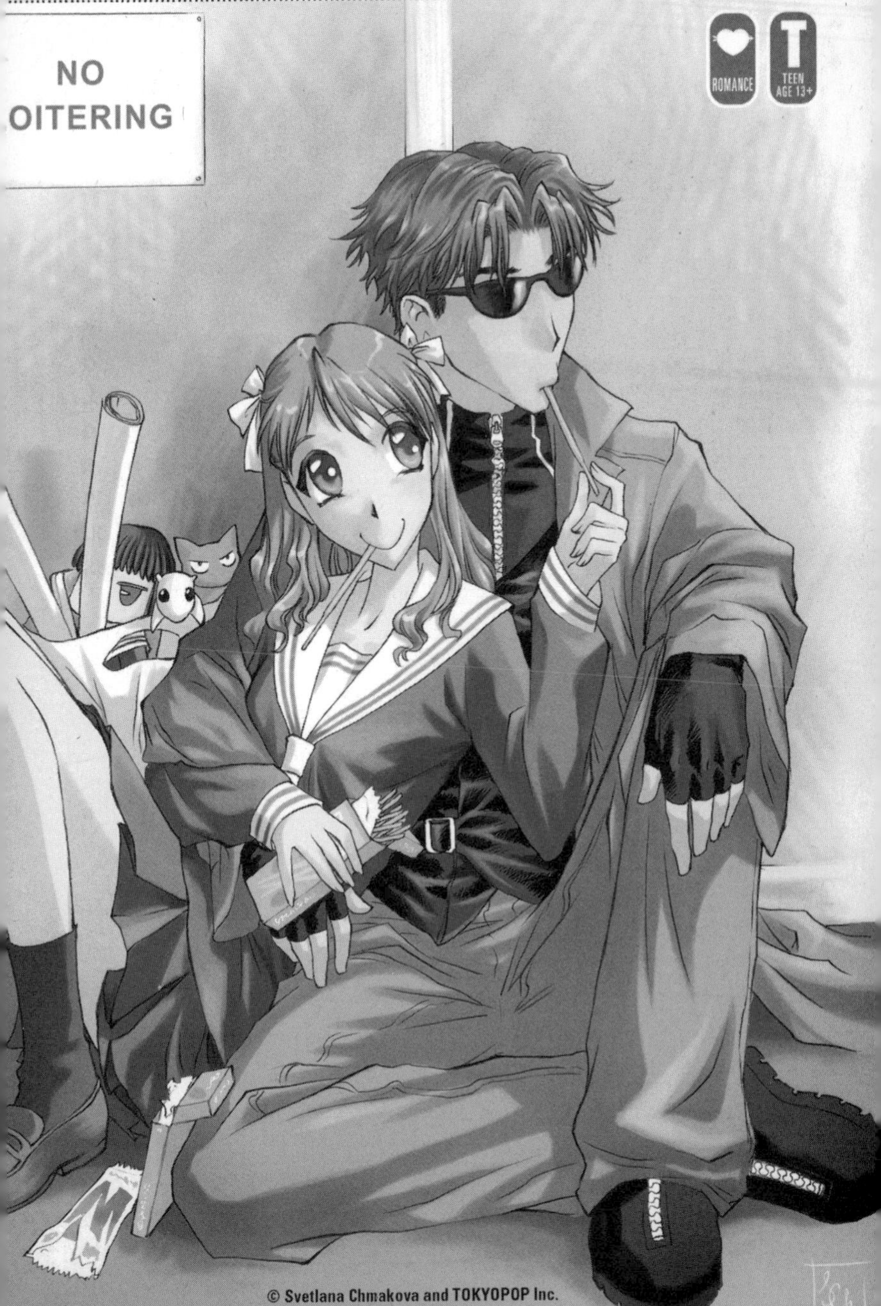
NO
OITERING
ROMANCE
T
TEEN
AGE 13+

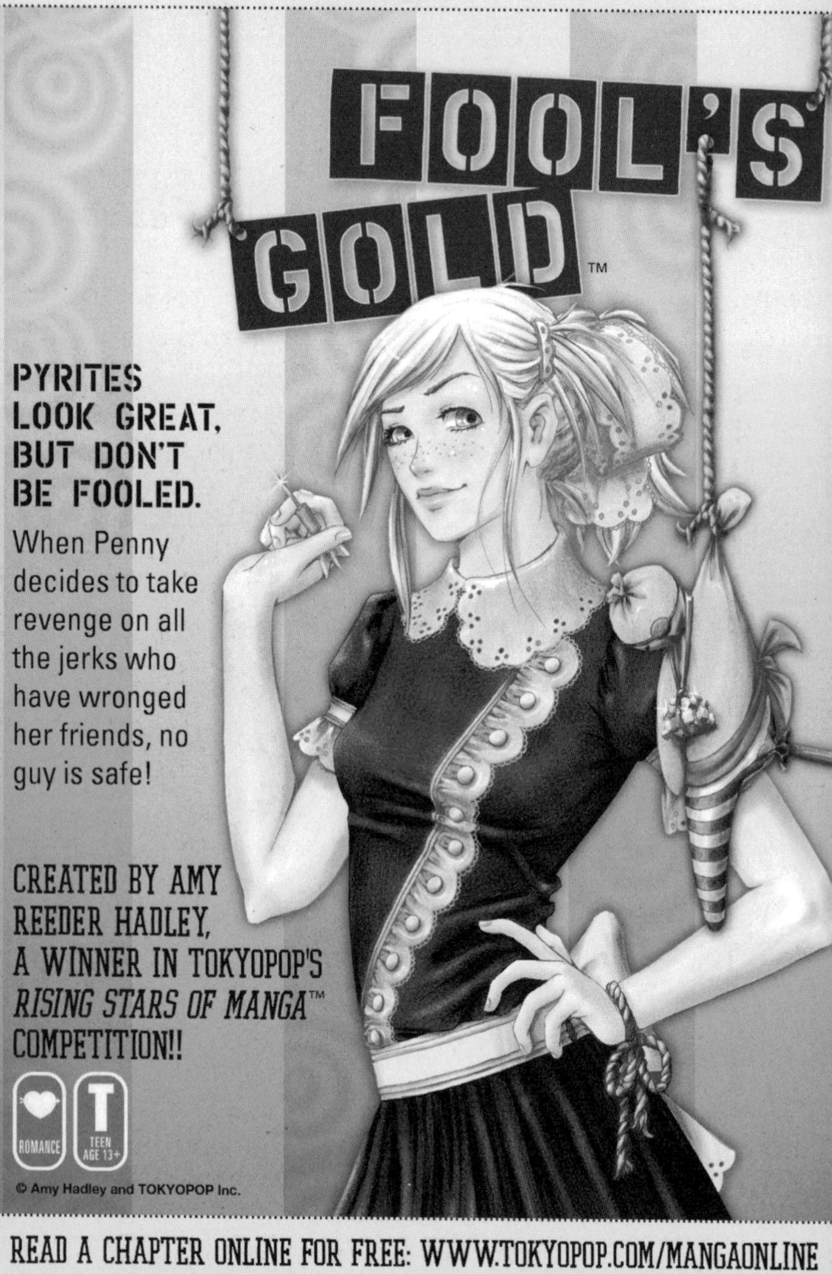
FOOL'S GOLD™
PYRITES LOOK GREAT, BUT DON'T BE FOOLED.
When Penny decides to take revenge on all the jerks who have wronged her friends, no guy is safe!
CREATED BY AMY REEDER HADLEY, A WINNER IN TOKYOPOP'S *RISING STARS OF MANGA*™ COMPETITION!!
ROMANCE
T
TEEN AGE 13+
© Amy Hadley and TOKYOPOP Inc.